*continued . . .*

# Archangel's Shadows

## Nalini Singh

JOVE BOOKS, NEW YORK

**THE BERKLEY PUBLISHING GROUP**
**Published by the Penguin Group**
**Penguin Group (USA) LLC**
**375 Hudson Street, New York, New York 10014**

USA • Canada • UK • Ireland • Australia • New Zealand • India • South Africa • China

penguin.com

A Penguin Random House Company

ARCHANGEL'S SHADOWS

A Jove Book / published by arrangement with the author

For information, address: The Berkley Publishing Group,
a division of Penguin Group (USA) LLC,
375 Hudson Street, New York, New York 10014.

ISBN: 978-0-425-25117-1

PUBLISHING HISTORY
Jove mass-market edition / November 2014

PRINTED IN THE UNITED STATES OF AMERICA

10  9  8  7  6  5  4  3  2  1

Cover art by Tony Mauro.
Cover design by George Long.
Text design by Kristin del Rosario.

# Archangel's Shadows

# Shadow Team

Ashwini navigated the darkened stairwell with quick steps, careful not to make a sound. Given the layout of the stairs—a kind of square spiral complete with a well in the center that went from the top of the seventy-three-story building to the basement—the echoes would bounce off the walls into a thundering racket.

It was unlikely anyone would hear the noise with the archangelic battle going on in the skies of New York while vampires fought the scourge of the reborn below, but getting cocky was a good way to end up dead. It was why Janvier had cut power to this part of the building, and why Naasir had set up a relay of small explosions to distract the enemy.

A bead of sweat rolling down her spine, she plastered herself to the wall when a door opened on a higher floor.

"There's no light," the irritated male voice boomed, magnified by the terrible acoustics for what was meant to be an office building, albeit one designed by an architect known for his "edgy" work. "Raphael's most recent strike must've damaged the building."

"No." A female this time. "He has people on this side of the line. Lock the doors to the main part of the floor on both sides. I'll alert our people to do the same throughout the building."

Ashwini's lips curved. She didn't need to get onto the floor itself to do what she'd come to do. Not in this particular building.

Continuing up as soon as the enemy guards left, she found herself considering Naasir's name for their small team: *shadow fighters*. It was a far more apt description than "spy" or even "soldier." Together, Ashwini, Janvier, and Naasir's job was to discomfort, discombobulate, and otherwise aggravate the enemy forces in the heart of the hostile encampment. For a three-person team, she thought they'd done one hell of a job.

This would be the icing on the cake.

Reaching the floor directly below the roof, she took off her small backpack and removed the charges. Ten seconds, that was all she needed to place and arm a device. The resulting explosion might not collapse the roof, but it should do enough damage to throw the invading force off its game. "Set," she murmured into the mouthpiece of the sleek communications device she wore hooked over her right ear.

"Get out, *cher*." A voice as languid as a hazy summer's day—if you didn't notice the steel beneath. "Your presence has been detected."

"I'm moving." Backpack on, she'd barely covered two flights when boots thundered some distance below, intermingled with shouts and war cries.

*Time for plan B.*

She slid off the backpack and retrieved the rappelling rope curled inside. Once it was anchored to the stairwell rail, she could use it to slide past and below any pursuers before they knew she was gone. The leather half-gloves she'd added to her outfit weren't a fashion statement, but preparation for just this contingency. Else, her palms would be shredded by the end.

Locking the heavy-duty carabiner directly to the railing after testing the metal would hold—at least long enough for her to get below her pursuers—she threw the rope down into the well at the center of the building. It uncoiled in swift silence, the metallic rasp of the carabiner moving against the railing hidden by the noise of the hostile fighters heading her way. Leaving the empty backpack, she went to swing over . . . and realized she could feel a draft of warm air on her nape.

She turned, going in low, but she was too slow. The male who'd entered silently through the door at her back slammed into her. The carabiner clanged against the rail in a hard beat of sound this time, the lump of it digging into her lower back as her attacker shoved his arm to her throat.

Fangs flashed in her face. "It's so nice when lunch has the manners to present itself on the doorstep."

Having used his self-congratulatory pause to drop a knife into each palm from the arm sheaths hidden under her jacket, she thrust up through his gut. Her trapped position made a deep cut impossible, but she got his attention, his blood on her blade. He howled in anger, punched her in the stomach—and took a step back.

It was all she needed.

Breathing past the agony from his blow, she sliced out again. Connected hard and true enough to puncture a lung. It would've taken down a mortal, but her opponent wasn't mortal.

A sound of frothing rage, his eyes appearing to glow in the dark. "Bitch." When he swung back, it wasn't with his fist.

Ashwini was skilled at close-contact combat, but she was in a tight space in the dark against a vampire who was clearly no neophyte in the art himself. And he had what felt like a broadsword. She brought up her knives to ward off the blow, but it was too heavy, too true a strike, the jarring impact brutal. Her blades clattered to the floor as he split her left palm and the underside of her right forearm open with the tip of the blade, and then that blade was cold fire across her chest.

Iron scent, wet and dark, filled her nostrils, her breath coming in shallow pants.

The vampire laughed.

Conscious she couldn't get out of this now, not with the heavy clamor of enemy boots only a floor below and the sword-wielding vampire in front of her, she managed to make her right hand work well enough to grab the gun from her thigh holster. Becoming a prisoner of war was not an option; never again would she let anyone lock her up. Of course, that was unlikely to be an issue given that Lijuan liked to *eat* people, the husk that remained after the Archangel of China fed turning to dust in the hand.

"Sorry, *cher*," she whispered to the man on the other end of the comm device, the man who'd taught her to play long after the end of her farcical childhood, and fired. The blunt, hard sound of her gun spitting fire filled the stairwell, the bullets passing through her vampire assailant to ricochet off the walls. Grunting from the impact, the vamp staggered back. Only to recover to scream obscenities at her; in the flashes from the gun, she saw him lift his broadsword for a fatal strike.

That sword clattered to the floor before it ever reached her, blood spraying her face in a hot gush. She stopped firing . . . and heard the dull, wet thud of his head bouncing down the steps, knew it had been sliced off by a fluid steel blade that wasn't a sword or a knife but something in between, as sharp as a scythe and even deadlier.

"No apologies between us, sugar," Janvier said and, scooping her up in his arms, ran *up* the stairs.

No point in protesting. Wounded as badly as she was, she'd only slow them down if she insisted on moving under her own steam. Instead, she reached her bloody left hand around his side for the gun she knew he wore in a holster at his waist. It took a second to get a grip, his breath warm on her neck, and his muscles bunching and flexing against her as he pounded up the steps.

Trying not to think about the fact that her chest was all but sliced in half, she sat up and pointed both guns, his and hers, over his shoulders. "Your ears are going to take a beating."

"I'll live."

She pressed the trigger on both guns.

Their pursuers fell back under the barrage, but she knew that wouldn't last. Not only would she soon run out of bullets— and that was counting the two spare clips she had on her—she had to take out a vamp's heart or the brain to kill with a gun. Even then, it depended on the age and strength of the vampire in question. Ashwini had once emptied an entire clip into a psychotic vamp's brain only for him to lunge at her.

Janvier jerked at that instant, but didn't slow his momentum.

She touched his shoulder, felt the warm slickness of fresh blood. Her stomach roiled. "You've been hit by a ricochet."

"Don't stop," he ordered. "Keep them distracted."

The scent of his blood igniting her deepest, most primal instincts, she did as he asked, mowing down a vampire about to leap up to them. Three bullets in the brain, her aim true thanks to the eerily staccato glimpse she caught in the split second of a muzzle flash, and he stayed down, giving his fellows pause. Her gun clicked on empty on the final shot. However, when she tried to use the breathing room to slot in a fresh clip, she almost dropped the gun to the floor.

"I'm getting fuzzy," she said, her tongue thick in her mouth. "Leave me. Go."

He could get out the same way he'd no doubt gotten in—by scaling the side of the high-rise. Janvier could climb even the sheerest wall without problem, his movements as beautiful as they were *other*, a reminder that he wasn't human.

"You can drink my blood." The words came out slurred, but she got off another shot when a clatter of sound betrayed an enemy vamp who'd poked up his head. It bought them a few more seconds. "For strength."

"I would love to." Pulse thudding against her as her face fell into his neck, the guns hanging limp from her fingers, he said, "But I'd rather you were sucking my cock at the time."

She tried to snarl a response, but the words wouldn't come.

"Don't you go, Ash. *Don't you fucking go.*" Harsh, unforgiving words as he came to a stop on the final landing, the same place where she'd placed the charges.

"'m here," she managed to mumble, patting at his cheek with a bloody hand. He was so sinfully pretty, was Janvier, with his green eyes and dark brown hair that got all coppery under the summer sun. She wished she'd kissed him for real, wished she'd hauled him into bed and bitten him on that tight butt of his.

"We can rectify that later," he said and shifted his grip to hold her full-length against him, one arm around her waist. "Arms around my neck. Come on, sugar. Don't let me down now."

Her limbs were so heavy, her blood dripping over her skin to soak the waistband of her jeans, but she managed to link her arms around his neck. "Window?"

"No, my entrance route will have been plugged by now. We're going down." Using a rope he must've anchored to the railing when he arrived, he swung over the side and slid down at breathtaking speed.

Shouts and screams came from above, but all Ashwini could think was that he wasn't wearing a glove.

A slamming halt as he swung them to a stop on a lower floor, below their pursuers but not home free. It was perfectly timed: she heard the rope slither past a heartbeat later, having been severed from above. Janvier was already racing down the steps, Ashwini once more cradled against his chest.

They rocketed past the first floor and down into the garage. A vampire with hair of metallic silver and eyes of the same startling shade against skin of rich, strokable brown was waiting for them, the door held open. Shoving it shut behind them, Naasir mangled the opening mechanism by bending part of it with brute strength. "Go! I'll take care of any pursuit!"

A small boom reverberated through the building at that instant, dust falling onto her face from the concrete of the garage ceiling. "We did it," she tried to whisper, but her throat wouldn't work . . . and her heartbeat, it was a sluggish crawl. As if her body no longer had blood to pump.

"Ashwini!"

Janvier's voice was the last thing she heard before the lights went out.

# 1

A fetid breath on the back of the neck.
A chill of bones. A cold whisper in the darkness.
There are those things that should not exist, should not
    walk, should not breathe, should not be named.
There are those nightmares that, once given form, can
    never be put back into the dreamscape.
          —*Scroll of the Unknown Ancient, Refuge Library*

There had been a war. Archangel against archangel. Squadrons of angels in the air and troops of vampires on the ground. He'd told it that when he returned. The being who no longer remembered its name, who no longer knew if it lived or was caught in endless purgatory, had heard the fighting. But it didn't care. That war existed on another world, not in the small darkness that was its own.

Here, it fought its own war, screaming at the faint sound of the dragging scrape-shuffle that announced the monster's approaching footsteps. But even as it screamed through a throat cracked and raw, it knew it was making no sound, its chest painful from a lack of air. Panic had clamped its cruel hand around its throat and now it squeezed, *squeezed*.

"No, no, no," the trapped creature whimpered inside its skull, mouth remaining locked in that silent scream.

Part of who it had once been understood that its mind was broken and would never recover. That part was a tiny kernel hidden in a distant part of its psyche. The rest of it was clawing horror and fear . . . and sadness. Tears rolled down its face, caught in its ravaged throat, but the haunting sense of despair was soon crushed under the suffocating weight of naked fear.

Then light hit the eyes that must be its own in an agonizing blindness and its pulse froze.

The monster was here.

# 2

Three weeks after losing most of the blood in her body, Ashwini was considering painting one of her living room walls pink with purple polka dots when her phone began to buzz. Grabbing it from the exquisitely scarred wooden coffee table she'd restored the previous year, she answered to find Sara on the other end.

The Guild Director had a job for her. "Something weird's been happening in the Vampire Quarter," she said. "Dogs and cats disappearing. First report was postbattle, but it could've been going on for longer with the strays no one tracks." Faint rustling sounds, pages being turned. "A canine body finally turned up in a sewer drain and reports are that it's desiccated. 'Like a mummy,' according to the vet who called me. I want you to check it out."

"You want me to investigate a mummified dog?" Ashwini loved animals, would have a big slobbering pup of her own if she didn't live in an apartment in Manhattan, but this was hardly her area of expertise. "I'm no Egyptologist. I also don't like sewers."

"Dog's not in the sewer anymore, so you're safe," Sara said

without missing a beat. "Could be we have a crazy vampire feeding off pets. Just check it out."

Narrowing her eyes, Ashwini glared at the view of the city's cloud-piercing Archangel Tower through the reinforced glass of the living room wall opposite the one she'd been considering earlier, the oil-paint orange of the late afternoon sunlight brushing the angelic wings in her line of sight in shades of auburn and sienna. It was Ellie who'd told her about this building—the other hunter had had an apartment in a similar building next door before she fell in love with the bone-chillingly dangerous male who controlled North America from that Tower.

"Seriously, Sara," she said, following the erratic flight path of an angel who appeared to be testing a lately injured wing, "you couldn't find anything *less* dangerous? Like sending me to find a little old lady's lost knitting needle?"

The Guild Director laughed, utterly unabashed. "Hey, you now hold the Guild record for the most stitches in one sitting— enjoy the time off."

"I want a real hunt after this." She scowled, but her hand was fisted as she silently urged on the unknown angel who was attempting to make a landing on a rooftop adjacent to the Tower. "Or I'm going to hunt Janvier on principle." The damn vampire had been *nice* to her for weeks, ever since she got sliced up during the battle to hold New York against the invading force marshaled by the archangel Lijuan.

The angel who'd just made a good if shaky landing on that rooftop in the distance had no doubt been injured in the same battle.

"Excellent," Sara said, as if Ashwini had just told her that unicorns not only existed but were currently granting wishes in Central Park. "Let me know when so I can buy tickets. Now go look at the canine mummy."

"Grr." She hung up after making the snarling sound she'd picked up from Naasir during the time she, Janvier, and Naasir had worked as a team behind enemy lines.

Walking into her bedroom, she pulled curtains of deep citrine across the sliding doors that led out onto her tiny balcony. That balcony was what had made Ellie recommend this apartment to her when she'd seen it go on the market—Ashwini had once told Ellie how much she liked the way Ellie's balcony offered a sense of freedom even so high up in a skyscraper.

The block color of the curtains was vibrant against the crisp white walls Ashwini had left untouched, and a vivid contrast to the fuchsia pink of the throw pillows on her bed. The sheets were cream with fine pink stripes, the carpet a pale gold. A spiral sculpture of cerulean blue glass sat on a tall black wooden stool in one corner; she'd found the sculpture on the curb in Greenwich Village, after the previous owner threw it out just because the base was chipped. Their loss if they couldn't see beauty in the fractured, the scarred.

The room might hold too much color for many, but after the genteel elegance of the place in which she'd spent five months of her fifteenth year of life, she couldn't stand the stark or the minimalist. Texture, color, story, that was what she wanted around her, why she collected pieces others had discarded and gave them new life.

She, too, had once been considered too broken to be of any use.

Her fingers brushed the scar that diagonally bisected her chest as she pulled off her gray tee, the mark a reminder she'd almost been fatally broken. Opening up her closet door to reveal the tall mirror mounted on the other side, she took in the clean line that stated the skill of the vampire who'd wielded the sword. It was no longer raw and red, and it would eventually fade to the pale honey that was the shade of the other, smaller scars on her skin.

The memories, however, those would never fade.

*"Don't you go, Ash. Don't you fucking go."*

Janvier's voice had been the last thing Ashwini heard before blacking out, and the first after she woke. *"It's bad manners to snarl at the nice doctor, Ashblade."*

In truth, she'd been too weak to snarl, but she'd made her dislike of the institutional setting clear. So Janvier had brought her home, tucked her into her own bed, and *made her soup.* From scratch! Who did that? No one else ever had for her and she didn't know how to handle the strange, lost feeling the memory aroused in her. So she just shut the door on it, as she'd been doing for the two weeks since she'd kicked him out, and focused on the scar.

Early on, she'd worried the wound had caused muscle damage that would limit her range of motion. A visit with the Guild's senior medic a week prior, in concert with her increasing mobility, had erased that concern. Since she planned on keeping her recovery on track, she picked up the bottle of special oil Saki had given her. "Rub it in twice a day after the stitches dissolve," the veteran hunter had said. "It'll help with deep-tissue healing."

Given Saki's impressive record of injuries, Ashwini wasn't about to argue.

The sweet-smelling oil rubbed in, she wove her hair into a loose braid, then took off her yoga pants to change into winter-appropriate jeans, hunting boots, a mohair turtleneck in vibrant orange over a thin, long-sleeved tee designed to retain body heat, and a thermal-lined black leather jacket that hit her at the hip. She found her gloves stuffed into the pockets of the jacket, so that saved her from hunting for them.

Deciding to leave in the dangly hoop earrings she was wearing—if the poor dead dog managed to rise up and attack her, it deserved to rip off her earlobes—she began to slot in her weapons. Knives in arm sheaths as well as one in her left boot, plus a gun in a concealed shoulder holster and another in a visible thigh holster.

Grabbing her Guild ID, she slipped it into an easily accessible pocket. Most of the local cops knew the hunters who lived in the area, but there were always the rookies. Since it would suck to be shot dead by a trigger-happy hotshot, especially after surviving an immortal war, she'd make it painless for them to confirm her identity.

That done, she considered her crossbow. Though she adored it almost as much as the portable grenade launcher she stored in a weapons locker at Guild HQ, it seemed a tad extreme for a visit to a vet.

"God, Sara," she muttered into the air at the reminder of her so-safe-it-was-a-joke assignment. "I'm almost convinced you're punking me."

However, even that was better than sitting around twiddling her thumbs—or destroying her apartment with boredom-induced decorating choices.

Before she spun the dial to lock the weapons safe hidden in

the back of her closet, she slipped on the glossy black bangle
Janvier had sent her in the mail a year before. Snap it apart to
reveal the wire within, and you were holding a lethally effective
garrote. The damn male knew her far too well. Which was why
she couldn't understand his behavior after her injury. The two
of them had an understanding; they irritated and challenged
one another, and yes, they flirted, but the rest . . . the kindness,
the tenderness, it was crossing a line.

He'd cradled her against his chest when she had trouble
sitting up, fed her soup spoonful by spoonful. It had felt warm
and safe and terrifying and enraging. Because he was the one
thing she could not have—and now he'd wrecked her hard-won
equilibrium by showing her what she was missing.

Angrily hiding a few more knives on her body for good
measure, she strode to the front door and yanked it open.

"There you are, sugar," said the two-hundred-and-forty-
seven-year-old vampire on her doorstep, his hair the rich shade
of the chicory coffee he'd once made her, and his skin a bur-
nished gold.

She bared her teeth at him in a way that couldn't faintly be
taken as a smile. "I thought I told you to go away." Last time
he'd "been in the neighborhood," he'd brought her mint chocolate chip ice cream. Her favorite. She'd taken the ice cream
and shut the door in his face in an effort to teach him a lesson.
He'd laughed, the wild, unabashed sound penetrating the flimsy
shield of the door to sink into her bones, make her soul ache.

"I did go away," he pointed out in that voice accented with
the unique cadence of his homeland, his shoulders moving
beneath the butter-soft tan leather of his jacket as he folded his
arms. "For an entire week."

"In what version of going away does it mean you send take-
out deliverymen to my doorstep?"

Eyes the shade of bayou moss, sunlight over shadow,
scanned her head to toe. "How else was I to make sure you
weren't lying collapsed in the bathroom because you were too
stubborn to call for help?"

"I didn't get hit with the stupid stick anytime in the past
couple of weeks." And, despite the somber predictions of her
father in childhood, she had friends. Honor had been by every
couple of days, alternating with Ransom, Demarco, and Elena.

Naasir had filled her freezer with meat before he left for Japan forty-eight hours after the battle.

"Protein will help you heal," had been his succinct summation. "Eat it."

A number of other hunters had dropped by to compare battle scars after they escaped hospital arrest. Saki had stayed for two nights, caught Ashwini up on her parents in Oregon. The older couple had once done Ashwini a great kindness, and while she'd been too damaged then to trust them enough to forge an emotional bond, never would she forget their generosity. As she couldn't forget the way Janvier had held her in his lap in the old armchair by the window, his hand stroking her hair as snow fell over the city.

It was a moment she'd wanted to live in forever. But she *couldn't*. "Out of the way," she said, her anger at fate a cold, clawing thing inside her she'd never been able to tame despite her decision to live life full throttle. "I'm heading to a job."

No more lazy grace, his expression grim. "You're not fully recovered."

Stepping out and locking the door behind her, she strode down the hallway. "The doctor gave me a clean bill of health." Even if he hadn't, Ashwini knew her body. It had been in hunter condition before the injury and she'd begun exercising as much as she could the instant there was no longer any danger she'd tear the wound open.

"Ash." Janvier touched his hand to her lower back.

"No touching." Gritting her teeth against the impact of him, she reached out to push the button to summon the elevator.

Janvier used his body to block her. "I'm coming with you."

Her mind flashed back to the last time he'd said something similar, to the first mission they'd worked together. Back then, they'd been antagonists who'd declared a temporary truce, and the problem had been a clusterfuck in Atlanta. Now, he was openly attached to the Tower, which technically put them on the same side. They'd worked like a well-honed partnership in Atlanta, fallen back into the same flawless rhythm during the battle. As if they had always been meant to be a pair.

And that just sucked.

"Fine." Refusing to face the awful, painful grief that lurked beneath her anger, she stepped into the elevator when it opened to disgorge one of her neighbors.

Janvier waited until after the other woman was out of earshot to say, "I don't trust it when you cooperate." Narrowed eyes.

"Don't come, then."

"You're not getting rid of me that easily, *cher*." Slamming out one hand to block the closing door, he got in.

The first time he'd called her *cher*, it had been a wicked flirt. Somehow, the term had become more in the years since, an endearment reserved for her. Never did she hear him use it with anyone else.

Today, he stood too close to her on the ride down, his scent a sexy, infuriating bite against her senses. A great big part of her wanted to haul him down to her mouth. She knew full well that seconds after she did, he'd have her slammed against the wall, her legs wrapped around his waist as he pounded his cock into her, their hands and mouths greedy to touch, to possess, to taste.

Her and Janvier's chemistry had never been in question.

When he walked out the elevator in front of her, she couldn't help but admire the sleek danger of him. Built long and lean, his muscles that of a runner or a swimmer, he moved with a sensual grace that fooled people into thinking he wasn't a threat.

Ashwini knew different.

Just under a year prior, he'd sent in three decapitated heads to the Tower to signal the end of an execution order. Those heads had belonged to vampires who'd sliced Ashwini up after cornering her in a pack. She'd killed two of the cowards, wounded the others, and it was the others Janvier had delivered.

Of course, he'd never claimed responsibility for the act; most everyone thought the vampires had been executed by their angel. Ashwini knew the truth only because Sara had had it direct from Dmitri, second to the archangel Raphael and the most powerful vampire in the country.

One eyebrow raised, the Guild Director had repeated Dmitri's response to her notice that the Guild was sending in a team to capture the rogue vamps. "No need. The Cajun's taken care of it. The dead morons touched his hunter."

That was when Ashwani had first tried to put distance be-tween them, first tried to cut off the connection that could not be permitted to grow. Janvier had made that an impossible task. He'd tracked her down in remote corners of the world, aggra-vated her to the point where she'd once tied him up and emptied a large pot of honey on his head, before pretending to leave him for the insects.

He'd laughed in delight and cut himself free using a hidden blade, then chased her through the trees, threatening to make her lick every drop of the sweet, sticky stuff off his body. The interaction had left her feeling more alive than she had in all the weeks since she'd decided to walk away from him. And so she'd been selfish, continued to play with him without telling him their flirtation could never be anything permanent.

Her wishes didn't matter. His didn't, either. There was no choice.

# 3

Straddling the hot red of his motorcycle, parked illegally in front of her building and gilded by the rays of dense orange that shot out of the winter sky, Janvier lifted up the helmet he'd left hooked on the handlebar and held it out to her.

"You realize this is Manhattan?" she asked with a pointed look at the foot traffic, not sure it was a good idea to get that close to him. The fact was, Ashwini didn't trust herself around Janvier. Not anymore. Not when the angry part of her wanted to steal time with him any way it could.

Strangling the voice that said it'd be much more fun to ride him and not the bike, she folded her arms. "Did you leave the key in the ignition, too?"

He shrugged, lips curving but eyes sharp, watchful. "This bike doesn't need a key, my *khoobsurat* Ash. Hop on and I'll show you my darling's fancy electronics."

His use of the language she'd learned at her grandmother's knee didn't surprise her; he had served out his hundred-year Contract in Neha's court, after all. *"Chaque hibou aime son bébé,"* she said in return, having discovered the quirky saying online while trying to figure out something he'd said to her.

A sinful grin that lit up his eyes and made her stomach

somersault. "I protest at being labeled an owl—I haven't eaten any mice lately. But I do love this beast. Come, let me give you a ride."

Accepting the helmet despite her reservations, she put it on, scowled when he remained bareheaded. "Vampirism doesn't protect against no-brain syndrome." She rapped her knuckles lightly against the back of his head. "You better have another helmet."

"Just checking if you still care." He retrieved a second helmet from where he'd apparently left it hooked somewhere on the part of the bike not in her line of sight. The man really wanted to get his stuff stolen. Then again, she thought, her eyes landing on the small set of black wings on the glossy red paint-work of the side panel, it'd be a stupid thief who took property marked as belonging to the Tower.

"Junkies don't care," she said, pointing at the emblem. "Their wiring is too scrambled."

"That's why I asked the doorman to keep an eye on it." He winked at her for having jerked her chain this long, his lashes thick and curling slightly at the ends. "Where do you want to go? I am but your loyal steed today."

Swinging over behind him, she put one gloved hand on his shoulder and told him the address of the veterinary clinic. He smelled even more delicious up close, the dangerous bite of him layered with an earthy undertone that echoed his person-ality: Janvier could pull off sophisticated, of that she had no doubt, but his real skin was full of sexily rough edges.

The motorbike came to life with a throaty roar that vibrated between her legs. Sucking in a breath, she grabbed his wrist when he would've reached back to stroke her thigh. "Hands and eyes front."

Chuckling, he put his hands back where they should be after tugging on his gloves. "Hold on."

Ashwini controlled her position with her thighs as he slipped into the heavy traffic, keeping just the one hand on his shoulder to balance herself. His beaten-up leather jacket did nothing to insulate her from the intimacy of feeling his body move, muscle and tendon and bone shifting under her touch as he maneuvered the bike through the sea of cars.

When an angel swept down to skim over the vehicles, the

distinctive blue of his wings causing motorists to slow down in a wonder that never faded, Janvier raised a hand in casual acknowledgment. Rather than returning the salute, Illium pointed to the curb and Janvier immediately slid the bike out of the flow of traffic and to another illegal parking spot in front of a fire hydrant.

Illium landed on the sidewalk at almost the same instant, folding in his wings in a susurrous whisper of sound. Golden eyed with ink black hair dipped in blue and flawless bone structure, he was one of the most astonishingly beautiful angels Ashwini had ever seen. Yet he did nothing for her, might as well have been a marble sculpture created by a master.

It was only Janvier who'd penetrated the wary steel of her defenses, made himself at home. As he had on her couch two and a half weeks back, his arm wrapped around her while they stretched out to watch an old black-and-white movie. When she'd started to fall asleep, her body not yet at full strength, he'd tucked her in with a kiss on the forehead she could feel even now.

"Ash," Illium said, a distinct glint in the gold. "I thought for certain I'd be organizing Janvier's funeral when he said he was planning to beard you in your den. I even called an undertaker."

She pushed up the visor of her helmet. "Keep the number. It might be useful one of these days."

"How you keep wounding me." Janvier slapped a hand dramatically over his heart before flipping up the visor of his own helmet. "Why did you pull us aside, sweet Bluebell? Can you not see that I'm acting as my Ashblade's chauffeur?"

Illium thrust a hand through his hair, pushing back the overlong strands that had fallen across his face. "Give me one of your blades," he demanded. "I need to cut this before it blinds me."

"You do it here and there'll be a stampede to get the discards," Janvier pointed out. "Not to mention the distress such barbarity will cause in the tender hearts of all those who worship your fine form."

Illium muttered something uncomplimentary about Cajuns who should be dropped off buildings that did nothing to dim Janvier's amusement. His hair brushed his nape, too, but he was comfortable with that length, and Ashwini liked it on him.

Too much. Running her fingers through the heavy silk of it was a bone-deep pleasure she'd indulged in only a rare few times, all too aware it could become an addiction.

"There's a situation I need you to handle," Illium said after pushing back his hair again. "Details have been sent to your phone."

Ashwini met the angel's gaze. "Shall I plug my ears?" Hunters had fought alongside immortals in the battle to hold their city, would do so again should the situation call for it, but when it came to everyday existence, getting involved in Tower business could be perilous to a mortal's health. "Or I can jump on the subway," she offered, taking her hand off Janvier's shoulder.

"No," he said, at the same time that Illium spoke the word. "There, *cher*," Janvier added. "You would not break both our hearts, would you?"

"What's the situation?" she asked Illium, trying to ignore the way Janvier's voice wrapped around her, as sensual and luscious as caramel. Despite the fact that he'd been Made over two centuries before, he'd lost neither his bayou roots nor its music from his speech, though the rhythm of his words had altered over time.

"A vampire's cattle are charging him with ill-treatment."

Ashwini winced at the derogatory term—used to describe humans who volunteered to act as a particular vampire's living food source—but couldn't take Illium to task for using it. These people chose to be "kept" by vampires, *chose* to be seen as livestock, petted and cosseted though they might be. "I didn't realize cattle had any rights."

Janvier was the one to reply, his eyes on the screen of his phone as he scrolled through the information he'd been forwarded. "Not every vampire enjoys seducing his food anew each night, or relying on blood banks. It is bad for the vampiric population for such arrangements to turn abusive."

Illium folded his arms, the clean line of his jaw set in a hard line. "If word spreads, mortals might become gun-shy."

"You'd think so, wouldn't you?" Ashwini said, recalling the hundreds of thousands who petitioned to be Made every year, despite witnessing countless examples of the brutality and violence that might be their lot. Because near-immortality came at a price: a hundred years of service to the angels, after which eternity awaited.

If you survived the Contract period with your mind unbroken.

"There will always be self-destructive idiots in the world." She squeezed Janvier's shoulder in an unspoken coda. He was a vampire not because of a lust for endless life, but because he'd fallen in love with another vampire as a "callow youth." His own words. She felt for the mortal man he'd been, because she knew in this way, she and Janvier were the same: when they loved, they loved desperately, holding on even when it threatened to destroy them.

"Is it urgent?" Janvier leaned back into her touch. "Ash is headed toward the same general part of the city, so we can deal with her task and go on to this."

"It's a relatively low-level rumor at present," Illium said. "An hour or two won't make any difference." Spreading his wings to their full breadth, to the delight of the teenagers who'd gathered in the portico of the building behind him, he readied himself for flight. "I almost forgot—there's to be a celebration in just over a month."

Ashwini blinked. "Not an angelic ball?" As far as she knew, Elena had an avowed dislike of the "excruciatingly formal" events. She'd been heard to mutter that she'd rather stick a fork in her eye. Ashwini couldn't see her fellow hunter changing her mind in the aftermath of a war. Even if she was hooked up with a scary-ass archangel.

Illium's laughter lit up his eyes and sent a woman on the sidewalk into a swoon broken by the thick arms of a nearby cop. "Ellie has threatened to shoot anyone who even suggests such a travesty."

"Thank God," Ashwini said with a shudder. "I thought for a second that she'd lost her mind and we'd have to stage an intervention."

"This is to be a 'block party,' as Ellie terms it, open to any and all citizens of the city. It's to be held in the streets and on the rooftops around the Tower."

"That's a really great idea." While crowds weren't Ashwini's thing, she wouldn't mind ending up on one of the rooftops with a group of friends. Each and every one of them had mourned in the aftermath of the war, for the fighters, mortal and immortal, who'd lost their lives. Now it was time to lift a drink to their fallen comrades, and to fully reclaim their city from the shadows of war—while giving a giant finger to those who'd sought to cripple it.

Janvier revved the bike at that instant. "I'll report back once I've checked out the abuse report."

"I'll be at the Tower." Illium took off in a powerful beat of wild blue accented with silver.

# 4

Wondering if the Cajun would catch his dark-eyed hunter this time around, Illium rode the winter winds directly to the balcony outside Dmitri's office. It was swept clear of snow, a task usually assigned to the youngest in the troop ranks, vampire or angel. Right now, with so many of the young injured, it was done by whoever had ten free minutes and didn't mind a little manual labor.

From the damp in Dmitri's hair where he stood behind his desk, his body clad in a simple black T-shirt and black cargo pants, Illium had the feeling Dmitri had cleared this himself. Not many who stood second to an archangel would do such a task, but this was why Dmitri was so trusted by Raphael's men—despite his power, he was, and had always been, one of them.

Glancing up at Illium's entry, his eyes having been on a map that showed the current position of Lijuan's forces in China, Dmitri said, "Did you find it?"

"Trace did." Illium had asked the slender vampire to follow the trail because most vampires outside the Tower had no idea he was Raphael's man. "It's called Umber." He placed a tiny vial of a reddish brown substance on Dmitri's desk, but while the color echoed the pigment for which it was named, the texture was unusual.

The contents glittered like tiny shards of glass—or crushed hard candy.

Dmitri picked it up, angled it to the light.

It was, Illium saw, oddly beautiful, despite the fact that light revealed the crystals to have an undertone of sickly yellow.

"Chewed?"

He nodded at Dmitri's question. "That seems to be the preferred method of ingestion with the users Trace was able to pinpoint. The supplier is taking extreme care to keep this underground and available to only a select clientele."

"Exclusivity makes it more valuable." Dmitri put the vial back down. "Effects?"

"Sexual high and addictive with a single hit." Trace had reported seeing the woman from whom he'd seduced the sample quivering in carnal pleasure after she ate a sliver, her hands cupping her breasts and her eyes heavy lidded. "Long-term effects are unknown—Trace was able to confirm the drug only hit the streets two days past. We were lucky to pick up on it."

"No. We weren't lucky; we were prepared." Dmitri had begun to create a network of informants throughout the city during the lead-up to the battle, and it was those informants who had reported a rising excitement in the wealthy vampire populace. All of it related to a mysterious new high.

Many of these new informants were human and a number were blood donors, specifically genetically blessed donors who came into contact with older, more powerful vampires on a regular basis. The trick was that none of the informants knew they served the Tower. One set of exclusive donors, for example, reported to the woman who ran the city's top vampire club, in return for the cachet of being in her inner circle.

The idea of the subtle but powerful network had come from Raphael.

"Elena," the archangel had said, "has made me realize we're not fully utilizing all our assets."

They'd been standing on the Tower roof at the time, the wind a savage beast. When Raphael turned to Dmitri, midnight black strands of hair had whipped across his face. "The mortals see things we do not, pay attention to those we might otherwise dismiss." Facing the wind once again, Raphael had continued. "We need that information, but I will not drag Elena's friends too deeply into the immortal world." An instant of piercing eye contact. "Such can end only badly for them."

Dmitri knew Raphael was no longer talking about Elena's friends, but about the horror of Dmitri's own past. "I do not blame you, sire. I never have." He blamed the vicious angel who had tortured them both. "Without you, I would've carved out my heart and been lying dead in a distant grave an eon ago."

"I blame myself, Dmitri, and I would not have Elena feel the same. Set up the network using mortals who have freely chosen to linger on the fringes of the immortal world as the base."

"Raphael." When the archangel turned to look at him with those eyes that burned with power, Dmitri had extended his arm. "The past is past, and if there ever was a debt between us, it was wiped clean the day you Made Honor." Those vampires Made by an archangel were stronger from day one, harder to injure or kill. "You are my liege, but you will always first be my friend."

Raphael's hand had closed over his forearm, his over the archangel's. "I hope to hear the same words a thousand years hence."

"You will." Both Dmitri and Raphael had come close to losing themselves to the insidious cold of eternity, but that was no longer a threat.

Today, it was Illium who concerned Dmitri. The majority of people, mortal and immortal, saw charm and a vivid zest for life when they looked at the blue-winged angel. Dmitri saw increasing power and an increasing darkness. All that held the darkness at bay was Illium's tight-knit connection to Elena and Raphael, and to the Seven. But there would come a time when Illium became too much a power to remain in the city.

Then who would keep him . . . human?

"How long does the Umber high last?" Dmitri asked, making a mental note to speak to Raphael about Illium's slow and near-imperceptible descent into the icy abyss that had nearly consumed the two of them. Unlike the others in the Seven, Illium couldn't be seconded back to the Refuge to assist Galen and Venom; the distance from Elena and Aodhan, in particular, would indisputably hasten the ravages of the kind of power at Illium's command.

"Longer than the high from a honey feed," the blue-winged angel said in response to his question.

Dmitri frowned. A vampire's metabolism differed from a mortal's, meaning normal drugs, no matter how hard, metabolized too quickly to be worth the cost or the bother. A honey feed—drawing blood directly from the vein of a drug-addicted mortal who'd just shot up, snorted, or otherwise ingested their poison of choice, provided a trip that could last for up to ten minutes.

"How much better?"

"An hour per half gram of Umber."

Dmitri went motionless. "An hour." No other known drug on the planet had such an intense effect on the vampire population. "Unsurprising, then, that it's become so coveted so quickly."

"Trace has been able to pinpoint ten users so far, all gilded lilies."

Dmitri knew the type: pretty but useless. Older, wealthy vampires who existed only to discover new indulgences, new sins. Anything to break the ennui. Dmitri had once, during the worst of his pain, joined them—only to discover he couldn't spend his days doing nothing. It was a vapid, empty existence, and even as self-destructive as he'd been, he couldn't sink into it. "They're probably the only ones who can afford the drug."

"It's not all good times." Illium shoved his hair back with an impatient hand. "During the high, a percentage of the junkies are hit by the urge to feed voraciously. At least one of the lilies is currently going through a vicious detox because he refuses to touch the stuff again."

Dmitri raised an eyebrow. "Not much worries them in their pursuit of sensation." Numb inside from centuries of indulging their every whim, the lilies' need to grasp at the new, the bright, held a pitiable desperation.

"This lily is part of a long-term pair," Illium told him. "He fed on his partner during the high and he wasn't gentle—her neck was raw meat by the end, her spinal cord exposed. A few more minutes and he might've severed that, killed her."

Dmitri understood the depth of the male's horror. Such

deeply loyal connections were rare among immortals, much less in the world of the lilies, and to be protected. Dmitri would end himself before laying a finger on Honor in violence. "Drop this downstairs," he said, tapping the vial. "Have it tested for everything."

Illium took the vial.

"Tell Trace he can report directly to me," Dmitri added. "I want you focusing on the men and women the healers have discharged." A significant percentage of the Tower's forces remained down, but enough injured fighters were now walking under their own steam that he needed Illium to take charge of their physical training. It would take skillful work to get them back to full strength in a short time frame.

"Talk to Galen, come up with a workable regimen." The weapons-master couldn't leave the Refuge, especially after the recent tensions there, but that didn't mean he wasn't available to the rest of the Seven. "He's already sent through his first set of orders, has people moving."

Illium bowed deeply, adding an elegant flourish with one hand. "Yes, O Dark Overlord."

Lips twitching, Dmitri hoped with every cell in his body that Illium would find his way through the crushing pressures of immortality and power, that he wouldn't lose the joie de vivre that had been a part of him since he was a fledgling. Dmitri had once witnessed a tiny blue-winged baby angel fall hard to the earth after tangling his wings, his flight path prior to the fall that of a drunken bumblebee. Despite running full-tilt, Dmitri had been too far away to catch him.

When he'd reached the site of the accident, he'd expected to find a sobbing, hurt child. Hurt he had been, one wing crumpled, but Illium was already on his feet, his bruised and scraped arms thrust up and his hands fisted, face aglow. "I flew so far! Did you see?"

Dmitri had never forgotten that first meeting with a boy who'd reminded him of the irrepressible spirit of his own son. Illium's life had not always been painless, and it had left scars, but none of it had been as dangerous as the power now gathering inside him. However, the issue wasn't critical.

Not quite yet.

"Begone, Bluebell," he said, an image of the tiny boy he'd

carried home to his frantic mother that day at the forefront of his mind. "The Dark Overlord needs to talk to a certain spymaster."

Walking backward to the door, Illium said, "Jason's back in the country?"

"He returned from China last night." From the territory of the insane archangel who thought herself a goddess. "Managed to get past the border and all the way to her innermost citadel." Dmitri had no idea how, but that was why Jason was Raphael's spymaster and Dmitri was his blade and his second.

A rustle of wings announced Jason's presence at the balcony door.

It was time to discuss the heart of enemy territory.

Ashwini and Janvier reached the veterinary clinic in a comparatively short time thanks to Janvier's skill at weaving through the traffic, the blue of the sky still edged with puffs of orange-pink that bathed everything in a forgiving light. Nothing, however, could soften the impact of seeing the body that awaited them at the run-down but clean clinic in Chinatown.

Sara had been right. This small, helpless animal victim needed a hunter's attention rather than the vet's. Not only was the cocker spaniel shriveled and bloodless, its throat had been ravaged as if by a wild beast. "Setting aside the loss of blood," she said to the vet, "is it possible these wounds could've been made by another, bigger animal?"

The tall, mixed-race woman, her features sharp, striking, pushed her glasses farther up her nose and dragged her eyes off Janvier. "The dirty water in the drain where he was found did a good job of messing with the wound, and I'm pretty sure rats have been at this sweet boy, too." She touched her hand to the dog's emaciated head. "No telling how long he was down there. Could be days, could be weeks. Even if it *was* a vicious dog . . ."

"Yes, no animal sucked out every drop of blood in his body." A chill in her bones, Ashwini checked the cocker spaniel's teeth, the dog's skin having tightly retracted to expose the gum line; the enamel was stained and cracked. Even if he had bitten his attacker, the evidence was already too contaminated to be of any forensic use. "Who found him?"

"A homeless man who hangs around the area. Poor thing was heartbroken over it." A sudden stiffening of the vet's body, her eyes flashing behind the clear lenses of her glasses. "He's harmless—I'm sure he had nothing to do with this."

"I'm not planning to hunt him down." What Ashwini was looking at wasn't a mortal crime. It had all the hallmarks of immortal involvement—though she'd dig up information on the subject of natural mummification, too, on the off chance that it was a possibility. "Can you autopsy the body?"

"It's called a necropsy when it's an animal—and sure. If someone's going to pay for it." Her gaze went from Ashwini to Janvier and back. "As you can see"—a wave around the shabby examination room, the paint peeling off the walls and the linoleum worn—"I don't exactly charge my clients a lot, so I need the money from those who can afford it."

"Guild will cover it. Look for anything strange—beyond the obvious."

"It'll have to be tomorrow. I promised my daughter I'd be home for dinner tonight." The vet took off her glasses to pinch the bridge of her nose between forefinger and thumb. "With the battle and all, she needs her mom."

Ashwini's throat grew thick; she knew all about needing her mom. Coughing slightly in an effort to clear the obstruction, she said, "Call me when you're done." She didn't really expect the vet to find anything significant, but better to check and make certain than miss a crucial fact. "You understand this is confidential?"

"I'm not about to mess with the Tower or the Guild by blabbing."

Exiting the clinic a few minutes later, Ashwini glanced at Janvier. "Has an animal ever become infected with vampirism?"

"It's not a disease, *cher*."

"You know what I mean."

"As far as I know," he said, passing her a helmet, "no animal has ever become a vampire, but I'm comparatively young in immortal terms. Do you want me to check with Dmitri?"

"Yeah, I guess if anyone would know, it'd be him."

His thighs defined against the denim of his jeans as he straddled the bike, Janvier picked up his own helmet. "The body," he said, holding her gaze, "it reminds me of the atrocity we witnessed during the battle."

A shudder rippled through her. "Me, too."

Ashwini, Janvier, and Naasir had watched Lijuan bury her face in the neck of one of her soldiers, her mouth open and teeth glinting. When she lifted her face back up, the lower half was a macabre mask of red, and she was bloated with power, her wounds healed, while the soldier lay a dead husk at her feet, a willing sacrifice.

"But," Ashwini pointed out, "even if Lijuan has somehow resurrected herself since the battle"—though she couldn't imagine how, when Raphael had blown the crazy bitch to smithereens—"I can't see an archangel who believes herself a goddess feeding off animals. I think she'd rather starve."

Janvier slipped on his helmet. "The dog was also not desiccated enough for this to be Lijuan."

"You're right." The empty husks that evidenced Lijuan's feeds had been so fragile, Naasir had crumbled one into countless fragments when he tried to carry it off as proof. In the end, they'd had to leave the husks where they'd fallen—after Ashwini took multiple photographs using her phone.

When Janvier and Naasir returned to the site after Lijuan's defeat, it was to discover the reborn had stampeded through it, crushing the remains to dust. "What's the chance that Lijuan *is* fully dead?" Putting on her helmet, she got on the bike behind Janvier.

"Low," he said over the throaty rumble of the bike's engine. "Archangels don't die easily, and Lijuan is the oldest of the Cadre, if we don't include Raphael's mother."

It wasn't the news Ashwini wanted to hear. Because who the fuck knew what a half-dead archangel could do even after her body had been annihilated?

# 5

Elena stretched her shoulders as she sat on the rooftop of the building given over to the Legion, her legs hanging over the side and her wings resting against the rough concrete surface. Her position gave her a direct view of the Tower, its windows blazing with the reflected glory of what promised to be a dazzling sunset.

Beside her crouched the Primary, in the Legion's distinctive gargoyle-like resting pose. Wings arched high and one arm braced on his knee, he was dressed in what had been unrelieved black, but was now dusty, the dark of his hair the same. He still wasn't "human" in any sense, but he no longer made the hairs rise on the back of her neck.

Most of the time.

"You are tired."

Elena reached up to fix her ponytail, her hair damp from the quick shower she'd grabbed, else she'd be as covered in dust and grit as the Primary. "Busy day." She'd spent it ferrying materials to facilitate the repair of one of the outlying high-rises that had been damaged during the battle. "How are the modifications to this building going?"

"It was not built for winged residents."

The eerie, risen-from-the-depths male was getting verbose on her, she thought dryly. "Yes, there's a lot of work to be done." Railingless balconies had to be added, internal walls knocked down, windows turned into doors—what was safe and comfortable for mortals and vampires was annoying and stifling for winged beings.

The overhaul would take time, but a technical assessment by a specialist team had shown it would still be faster and more efficient to modify an existing building to the Legion's requirements than to build a new one from the ground up.

"Are your people handling it all right for now?" One thing the Primary had told them was that while the Legion did not need sleep, his men didn't do well cut off from one another so soon after their rising.

"Yes. We gather on the roof."

Elena knew that. The first night she'd looked across from the Tower at midnight and seen their crouched forms, those hairs on the back of her neck had stood straight up. She wondered if the Legion had any idea how seriously *other* they could sometimes be. "If the snow's too cold, we can organize—"

"The roof is acceptable."

"Do you miss the sea?"

A long pause, the answer halting, as if she had asked him a question he hadn't considered until that instant. "Yes . . . there was peace . . . and wonder . . . more than mortal or immortal eyes . . . ever see."

Elena could do nothing but nod; she'd had but a glimpse of the Legion's domain, and it had been of haunting beauty in the endless dark. "I had another home, too, once," she told him, pointing past the Tower. "An apartment in that building with the serrated roof."

The Primary's response appeared a non sequitur, but she could almost see how he'd worked his way to it. "You are not mortal and yet you are."

"I guess that describes me pretty well." Angling her face to the caressing wind, she drew in the myriad scents of her city. A city made of spirit and grit and sheer bloody-mindedness.

Just like its people.

And then the fresh kiss of the rain, the crash of the sea was in her mind, Raphael's wings magnificent in flight as he took off from the Tower balcony where he'd been speaking with Dmitri and Jason. Breath in her throat at the power and skill of his flight, Elena didn't move. Five seconds later, he brought himself to a hover a few feet from her, making the maneuver look effortless when Elena knew from experience that holding a hover took brutal muscle control.

Dressed in sleeveless combat leathers similar to the Primary's, though his were a deep brown, he looked to the leader of the Legion. "My second wishes to speak to you." A ray of the setting sun struck the violent wildfire blue of the complex and extraordinary mark that ran from his right temple to the top of his cheekbone.

A stylized dragon, that was what Elena's mind had said of the mark the first time she'd seen it as a whole, but the truth was that it was difficult to clearly describe. The impact was visceral, as if the jagged lines held an impossible power.

"Sire." The Primary took off in silence.

Elena shivered. "I can't get used to the fact that their wings don't rustle." The Legion had wings more comparable to bats' than angelkind's, strong and webbed and frighteningly quiet.

"They are built for stealth," Raphael answered, the shattering hue of his eyes focused on her alone, the blue so pure it almost hurt. *Homeward,* hbeebti?

Everything in her resonated at the incredible power of that question, of the foundation that lay beneath it. *Home* was a truth for them both now. "Yes, unless the drug situation you mentioned means we have to stay at the Tower." She didn't like the sound of this Umber stuff.

"Dmitri has the matter in hand, and Illium will take the night watch over the Tower, with Aodhan for company." A glint of laughter in his eyes, her archangel who was no longer the glacial, inhuman being who'd made her close her hand over a blade, her blood dripping hot and red to the Tower roof. "Naasir is to arrive this eve."

Elena scowled. Raphael continued to refuse to tell her the truth about Naasir, the vampire who was unlike any other vampire she'd ever met. "Revenge will be mine," she threatened. "I'd sleep with one eye open if I were you."

The covetous wind pushed strands of the obsidian silk that was his hair across his cheek. "I remind you of your own conclusion that our butler would not be impressed with blood-drenched sheets."

His solemn words startled her into a grin. "I'm surprised Naasir was able to get back here so soon." The vampire had returned to Amanat, the territory held by Raphael's mother, Caliane, just over two and a half weeks past. "Don't we need him to keep an eye across the water at Lijuan's territory?" Jason went in and out, but the spymaster couldn't always be in one place.

"Venom has taken Naasir's place temporarily." This time, the amusement that shaped Raphael's lips was acute. "My mother called to ask what else I have in my menagerie."

Elena snorted, in no doubt of Caliane's acerbic tone. "Can you blame her? First you send her a tiger creature who eats people he doesn't like, and then a vampire with the eyes and fangs of a viper." She held up a finger. "Oh, and let's not forget the mortal you keep as a pet."

"My mother does not consider you my pet, Elena. She is very kind to pets."

"Oh, ouch!"

Amusement fading, Raphael closed the distance between them to cup her jaw. "You were in the infirmary after you bathed."

"Yes." It had become habit to drop in a couple of times a day. And if it continued to terrify her to build bonds with so many men and women who could die in the battles to come, each death cutting away another piece of her heart, she was taking it one day, one friendship, at a time.

"Mood is upbeat," she told Raphael after wrapping her arms around his neck, "especially since Galen has given the order that anyone remotely ambulatory is to be up and active *or else*." Her lips curved. "I heard him cursed in at least eight different languages, threatened with murder and other more creative forms of revenge by a number of very sweaty angels and vampires." All of whom had been injured either in the Falling or in the fight against Lijuan. "My personal favorite had to do with marmalade, spiders, rope bondage, and a giant vat."

"Then it is as well my weapons-master is in the Refuge."

"As if any of that would faze Galen. He'd probably eat the spiders and tear the ropes apart with his bare hands." The angel, built like a tank, was a force of nature. "But beneath the complaining, all I saw was relief. The ones who're up are happy to be worked so hard, treated like the warriors they are, and the ones who aren't yet mobile have both a source of amusement and a goal."

Raphael slid his arms around her waist and pulled her off her perch as he turned at an impossible angle, his wing arching across her vision before he brought them to a vertical hover. "So, tonight," he said, his breath a kiss against her lips, "our people are safe, the city is under watch, and I can spend the night with my consort."

Stealing a kiss from the archangel who was her own personal and very private drug, Elena said, "Now," and he released her.

She spread her wings, swept out into the cold breeze, her joy in flight a living thing inside her. The sky was a brilliant show of scarlet and orange now, the snowy sprawl of Central Park ablaze and the skyscrapers glowing like faceted gemstones. In contrast to the wild color of the sky, the air was crystalline, frosty with cold. Her lungs expanded in pure physical pleasure. Then she glanced to the left and felt her forehead wrinkle.

Raphael had dipped lower than her, and the white fire that had become more and more apparent to her licked sunset-kissed flames over his feathers. *You're burning again, and don't tell me it's an illusion.*

Banking right, Raphael soared up, then swept back down beside her. *It makes no rational sense for my wings to become aflame—what use is an archangel who cannot fly?*

*Are you having any difficulty at the moment?*

*No.* A short pause. *In point of fact, I'm cutting through the wind more smoothly than usual.*

Given that Raphael's usual skills were phenomenal, that was a serious asset. *The edge of your wing is totally engulfed in white fire all the way up to your secondary coverts,* she told him. *Come closer and under me so I can touch your wing.* Elena was getting better at flight with every day that passed, but that kind of a fine maneuver was currently beyond her.

Raphael shifted into the position she'd requested, part of his wing under her hand. Reaching out, she touched her fingers to the white fire. *I can feel your feathers beneath the fire.* Silky and strong and as they'd always been. *But the flame is playing over my fingers. It's cool to the touch and it feels like you.*

Impossible as it was to explain, she could feel the rain and the wind against her fingertips, sense the crashing sea.

Raphael swept up to fly beside her. *Once again we have company.*

*Damn it. I wish they'd wear bells or something.* She'd totally missed the Legion fighters who'd come alongside them, both of them dressed in basic black combat leathers, no sleeves.

When she glanced at the one to her left, it was to find him staring at her.

Black haired and golden skinned, he had pale, *pale* eyes ringed in a pure blue that echoed Raphael's, his wings a beaten gold where an angel's largest flight feathers would be. In contrast, where the Legion fighter's wings grew out of his back, the leathery texture was a black identical to the black in Elena's wings, the color bleeding into a midnight blue that merged with the gold.

It was the same exact coloring as the Primary had, the Legion all minted on the same press, but she knew this wasn't the Primary. While the leader of the Legion gave off a sense of terrible age, of infinite memory, this fighter appeared oddly young to Elena's senses. As if he'd been barely formed before their eons-long Sleep in the deep.

Raising her hand, she waved, just to see what he would do. Only the Primary had spoken to Elena and Raphael thus far. Interaction such as she'd had with him on the rooftop that day was even rarer. "Hello!" she called out in concert with her wave.

The Legion fighter tilted his head to the side like a curious bird and swung closer. Then he raised his hand and echoed Elena's move. Delighted, she laughed and waved back. His lips moved, as if he were trying to figure out how to laugh or smile. Though he gave up the attempt soon afterward, he stayed by her side across the Hudson.

*Do you wish me to command them to stop the escort?*

Elena shook her head at Raphael's question. *They seem to like doing it for some reason and it's harmless enough.* The escort home—whether to the Enclave or to the Tower—had begun quietly, soon after the initial postbattle repairs were complete, and was now a ritual. *Unless you're planning to sweep me up into a dance . . .*

*Are you agreeing to be naked above Manhattan?*

*Not this century.* Skin heating at even the idea of it, though not all of that heat was mortification, she swept down to the river. The Legion fighter dropped with her and skimmed over the rippling water at her side, a puzzled expression on his face. *I think he's trying to figure out why I'd want to do this.*

*I do not think the Legion yet understands joy.* Raphael winged down to join her before the two of them soared back up almost vertically to reach the top of the cliff beyond which sat their home. Elena's muscles strained at the ascent but she was exhilarated at completing it without faltering.

"Yes!" She pumped her arm up and down as she joined Raphael on the lawn.

The Legion fighter landed beside her, while his partner came down next to Raphael. Turning to her archangel, she said, "How was my form?" It was a serious question.

"You're listing slightly to the left."

"I had that feeling. I can't quite get the balance right." Frowning, she settled her wings and looked to the Legion fighter who'd waved at her. "Any tips?"

"You are accustomed to carrying a crossbow on the right side of your body, and you tilt to balance yourself out even when you don't have it strapped on."

Elena stared. *Did I just imagine that or did he speak?*

*He spoke.* Raphael shifted his attention to the fighter. "Your insight is acute." Turning to Elena when the fighter inclined his head toward him, in the way the Legion had of doing with Raphael, he said, "You don't need to fix the listing. Learn to be aware of it and conscious of how it affects your balance when you don't have the crossbow."

Elena nodded, thanked the Legion fighter, then said, "Want to come for a walk?" to him and his partner both. "I'm heading to the greenhouse."

*Guild Hunter, what are you doing?*

*Trying to humanize them, so to speak.* She couldn't keep being disturbed by a force that belonged so deeply to her and Raphael that the knowledge was a hum in her bones. *Wouldn't you need a few pointers if you'd been buried at the bottom of the ocean for millennia?*

"I will tell Montgomery to send refreshments to you."

When Elena swiveled on her heel to walk toward the

greenhouse, both Legion fighters fell in with her. *Hah,* she said to Raphael, *bet you didn't think they'd accept my invitation.*

*You would win that bet.*

Blowing him a kiss over her shoulder, she carried on to the greenhouse. She usually took off most of her weapons once inside the warm, humid haven, though she kept them within easy reach, but today she didn't unstrap a single knife. It was one thing to try to get to know them, another to blindly trust a millennia-old force that had come out of nowhere, hum in the bones or not.

She was hyperconscious of the fighters standing silently on either side of the doorway while she checked her plants. When Montgomery, dressed as per usual in an elegant black suit, his shirt white, arrived with a tray of coffee and small, delicious things, she said, "Have I told you how much I love you, Montgomery?"

"Not today, my lady."

Elena winced inwardly. The butler had become used to calling her "Guild Hunter," and then the battle had happened and he'd reverted. "What did you bring?" she asked, knowing Montgomery would've already noted his mistake.

"Éclairs made fresh by Sivya, blueberry muffins, and fruit." Pouring the coffee into a mug for her and adding two sugars, he placed it on her bench. "Would the gentlemen like a drink?"

Elena looked to the fighters, held up her mug in a silent question.

One of them finally spoke. "We do not require fuel."

"Then I will leave you to your work, Guild Hunter."

Figuring her two guests might have hit their limit when it came to new experiences, she returned to her plants . . . and became aware they'd closed the distance to her in deadly silence.

# 6

Skin prickling, she waited to see what they'd do.

Nothing.

Her eyes fell on the empty terra-cotta pots she'd lined up at the back of her bench. Inspired, she gave each fighter one, curious to see their response. "Could you fill these with soil for me? The bag's over there."

They moved to the bag as one and began to scoop out the rich potting soil using their hands. About to tell them to stop, put on gloves, she realized it would make no difference to the two. When asked, the Primary said the Legion were "of the earth, of life." Now, as they dug their hands into the soil, she saw an unexpected easing in the shoulders of both males, their lashes lowering and chests expanding.

*Raphael.*

*Do you need a rescue?*

*No.* Seeing her fighter had filled his pot, she said, "Why don't you transfer one of these seedlings?" She indicated the flat, shallow tray in which she'd nurtured several different plants to life.

As she watched, he removed one with care, placed it into the pot after scooping out a hole, then gently patted in the soil around it.

*I think we need to create gardens in the Legion building. Part of the roof, some of the larger planned balconies, areas under a skylight, all of them will work.*

Raphael's response was immediate. *They are of the earth, must be nourished by it in some way while they're active. It is why they are so often in Central Park.*

*That's what I think,* she said, seeing the second fighter join the first and, after a glance at her for permission, reach into the seedling tray.

*Are you able to take on the task of organizing the gardens?*

*Yes.* It would be a fascinating project, and perhaps one in which she could involve some of the injured who weren't yet ready for full duties.

"It is done."

Taking in the beautifully potted plants the fighters set in front of her, she said, "Want to do more?"

It was an hour later that she returned to the house, having left the two men in the greenhouse, after assuring them they could stay as long as they liked. She'd seen movement through the glass from the outside, their silhouetted hands touching the leaves of the overhanging ferns.

Heading upstairs, she changed, then tracked Raphael down in his study. After having come so close to never again feeling his touch, she didn't deny her need to be close to her archangel. Life was unpredictable—they might not have a quiet night together for another week or month if things went to shit again.

"Dinner will be a while," she said, sliding her arms around his waist. "I've decided to seduce you for my entrée."

The erotic, exotic taste of angel dust on her lips, on her skin, Raphael's silent response making her shiver. He was dipping his head toward her when a chime interrupted the silence. It came from the large video screen built into the wall to Elena's left. There were very few people who had the direct code, but that included his mother and the entire Cadre.

"It is Titus," Raphael said after glancing at the incoming caller ID.

Elena frantically brushed the incriminating shimmer of

angel dust off his lips and face, then tried to wipe her own using the bottom of her T-shirt, while her body continued to throb with sexual heat. "Well?"

Rubbing his thumb over the side of her mouth, Raphael fed her the bone-melting taste. "We should stay in the shadows."

Elena groaned but pulled the curtains shut to block out the last of the sunset, throwing the study into a mild gloom. "Okay, go."

She didn't always stay beside him when he answered such calls—she didn't have the kind of power to be involved at that political level and, frankly, she didn't want it. Her priority was on doing what was necessary to support Raphael. Titus, however, might be responding to the message she'd sent him in her role as Raphael's consort.

"Titus," Raphael said when the other archangel appeared on-screen.

Titus was dressed like the warrior he was, his breastplate shining gold against skin of jet. Elena knew the armor was unlikely to be actual gold but rather a tougher material coated in a thin layer of the precious metal. Because Titus wasn't a play warrior; he was the real deal. Built along the same lines as Galen, his features were rough-hewn, his presence forceful.

"Raphael." Eyes of impenetrable onyx shifted to Elena, his tone quieter than she would've expected from a man of his size and strength, the resonant tone compelling her attention. "Consort."

"I'm delighted to speak to you," Elena said, thankful for the instructions Jessamy had given her in how to interact with an archangel who was an ally but not yet a friend. The last thing she wanted to do was put her foot in it, when the alliances they made now could help save the world during the war to come. It was a certainty that the Archangel of China was going to rise from her regenerative sleep in a bad, bad mood.

"I thank you for your invitation," Titus said in reply to her words. "I will join you during your celebrations."

*Well, crap.* Elena had extended the invitation sure that Titus wouldn't accept. It had been more along the lines of fostering goodwill. The other archangels she'd invited had already sent their regrets, including Hannah and Elijah, who Elena would've been happy to see—but like Elena and Raphael, the other couple needed to be with their people right now.

As for Favashi and Astaad, both had scheduled private visits after the block party.

Knowing how Neha felt about Raphael, but also aware that to not invite her would be seen as an insult, Elena had sent the Queen of Snakes, of Poisons, a personal invitation. The response had been icily polite, but it had been handwritten by Neha herself, which Elena figured had to be better than dead silence.

Michaela was permanently off any guest list Elena made, as was Lijuan's buddy, Charisemnon.

"I look forward to making your acquaintance in truth," she said to Titus now, dredging up more of Jessamy's lessons. The historian and librarian of the angelic race had the patience of a saint, even when her pupil pretended to collapse and die from the mind-numbing complexity of angelic protocol.

"I, too, will be glad to see you, Titus," Raphael said, his wing sliding over her own. "You have contained the situation with Charisemnon?"

That situation was the reason Elena had expected Titus to stick close to his territory. He shared a land border with Charisemnon and the two archangels had never had a cordial relationship. Their constant back-and-forth had turned into all-out aggression when Charisemnon sided with Lijuan during the hostilities; not only had Charisemnon used his new ability to create disease to attack New York, he'd begun to send disease carriers over the border into Titus's lands.

"I have had confirmed reports that Charisemnon is sick."

"His mind?" Raphael had seen his own parents go mad with age, but Charisemnon was young in immortal terms.

"No. He is physically ill. My spies tell me he is bedridden, his body covered in sores."

"Archangels do not get ill." An immutable fact throughout angelic history.

"It appears Charisemnon is changing the rules." Titus put his hands on his waist, biceps bulging. "I have spoken to my healer and Keir both about the possible cause—they believe he overextended his ability and it turned on him."

Raphael considered that. "If we remove Lijuan from the picture, Charisemnon appeared to have the strongest Cascade-instigated gift."

The other archangel had taken down hundreds of Raphael's angels in a cowardly strike, leaving five dead and many so brutally injured they'd been little more than bleeding torsos. It would take months of excruciating pain before the youngest would recover, the crime of the Falling one Raphael would never forget. Vengeance among immortals was often a long and deadly process, and Raphael had learned the value of patience long ago.

"Yes." Titus's expression held grim pleasure. "The pestilent fool acted too fast, was too arrogant. Now he pays the price."

"There's another possibility."

Titus frowned at Elena's words, but made it clear she had his attention. Raphael knew that wasn't the African archangel's usual approach to women who were mated, married, or otherwise tied to a powerful male. It wasn't misogyny—Titus had a strong contingent of women in his army, including Galen's mother, Tanae.

It was that, in Titus's mind, there were two kinds of women—the warriors, and all the rest. The latter were to be cosseted and protected and indulged, but not taken seriously. It had, Raphael knew, taken Titus time to accept that Elena didn't fit into the second category.

Despite that, she remained young in angelic terms and wouldn't have had the power to hold the attention of an archangel of Titus's age had Titus not heard of her courage and loyalty during the final battle against Lijuan, when his hunter had chosen to die with him if it would save their people.

"She is a true consort," the other archangel had said to Raphael when the two of them spoke not long after Raphael's troops forced Lijuan's into retreat. "You are a blessed man."

An absolute truth.

"Lijuan," Elena said now, "was"—a pause—"*is* known to share power with those close to her. We saw that with her generals during the battle. They could go for longer, heal faster than our men and women, but the boost only lasted as long as she was in play."

"But to share power with one of the Cadre?" Titus's scowl was thunder, his arms folded across his chest. "It is not possible."

Raphael wasn't so certain. "Charisemnon shouldn't have been able to cause the Falling," he reminded Titus. "He most assuredly should not have been able to negatively affect the older and more powerful of my people."

"Yes." Scowl even heavier, Titus gave a hard nod. "I will think on this. But as matters stand, Charisemnon has pulled his troops back tight to his own borders, and my army is stronger than his, since he cannibalized so many of his foot soldiers by using them as carriers of disease." A dangerous smile. "It may be time I caused an earth tremor or two to remind the cur I do not need Lijuan to flex my ability."

"I would be happy to see Charisemnon disappear into a bottomless cavern."

Titus's laugh boomed through the speakers, the sound huge and open. "I am not yet so strong, but soon." Still grinning, he said, "Have you heard of Michaela's most recent grab for territory?"

"I received her message an hour past," Raphael said, and felt Elena's immediate negative response, though her face gave nothing away. *There is no cause for alarm, Guild Hunter. Michaela is simply slavering for Lijuan's lands.* Out loud, he said, "I plan to ignore her demand for a Cadre meeting to parcel out the land." It was far too soon to declare Lijuan dead, especially when all indications pointed to the opposite conclusion.

"As will I." Arms unfolding, Titus looked directly at Elena. "I am curious to experience a 'block party.' I have not heard of such."

*Guild Hunter, the floor is yours.*

"It'll be quite unlike an angelic ball," she warned with a bluntness Raphael knew Titus would appreciate. "I'm sure that wherever Lijuan is, it'll make her gasp in horror."

Titus's teeth flashed white against his skin. "That is no deterrent! I will be there unless the misbegotten son of an ass on my border manages to crawl out of his sickbed. Raphael. Consort." The African archangel signed off.

Raphael's hunter leaned forward to opaque the screen on

their end before turning to glare at him. "You told me the invite was pro forma."

"You will enjoy Titus, *hbeebti*. He is apt to ask you to spar with him as a sign of respect for your honor." Seeing her begin to look interested, he added, "I would have to refuse on your behalf, of course, since Titus has no subtlety to him and will treat you like a blooded angelic warrior, tearing off your head and limbs in the process."

Elena's mouth snapped shut after having fallen open at the first part of his sentence. "You may possibly have a point." Running her hands through the fall of hair she'd released from its tie, the shade akin to the white fire she'd seen on his wings, she sighed. "It's not that I don't like Titus. He seems okay from what I've seen of him, but I just want to celebrate our survival and victory with our city and our friends, not stress about doing the hostess deal."

"Then I can put your mind at rest." He closed his hand over the arch of her wing, stroked down.

Shivering, she pressed her hand to his chest, lashes falling.

Raphael repeated the intimate caress. The nerve endings in that part of an angel's wings were highly sensitive, and Elena's sensitivity had grown over the preceding months, until he could have her loose limbed and heavy lidded in bed with no touch but this. He'd summarily kill any other man who dared touch her there.

"Titus has no time for formality," he told her as she sagged against him. "He will be the easiest archangelic guest you will ever host—especially as the city will be holding a celebration at the time."

All but purring under his touch, it took her a half minute to respond. "Titus likes to party?"

Raphael laughed. "Yes. He will take pleasure in the energy of our city and seduce five or ten very willing women in the process."

Elena's lashes lifted, pupils hugely dilated against the gray of her irises, the rim of silver that announced her growing immortality dramatic in the dim light. "He doesn't have a harem of concubines?"

"No." Though women did live at Titus's home, they were

not his lovers, but rather those he had given safe harbor. "Titus does not have long liaisons. He spoils the woman he is with at the time, and then he moves on—yet his lovers appear to feel only affection for him." Raphael had seen that firsthand when he'd been a half-grown stripling in Titus's army, having signed on because he knew he could learn more from the archangel when it came to the skills of a warrior than he could from any other living angel.

Of honor, too, he had learned much while in Titus's army. "In all the years that I have known him, never have I heard a woman he has taken to his bed disparage Titus." And because he knew it would amuse his hunter, he added, "Mostly they just sigh at the sound of his name and lose their train of thought."

Elena's laughter was husky, her wing warm and strong under his touch. No one in angelkind had wings like Elena's, the evocative midnight of her feathers flowing into deepest indigo that shaded into blue and the shimmering hue of dawn, her primaries white-gold. "The man's clearly got game." Moaning in the back of her throat when he increased the pressure of his caresses, she nuzzled into the curve of his neck. "That feels so good. Can you do it all night?"

"If you make it worth my while." Reluctantly halting the touch that gave him as much pleasure as it did her, his body hard with arousal, he drew her out of the room. "Montgomery will soon be seeking us out for dinner. We should not shock him."

"I think Montgomery is unshockable at this point."

Raphael caught the butler's eye as they left the study—the vampire had appeared in the hallway when Raphael opened the study door. *It is a quiet evening, Montgomery. A gift after war and chaos. Perhaps you should invite Sivya to a walk along the cliffs.*

Montgomery's eyes reflected alarmed distress. *Sire, I assure you, we have not—*

*I am an archangel, Montgomery. I know those who are mine.* He began to climb the stairs with Elena. *To have two of my trusted people become one, it is not something to disdain.* Understanding the depth of Montgomery's loyalty, he made his approbation even clearer. *You have my sanction to court her, should you need it.*

Halting at the landing, he glimpsed the nervous hope in Montgomery's expression. It was odd to see the distinguished butler thus, but love had a way of making mortals of them all. Bowing deeply, Montgomery said, *Sire.*

"What was that about?" Elena asked the instant they were behind the closed doors to their bedroom. "I knew you two were talking."

Watching her remove her weapons, he said, "Why are you so heavily armed in our own home?" She'd changed into a scoop-necked T-shirt in sky blue and soft black pants that hugged her form, her feet bare. Yet she'd somehow managed to secrete away at least three knives.

"Huh." She stared at the knife she'd pulled from an ankle sheath. "Habit, I guess." Placing the weapons neatly in a bedside drawer, she said, *"So?"*

"Montgomery is courting Sivya."

"No! *Really?*"

"You must pretend not to notice," he cautioned her. "They would be appalled to think they'd been so remiss in their duties as to make you aware of their personal lives."

Elena pursed her lips, eyebrows drawn together, and began to tug off her T-shirt. "But you noticed." The sound came out slightly muffled.

"I am their liege. I am meant to notice and make certain they do not sacrifice their joy in the mistaken belief that I would find their coupling discourteous." He cupped her breasts after she threw the T-shirt over the back of a chair, his need to claim her a pounding in his blood.

He had come to within a split-second of igniting them both on the battlefield in a final attempt to defeat Lijuan's evil, come to within a split-second of never again holding Elena in his arms. The memory was yet raw. "As my consort," he said, dipping his head to press his lips to the curve of her shoulder, "your job is to notice when they are a pair, so as to assure their duties don't separate them any more than necessary."

Her hands were in his hair, her lips warm and wet against the line of his jaw. "It's weird to think of Montgomery and coupling in the same breath." A small gasp when he tugged at one tightly furled nipple. "I'm convinced he sleeps in his suit."

"Enough talk of others, *hbeebti*. It is time for our own coupling." Each hour, every hour of peace was a treasure. War boiled black and violent on the horizon, and when it came, it would engulf the world.

# 7

The sky was a smudgy gray with only the faintest tinge of orange by the time Ashwini and Janvier arrived at their next destination, located in neighboring Soho—though the area bore that name only until sunset. Then it became the Vampire Quarter. That was when the swanky shops and chichi cafés shut their doors, to be replaced by blood cafés and vampire clubs filled with the cruel and the beautiful.

*Hmm . . .*

Removing her helmet after Janvier parked down the street from a freestanding dual-level town house on the edge of the Quarter, she said, "The dog, it might be a vamp who's lost it."

He took off his own helmet and the silky mahogany of his hair tumbled out. She couldn't help it; she reached out and scraped her nails lightly from the front to the back of his scalp, the strands cool and the texture exquisite. Leaning his back against her chest, he made a sound deep in his throat.

Her breath caught, her breasts swelling against her bra.

She wanted to wrap her arms around his shoulders, nuzzle her face into the warm line of his throat, and lick him up. Clenching her fist so tight her nails dug into her palms, she got off the bike and hooked the helmet over a handlebar. Doing the same with his own, Janvier swung off the powerful machine with a lazy grace that always caught her attention—and that of any other female in the vicinity.

"Could be," he said, as if their conversation had never been interrupted by a caress she shouldn't have permitted herself to make. "You know some vamps don't do well after three hundred years or so."

The remembered feel of him burning against her palm, Ashwini unzipped her jacket to give her hands something to do. "What would drinking animal blood do to a vamp?"

Janvier leaned back against the bike after unzipping his own jacket to reveal the thin white T-shirt beneath. He wasn't, however, wearing the twin blades that were his weapons of choice. Pressed up against him on the bike, she'd felt nothing but Janvier, no sign of the crisscrossing holster he'd normally wear on his back, over the tee.

While he hadn't utilized the blades during their mission in Atlanta, she'd become used to seeing them on him since he came to New York. "Where are your kukris?" she asked before he could answer her question about animal blood.

He rubbed the back of his neck, a flush on his cheekbones. "The holster snapped this morning."

Ashwini bit the inside of her cheek in an effort to fight her smile. She'd told him to get the worn leather replaced after seeing the state of it while he'd been staying at her place. While the scabbards were metal, to prevent the razor-sharp blades from cutting through, the holster built around them had to be soft and flexible enough not to limit his range of movement. "That's too bad."

Shooting her a look of open suspicion at the bland response, he shrugged. "It'll take a specialist artisan a week to make a replacement once I send him the old holster. I have no hope of getting myself on Deacon's schedule for at least a year."

At that instant, he looked both sulky and irritated with himself. Knowing how naked she felt without her favorite weapons, she couldn't keep the secret any longer. "Or," she said, "you could use the holster Deacon dropped off at my apartment yesterday."

Janvier straightened. "For me?"

Folding her arms against the impact of the fierce delight in his voice, she nodded. "He used your old holster to make a blueprint for the new one while you were out getting me cake that day." She'd sent him to a specific and distant bakery for just that reason. "The scabbards should slide right in." Deacon did not make mistakes.

"But how? Deacon is booked years in advance."

"He always has time for hunters." Sara's husband had once been a hunter himself.

Janvier's smile was slow, deep, and so painfully real, it caught her heart and refused to let go. "I'm not a hunter."

*But you're mine.* Biting back the words she could never say, not if she cared for him in any way, she scowled. "Don't make a big deal about it or I'll dump it into the Hudson."

Cheeks creased and the sunlight in the bayou green of his eyes blinding, he shook his head. "I cannot help it, *cher.*"

Ashwini broke the eye contact; she couldn't resist him when he smiled that way. "You were telling me about what happens to vamps who drink animal blood."

"The blood of animals is too weak to provide nourishment," he said, his voice liquid warmth that seeped into every cell of her body. "I remember hearing of a vampire who fed on animals for two months after becoming lost in the mountains. *Moitié fou* Billy, they called him. But since he was so weak, he wasn't dangerous."

Ashwini had picked up enough Cajun French from being around Janvier to know he'd just indicated the vamp had gone half-crazy. "So our hypothetical animal-blood drinker might already be out for the count."

A nod. "But there is the desiccation—it's unnatural, unless the pup died in an environment that would produce that result."

Ashwini's phone beeped at that instant. Glancing at the screen, she saw a note from the vet. "Dr. Shamar decided to have another look at the dog before she left for the night, discovered he had a chip embedded under his skin. Kind of thing pet owners put in so cats and dogs can be ID'd if animal control picks them up." The doctor had missed it during her initial examination because the chip had slipped between two ridges of bone.

"She was able to scan it, look up the dog in the system.

Apparently it went missing a couple of days after the end of the fighting." Dr. Shamar had added a note that she'd made no notification to the owners and wouldn't do so until advised otherwise. After thanking the other woman, Ashwini looked at Janvier. "Is that enough time for natural mummification, even in an optimum environment?"

Janvier spread his hands. "We shall have to ask a scientist."

"Honor might know someone." Her best friend was an expert in ancient languages and history and had a wide range of contacts. "I'll give her a call tomorrow." Sliding away her phone, she braced herself against a sudden, chilling wind that tasted of snow. "It's possible Lijuan shared her ability to suck the life out of people with someone else."

Janvier closed the distance between them, his body heat a caress. "It was her ace in the hole. I can't see her giving that away, can you, *cher*?"

"No." It was Naasir who'd told them the Archangel of China could share strength with her generals, but it wasn't a permanent transfer. As soon as Lijuan was out of the equation, those generals had crumpled.

Hands on her hips, she chewed on another possibility. "Lijuan's creations tend to be infectious." The archangel's horrific reborn had been a plague. "Only"—Ashwini frowned—"she wasn't creating when she fed. The sacrifices ended up shells, so I guess we're back to square one on that."

Janvier shifted to take the brunt of a fresh gust of wind. "I'll report our theories to Raphael nonetheless. He must be alerted to the possibility that Lijuan may have left a lingering taint in the city."

Ashwini raised both eyebrows. "Back in Atlanta, you said you'd never met him, and now you're on a first-name basis?"

"I hadn't met him then," he said, that sneakily seductive sunlight still in his eyes. "Vampires my age do not usually ever have personal contact with the archangel to whom we give our allegiance."

"Most vampires your age aren't as strong as you." Or as smart, as tough. Having long ago fulfilled the terms of his Contract, Janvier didn't have to serve anyone. He chose to do so. "You're an asset."

"And the sire"—Janvier cupped her cheek—"treats his assets well."

Not wanting to understand the implicit message, she broke the contact to focus on a car in the distance, its brake lights glowing rubies in the gray light of dusk. "I'll do some research in the Guild Archives, see if I can find any similar cases."

Janvier began to walk toward the town house that was his objective, his expression telling her he saw too much. "I'll let you know if Dmitri has any insights." Metal creaked as he pushed open the decorative wrought-iron gate that fronted the short pathway to the town house. "Let us see to the health of these cattle first."

Ashwini took in the town house as they walked, grasping at the distraction from the need that was a wrenching tug low in her belly. The building appeared new; the walls gleamed a stylish black, but the door was painted the same glossy orange-red as the gate, as was the trim. "Nice place." If you had a million or ten lying around.

"Want one?" said the vampire by her side. "I can buy it, allow you to live rent free on the premises."

"Yeah?" she said, playing along because she only had so much self-control when it came to Janvier, and she wasn't about to use it to handle his flirting . . . didn't want to shut that down. "On what condition?"

"I would have a key, of course. To make sure you are keeping my property in good repair." His innocent look had probably spelled the downfall of at least a hundred virgins in his lifetime.

"Such a conscientious landlord. Would you fix the plumbing, too?"

"If you let me put my pipe in your sprocket." Pure wickedness in his smile at her groan, he ignored the door knocker shaped like a snarling lion to rap his knuckles directly against the gleaming paint.

She wanted so badly to kiss him that the craving was a ferocious beast inside her. Smile fading as his pupils dilated, Janvier went to angle his body toward her when the door opened to bring her face-to-face with the last person she'd expected to see here. "Arvi?" She stared incredulously at the tall man with aquiline features, silver-dusted black hair, and skin the exact shade as her own.

Her brother stared at her. "What are you doing here?"

"She's with me." No charm in Janvier's expression now, only a cool, deadly intensity that had never been directed at Ashwini. "You aren't one of the cattle."

Arvi flinched. "Certainly not. I was called here to provide medical assistance."

"I wasn't aware you did house calls," Ashwini said, her brain running on automatic.

"It was a favor for a friend." He pinned her with the near black of his eyes. "I'll expect you for dinner in the next week."

Ashwini stared after him as he strode past her and down the pathway on that command. She hadn't seen him for two months, but though the silver in his hair might be a touch more apparent, his face remained unlined. Arvan Taj was a man who'd age into handsome elegance. And his smile? It could devastate; she knew that despite having seen it only once since she was nine.

"He's the one, isn't he?" Janvier asked, voice rough and expression dark. "The boy whose photo you carry in your phone, the one who hurt you."

She realized he'd gotten the wrong idea, but the door filled with another body before she could correct him. The blonde's stunning blue-green eyes were round with worry until they alighted on Janvier. "Janni!" She leaped into his arms.

Catching her, he chuckled, the grating emotion Ashwini had just heard in his tone no longer in evidence when he said, "*Petite* Marie May."

Folding her arms, Ashwini leaned against the wall as the giggling girl tried to kiss Janvier on the mouth. He deflected it as smoothly as he did everything else, taking the kiss on his cheek before setting her down. "What are you doing here, Marie?" he asked with what Ashwini recognized as genuine concern. "Last I saw you, you were set on becoming a star of the silver screen, *non*?"

Marie beamed, her expression so earnest, it was scary. "I live with Giorgio." She stroked her hands down her ankle-length gown of cream lace, the bodice modest and the sleeves long. "I serve him."

"When did this happen?" A soft question. "You are barely out of pigtails."

Marie's curls bounced as she slapped Janvier playfully on the chest, clearly not realizing how angry he'd become. "Janni! I'm *nineteen* next month." An antique amethyst ring sparkled on her index finger. "Giorgio and I met at the studios—he's a producer, you know."

"I see. He plans to share your talent with the world?"

"Not yet." Marie made a face. "He says I'm too young for the piranha pit and should be twenty-one at least before I start. He got me into the most incredible acting master class, though"—a clap of her hands, the smile back on high beam—"so I'll be ready when it's time!"

Not sure what to think of this Giorgio, Ashwini held her silence while Janvier whispered in Marie's ear, the rich brown strands of his hair sliding to touch the gold of hers. The sight should've made Ashwini jealous. It didn't. Because Janvier's capacity for loyalty was unrelenting and she had his unspoken promise . . . even though she'd done her hardest to give it back, regardless of her desire to hoard it close.

Smile washing away to a faded watercolor of its previous self, Marie bit down on her lower lip, her mouth a perfect pink bow, and glanced over her shoulder. "I shouldn't say." It was a whisper.

"Marie." Janvier touched his finger to the creamy skin of her cheek, a coaxing smile on his face. "It is a complaint. You know I must investigate."

Marie glanced over her shoulder again, then gestured him closer after shooting a wary look at Ashwini. "It's not all of us, just Brooke." Her nose scrunched up. "She's been with Giorgio the longest and she was mad because she thought Giorgio was paying more attention to me and Leisel than to her, so she started telling people he was hurting her."

Taking a breath, Marie continued. "Today she even cut herself! Now that Giorgio's been so good to her with the doctor and everything, she's sorry, but the rumors have already started." The stamp of a small foot under the lace of the dress. "It's *so* unfair."

"I'll need to talk to Brooke."

"I'll get her." All the fury leaked out of her as quickly as it had built up. "Don't be angry at her, okay?" Her eyes pleaded with Janvier. "She's crazy about Giorgio. She thinks . . ."

"What, *bébé*?" Janvier tucked her hair behind her ear, his voice gentle.

Marie melted.

He was good at that, Ashwini thought, at making women trust him. Funny thing was, he never tried his tricks on her, except in play, both of them fully aware of his motives and desires. Quite unlike the innocent Marie May.

"Brooke thinks she's getting old," the girl whispered, blinking back tears. "Even though Giorgio loves her, she doesn't believe him."

There it was, one immutable reason why a relationship between a mortal and an immortal could never work long-term. The mortal would inevitably fade, and even if the love survived, it would leave the immortal broken when his lover died. Especially, she thought, her eyes lingering on Janvier, when the immortal was the kind of man who knew how to be loyal.

"Hush." Janvier bent his legs to bring himself down to Marie's height. "I will be kind." He drew the girl into his arms. "You know I do not hurt women."

A jerky nod, Marie's throat moving as she drew back. "I'll go find Brooke."

"Is it only the three of you who serve as Giorgio's blood family?"

Shaking her head, Marie said, "Penelope and Laura do, too."

"Fetch them all, won't you, Marie."

"I will. You can wait in the parlor." Leading them to the room, the girl left in a rush of sweet, floral perfume.

Ashwini and Janvier stood there in silence, tension a taut thread that tied them to one another. The expensive but cold décor—white walls, white sofas overflowing with black cushions, the paintwork on the wall a dripping canvas of darkest red—only intensified the silent, *intimate* thing that pulsed between them.

As if they had become lovers long ago.

# 8

When Marie returned, it was with four others: a gorgeous black woman as dewy skinned and soft as Marie, whom Ashwini pegged as Leisel, two leggy brunettes apt to be Penelope and Laura, and a handsome auburn haired woman in her late twenties with a small bandage on the pale skin of her right cheek. Brooke, unless she was mistaken.

All the women were dressed in a style Ashwini had termed "vamp couture." Leisel's dress was heavy aqua silk bordered with lace of the same shade, the lush fabric and simple style throwing the rich hue of her skin into sharp relief. A thin bracelet circled her wrist, its cost probably equal to Ashwini's pay from a difficult hunt.

One of the brunettes wore tight black pants with a cherry red top, the tails tucked into her waistband and the sleeves slashed to expose the delicate gold of her skin. Around her neck was an intricate gold choker with a small padlock in front. Her fellow brunette wore an identical outfit, except that her top was emerald green and the choker silver.

A matched pair. Cute. Or stomach churning.

Brooke, meanwhile, was in a tailored gown that hugged her curves, the fabric a pale peach striped with vertical lines of raspberry. No lace on the gown, but she'd sheathed her hands in fine lace gloves that exactly matched the peach of the gown, her hair twisted up into a chignon anchored by jeweled combs.

"Ah, we must have drinks for our guests!" The words came from the vampire who'd followed the women into the room. Against the royal blue of his fitted velvet coat, his skin glowed a white as true as the fall of lace at his throat and wrists, his eyes a brilliant topaz and the thick golden waves of his hair shining in the light thrown from the crystal chandelier above. Giorgio was a living, breathing advertisement of the beauty that could come with vampirism.

It made Ashwini think of what Janvier would look like in another five hundred years. She didn't think he'd ever be this glossy, this uncomfortably perfect—as with Dmitri, his rough edges were internal and part of what made him Janvier. Never did she want him to lose the heart of the bayou-born boy he'd once been.

Melancholy threatened on the heels of that thought, because no matter what, she'd be long dead before he ever reached Giorgio's age, which she estimated to be around six or seven hundred.

"Janvier." Giorgio extended both hands, the lace frothing over what looked to be a diamond-studded identity bracelet on one wrist, a platinum watch on the other. Another diamond winked in his left ear. "It has been too long, *mon ami*."

Used to Janvier's charm and tendency to never make enemies when he could as easily make friends, Ashwini was surprised when he didn't return the gesture, instead saying, "Drinks aren't necessary, Giorgio. I simply need to talk to Brooke and your other women. Alone."

Smile not dimming a fraction, Giorgio put his arm around Brooke. "Of course." Kissing her uninjured cheek, to the possessive stroke of her hand over his chest, he left the room.

"Ash," Janvier said, "will you wait with Marie and the others while I speak to Brooke?"

"No problem."

The instant he was alone with Brooke, Janvier focused on the butterfly bandage high on her right cheek. "You've been hurt."

"I did it myself," Brooke answered without hesitation, heat under the pale cream of her skin. "It was foolish and done in a moment of pique. I'm so very sorry to have brought you out here for nothing." Twisting her hands in front of her, she hunched her shoulders inward. "Giorgio is a wonderful master and I am ashamed of my actions."

Stepping closer to her, Janvier lowered his tone to the same gentleness he'd used on Marie. "No one will do you harm." As far as Janvier was concerned, the abuse of women was an unforgivable crime. "You have my protection. Speak the truth."

Brooke's eyes shone wet, her lower lip trembling. Raising her hands, she placed them against Janvier's chest. "I am," she rasped. "From the bottom of my heart, I am. If there is to be punishment for wasting the Tower's time, I will take it." She inhaled a shaky breath, her smile piercing. "My Giorgio is innocent of all but loving me even when I am foolish." A single tear hit Janvier's hand where he cupped Brooke's cheek, her other cheek holding a trail of wet.

She couldn't have appeared more romantically tragic if she'd tried.

Janvier spoke to Brooke for another ten minutes, but the most senior of Giorgio's cattle stood firm in her assertions. Releasing her, he talked to Marie, Leisel, Laura, and Penelope one at a time. All backed up Brooke's statement that she'd done the injury to herself and that Giorgio didn't mistreat his women.

The five held hands when united again, unanimous in their declaration that Giorgio was a good and fair "master."

"We aren't prisoners, Janni," Marie said, eyes bright and naïve and fervent to Ashwini's gaze. "Any one of us is free to do as she wishes. Laura's leaving in a few days, aren't you?"

The brunette nodded, her smile poignant. "I'll miss Giorgio and the rest of my blood family desperately, but I'm homesick. The master bought me a first-class ticket home to Nebraska, and he says he'll pay for me to return if I ever change my mind."

"I'm thinking of joining her." Penelope squeezed her friend's hand, her fingernails decorated in gold polish with a tiny constellation of diamantés in the top left corners. "At least for a visit." A sweet, affectionate kiss to Laura's cheek. "Giorgio knows how close we are. He's offered to pay for me to go to visit her."

"He treasures us." The words were Brooke's but the sentiment was clearly shared by all five women.

The fatuous devotion on their faces made Ashwini's skin crawl.

"Brooke and the others," she said to Janvier when they left the town house five minutes later, "are as much junkies as those mainlining coke." Not every vampire could give pleasure with his bite, but the thrill of having fangs at the jugular or the carotid was rush enough for many. "Add in Giorgio's kind of beauty, and they mistake dependency for love. It's like he has his own miniature cult."

Janvier straddled the bike, passed her a helmet. "Let's ride. I need to get the sickly devotion of it all out of my head."

Initiating the throaty roar of the engine once she was on, he took them through Greenwich Village to Chelsea Piers, then hugged the edge of Manhattan until they reached the George Washington Bridge. Powering over it in the winter dark that had fallen while they'd been inside the town house, he drove to the cliffs of the Angel Enclave, his bike obviously well known enough that none of the angelic guards stopped him.

When he brought the bike to a halt, it was mere feet from a snowy cliff that overlooked the river they'd just crossed. Ashwini couldn't see any houses, only towering trees on either side of this narrow clearing, so either this land was unclaimed or—more probably—on the far edge of an angel's property line. Taking off her helmet as Janvier removed his, she swung off the bike, placed the helmet on the ground, and walked to the edge of the cliff. The lights of Manhattan sparkled on the other side of the water that moved slumberous and sullen tonight.

Drawing in deep drafts of the bitingly cold air, she tried to shake off the crawling sensation she'd felt inside Giorgio's elegant town house. New as the house was, she'd picked up nothing from the walls, no embedded whispers of horror. Her response derived solely from, as Janvier had put it, "the sickly devotion of it all."

Having remained on the bike, Janvier said, "Giorgio's household has little to recommend it."

Ashwini frowned, shifted on her heel so she could see his face. "You say that like the cattle-master relationship isn't a bad idea full stop."

"It's not always about exploitation." He leaned forward on the handlebars, leather jacket unzipped and hair a sexy mess. "I know vampires who have had the same cattle for decades. They truly treat the men and women as family, are more loyal to them than to other vampires, mourn each who passes. Some of the most haunting memorials I've seen in the graveyards of New Orleans are to blood family members."

"Could be it's just about keeping the food happy."

"Food is not so difficult to find, *cher.*" A liquid shrug. "Vampirism gives the old ones astonishing physical beauty and many are also wealthy and powerful. Mortals are drawn to them like flies, yet it is the oldest of my kind who most often have cattle.

"Unlike Giorgio, the majority don't view it as a sexual relationship or treat those in their blood family as trophies, the physical appearance of their cattle an unimportant consideration. Friendship, affection, respect, these are the keys. I once asked a six-hundred-year-old friend why he kept cattle, and he said he was tired of the constant round of meaningless seduction, wanted only the intimacy and comfort of family around him."

Sitting back up, he played with a blade he must've slipped out from his boot. "You must remember that many of my kind were born in a time when to be a family was to live in a single home, several generations one on top of the other, newborns sharing rooms with grandparents, and warriors seated side by side with younger siblings, cousins, and fosters. That is what they seek to recreate, for the old ones often find loneliness the worst pain of all."

His words stopped Ashwini; she'd never considered things from that angle and it made a heartrending kind of sense. "I grew up like that," she found herself saying when most of the time, she did her best not to think of the past. "My paternal grandparents lived with us, as did an aunt before she got married, and another who'd been through a divorce." It had never been quiet in the Taj household.

Janvier's expression was intent. "So you understand."

"The need to create a family? Yes." Wasn't that what she'd done with the Guild when her own broke into too many pieces to put back together? "But that's not what we saw today."

"No." He stared out toward the water. "Giorgio treats his

women as pretty dolls. His to own, to dress, to bejewel. Marie May had such a fire in her when I first met her—that fire is now all focused on Giorgio. Soon she will forget her dreams."

"And when she gets too old for him, he'll nudge her out like he's doing with Laura and Penelope."

"*Oui*. What they see as kindness is simply Giorgio's way of creating space for new playthings."

Red in her vision at the memory of the smug bastard who, it was clear, would soon push poor, lovesick Brooke to the curb, she folded her arms. "Can you get the young ones out?"

"No." Jaw tight, he said, "They are of age and the Tower cannot interfere in domestic arrangements without cause." That fact clearly not sitting well with him, he swung his leg off the bike and came to stand beside her. "I'll call Marie tomorrow and reiterate that she and the others can come to me at any time, but I can do nothing about their mental and emotional enslavement when they go into it with eyes wide open."

"Five minutes alone with Brooke," Ashwini said, "and I'd know for certain if she was telling the truth." Memory echoes were the strongest in old ones like the angel Nazarach, but with a little more effort, Ashwini could pick them up from those under four hundred. The latter limitation was why she could continue to work as a hunter—it was extremely rare for the Guild to be contracted to hunt an older vamp. The angels usually took care of any problems at that level themselves.

Unfortunately, the limitation wasn't set in stone. Janvier was opaque to her—had always been that way—but usually, the better she knew someone, the more chance she'd connect with them regardless of age. And every so often, even a young stranger would set off her senses, drag her under. It was why she was so careful about physical contact.

Janvier ran his knuckles down the line of her spine. "If you find darkness in Giorgio's blood slave, it'll live in you forever. No, I won't permit this."

"Since when do you have the right to 'permit' me anything?" she said, turning away.

He grabbed hold of one of her wrists, his grip gentle but unbreakable. "Who was he?"

Her response was instinctive, her mind shying away from the agony of it all. "None of your business."

Hauling her to him, Janvier held her wrist against his chest, his heart pumping steady and strong under the thin barrier of the T-shirt, his body so warm she wanted to stretch out into it like a cat before a fire. "We are beyond that, and you know it. That's why you've been running so hard from me."

"I seem to recall hunting you," she said, her traitorous fingers curling into the heat of him.

He tugged her closer, and his voice, it held so many layers when he spoke. "I see such pain in your eyes, such loss." Breath shallow and shoulders rigid, he whispered, "Did you love him so much?"

At that instant, she knew she could strike a blow that would be a sledgehammer to the strange, nameless, precious thing between them, the connection that had formed the first day they came eye to eye. He'd grinned at her as she notched a crossbow bolt in place, then blown her a kiss and moved with the rapid grace she'd come to associate always and only with him. She'd almost smiled in return before remembering she was there to bring him in to face a very irate angel.

That angel had pulled the hunt order seventy-two hours later, after Janvier made nice. She'd walked into the angel's residence to find him laughing with Janvier, while the damn Cajun who'd led her into a swamp, before escaping with a slickness she'd reluctantly admired, lay sprawled in a heavy green armchair, long legs kicked out. It was the first time he'd called her *cher*, asking her when they'd play again.

*Et quand en va rejouer, cher?*

"I have photos of all my family on my phone," she whispered, unable to destroy their relationship with a lie that would forever alter the honesty at its core. "You just saw Arvi's that day . . . my brother."

Janvier released a harsh breath, a shudder rippling through his body. "He's at least twenty years older than you."

"Nineteen," she said. "I was a late-in-life oops baby." A mistake, a regret. "In many ways he was my father. That's why he talks to me like that, assumes I'll do what he says."

"Your parents?"

"You didn't already hack into a database and look it all up?" It was stupid to avoid the question, but she'd been doing it so long it was habit.

Thumb moving over her skin, Janvier waited until she met his eyes to say, "That would've been against the rules."

Ashwini couldn't pretend she didn't know the rules. "My mother and father died when I was nine."

"An accident?"

"Yes. That's when we lost our sister, Tanu, too." The words were a lie wrapped in a devastating truth but this one secret she couldn't share. Not today. Not until she no longer had a choice. "After they were gone, Arvi stepped up, took charge of everything." She'd thought he hung the moon, her smart, handsome brother.

"Love does not cause such shadows as I see in you, my fierce Ashblade."

# 9

Unable to bear the naked emotion in his eyes, because it was a mirror of her own, she used her Guild training to break his hold. The fact that she'd waited until now was another danger sign, another warning. "I didn't fit," she said, and it was all she could say right then without breaking completely.

Moving to the very edge of the cliff, the snow crunching beneath her boots, she turned the conversation back to what she could handle. "My brother is a neurosurgeon." One of the most revered in the profession. "Dr. Arvan Taj *does not* do house calls, not for anyone. And he definitely doesn't treat cattle."

"Giorgio was once a renowned physician." Janvier's boots broke through the ice crust over the snow as he came to join her. "He was responsible for a number of significant breakthroughs in his time and remains respected in medical circles. Perhaps because it is only in the past four decades that he has chosen to abandon his vocation for the pursuit of a selfish pleasure that does not care who it hurts."

Catching something unexpected in his tone, she frowned. "He called you *mon ami*. You were friends?"

"No, but there was a time when that address would've made me proud." Pushing a hand through his hair, he said, "I spent a month in his château in the Alps a long time ago. He was having a salon featuring a select number of the world's best minds and I stumbled into it when I was tasked with delivering an important letter." Eyes distant, he shook his head. "For some reason, he invited me to remain, though I was an ignorant courier with barely half a century of vampirism behind him."

"You've always been smart." It was a flame in him, the desire to grasp at life with both hands, absorbing knowledge in a thousand different fragments.

"I am happy to know you think so, *cher*, for your mind seduced me long ago." The faint hint of a smile lay on his lips, Janvier a man who was never dark for long. "But I was out of my league there, the others around the fire scientists and artists, philosophers and explorers." A sigh, his throat arched as he looked up at a night sky become hazy with clouds. "It could be those great men and women decided they needed an audience. It doesn't matter—I drank in the knowledge they shared as if it were rain and my soul a thirsty plain."

It was an image that tugged at her soul, made her want to lock herself in a room with him for days, weeks, months, just so she could hear of the roads he'd traveled, the places he'd been, the people he'd met. Time was running out from between her clenched fists, and she had so many things she didn't yet know about him.

"Did Giorgio have cattle then?" she asked through the ache of need.

"Yes, and he has always had an eye for nubile beauty, but such is true of many men, mortal or immortal, *non*?"

Ashwini nodded, thinking of the septuagenarian who lived in her building, his companion a foxy redhead in her thirties.

"But back then," Janvier continued, "Giorgio treated the older of his cattle with love and respect even after their youth faded—during my time in the château, I met one who was in her sixth decade. To her, Giorgio was family, and the feeling was reciprocated."

Ashwini couldn't get her head around the idea that the vampire they'd just left had once been such a different man, a sudden fear choking off her breath. "Don't let immortality do that to you," she whispered. "Don't let it steal your soul."

Moss green eyes held her own. "It is, others tell me, far easier to stay human if you split your heart in two and give one part to another to keep."

*Give it to me,* she wanted to say. *I'll protect it with my life . . . and I'll give you my heart in return.* Folding her arms against the urge that would ultimately cause him pain so terrible it permanently scarred, she broke the searing intimacy of the eye contact to stare out toward the dazzle of Manhattan. "I guess Arvi might do a favor for a friend. He and Giorgio probably met at a charity gala or some other black-tie affair, became acquainted."

Her brother was at home at such events, the perfect, urbane date. Because though Arvi was a man born to be the head of a family, the mantle sitting on his shoulders as if he'd been made to wear it, he had never married. A decade back, Ashwini had thought that was about to change, but the gifted female surgeon whom she was dead certain Arvi loved passionately had gone on to become another man's bride. Since then, Arvi had played the field. It didn't suit him, but she understood why he did it.

"You've never mentioned your brother before." Janvier stroked strands of her hair between his fingertips.

The tiny tugs on her scalp reaching deep inside her, Ashwini looked up at a wash of wind to see a squadron of angels passing overhead on a low flight path. They dipped their wings as a unit as they passed, and she knew Janvier had been spotted. He raised his free hand in acknowledgment right as a fresh gust of wind blew his hair back from his face.

That face could never be called beautiful. It had too many rough edges. But sexy? Yes, Janvier was sexy in every way a man could be sexy. The curve of his lips, the dark shadow of scruff on his jaw that said he didn't fuss about being pretty, the glint of sinful knowledge in his eyes, the lazy way he moved, it added up to a package a woman would have to exercise incredible willpower to repudiate.

Ashwini's willpower was at an all-time low.

As if he sensed that, Janvier slid his hand down her back to hook one thumb into her back right pocket. It was pushing at her boundaries and it was what he always did. If he ever stopped flirting with her, a part of her would die. "Do you have to report in to Illium in person?" she asked, ignoring his implied question about her brother, unable to go there, to talk about the agony that both divided and united her and Arvi; she couldn't forget his betrayal, and Arvi couldn't forgive what he saw as hers.

"I can call in the information." Janvier's gaze was acute, but his words easy. "You?"

"I'll do the same."

Separating to opposite ends of the cliff, she rang Sara while he contacted Illium.

Ashwini updated the Guild Director on the details, then said, "My instincts are screaming that the dog is a harbinger of worse to come." The feeling had nothing to do with her more unusual abilities; it was pure hunter instinct. "I'm going to keep an eye on the area, work my contacts to see if I can shake anything loose."

"I'm not putting you on an active hunt for another two weeks at least," Sara replied, "so take the time and keep me in the loop. No heroics." It was a command. "I damn well don't intend to watch the undertakers put another one of my people in the ground."

There had been far too many funerals after the battle that had thundered in the air, on the rooftops, and along the streets of Manhattan. Hunters, vampires, angels . . . the wave of death had been indiscriminate, the grief left in its wake a heavy shadow that colored Sara's order tonight. "Noted," Ashwini said to the other woman before hanging up.

Then she turned, looked at the man who walked toward her, his hair wind-tumbled and his smile an invitation, and knew she was about ten seconds away from making what might be the worst mistake of both their lives.

Janvier wanted Ashwini. He'd wanted her since their first meeting in the luxuriant green humidity of a cypress swamp, her skin beaded with sweat and dragonflies buzzing in the air. It had taken everything he had not to attempt to seduce her then and there, the desire to lick up the salt-laced tang of her as he drove his cock into her body a sudden, violent craving.

The fact that she had a crossbow aimed at his gut hadn't dampened his lust, just heightened it, but the lust had only been the start. Each time they tangled, he'd learned a little more about his Ashblade, until having her body would no longer be enough. Janvier wanted all of the gifted, complicated, skilled woman in front of him.

Including her trust.

Today, the rich brown eyes he'd seen laughing, infuriated, amused, were sad and brittle. A small push and he knew she'd permit the seduction, allow him to use his body to make her forget the pain that lived in her, that huge thing too terrible for a mortal to possess. He could kiss her, taste her in an effort to assuage the need inside him, even thrust his cock so deep into her that she cried out. And when it was over, he'd have destroyed the most beautiful thing he'd encountered, that he'd *felt*, in all eternity.

"It's a great night for a long ride," he said before she could speak. "No real wind, and I can handle any snow that falls. You game?"

A pregnant pause, those mysterious eyes locked on his face.

His nerves stretched taut; Janvier didn't know if he had the strength to refuse her if she made him a different offer, even knowing it would be a devastating mistake. She was his Achilles' heel, his personal, luminous madness.

"Yes," she said at last. "Let's go."

Grabbing the helmet he'd bought especially for her and that he never lent to anyone else, he put it on her with his own hands, flipping down the fog-resistant visor to protect her face. Then, zipping up his jacket after a glance at Ash to make sure hers was secure, he put on his helmet and straddled the bike. She hesitated for a second before swinging up behind him, long and sleek and the most complex, fascinating creature he'd ever met.

Not interrupting the silence that had fallen between them, he drove down the narrow cliff access road with care; he might have a daredevil streak, but despite her grit and determination, Ash was mortal. If he totaled the bike, she could die. His gut tightened, his spine locking.

*Only a few more decades. Then it'll be time for a new hunter to chase you.*

She'd said that to him the first time she ever asked him for help. They'd gone into Nazarach's territory, survived the sadistic angel, shared a decadent promise of a kiss on a train platform before she left him, his wild windstorm of a lover. Because she *was* very much his lover, even if they'd never been skin to skin. The idea of being with any other woman after he met her had simply been out of the question.

He would not—*could* not—let her die. Not the tempestuous storm that was her.

The light would go out of the world if she was gone.

The only impediment to her becoming near-immortal was Ash's own resistance to the idea. Raphael had been aware of Ash since long before Janvier's fateful meeting with her in that swamp; the archangel would be more than happy to have a woman with her abilities in his Tower. Somehow, Janvier had to make Ash see that living hundreds, perhaps thousands of years wouldn't be the nightmare she imagined.

Once out of the Enclave, he turned the bike in the direction of the Adirondacks. The night wind whistled past them and other vehicles overtook on the left because he kept the speed undemanding, the snow on the sides of the road glittering in the beam of his headlight when they passed out of the more populated areas, the trees clean silhouettes against the night.

Flicking on the microphone and speaker system embedded in his helmet with a tilt of his head, he said, "There's something about going for a ride with a beautiful woman wrapped around me."

It took her a couple of seconds to figure out the system on her end. "Since when is a hand on your shoulder 'wrapped around you'?"

The old sadness and older hurt he'd sensed in her since the instant she came face-to-face with her brother was still there, but he could hear his Ash rising through it. "Ah, perhaps I am simply indulging in a fantasy. Foolish male that I am."

A snort sounded from behind him . . . but then she slid her arms around his body, pressing her chest flush to his back, the strength of her grip making him feel possessed, owned. The contact eased the aged, potent need inside him enough that his chest no longer hurt, air filling his lungs again.

"So, I ask and I receive. You're in a generous mood."

"Don't get too cocky, cuddlebunny."

His grin was bright. "What's a cuddlebunny?" he asked, genuinely curious.

"You, at the moment. Sexy, *non*?"

He loved it when she teased him. "*Oui*, if it makes you cuddle so close."

Her laughter was husky, and it was all he needed to hear.

They rode for hours, taking a break now and then to stretch their legs or admire a view—or for Ashwini to get some hot coffee into her.

"I'm going to hit caffeine overload at this rate," she pointed out the second time Janvier made a quick pit stop at a diner, the snow that had begun to fall soft and pretty and no challenge to Janvier's skill at handling the bike.

"Humor me, *cher*. I don't want you frozen." A wicked smile. "I like your blood running hot."

"Stop thinking about my blood."

"Now you ask for the impossible from your cuddlebunny."

With each mile that passed, each playful word from him, Ashwini felt more and more of the strain caused by the unexpected encounter with Arvi leaching away . . . and more and more of her heart falling into the hands of the man who'd seen the fractures in her and given her laughter to heal it.

What was she going to do about this, about them? It no longer seemed as simple as keeping a secret, keeping her distance. Because, as proven by her current position, the latter had proved a *spectacular* failure, and the former seemed a betrayal of everything they'd become to each other. "Naasir is right," she said when Janvier brought the bike to a halt at a gas station on their way back to Manhattan, the air clear of snow once more.

Taking off his helmet, Janvier looked over his shoulder at her. "About what?"

"About people making things too complicated for—" A loud

buzzing interrupted her words. "Hold on," she said, her heart slamming into her ribs because the decision about what to tell Janvier might just have been made for her.

However, the late night call wasn't from Banli House.

"It's Sara." Ashwini felt her blood go cold; the Guild Director wouldn't be calling her at a quarter after eleven unless there was a serious problem. "Sara, what's happened?"

"Cops just contacted me. They have a body they've tagged as Guild business. From the description, it's in the same condition as the dog."

Ashwini had steeled herself for bad news, but Sara's words knocked the air out of her nonetheless. "Damn it." Fisting her hand against Janvier's shoulder, she closed her eyes for a second before flicking them open. "I'll handle this."

"You're not in hunting condition, Ash. You know that."

Janvier tapped her thigh and made a motion for her to cover the phone so they could speak.

"One second, Sara."

"I couldn't hear her clearly," Janvier said as soon as she blocked the receiver, "but did she say a body connected to the dog?" At her nod, his face grew grim. "The city doesn't need this right now, so soon after the battle. It's barely begun to heal."

"Are you offering Tower assistance?"

"No way around Tower involvement," he pointed out. "Guild would have to report this to Dmitri sooner or later. Might as well work together from the start."

Ashwini couldn't argue with him—this was no normal Guild case. "I've got Tower assistance," she said to Sara. Annoyed as she was about having to fight to do her job, she also knew the Guild Director was right; she wasn't in the physical condition to handle this on her own. It'd be stupid not to have backup in case things turned to shit.

"Janvier?" Sara asked.

"Yes." She passed on what he'd said about the city's psychological state.

"He has a point." A faint tapping sound came through the connection, Sara likely drumming her pen against her desk. "I assume Janvier will pass on the details to Dmitri?"

"Yes."

"All right. I'll contact Dmitri in the morning, sort out our game plan, but for now, work under the assumption that the investigation needs to fly under the radar."

"So the case is mine?"

"I'll tell the cops to hold the scene for you."

# 10

Ashwini and Janvier arrived back in Manhattan in half the time it should've taken. It was the most exhilarating ride of her life, the bike moving as smooth as a ribbon of water along a well-worn channel. Pure silk and steel and speed.

That exhilaration was replaced by bright, hard anger the instant they reached the scene.

The victim had been found in a Dumpster behind a restaurant officially located in Little Italy. In actuality, it hugged up against the far edge of the Vampire Quarter. One street over from this quiet one, and the clubs were questionable at best, deadly at worst.

Last time she'd been in the area—chasing a vamp who'd skipped out on his Contract and decided to hide in the dark underbelly of the city—she'd walked into one of those clubs and come across a blissed-out junkie passed out in the lap of a well-groomed and elegant vampire with a tinge of red in his eyes. He had the junkie's sequined mini shoved off her shoulder, his hand molding her bare breast as he drank from her neck.

Another male vamp had his fangs buried in her inner thigh.

Ashwini had known she was wasting her time, but she'd made them stop, then waited until the woman was conscious.

At which point the junkie had called Ash a bitch who needed to get fucked. Then she'd spread her legs lewdly to reveal she wore no panties, and shoved one of the vampires down between her thighs, telling him to feed. Her eyes had rolled back in her head an instant later, orgasmic cries torn out of her throat.

A week later, Ashwini had seen the same woman's face in a Guild bulletin. She'd been found drained of blood, fanged all to hell. Saddened but unsurprised, Ashwini had told the hunter on the case about the vamps she'd seen with the victim. Turned out the two had been in San Francisco at the time, the junkie killed by another of her customers.

That was only the tip of the iceberg.

Certain parts of the Vampire Quarter were a meat market—for blood, for sex, for pain. Not all of it in the dives. Two of the most dangerous Quarter clubs were also the most sophisticated and exclusive, catering to a highly select clientele. Old, *old* vampires who no longer liked anything vanilla.

The Guild did its best to keep an eye on things, but the hunters weren't anyone's big brother, and if the meat walked in and wanted to be eaten, it wasn't anyone's business but that of the adults involved.

Minors were a whole other story.

Ashwini's skin pebbled at the memory of the report that had been part of the file she'd been given when she entered the Academy at sixteen—the Guild had a policy of making sure all its students were fully aware of the world in which they'd be moving should they complete their training.

The younger students received redacted data, what their minds could handle at the time, with more to follow as they grew. Older entrants, in contrast, were given the hard facts with both barrels from the word go. In that never-forgotten case, the vampire in question had been sent to a special prison for near-immortals and sentenced to have his skin flayed off once every fourteen days, no anesthetic, the tool to be a whip or a scalpel.

Apparently, he had to choose which tool was used each and every time. If that wasn't terrifying enough, once every month, the jailors cut off his tongue and genitals in specific punishment for the fact he'd preyed on children. The timing was calculated to be precisely long enough for everything to grow back, given his age, and for him to have two days of perfect health.

*Forty-eight hours in which to dread what is to come,* Janvier had said to her once while they'd been discussing punishment in the realm of immortals and almost-immortals. *It's a stupid man indeed who seeks to break a law when the penalty is in Dmitri's hands.*

Parole wasn't even a possibility until the vampire had served a hundred years.

As far as Ashwini was concerned, it was the perfect god-damn punishment. The vamp had been fucking and sucking from a thirteen-year-old boy and a twelve-year-old girl, both of whom had been raised in his household, the children of servants. Instead of protecting the innocents who'd looked up to him, he'd used their trust and that of their parents to systemi-cally abuse.

He'd even groomed his victims to the point that they believed the abuse to be a normal part of life.

The two children had been damaged on such a deep level, Ashwini knew the prognosis for their future psychological health had been bleak at best. She'd heard rumors that it was one of the rare times Raphael had personally involved himself in the lives of mortals—this was long before Elena became his consort.

According to the rumor mill, he'd done something to the children's minds that allowed them to heal. Ashwini had always hoped the rumor was true, that the kids had made it, were living safe and happy lives as the adults they'd now be . . . and that no other monster had invaded their existence.

Like the one who had preyed on this victim.

The female—who wasn't any longer in the Dumpster, but had been put on a tarp on the fresh-fallen snow beside it, a white tablecloth protecting her from exposure—wasn't a child. That much was clear when Ashwini and Janvier lifted one edge of the tablecloth to look underneath with the help of the high-powered flashlight she'd borrowed from one of the two cops who'd responded to the report of a body.

"I knew it was a Guild case soon as I saw it," the senior member of the duo had said, her gray hair worn in a neat bun at the back of her head and her breath frosting the air. "Things I've seen on this job, you'd think I'd be immune to surprise. Never come across anything like this before, though."

The victim, her hair like straw stripped of color, wasn't a total mummy, had some shape to her. Enough that Ashwini could tell her face had the bone structure of an adult and her breasts had developed beyond adolescence. Her height appeared to be near the five-four mark and, with the skin around her mouth having receded, her dentition was clear and testified to her humanity. No fangs, not even baby ones. The marks on her body were myriad. The light reflected off the shiny white of long-term scarring, sank into the fresh purple-green of new bruising, was torn up by the mess that had been her throat.

Someone had hurt this woman over a long period of time.

Anger throbbing in her gut, Ashwini knew any further examination would have to wait for the cold clarity of the Guild morgue. "Why did you move her?" she asked the senior patrol cop.

Her partner, young and buff and a touch green around the gills, was on guard at the entrance to the alley/drive that serviced the back of the businesses along this stretch.

"Wasn't me, ma'am." A subtle jerk of her head. "Restaurant owner, he had her out before we got here. Name's Tony Rocco."

Glancing behind the uniformed cop, Ashwini took in the short and solid-appearing man who stood red-eyed in the open back doorway of the restaurant. She rose, giving the waiting crime scene techs the go-ahead to process the scene. The two weren't Guild, but had worked cases for and with them before and could be trusted not to leak anything to the media.

"Thanks for coming out so late, guys," she said before walking over to Tony Rocco.

Janvier held back, talking quietly with the techs.

"Sir," she said on reaching the restaurant owner. "My name is Ash. I'm with the Guild."

He didn't ask to see her ID, just shook his head, his thick hair the same deep black as his neatly groomed mustache, his skin pasty with shock. "I couldn't leave her in there, like garbage. I know I'm not supposed to touch if I find something like that, but I just couldn't." His lower lip shook, his voice hoarse. "She's someone's little girl."

At least, Ashwini thought, the victim had had this, a moment of care, of humanity after the horror. "I understand, Mr. Rocco," she said, keeping her voice gentle. "But can you tell me how you found her? Was there rubbish on top of her?"

Instead of answering, he turned in the doorway to call out, "Coby!"

A lanky teenage boy with the same facial structure as Tony, but a foot more in height and skin several shades darker, appeared behind the older male. "Yes, Pa?"

"Show the lady the photos."

The teenager took out his phone, touched the screen to bring up his photo files, then handed it to Ashwini. "I watch the crime shows . . . but I never expected to see anything for real." His Adam's apple bobbed. "I made Pa wait a minute to take her out. I helped him then, even though I knew we shouldn't."

Gripping his father's hand as he must've done as a younger child, Coby blinked rapidly, added, "She was just thrown away. I didn't know people did that for real. I thought they made that stuff up for TV." His voice shook.

Ashwini met a lot of bad people in her line of work, mortal and immortal. A few were plain stupid and violent, others evil and cruel, a percentage selfish and narcissistic. Then she met people like Coby and his father and it renewed her faith in the world. "Thank you." Forwarding herself the photos from the boy's phone and deleting his copies so Coby wouldn't have to do it himself, she said, "Do you usually put out the garbage around the time she was found?"

Tony Rocco nodded after putting his arm around his son and hugging the teenager to his side. "Yes. We clean up for the next morning and—"

"It would've been around eleven," Coby said when his father broke off, the older man's voice swallowed up by grief.

"Anyone else use this Dumpster?"

"Street people Dumpster dive now and then," Coby said, "but we try to give them leftovers so they don't have to." Another jagged swallow, but the boy kept going. "It's so cold now that they don't come around at night anymore. Mostly it's us and the place next door, only they were closed today."

Coby's father pointed a shaking finger toward the black garbage bags on the ground beside the Dumpster. "Who does that?" Making his hand into a fist, he thumped it against his heart. "Who just throws a human being away?"

Ashwini had no answer for him. "Did you come out here earlier in the day?"

"I did," Coby said. "I do the cleanup after the lunch rush. It would've been maybe two thirty, three at the latest." He rubbed his hands over his sweater-covered arms. "She wasn't in the Dumpster and I didn't see no one hanging around."

Ashwini made a note to check for surveillance cameras anywhere nearby, the cops having already ascertained that the restaurant didn't have one. She didn't have high hopes; the area wasn't wealthy enough for cameras to be an automatic add-on, but not crime-ridden enough that surveillance was a prerequisite for insurance. Here, neighbors looked out for one another, but most places would've closed at least an hour before, and while this restaurant butted up against the Vampire Quarter, it wasn't on a popular pedestrian route for clubgoers, making it doubtful she'd be able to locate any eyewitnesses.

It all added up to tell her that the person who'd chosen this Dumpster knew the area well; he or she was either a local or lived nearby. Unfortunately that left her with a massive pool of suspects. Meeting Coby's dark eyes, then Tony's, she said, "Do either of you remember if there were other footprints in the snow when you came out tonight? Your own from before?"

"No, there was fresh snow, with only a cat's paw prints," Coby answered. "I remember, 'cause I stood in the doorway and thought about how it would make an awesome decoration for a cake, tiny paw prints on white icing, maybe a cat sitting on the edge." He began to smile, but it faded a heartbeat later. "That was before . . ."

His father reached up to pat his boy's face. "No, you don't let anyone steal your dreams, especially some piece of scum who'd hurt a woman that way." Pulling down his son's face with weathered hands on his cheeks, Tony said, "We'll go bake that cake and we'll share it with our guests tomorrow, celebrate this woman's life, give her something better than the ugliness of her death."

Waiting until his son had nodded in response to his empathetic words, Rocco looked at Ashwini. "If she doesn't have family, we'll take care of her funeral, make sure she's treated right."

"Thank you," she said, conscious it would be a monetary sacrifice for what appeared to be a small family business. "I'll contact you once we know her circumstances and the details of when the pathologist will release her remains." It would be as ashes, the state of the woman's body too explosive to risk further exposure.

Tony nodded and led his son away. "I'll leave the door open," he said over his shoulder. "Anyone needs coffee, you come in."

The older cop accepted his offer on behalf of herself and her partner, both of them having been out here for over an hour. Shaking her head when the cop stopped in the doorway to check if Ashwini wanted some, she walked over to Janvier and showed him the photos Coby had taken. "She was dumped sometime between two thirty in the afternoon and eleven at night, when the boy discovered her. We can narrow that down if we find out when it snowed in this area after two thirty."

Janvier handed back her phone, his anger an icy film over the green of his eyes. "Before we do anything else," he said, his voice rigid with control, "we have to make sure news about the condition of the body won't spread. She deserves better, but this could affect an entire territory."

Ashwini normally had no time for politics, but this particular political situation could quickly turn deadly—the archangels were all watching New York for any signs of fresh weakness. More, as Janvier had pointed out earlier, the city had only just started to heal from its losses. One more kick could tear the wounds open again.

"The senior cop told me she didn't radio in any details, only the fact that they'd found a deceased female." Ashwini had serious respect for the officer and her quick-thinking response in contacting the Guild by using her phone rather than the radio. "With this location, anyone listening in would've assumed she was a honey feed who serviced one of the fringe clubs. The media aren't going to respond to anything as 'routine' as a honey feed death."

The honey feeds—male and female—were part of the gray world. Light didn't penetrate that world and it was one that "ordinary" people didn't like to think about. Once lost, the people in the gray were forgotten, and that was both sad and an ugly indictment on society.

This time, however, that callous attitude would work to their advantage.

"That leaves the restaurant owner and his son," Janvier said, his eyes on the open doorway through which the senior cop had exited a couple of minutes earlier with two steaming mugs of coffee. Both patrol officers were now at the open end of the service passage. "Boy had the photos."

Ashwini frowned. Yes, she'd deleted the images, but Coby had had plenty of time to e-mail a copy to himself, or to someone else. "I'll talk to them," she said, fairly certain the teenager wasn't the type to leverage fame out of atrocity.

"No." Stripped of any hint of charm, Janvier's expression exposed the relentless will at the core of his nature. "We'll talk to the boy and his father together."

"These are good people." Ashwini folded her arms. "They don't need to be terrified in repayment for being honest enough to call in the body when they could've allowed sanitation to pick it up, no one the wiser." Where Coby and his father had seen a person, many others would've seen garbage.

Janvier touched his fingers to her jaw, a cool, slightly rough brush that was over before she could protest. "Fear is what keeps the mortals alive in a world of predators." Unspoken was that he was one of the predators.

Ashwini had always known that, always seen the complex strata of him, because the charm? It was real, too. "I'll do the talking." Taking a minute to speak to the crime scene techs to make sure the victim would be transported to the Guild morgue as fast as possible, she headed toward the restaurant.

"You don't want her out in the cold," Janvier said, stopping her on the doorstep.

Ashwini didn't deny her irrational but visceral impulse. No one should have to lie in the cold dark after having been so brutally tortured. "Come on," she said, forcing her eyes away from the body so emaciated that it made barely a ripple underneath the tablecloth that was its shroud, "let's do this."

# 11

Inside the restaurant, father and son were cleaning up, the scent of baking in the air.

"Would you like a cup of coffee?" Coby asked.

"No, thank you," Ashwini said to the sad-eyed teenager and reached out in unspoken sympathy—to close her hand over his where it lay on the counter. She saw Janvier start to move toward her, shot him a look that told him to back off. His expression became flat, shoulders unyielding, but he didn't interrupt, though his gaze remained locked on her face.

Coby was too young for her to sense anything accidentally. It would've been different had he been a friend or family. That painful quirk was why she'd known things as a child no girl should know—like the fact that her divorced aunt picked up strange men in bars every Friday and that her grandfather mourned the death of the unsuitable girl he hadn't been permitted to marry.

Tonight, she consciously focused her ability as she did only in rare circumstances, and all of Coby slammed into her: naked pain and heartache, love for a girl and for his family, the horror and pity he'd felt at seeing the body, worry for his father . . . so many pieces of the teenager's soul.

Ashwini didn't like drowning in another's life, was afraid one day she'd go under and not find her way out. But she didn't want Coby to be hurt, didn't want Janvier to become a monster to the boy and his father. So she ignored the fear, found what she needed in relation to both, the boy's memories of his father enough to reinforce her gut feeling about the man.

Breaking contact, she said, "Thank you for what you did today."

Eyes shining, the teenager looked away, while his father allowed his tears to fall.

"Please don't mention the details of what you saw to anyone."

"I don't ever want to put that nightmare in anyone else's head," Tony said to his son's jerky nod.

Janvier held his silence until they were outside and far enough away from the patrol officers that they wouldn't be overheard. When he spoke, his voice vibrated with fury. "You opened yourself up to everything in the boy's head."

"Yes, I did." It had been a violation, but she told her conscience that she'd saved Coby from a far bigger violation. Should the Tower even *think* Coby or his father had—or would—disseminate any information, the reprisal would be icily cold, darkly terrifying.

"I've survived far worse than the memories of a sweet boy and his father." An angel had once gripped her wrist, twisted it in an effort to haul her close so he could "taste" her. She'd thrust a heavy-duty hunting knife into his eye, because there really was no way to escape an angel that old except with surprise and speed and smarts.

She'd done so by the skin of her teeth—and with so much of the creep's life stuffed into her head that she'd thrown up the instant she was in a hideout. "You might have lived more than two hundred years," she said to Janvier, "but I don't think you know the depth of cruelty and horror some immortals are capable of."

Jaw working, Janvier lifted his hands as if to grab her upper arms but dropped them halfway. "You infuriate me." She had no care for herself. He'd seen her in agony after unavoidable contact with an immortal old and twisted—never in public, of course, never where anyone could see the weakness.

Janvier had simply happened to be there and he knew her well enough to pick up the signs of pain she was so good at concealing. So he'd engineered their exit, gotten her into a room where she could collapse, her hands clutched to her stomach. He'd never felt as helpless as when he'd had to watch her suffer without being able to do a fucking thing about it.

Now, she planted her feet in a combative stance, hands on her hips. "Yeah, well, you're infuriating me right back."

The two of them went silent as the morgue van pulled in, the body loaded into it with care, the doors shut. The crime scene techs continued to work, but it was obvious they weren't getting much.

However, that wasn't Janvier's priority right now. "You took a dangerous risk."

"He's a *boy*. There was no horror in him, only sorrow."

Janvier knew she hadn't given him the right, but he took it anyway, reaching out to grip the side of her neck with his hand, shift his body close to hers. "You didn't know that when you touched him." He was so angry at her for putting herself in that position. "You didn't know what would rush into your head, *sorcière*."

"I told you"—her eyes burned into him, full of a thousand secrets—"witches were burned at the stake. I'm just a woman."

A woman who saw through the veil people put between themselves and the world, who could strip away lies to reveal the heart of darkness that lived within mortal and immortal both . . . and for whom immortals were the enemy of her sanity. He ran his thumb over her pulse, but she wasn't there any longer, having escaped his grip with hunter slickness.

Walking to the techs, she hunkered down to talk to them, clearly hoping to find something, though she had to know the chance was low. Criminals could be stupid, but Janvier didn't think this was one of those times. There was something very *cold* about throwing a human being in the garbage. It took a soul of ice to do that and walk away, and someone that devoid of feeling would cover his or her tracks with the same calculated coldness.

Again, he thought of Lijuan and of how the Archangel of China had fed from her troops. Naasir had run through brutal fighting to get word to Raphael about the enemy archangel's ability to regenerate using the life force of others, had ended up with his back all but sliced open. Still behind enemy lines, Ashwini and Janvier had worked to slow down the hostile forces any way they could.

*"Is she yours?"*

Naasir's question, silver eyes gleaming against the rich brown of his skin.

*"Touch her and find out."*

*"You better hurry, Cajun."*

Janvier was going as fast as he dared, but he feared it wasn't fast enough. Ashwini was a hunter; hazard pay was a standard part of hunter contracts for a reason. And if—*when*—war came to the city again, she'd fight the enemy right beside him. The diagonal slice through her torso in the final hours of this battle had come within a hairsbreadth of nicking her heart and perforating other internal organs. Death could've stolen her from him had the vampire who'd attacked her shifted position a single inch before he struck.

Furious defiance burned under his skin.

He'd watched everyone he ever loved die of old age. They had wanted to go, having lived happy, contented lives, and he hadn't tried to force them to hold on, to apply for a chance at vampirism and near-immortal life. He was too selfish to be that understanding when it came to Ashwini; he would not watch her star go out.

Not her.

# 12

Dmitri moved his bishop on the chessboard in the flickering light of the candle that burned in a holder to his left. It put him in prime position to capture Aodhan's king.

Illium leaned back on his hands, wings lying spread on the carpet. "Looks like he has you, Sparkle."

"I need to kill you. Later," Aodhan muttered, staring at the board.

The three of them were sitting in the aerie at the very top of the Tower. It had been Dmitri's lookout during the battle, the wraparound windows offering three-hundred-and-sixty-degree visibility. New York glittered beneath them in every direction, the Tower planted on a field of stars.

It reminded Dmitri of the brilliant quiet of a tiny cottage on a small farm long ago, before either Illium or Aodhan had been born. The nights had been so clear above his long-ago home that he'd stayed awake long past when a farmer should be asleep, simply to watch the stars with his wife.

The memory of Ingrede's smile, her kiss under the starlight, it no longer drew heart's blood. Because his heart had come back to him. She was changed and so was he, but they were who they needed to be for each other.

Honor loved it in the aerie and often kept him company when he had care of the Tower at night. Tonight, however, she was working on an intriguing historical document in their apartment, having laughingly told him to have fun with the "boys." The "boys" were the two lethal angels with him—one sprawled to his left, the other frowning in concentration in front of him.

The aerie had no furniture, the three of them seated on the floor.

Not that it was spartan now that it was no longer a war room. The floor was covered by a fine Persian rug Dmitri had brought out of personal storage, having picked it up a hundred years past, in a market along the old Silk Road. It had been hand-knotted by a gifted artisan, the colors ruby red and yellow-gold with hints of midnight blue.

On top of it lay the large, flat multihued cushions Montgomery had supplied from the warehouse where he stored so many things, Dmitri had no idea of the inventory. That was strictly Montgomery's domain—except when the butler took offense at how another immortal was treating a priceless work of art and decided to "relocate" it to his own care.

Thankfully, Dmitri had only had to handle that once. It had taken him three hours in the warehouse to unearth the four inch-tall statue of a goddess of the erotic arts. The piece had been exquisite enough to prompt Dmitri to offer to buy it from the vampire who owned it, but the man wouldn't part with his treasure until a decade ago. At which point Dmitri had placed the statue in Montgomery's private sitting room at the Enclave house.

Most often, the butler displayed his purloined items in Raphael's home, and the archangel made sure each piece was quietly reunited with its owner. Many men—angel, vampire, or human—would've dismissed a servant with such a peccadillo, but Montgomery was as loyal to Raphael as any of the Seven, and the sire understood the value of such loyalty.

"A flaw does not make a man worthless," Raphael had once said to Dmitri. "Else I would've been discarded long ago."

Now, Illium snacked on the sugared dates Montgomery had supplied, the sweetmeats part of an array of food that would tempt any appetite. Reaching out, Dmitri took a single grape,

enjoying the fresh, sweet flavor and imagining feeding Honor
the taste from his lips.

"Date?" Illium said with a glint in his eye.

Dmitri ignored the painted wooden bowl the angel held out.
"I'm going to help Aodhan kill you—after I torture you by
making you drink champagne while listening to Mozart." The
blue-winged angel hated both.

Illium grinned, unafraid of Dmitri and Aodhan's combined
wrath. "Don't tell me you're still heartbroken over Favashi,"
he said, naming the archangel who had vast date plantations
in her lands. "I won't believe you—I admit I wasn't even a
twinkle in my mother's eye during your liaison with the lovely
Archangel of Persia, but I've since seen you together, and you
never looked at her the way you look at Honor."

"Illium has the right of it in this, Dmitri. Honor is your
heart." Aodhan's crystalline eyes refracted Dmitri's face into
countless fragments, the fine grooves around the angel's mouth
the only sign of the pain he continued to bear as his injuries
healed.

The neck wound had closed first, his immortal body con-
centrating its efforts on the most dangerous threat. His damaged wing had come next, but while Aodhan could fly short
distances, and had been encouraged to do so by the healers in
order to strengthen the weak new muscle, it'd be several more
weeks before he could return to full flight status.

His broken bones had healed, but his left arm, as the most
minor injury in immortal terms, had only regenerated partway
to his elbow at this stage. It was currently covered by a neatly
pinned white shirtsleeve in deference to the fact that cold could
sometimes retard healing by diverting the body's resources
into generating warmth.

It spoke to the power in Aodhan's veins that he'd healed at
such speed. Most angels his age would've still been bed-bound,
their recovery counted in months, not weeks. The best news,
however, had nothing to do with Aodhan's physical health. No, it
had to do with a slow but deep healing of the soul.

Illium's voice broke into Dmitri's assessment of the injured
angel. "I think our honored second is stalling. Why does the
memory of the steel hand in a velvet glove that is Favashi make
you gnash your teeth?"

"It's not the memory of Favashi that aggravates me." Dmitri scowled. "It's the memory of my own stupidity." The female archangel had nearly manipulated him into becoming her personal weapon.

Dmitri had no argument with being the blade of the person he loved—he was lethal and there was honor in protecting that which was precious to the heart and the soul. He did have a problem with being used for a fool. "It took me far too long to see through her machinations." He ate another grape. "At least Michaela wears her self-interest and narcissism openly, while Favashi pretends to be kindness and grace while having the soul of a cobra."

Aodhan shook his head. "She did nothing a male archangel wouldn't do in seeking to secure a strong immortal to his court. It is wrong of you to compare her to Michaela."

Dmitri knew Aodhan was right; immortal politics didn't permit any but the ruthless to survive. In truth, Favashi and Michaela had little in common beyond their gender. Yet the whole idea of manipulating strong immortals into service continued to irritate him. "We all serve Raphael of our own free will. You'd think the lesson would be clear."

Hair glittering diamond bright even in the muted light, Aodhan said, "You forget, Dmitri. Raphael is yet considered young. We are an experiment—most of the old ones expect you in particular to rise up and rebel any day now."

Aodhan had always been closest to Illium, Dmitri over five hundred years old when Aodhan was born. So he hadn't realized until now how much he'd missed the angel. Aodhan had always seen the world through an incisive lens, something that was visible in his artwork.

"Sometimes," Dmitri said, "I think I'll never understand angelkind." A thousand years he'd been by Raphael's side—with minor deviations along the way—and still people refused to believe that theirs wasn't only the relationship of an archangel and his second, but a friendship.

"You aren't alone," Aodhan said. "I think some of the old ones have become so insular, so ensconced within their coterie of like-minded friends, that they no longer grow. They are like the butterflies Lijuan kept pinned to her walls."

In contrast, Raphael lived in the center of one of the world's most vibrant cities, his Seven traveled continents on a regular basis, and, critically, both Dmitri and his sire had fallen for extraordinary women whom angelkind did not truly understand.

One old angel had said, "Your wife is beautiful," to Dmitri, a puzzled look on his face. "But why did you marry her? Would she not have served better as a concubine?"

The only reason Dmitri hadn't ended the other man's life then and there had been the true confusion in the question. The angel had no comprehension of love, and that was a tragedy so terrible, Dmitri could offer no harsher punishment. Love had savaged him once, but it had also given him the greatest joys of his life.

The memory of his children's sweet faces might be painful beyond bearing, but no evil could ever steal the tender joy that was the sensory echo of holding them in his arms, of Misha's laughter and Caterina's gurgling smile. And then had come Honor, bringing with her an incandescent light.

"I think you're right about the hidebound old ones," he said to the angel across from him. "Now, Sparkle, are you intending to move or do you concede defeat?"

Aodhan was, in many ways, the most even-tempered of all the Seven. So when he looked up with eyes glowing and power crackling at his fingertips, it was an unexpected sight. Especially given the lighthearted provocation. Then the angel smiled slowly and moved a single piece on the board. "Check. And mate."

Dmitri looked down in disbelief. "No," he said, trying to figure out how Aodhan had pulled off the impossible.

"There, there," said a new voice. "You can beat me and feel better about your skills."

All three of them looked up and muttered various imprecations, Illium's the most creative welcome. Naasir bared his teeth in return, silver eyes reflecting the candlelight.

"How the fuck did you get into the city without alerting any of the sentries?" Dmitri had put the entire security team, as well as the general warrior population, on high alert. This time around, he'd also alerted the Guild to be on the lookout, his respect for their abilities having grown during the course of the battle.

It was all part of a game Naasir had been playing with the others in the Seven for centuries. As a child, when he'd first been brought to Raphael's stronghold, he'd tended to lie in wait below Dmitri's desk or pounce from the top of the bookshelves in the stronghold library, giggling like a maniac when he was found out—or when he captured his "prey."

Naasir had been tiny then, as small as Misha had been when he died. Four in human terms, but he'd lived three decades by then. Still, he'd been a child. A feral one, but a child nonetheless, and the game was one of the few things he did that was free from the rage inside his small body. So Dmitri had let him play, Raphael in agreement with his decision.

As Naasir grew from babe to boy, he'd found it funny to sneak into places where he shouldn't be—on one memorable occasion, he'd decided to infiltrate Lijuan's dining room. He'd apparently been seated at the head of the table pretending to eat a live pet cat when the Archangel of China discovered him. Lijuan, relatively normal back then, had found the incident amusing, and Naasir had escaped with his life.

It had been one of the few times Dmitri had come down hard on him, managing to drum it into his head that Lijuan and the others in the Cadre were dangerous. He'd never forget what Naasir had said to him when Dmitri yelled that he didn't intend to bury another child and that Naasir needed to have a care for his life.

"Am I a person, Dmitri? Will you be sad if I die?"

Hardened and cruel though he'd become, the innocent question had shaken him. "Yes," he'd said, as honest in his answer as Naasir had been in his question. "You are a person. You are *Naasir*. I'll lose a piece of me if you die and it's a piece I'll never get back."

Naasir had stared at him for a long time before coming over to hug him. "Okay, Dmitri. I'm sorry. I didn't know I was a person before."

As a result of the fact that Naasir had grown up under Dmitri's care, their relationship was unlike the relationship he had with the others in the Seven. Naasir still obeyed his every order, still asked him questions a child might ask a father. Dmitri often thought the sliver of humanity that had survived in him until he found Honor, had survived because of the tiny, feral boy with silver eyes who had pelted out to see him when he returned to the Refuge after an absence.

The same way Misha had run to him after his trips to the market.

It had torn his heart to pieces each time Naasir did the same, but Dmitri had caught him in his arms without fail, unable to bruise the spirit of the wild boy who didn't know that Dmitri was meant to be without heart, without hope.

That boy had never lost his delight in his favorite game.

These days, Naasir liked to sneak into cities and territories. Not only did the penchant make him the best scout in Raphael's forces, but Naasir's abilities were an excellent test of a city's defenses. The fact that it amused him was a bonus.

Coming down to the carpet in a movement as graceful as a cat's, the vampire who wasn't quite a vampire grabbed a large plate that held an entire chicken. "The sentry on the building with the blue lights almost caught me," he said, ripping off a drumstick after sniffing at the meat and making a face. "She's good."

"Do we have holes in our defenses? If so, they have to be immediately plugged."

"Only if the scout is someone better than me."

Dmitri relaxed. Naasir's skills at covert infiltration were unmatched, part of the reason he'd led the small team of saboteurs during the battle. "I just received a message from Janvier." It had come in while he spoke to Aodhan about angelkind's inability to comprehend certain truths. "He's heading this way." The news, the vampire had indicated, was bad.

"Is his hunter with the Cajun?"

"Not tonight."

Having finished off the drumstick, Naasir crunched the bone in a way that made Illium and Dmitri both wince. "One day," Illium said, "you're going to get a bone shard stuck in your gullet."

Naasir shrugged and tore off the other leg. "Let's play chess."

"Last time we played chess," Illium replied dryly, "you threw the pieces out a Refuge window and down into the gorge."

"I'm better at it now." Naasir growled, but it wasn't anger, simply an emphasis on his words. "Caliane is trying to civilize me."

Having accepted the piece of meat Naasir held out, like a lion sharing with his pride, Illium said, "How is that progressing?"

Naasir gave some meat to Aodhan, too. He never did that with Dmitri because, in his mind, Dmitri was another predator who would be insulted by the offer. Dmitri wondered if Illium and Aodhan realized Naasir saw them as younger cubs who had to be fed by the top predator. He was the same with Venom. Not Jason or Galen, though. Jason, like Dmitri, had been an adult while Naasir was a child. Galen wasn't that much older than Naasir in angelic terms, but the two had never known one another as children.

"I told Caliane that trying to civilize me is like trying to civilize a jungle cat," Naasir said with a shrug. "We pretend to like people until we get hungry and want fresh meat." A glance around, a glint in his eye. "I honestly do like you all. I haven't thought about eating you for at least two centuries."

Aodhan looked at the vampire. "I am relieved," he said in a tone as serious as Naasir's.

"Really, Sparkle?" Naasir moved out of the way with quick-silver speed before Aodhan's very well-aimed bishop would've hit him dead smack in the center of his forehead, the vampire's laughter as wild and gleeful as when he'd been a boy who'd managed to startle Dmitri by grabbing on to his leg under the desk.

Dmitri was rescuing the bishop when Janvier appeared in the doorway. Naasir hauled him into a back-slapping hug, the younger vampire returning the embrace as enthusiastically. When they drew apart, Naasir took a sniff of Janvier. "You smell of our hunter. Where is she?"

"Resting." Janvier's smile faded. "I have some bad news."

# 13

Ashwini knew she should stay home, sleep, but her body wasn't hurting, while her heart was in agony. After giving Janvier the holster she'd had made for him, she waited until he'd driven off before she left her apartment building again, having arranged to borrow a car from her doorman's cousin as she'd done a couple of times before. She figured the money might as well go to a young couple raising a family as to a rental place.

"Thanks," she said when the stocky blond handed over the keys. "I was planning to jump on the subway to your place, but Nic told me you were already on your way."

"I needed the drive and it wasn't like I was asleep." Yawning, the twentysomething male stretched, bones popping one after another. "Anyway, I better get back home before my wife decides to divorce me for leaving her alone with the baby." A good-natured laugh. "The lungs on her come from her ma, no doubt about it."

Ashwini frowned when he turned to head to the nearest subway station. "Hop in with me," she said. "I'll drop you off on my way out."

He scratched his head. "You sure? You paid for it fair and square—more than fair."

"It won't take me out of my way," she lied. "The company would be nice."

"In that case, I won't say no."

He *was* good company. Easygoing and besotted with his wife and baby both. Listening to him patter on about the two of them distracted her for the time it took to drive him back to his apartment building. Once there, she saw him stop in front of the stoop to wave up at the silhouette of a woman in a third-story window, her arms rocking a baby.

Ashwini sat there for another minute and she didn't even know why until she saw the silhouette change, mother and child joined by a masculine form, stocky and with arms that went around them both. Wrenching her eyes away from a scene that would never be a part of her own life, she drove off.

It was stupid to do this, she knew that. Once she was outside Manhattan, the drive would take eighty minutes or more there, the same back, and she planned to wake early to attend the autopsy. But a night without sleep wouldn't kill her, and her gut pulsed with the remorseless tug she felt only during the worst episodes, when neither medication nor therapy would fight the monsters. Oddly, Ashwini's voice, reading from a piece of classic literature, had proven the best panacea when things began to go downhill . . . as was happening more and more frequently.

She reached her destination just under an hour and a half later, was welcomed by a familiar nurse, his red hair combed in a simple style. All the senior staff knew Ashwini had permission to visit at any time.

Carl's face made it clear her instincts hadn't let her down. "How bad?" she asked.

"Most severe end of the scale."

"Did anyone unauthorized go into the room?"

Shaking his head, Carl said, "I double-checked. The episodes are simply getting worse, Ash."

It was a fact she'd admitted to herself three months back. "Have you told Arvi?" Unlike her, he refused to face the truth even a blind man could see.

"Yes. He's here, but you know your voice is the only one that seems to help." Blue eyes sad against the freckled paleness of his skin, he spread his hands, palms out. "I would've called you, but it was so late and with your injury . . ."

"It's all right, Carl." Leaving the nurse at his station, she strode down the thick gray carpet of the hallway toward the corner suite, the walls around her hung with elegant pieces of art, and the arched window at the end reaching the floor. It allowed sunlight to pour in during the day while showcasing the hedge maze that was part of the extensive gardens.

Tonight it revealed only stygian darkness.

The book was waiting for her on the little hallway table beside the closed door, the soundproofing so good that she couldn't hear anything beyond it.

Arvi sat on a chair beside the table. His head was in his hands, his shoulders slumped and the white of his business shirt stretched across the breadth of them. He'd always seemed so big to her, larger than life. Yet he was only a man, a man who was in pain. She went to reach out, closed her hand into a fist before she could make contact.

Turning, she picked up the book . . . and Arvi's hand closed over her wrist, the leather of her jacket insulating her from the skin-to-skin contact that might have plunged her into her brother's life and his secrets against her will. Chest thick with a thousand unsaid things, she shifted to look at him.

When his shoulders shook, a harsh sound escaping his throat, she turned completely and held his head against her stomach as he cried. Her own tears were locked up inside her, knotted up with fear and anger and loss. But she held Arvi as he cried, her strong, determined older brother who couldn't fix this one thing that had changed everything.

The past. The present. The future.

*Janvier.*

He could've been her future in another world, another time, when Arvi's rough tears didn't hold pure heartbreak and the knots inside her weren't formed of a terrible, inevitable truth. Because Ashwini would never permit herself to be the one on the other side of the locked door.

No matter what.

Raphael walked downstairs long past midnight, his city swathed in a moonless and velvet dark while his consort lay peacefully in their bed. She'd been sleeping with her hand over his heart until he left. Though Elena had gone to bed tired but happy and he didn't expect the nightmares to find her, he didn't like to leave her in the twilight hours. However, Dmitri had made direct contact, and his second didn't interrupt Raphael at such times for trivialities.

*A woman is dead,* Dmitri had told him, *and her body bears hints of Lijuan's hand. Janvier is on his way to the Enclave to give you a report.*

Icy fury filled Raphael at the thought of the archangel who'd sought to harm his people in her lust for power. He wanted no taint of her in his territory. That thought uppermost in his mind, he turned at the bottom of the steps and made his way to the library.

The man who stood facing the sliding glass doors that looked out to the Hudson, and beyond it, the million pinpricks of light that was Manhattan, held himself like a fighter, his stance light. He wore a white T-shirt and over it, a holster that crisscrossed his back. That holster wasn't the weathered brown one Raphael had previously noted; the supple leather of this was golden in color, the blades it held distinctive.

Those blades had been lethal in combat.

Raphael was well aware that Janvier, along with Naasir and Ashwini, had done far more behind enemy lines than was known even among their own troops. The three had a way of making it all seem a game, not to be taken seriously. A number of their actions during the battle might have appeared foolish to others, but he'd seen the strategic calculation behind it— distracting, annoying, or frustrating the enemy at a critical juncture could be as deadly a strike as a cleaving blow with a sword.

Turning the instant Raphael stepped into the room, Janvier put his hands behind his back, his stance altering to that of a soldier with his liege. "Sire."

"Janvier."

The other man didn't dally, giving him a crisp, clean report of the night's discovery. "While the final state of the victim's body hints at Lijuan," he added, "the scars and bruises point to long-term abuse.

"As it is, we all know Lijuan can't have regenerated already. Even if she had, she'd hardly be interested in prowling the streets, attacking pets and women—but I also can't see Lijuan sharing this particular power."

Raphael had witnessed Lijuan fly apart into a thousand shards and, regardless of her attempts to convince the world that she was a goddess, he was certain she needed her physical body. He'd injured that body multiple times during the battle and the only reason she'd been able to so quickly erase the wounds was because she'd fed on the life force of her soldiers.

And for that, she'd needed her mouth.

Even an archangel couldn't regenerate the mouth without first regenerating the brain and all the systems of the body that kept that brain alive. Lijuan wasn't dead, of that he was in no doubt, but neither was she a goddess. It would take her considerable time to repair her physical form, especially taking into account that he'd obliterated her using a combination of wildfire and angelfire.

The former was a new, Cascade-born gift, and it had proven to have a debilitating effect on Lijuan. Raphael hadn't mentioned it to anyone but Elena and Dmitri, but he believed the wildfire had caused damage it would take Lijuan much longer than usual to rectify.

"You're right about her not sharing this ability," he said to Janvier. "She's both too used to controlling her people through the leash of doling out power, and too greedy. You say this victim wasn't an empty husk as you witnessed in battle?"

"No, she still had a sense of humanity and of flesh about her, enough that we could immediately identify her as female."

Whereas Lijuan's victims had been so shriveled into themselves, determining gender had been impossible from a visual scan of the high-resolution photographs Janvier's hunter had taken. The shadow team had all three reported being unable to make the determination at the scene, either—except, of course, for those they'd personally witnessed being consumed.

"Fang marks?" A vampire could conceivably drain a victim of all her blood, given a long enough time frame.

"Yes, but not at the site of the fatal throat wound. There was too much damage to determine what caused that injury— similarly to the dog, she appeared gnawed on."

That didn't exclude vampires; it could be one of the Made who'd given in to bloodlust, torn and ripped and chewed at the flesh in his feeding. "Can the situation be contained?" Raphael had to be ruthless; a mortal had lost her life and deserved justice, but that justice could not happen on a public stage. Not this time.

"I'm confident Ash and I can deal with this quietly, with help from the Guild and Tower as necessary. The two witnesses, responding officers, and crime scene techs can be trusted to keep their silence."

Before Elena, Raphael would've made a hundred percent sure of that by wiping the memories of the people involved, but now he'd seen mortals through her eyes, understood that these people were her friends and colleagues and she would protect them—because memories were what made a person.

*I would rather die as Elena than live as a shadow.*

The echo of what she'd said to him soon after they first met, paired with her passionate words before the battle, made him no less ruthless when it came to his city, but he did consider other options before taking this particular measure.

"I'll have Dmitri put a watch on all their communications as a contingency." Greed could sink its hooks into the most unexpected of people, and this information had value to the media. "Do you expect to uncover any further information tonight?"

"*Non.* The late hour means we'll have to explore other avenues come morning." The languid rhythm of Janvier's voice belied the hard edge in his eyes. "Even the victim's fingerprints can't be used to search for her identity until the pathologist rehydrates her fingertips."

"Take care of her, Janvier," Raphael said. "I will not have the mortals in my territory become hunted." Human lives might be a fleeting firefly flicker in comparison to the endless span of an angel's, but Raphael now knew their light could burn so bright, it had the strength to vanquish the ice of eternity itself.

"Sire."

Walking to a small cherrywood table on which sat a faceted crystal decanter and six tumblers, Raphael poured out two measures of the carefully aged amber liquid in the decanter. He handed one of the tumblers to Janvier and said, "Your blades are from Neha's land." The Cajun, as all called Janvier, was now one of his trusted people, but they didn't have between them the relationship Raphael had with his Seven.

That was to be expected. Janvier wasn't yet past his third century—even Venom, the youngest of the Seven, had over a hundred years on the vampire with the bayou in his voice. However, Raphael saw in Janvier the same thing he'd seen in Venom, in Aodhan, in Illium, and in the others of his Seven: the Cajun had honor so deeply woven into his bones that it would take a cataclysm to shatter it.

Dmitri hadn't lost it even during the worst years of his existence.

"Yes." Janvier took the drink, his posture easing now that the report was done. "Neha gifted them to me when I left her court, said she had a feeling I'd be getting into trouble and she enjoyed my wit too much to hear I'd lost my head because I didn't have adequate weapons." Reaching back, the vampire withdrew one distinctively curved blade in a smooth motion, held it out handle first toward Raphael.

He took it, tested the weight and heft. It was heavier than it appeared when Janvier used it. That weight, along with the razored edge, explained how the Cajun was able to slice off heads with a single swipe. Interestingly, however, the weapon appeared decorative at first glance, the carved bone handle inset with small gemstones that sparkled prettily, drawing the eye away from the honed death of the blade itself.

"Neha favored you." More than Raphael had realized— because he recognized the workmanship behind Janvier's blades now that he'd handled one. "These were created by Rhys himself, if I'm not mistaken." Neha's trusted general, a man who'd been a weapons maker in his youth, and to this day made blades renowned for their strength and handling.

It was said he only created a new set once every decade.

Janvier took the blade back, slid it into the specially designed scabbard. "Rhys is responsible for much of my skill at the kukri."

"And, like Venom, you keep those ties." The youngest member of his Seven had been Made by the Queen of Poisons herself. "He manages to make himself welcome in her lands even when Neha carries a grudge against me."

"Perhaps that's why she's been known to refer to the two of us as Charm and Guile." A faint smile. "I've never worked out which one of us is which."

They spoke for several more minutes before Raphael walked with the vampire to the front door.

"Sire." Janvier paused on the doorstep after shrugging on the leather jacket he'd left with Montgomery, the gleaming red of his motorcycle visible behind him. "Ash—her Making—is it still—"

"She is cleared." Had been for a number of years, ever since her abilities first came to the attention of the Tower, her blood covertly obtained and tested for compatibility with the process that led to vampirism. "But, Janvier"—he held the other man's eyes—"she has shown no inclination toward accepting the offer quietly made her."

Janvier clenched his jaw, looked away before facing Raphael once more, a bleak hollowness to his gaze. "That is the thing . . . I don't think anything could convince her to choose a life among immortals."

# 14

Janvier picked Ashwini up at eight that morning. "You didn't sleep well," he said, eyes on the dark smudges beneath her eyes.

"It's not the first sleepless night I've ever had—I'm fine." Unable to resist the craving to touch him, she put her hand on his shoulder and swung up onto the bike. Warm and strong, his scent earthy and familiar, he made the bruises inside her hurt less, her muscles no longer as taut.

"I checked on the snowfall records," he said. "Last fall in Manhattan before the body was found was around ten p.m., but there were earlier flurries."

"That still leaves us with a wide window for the body dump." She chewed on the information as she put on the helmet he passed over. "I don't think this was done in the light."

"No—there would've been too high a risk of being seen."

"It's dark by roughly six, but the shops in that area are open and busy till eight, the restaurants for longer. Even with the place next door to Rocco's being closed at the time, I'd bet on the body being dumped very close to ten."

"I agree." He stroked his hand over her thigh.

She didn't protest; there was something more tender than

sexy in that touch and it closed up her throat. "The autopsy's starting soon," she managed to say, before putting her hand on his shoulder again. "Let's go."

"There isn't a drop of blood left in her," the pathologist confirmed thirty minutes into his examination of the body, "but if this was a vampire, he's the messiest eater I've ever seen. I'll do cross sections of her throat, but I don't have much hope of finding deep tissue wounds that confirm fangs."

"Her other injuries?" Janvier asked, echoing Ashwini's thoughts.

"Long-term abuse." The pathologist pointed to a set of scars on the victim's breasts. "At *least* three months old, though I'd hazard they were made even earlier. And I'm sure you noticed the fang marks elsewhere on her body. Whoever fed from her didn't bother to seal up the wounds except over major veins and arteries, and even there, he or she only did the bare minimum to stop the bleeding."

Ashwini's best friend had been kidnapped and kept by a predatory group of vampires for two long months. Honor had survived, but she'd been brutalized. Ashwini would never forget the wounds on her friend's body when they'd found her, the despair in the midnight green of Honor's eyes. A little longer and she might have lost her friend forever.

The woman on the steel table in front of her hadn't been found in time, the monsters hurting her terribly before they killed her.

*I'll get justice for you,* she promised silently, before looking at the pathologist again. "Were you able to confirm when she died?"

"It's best-guess at this stage, but from the signs of decomposition in the tissue she does have left, I'd say it was within the past week."

"Any distinguishing marks on her body?"

"Tattoo on her outer left ankle of what looks like a rainbow-colored dolphin. That has to be unusual."

Using her phone, Ashwini took a close-up of the image with the pathologist holding the skin taut. It wrinkled in on itself as soon as he let go, and the sight was at once sad and enraging. No one had the right to treat another being as if they had no value.

*"This is for your own benefit."*

*"But, Arvi—"*

*"No arguments. This . . . thing inside you is never going to permit you to be normal. The doctors will change that."*

Shaking off the memory of the greatest betrayal of her life, she watched with care as the pathologist turned the pitiable shell of the body to check the victim's back. "No other tattoos or distinctive scars," the doctor said after laying her down in the supine position again. "But there's something else you should know."

Ashwini frowned as the man picked up a limp hand. "That wrist wasn't broken when she was loaded for transport."

"Exactly." The pathologist picked up the victim's other arm. "I'm sorry to have to do this, but you need to see how bad it is." With a quiet murmur that Ashwini couldn't make out, but which appeared to be directed at the woman on the autopsy table, the pathologist snapped the ulna like it was driftwood.

Janvier hissed out a breath. "All her bones are so weak?"

"I'll do scans to confirm, but yes. They're porous to the point that I broke her wrist while doing an initial examination." Placing the victim's arm back down gently, he said, "Her teeth are cracked, and her skin's so delicate it's like paper. See how the bone shard's gone straight through."

Pity and anger entwined inside Ashwini. "Anything else?" she said, fighting to keep her voice level.

"Not yet. I'll forward you the blood test results and any other forensic evidence."

"Her fingerprints could significantly speed up identification," Janvier said, white grooves at the corners of his mouth.

"I'll get started on them right away."

Thanking the pathologist, Ashwini stepped out of the morgue and into the cool white corridor empty of all other life. It was odd; every time she came to the morgue, it was to exit into this cool quiet and yet it never failed to unsettle her, despite the fact that, to her ability, this place was almost peaceful. The dead kept their secrets.

Striding through the silence, she didn't refer to what the pathologist had shown them; there was nothing to say, Janvier's anger as white-hot as her own. "I've sent the image of the tattoo to the Guild computer team, asked them to run a search against all possible databases. They'll do the same as soon as the fingerprints come through, liaise with the Tower team throughout."

"What about the face?" Janvier zipped up his jacket as they stepped outside into the light snow that had begun to fall. "The Tower has access to an artist who can rebuild it."

Zipping up her own jacket and flipping up the collar, she said, "Can he—she—do it without the skull? I don't want to strip away the skin the victim has left." She should be allowed that dignity at least.

"I'll ask," Janvier said, not questioning her irrational choice. "It may be possible with high-resolution scans and X-rays."

When he went to hand her a helmet, she shook her head. "I'm going to walk to Guild Academy, see if I can pick up useful scuttlebutt from the other hunters." Her brethren might have seen or heard something useful without realizing its significance. "I'll also drop by the other businesses in the area near the restaurant, see if anyone has security footage or was around late last night."

"I can join you."

"No, I think it's better I do this myself. Even a hint of Tower interest and people start getting nervous—not to mention, your presence will raise questions." Ashwini, on the other hand, could explain hers away by saying she was doing a favor for a cop friend in order to assuage the boredom of being on mandatory sick leave.

Stowing the helmet, Janvier straddled his bike. "When will you tell me about your brother, *cher*?" he asked in a voice as dark and as mysterious as the slow-moving waters in the land he called home.

Ashwini's thoughts filled with the terrible secret she'd carried within for so long. He had to know, that much had become clear to her during their ride . . . but she didn't have the courage to face the pain on this cold morning while the afterimage of death lingered on her retinas.

"Not today," she whispered.

Watching Ash walk away into the falling veil of snow, long and lithe and alone, Janvier fought the urge to haul her back, demand her trust. That would get him nothing. She was wounded deep inside and, like any wounded creature, would strike out in an effort to protect herself. Not only that, in attempting to force her, he'd lose the faith she already had in him.

And his Ashblade offered that faith with the wariness of one who'd once had the gift of it betrayed.

Revving the engine, he made himself leave. He might have been born in a time when a man protected his woman from the world, but he'd come of age in a changing world, and, unlike some vampires of his generation, he didn't cling to the nostalgia of what once was, choosing instead to embrace the new world while never forgetting his past.

Ash would die if caged.

Even were the cage built with love and a devoted need to protect her from harm.

The image an ugly one, he rode through the streets with pitiless focus, taking the bike directly into the Tower's underground garage. He knew he'd passed at least five levels of security by the time he brought it to a halt—security most people never glimpsed. Striding to the elevator afterward, he didn't jerk in surprise when Naasir dropped from the ceiling to stand beside him, having had his senses open for the vampire.

Feet bare under his jeans and the incongruously soft-looking black V-necked sweater he wore over a pale blue shirt with the ends hanging out, he said, "You didn't bring our hunter?"

Naasir had a feral charm that drew women to him—be they mortal, vampire, or angel. Janvier had seen more than one experienced immortal make a fool of herself over him. But despite the way the vampire liked to needle Janvier every so often, his interest in Ash wasn't romantic or sexual, the possessiveness he displayed more comparable to that he exhibited with Raphael and the Seven.

"She's at Guild Academy." Attempting to get his mind off the old pain he'd glimpsed in Ash's eyes before she walked away, he tested the texture of Naasir's sweater. "Is this cashmere?"

"So?" A growl. "It's cold here. I don't like the cold, and the shop lady said this would keep me warm."

Janvier was momentarily diverted from his thoughts by the idea of Naasir shopping in one of the exclusive department stores that sold this type of clothing; the stores were open all hours to cater to an immortal clientele. He had a hunch the vampire had walked into the first clothes shop he'd seen when the cold began to pinch. "Did the woman in the shop also tell you shoes might help?"

"I'll wear them when I go outside." Naasir raised his arm to rub the sleeve against the side of his face, his pleasure in the texture open. "Why is Ash at the Academy? She should be here. She's one of us."

"She disagrees." Immortality didn't hold the lure for her that it did for so many, and Janvier couldn't blame her. "You know what she can do—imagine her living in the world of immortals."

Naasir took time to think over his words. "I don't know how to fix that," he said at last, his silver eyes on Janvier. "This is bad, Cajun. I don't want to watch Ash die."

Wrenching pain in his gut at the idea of it. "I don't have an answer, either." The very things that made Ash who she was were also the same things that made immortality a bad choice for her. Janvier knew in his bones that she had the strength to handle the challenges, but he wasn't sure how to convince her of that.

Naasir narrowed his eyes as the elevator doors opened, and took off toward the stairs. When Janvier stepped out on the floor of the Tower that held Dmitri's office, high, *high* above the city, it was to see Naasir coming through the door on the other side. The vampire's face was pumped with energy, his hair falling around his face, but he wasn't even out of breath.

"Stupid race," the other man growled. "You didn't run."

"Yeah, I should have." He had too much energy inside his skin, too much pent-up *want*. "I'll race you down later."

They walked together to Dmitri's office. Raphael's second and the leader of the Seven was standing by the large wall of glass behind his desk that looked out over Manhattan, his hand cupping his wife's cheek. Dressed in black jeans paired with a fitted black jacket over a top the color of fresh raspberries, Honor St. Nicholas laughed up at her husband. Her eyes were an intense dark green that reminded Janvier of a shadowed jungle he'd once traversed as a courier, her hair soft ebony. Ashwini's best friend had come through the transformation to vampirism with a luminous physical beauty it took most vampires hundreds of years to achieve. Her physical appearance, however, wasn't what made her beautiful to Janvier. It was the way she looked at Dmitri. No one in the world could doubt her allegiance to the lethal vampire, her heart worn on her sleeve.

Hearing Janvier and Naasir at the door, she glanced toward them. "Oh, look at you!" Pure delight in her expression.

Janvier stared as Naasir ducked his head, his hands in the pockets of his jeans. Was he *blushing*? Impossible. Naasir didn't blush. But the vampire stayed in place as Honor closed the distance between them to stroke her hands over his shoulders. "It suits you," she said with open affection.

Naasir took his hands out of his pockets in response and put his arms around Honor. Then he held her, rubbing his cheek against her hair, his eyes closed. It was rare to see the vampire so quietly content. Janvier knew Naasir was staying in Honor and Dmitri's Tower suite—he didn't like living alone, eschewed his own quarters. He'd also stayed with the couple the two days he'd remained in the city after the final battle.

It was clear he'd bonded with Honor during their time together.

The hunter hugged him back with the same warmth, unafraid though she had to know she was being held by a predator. No, Janvier realized, that wasn't right. Despite the fact that Naasir's arms were around her upper body, hers around his waist, it was Honor who was doing the holding. Naasir had subtly ceded control of the embrace.

Janvier glanced at Dmitri, saw an intensity of emotion on his face that made his own heart squeeze. He'd never truly thought about the fact that Dmitri was over a thousand years old, the other man was so at home in this time period. Today, however, he felt the ache of memory within Dmitri, the weight of a history that had left scars on his soul, and he thought again of Ash, of the gift that could drown her in a stranger's past.

Beside him, Honor drew back and, rising on tiptoe, stroked the jagged cut of Naasir's hair off his face. "I have to go. I'm teaching a class at Guild Academy." Tugging him down, she kissed him on the cheek. "I didn't know you'd already bought clothes, so I picked up a few things for you earlier this morning. I put the packages in your room."

The rumble that came from Naasir's chest was so close to a purr that Janvier wasn't sure he hadn't imagined it. Sending Janvier a warm smile and Dmitri a far more tender look, Honor slipped out.

The strange, beautiful, unexpected moment ended with her departure.

Dmitri motioned for the two of them to walk out with him to the balcony, the light fall of snow having passed to leave the city glittering under a crystalline winter sun. "Tell me about the autopsy."

"It uncovered a tattoo that may help us track the victim's identity should the fingerprint search fail," Janvier said, then shared the details of the weakness in the bones, the skin. "However, the pathologist also confirmed the presence of fang bites as well as the long-term abuse we suspected."

"So while the bones echo what Lijuan did to her sacrifices, the long-term nature of this would seem to nudge us away from her."

"Yes, she ate up her people all at once," Naasir said, having crouched at the very edge of the railingless platform, his bare feet on the thin layer of snow that had collected on the flat surface. He stared out at the city below in unbridled fascination.

No one who didn't know him would ever expect such behavior. Janvier had seen the vampire act perfectly "normal," even appear sophisticated, cultured, and arrogant, as might be expected from a male of his age and strength, but that was all it was—an act.

"It's like putting on another skin," Naasir had said to him shortly after their first meeting a hundred and twenty-five or so years back. "The skin is not mine and it itches until I take it off."

Naasir only wore those skins around people he either didn't like or was yet making up his mind about. The latter could take him an instant or a year. Janvier had never had to deal with the vampire in any skin but his own—he'd met Naasir in a no-name vampire bar in Bolivia. To cut a long story short, they'd raised hell, broken furniture and a few jaws, and come out of it friends who understood the wildness in each other.

*"I like you, Cajun." A flash of gleaming fangs. "Where do you go from here?"*

*"I have to deliver a 'will you be my one and only concubine' proposal from an angel to a vampire."*

*"You're to ask this vampire to be a concubine on behalf of another? Why?"*

*"Because I'm a stupid* couillon *who lost a bet, but this Cajun doesn't go back on his word. So I'll play matchmaker. I just have to find the son of a bitch in the damn rain forest first; he's off licking his wounds after a lovers' quarrel."*

Naasir's eyes had lit up and Janvier had ended up with a companion on his hunt. They'd located the vampire and Janvier had delivered his message—to Naasir's silent laughter—then escorted the happy male back out to his contrite angel. It wasn't the first time the two of them had ended up playing or working together; it was through Naasir that Janvier had first come to see Raphael not simply as an archangel but as a man to whom he'd be proud to give his allegiance.

Now, he stepped up to where the vampire crouched, but instead of looking down at the ribbon of traffic far below, he turned his head in the direction of Guild Academy. "I'll continue to work with Ash, dig up everything we can on the victim, tug on all possible threads that could lead us to her murderer."

Dmitri shifted to stand on Naasir's other side. "I also need you to keep an eye on the vampire community on the ground. With Illium busy running drills, he doesn't have as much time to move in that arena."

"Do I need to look out for any specific problems?"

"If you hear anything about a drug called Umber, pass on the information to me immediately." The vampire gave him a briefing on the drug before adding, "In more general terms, the Made are aware the Tower's busy with a number of other matters at present."

Dmitri's eyes followed a Legion fighter coming in to land on the roof of the high-rise that was being modified for their use. "Repairs, the Legion, the archangelic political situation—they're sucking manpower and attention. And you know our kind."

*Yes.* Vampires were predators, the clawing hunger for blood existing just beneath the surface of their skin. Janvier had learned to control it long ago, as had Dmitri, but that didn't mean it wasn't there. Being a vampire wasn't a cosmetic choice; it affected the cells of the body itself, permanently altering its internal chemistry.

Bloodlust, if allowed free rein, could turn a vampire into a gluttonous killing machine.

# 15

"I've made it a point to be a presence in the vampire community since my return," Janvier said, understanding Dmitri's concern. New York—in particular, Manhattan—had a heavy vampire population. An outbreak of bloodlust could paint the city crimson-black, fragile mortal bodies lying in the streets like broken toys. "It was simple enough to slide back into the community, since I knew a number of people from previous visits to the city."

Dmitri's lips curved. "The ability to charm your enemies and make friends wherever you go has always been your gift, January."

Naasir snorted at the literal translation of Janvier's name. It was an unusual one, given to him by a girl of sixteen who was in love with her baby—a baby born during the first minute of a long-ago January night. The time and date were facts his mother had known only because right before she pushed her son out into the world, she'd heard the sky explode with fireworks as the wealthy mortals and immortals who lived in the nearby settlement celebrated the new year.

That sweet, romantic girl had loved him to the day she died as a tiny, wrinkled woman who'd lived a glorious life.

*"My Janvier. My New Year's gift."* Warm, soft hands on his cheeks, a brilliant smile that hadn't faded an iota in all the decades of her life. *"I am so proud of you."*

Warmed by the precious memory, he smirked at Dmitri. "At least people don't run screaming when they see me coming." The other vampire was simply too old to fully conceal the lethal depth of his power.

"Do you think I could jump to the ground from here?" Naasir asked conversationally.

"No," Dmitri replied. "I'd have to scrape you up with a shovel."

Naasir frowned, stared down at the distant city street. "Pity."

Sometimes, even Janvier didn't know if Naasir was kidding or asking a serious question. "If you don't need me to handle anything else immediately, I'm going to visit the injured." He'd gotten into the habit of dropping in, updating the fallen men and women on news of the outside world—the kinds of things that would make them laugh or groan.

"I'll hit the vampire clubs tonight," he added, "get a feel for things." If the computer searches on the tattoo and fingerprints came up empty, the clubs would also be a good starting point when it came to tracking the identity of his and Ash's victim.

As soon as her name formed in his mind, it was as if the past minutes hadn't existed. He was back on the snowy street outside the morgue, watching the woman he'd waited two lifetimes to find walk away from him.


Mulling over the strain he'd seen on Janvier's face before the Cajun left, Dmitri turned to the vampire who remained. Naasir was unique, the only one of his kind in known history. He was also dangerous to himself at times, with as little sense of self-preservation as a four-year-old. "If you crack your skull by falling over," he pointed out, "you won't get to have dinner with Elena and Raphael tonight."

Naasir jerked up his head, eyes shining. "Dinner?"

"Yes, you've been invited to the Enclave. Elena would like to welcome you back to the city."

Naasir crept away from the edge a fraction. "I want to go to dinner," he said decisively. "Will there be proper meat?"

"Montgomery will ensure you get fed." He was severely tempted to turn up at the dinner himself, just to see Elena's reaction to Naasir's unusual eating habits. "Tell me about Amanat." The lost city risen to the surface after an eon was home to the Ancient Caliane, Raphael's mother and a staggering power.

"Twice a week," Naasir said, "Caliane lowers the shield that protects the city so her people can go outside. They do so in small herds, scared and clinging to one another." There was no judgment in the words. "It may take months for them to overcome the fear seeded by the loss of one of their own."

Dmitri wasn't surprised. Caliane was strong, but the people who'd come with her into her long sleep were gentle, cultured beings with no real capacity to protect themselves. "Lijuan's territory?"

"I was able to infiltrate it without being detected after Jason gave me the advance data."

Dmitri had already received Jason's report, but the spymaster had focused on the politics, as well as on any news of Lijuan's whereabouts, while Naasir had been directed to pay attention to the populace.

"Her people are in the grip of a stunned kind of shock," the vampire said, "but there is no despair, not at the level there should be. They are waiting, and erecting shrines—where they kneel and pray for Lijuan's swift recovery."

"Damn." Dmitri had been hoping Raphael had managed to kill her off despite Raphael's own belief otherwise.

*Killing an archangel,* Raphael had said, *has always been a difficult task. Killing an Ancient might be an impossible one— and while Lijuan isn't an Ancient, she's close enough to it that I believe it'll take an extraordinary event to eliminate her.*

"I've thought of multiple methods to kill her," Naasir said. "Unfortunately, she keeps regenerating, even in my imagination."

That was the crux of it. If nothing could eradicate the threat of Lijuan, hell would erupt on earth. "Share your ideas with the sire." Naasir didn't think like the rest of them, had come up with surprising maneuvers before.

"Do I need to take a gift for Elena? Is that the thing to do?"

Dmitri fought the urge to tell him yes. Naasir's idea of a gift tended to be interesting at best. "Do what feels natural. Neither the sire nor the consort expect us to be anything other than who and what we are." That fact was at the core of why he served Raphael; there was no need for pretense.

"I'll take a gift," Naasir said after a minute. "It's what Jessamy taught me to do when invited to a special dinner at someone's home."

Dmitri wondered if Honor would mind if he changed their plans and invited them both to dinner at the Enclave.

## "It lives!"

Ashwini pointed her finger at Demarco. "I haven't shot anyone this week."

The streaky blond-brown of his hair more on the brown side right now, given the winter sunlight, the irrepressible hunter jumped over a table in the Academy dining hall to grab her shoulders and squeeze. It was his form of giving her a hug—most of the hunters who were her close friends knew she had trouble with too much physical contact.

Leaning forward, she hugged him. He was part of her family and she understood the value of such loyalty and affection in a way no one who hadn't lost a family could. It had all gone wrong so long ago, and now there was no way to fix the family into which she'd been born. But she could do this; she could hold on to the family she'd created.

"You teaching today?" she asked when she drew back.

Demarco flicked his finger at one of her earrings, the fall of bronze circles making a tiny metallic ping of sound. "Just finished doing a one-on-one strategy lesson with an older student." He led her back to where he'd been seated with a cup of coffee and a half-demolished banana chocolate chip muffin, the two of them detouring to the counter so she could pick up a muffin and a chocolate milk for herself.

They'd just sat down when Honor walked in.

"I thought I saw your name on the board," Demarco said. "Aren't you meant to be in class?"

"I postponed it for fifteen minutes to give the students time to change and catch a breath after a combat session that ran overtime." She slid into the chair next to Ashwini, nudging at Ash's shoulder with hers in hello before sneaking a piece of chocolate off Demarco's plate. "Mmm." She sighed, eyes closing. "I don't care how old I get, I'm never going to lose the taste for chocolate."

"I thought Dmitri gave good blood?" Demarco smirked.

"I'm going to murder Ellie," Honor said, her cheeks hot.

"Don't blame Ellie." Ashwini gave her friend a chunk of chocolate from her own muffin. "You start to stutter every time one of us asks about the blood drinking." Honor was the first hunter they all knew who'd become a vampire, and, family being family, they were nosy as hell about the experience.

"Then," Demarco added, "you go this amazing shade of red and seem to lose the ability to form words."

"Shuddup."

Laughing, Ashwini took a sip of her milk. She was happy to see her friend so alive and vibrant. Dmitri might be a bit of a bastard, but he'd brought Honor back from the bleak world in which she'd existed after the hell of her captivity, and for that, the vampire had a friend in Ashwini.

"Did Dmitri mention the case I'm working?" she asked her friend, feeling her way before she mentioned the details. The last thing she wanted to do was drag Honor back into the horror she'd survived.

"Yes." Honor's skin pulled taut over her bones, her voice vibrating with withheld emotion when she said, "I hope Raphael fries the evil bastard after you catch him."

Demarco leaned forward, lowered his voice. "What's the case?"

Reassured by Honor's anger that her friend wasn't in a bad headspace, Ashwini told him. She knew he wouldn't speak to anyone else about it unless she gave him the go-ahead. "Have either one of you heard anything that might help?"

"I wish I had," Honor said, her fury a thrum beneath her skin. "But I haven't really been on the streets since I got back, mostly teaching and at the Tower, helping Dmitri deal with the Legion. Now and then, the Primary will talk to me in an ancient language I've studied but never expected to hear. It's fascinating."

Ashwini shivered at the thought of the winged army that had appeared out of nowhere. Most people assumed the fighters had arisen from a secret compound that belonged to Raphael. Ash knew that was wrong, very, *very* wrong. Even from a distance, they gave off such a sense of age that it was a crushing pressure against her senses.

Sometimes it felt as if the entire ocean lay on top of her, the weight of it at once vast and strangely freeing. The last time she'd woken breathless from that particular dream, she'd walked out to her little balcony to see a Legion fighter sitting on the railing.

He'd stared at her. She'd stared at him, the hairs rising on her arms.

An instant later, he'd flown off, his batlike wings silent in the night-draped sky.

Demarco tapped his finger on the table, the sound tugging her back from the memory of the surreal encounter. "Ransom was saying something about his street friends having noticed a weird vibe in the clubs. You should talk to him."

"I was hoping he'd be here." A former street kid, Ransom had contacts the rest of them couldn't access, and with his leg currently in a cast that meant he couldn't actively hunt, he'd been drafted in as an Academy instructor for the duration.

Demarco glanced away, staring through the casement windows at the snow that had begun to fall again, the flakes fatter and heavier than when Ashwini had come inside. "He took the day off."

Ashwini caught Honor's eye. Turning to Demarco, they said, "Spill," in unison.

"Shit." He shoved a hand through his hair. "I can't. He'll skin me. You'll know tonight."

They trained their best "Talk or die" scowls on him, but he folded his arms and narrowed his eyes. Ashwini knew that look. He wasn't going to budge. "Fine," she muttered. "But you better have a damn good excuse for keeping it from us."

"Trust me." Grinning, he unfolded his arms, all open charm, but while she felt the affection of a friend for him, his smile did nothing for her as a woman.

Not like the smile of a certain vampire.

"Talking of secrets," Demarco drawled, "you and the Cajun—"

Ashwini thumped a blade into the table in front of the other hunter, left it quivering in a vertical position.

"Watch it, Dem"—Honor laughed—"or you might end up dog food."

The other hunter threw up his hands. "It was an innocent question."

"*Any*way," Ashwini said pointedly, "if you hear anything that might be useful, pass it on." She figured Ellie already had the info via Raphael.

"Will do." Demarco glanced at his watch. "Gotta go. Have to pick up a vampire who decided to skip out on his Contract."

Ashwini and Honor stared at him. "And you were sitting here eating a muffin?" Honor asked in a dumbfounded tone. "Isn't a pickup a little more, I don't know, important?"

"Genius booked a bus ticket. I swear to God," Demarco said, doing up the buttons on his pale brown corduroy jacket with leather patches of darker brown at the elbows. "Under the name Bill Smith."

Ashwini rolled her eyes. "I guess it's better than John Smith."

"No, that's his real name. Plus, since he was good enough to provide photo ID when he booked, I know it's my target." He grabbed a deep blue woolen scarf and wrapped it around his neck twice. "I know what you're thinking, that he's throwing me off the scent—but I did my research. Bill Smith is an accountant who goes by the book."

"Then why is he attempting to skip out on his Contract?" Only the morons, the deluded, and the arrogant tried to cheat the angels. Especially when the resulting punishments were known to be pitiless. Ashwini would've felt sorry for the vamps she brought back to face punishment except that no one *had* to choose vampirism. Once you made that bargain, though, it was your responsibility to keep it.

After all, there were no take-backs when it came to the near-immortality bestowed in return for the hundred years of Contracted service.

"Bill Smith thinks he found a loophole," Demarco answered

with a roll of his own eyes. "That's according to the certified letter he left his angel. And there might be a woman involved. Isn't there always?" A woebegone look. "Us poor males don't stand a chance." Gloves on, he left with a quick laughing salute, promising to message them if he did in fact pick up Bill Smith at the bus station.

Alone with Honor, Ashwini said, "Dmitri giving good blood aside, how's the vamp thing going?" They'd talked after Honor's return to the city, but her friend continued to adjust to her new life.

"It is a bit weird, realizing I'm not human any longer. I forget all the time and then something reminds me and I go through the surprise of it all over again." She snuck a taste of Ashwini's chocolate milk. "But no one's treated me any different—at the Guild, I mean. I was worried about that, you know?"

"Idiot." Only way a hunter lost his or her right to the loyalty of her brethren was if she betrayed them. "You do realize you'll now be a hunter for eternity?"

Honor's smile turned her eyes an incredible jeweled shade that was breathtaking, her immortality unmistakable at that instant. "I'm happy, Ash. Happier than I've ever been. Dmitri . . ." A shake of her head. "I don't have the words."

"You don't need them." Ashwini had sensed the soul-deep connection between Honor and Dmitri the first time she saw them together. As if two broken halves of a whole had found their way to each other, and in the process healed the fractures in one another.

Sometimes, she thought Janvier could do the same for her, if only she'd let him in.

Honor closed her hand over Ashwini's where it lay on the table, the two of them having been friends long enough that the other woman wasn't threatened by her abilities. Ashwini, in turn, had no problem dealing with Honor's touch. Even with the horror she'd suffered, Honor was Honor, no ugly surprises, just an old, *old* soul. The nightmares that had tormented her in the aftermath of her abduction were long gone, vanquished by a fierce spirit that had chosen love over darkness.

"It's a wonderful thing, Ash . . . and you can have it with Janvier. He adores you."

"I know." It was a rasp of sound, the need inside her a vast emptiness.

She adored him, too.

And because she did, she had to find a way to tell him the truth.

# 16

Standing on the roof of the Legion high-rise, the snow having passed, Elena looked at the architect cum structural engineer who had the task of converting it to the Legion's specifications. "Can you do something with the roof so we can insert a skylight?"

Twisting her lips, the stunning ebony-skinned vampire named Maeve glanced down at the flat surface. "I could, but if you're wanting to maximize natural light, I say we take off the entire roof and replace it with glass."

"Can we do that?" Adrenaline shot through Elena. "Structurally, I mean?"

"Don't see why not." Maeve's accent was so modern Manhattan, her clothes so edgy—like the kaleidoscope of color that was the structured, asymmetric ankle-length coat she wore—no one who didn't know would've guessed she'd been born on another continent over five hundred years ago.

The woman, with her high, slashing cheekbones and short crop of tight curls, had used the years to become multiqualified and was considered one of the best in her line of work. "Only thing is," Maeve continued, "I'd have to work out the weight tolerance—Legion might not be able to gather on it in such large groups."

Elena looked at the Primary, standing silent to her right. "Preference?"

"Glass." The rim of blue around his irises appeared to burn in the icy winter light. "If we can gather in a place of earth, we do not need the roof."

"So," Elena said, "we make the entire penthouse a glass box." With floor-to-ceiling windows designed to be opened so the Legion could fly in and out, though they'd have to figure out how to conserve heat in winter for the plants.

"No."

Maeve blinked at the Primary's interjection. "No?"

"Can you make the garden deeper?"

"You mean merge two or more floors?"

A curt nod.

"Yes," the other woman said slowly. "But I think what'll work best is if we don't take out the entire floor between the two levels—instead, we can cut it out in parts." She did a rough sketch on her tablet using a stylus. "See, like this?"

The sketch showed a hollowed-out interior with ledges coming out from the walls in what appeared to be a random formation over three floors, but Elena quickly realized the placement of those ledges meant light would be maximized, creating multiple areas for gardens, as well as landing sites for the Legion. "Brilliant."

The Primary touched the sketch. "Yes. Can the whole building be thus?"

Maeve blew out a breath, her hands squeezing the tablet. "Wow. Okay, I'm going to have to do more research on the structural aspects of the building to answer that question." She was making frantic notes as she spoke. "Top three floors, though, that's a definite."

Elena was wonderfully astonished at the idea of a high-rise turned into a giant greenhouse, its interior a branching tree through which a winged being could weave all the way to the ceiling. She crossed her fingers that Maeve would be able to come up with a solution.

"We might as well start on the top three floors, then," she said, after a glance at the Primary to see if he agreed. "Maeve, I know plants, but the building's going to be your ball game."

"I'm on it."

Leaving the other woman to talk to her team, Elena took the Primary to a gardening supplies warehouse, where she organized delivery of pots, soil, freestanding grow lights, and other items. Their next stop was a commercial greenhouse.

Two hours later, enough plants and supplies had been delivered that she put the Legion to work. It would take time for the modifications to the top floors to be completed; in the interim, she'd decided to transform the entire first floor into a place where plants could thrive and the Legion could rest.

Elena understood the need for a haven, a safe place.

With Maeve's consent and advice, the winged fighters had already knocked down walls that weren't load-bearing, opening up the space. They'd also ripped up the carpet and cleaned the floor so it was smooth. All of it since six that morning.

As she helped rig things up so this floor would have adequate heat and humidity, then showed the Legion fighters how to handle the more delicate plants, she began to feel her own body relax. Their pleasure in the earth was transcendent, the haunting peace of it wrapping her in its wings . . . until her skin rippled with a cold shiver, her heart punching into her rib cage.

She could hear them, the echo of whispers that together was a mind created of hundreds; it was a rushing, overwhelming sound inside her skull, like a wave crashing inside a cave. "Stop," she gasped out.

Silence.

The Primary was in front of her seconds later. "The consort does not wish to join our conversation?"

That was when Elena understood the voices had been an invitation. "One at a time," she said, not sure quite what she was doing but feeling an odd sense of . . . vulnerability around her. "I want to know you one at a time."

A rustling consternation.

"We are one," the Primary said. "We are the Legion."

"This," she said, brushing her hands over the miniature mandarin orange tree in front of her, "is one. The root systems, the trunk, the branches, the leaves, they all act together with one goal. Yet not one of the leaves is *exactly* the same. You can be one without being identical copies."

Muted whispers, the Legion attempting to be quiet for her benefit. It cut off when the Primary looked around the room.

Returning his gaze to Elena, he said, "We will consider the idea of being one without being one."

Elena was pretty sure the Legion continued their whispering discussion long after she left late in the afternoon. It had been eerie to be in a silent room when she'd known a heated debate was going on between its inhabitants.

Having showered and changed at the Tower, she swept out under the rays of the setting sun, more than ready to go home, be with Raphael and their friends. She'd only been in the air a matter of seconds when she received a message from Demarco.

*You owe me fifty bucks. Bill Smith was waiting patiently in line for his bus.*

She couldn't believe it; when they'd run into each other at their mutual favorite coffee place at dawn that morning, and he'd shared his plan for catching the vampire, she'd told him he was losing it. "Shows what I know," she muttered and sent him a reply before sliding her phone away into a zipped pocket.

*Archangel?* she said, unsure if she'd reach him. He'd taken a specialist squadron out over the sea to practice maneuvers. Now, more than ever, the Tower's defenses had to be airtight. New York couldn't appear wounded prey to the hostile forces who watched. On the other hand, their people were tired. It was why Dmitri had staggered exercises so every fighter would have more days off than usual in rotation.

The wind swept into her mind, licked with rain and the endless sea. *I'll be home soon, hbeebti. Naasir has said he will behave if he arrives first.*

*Well, he has promised not to eat me, so that's something.*

Illium fell into flight with her as Raphael's laughter lingered in her mind, while her Legion escort flew far enough overhead that it was unobtrusive. Angling her wings slightly so she could talk to the blue-winged angel beside her, the silver filaments in his feathers catching the fading light, she said, "Are you coming to dinner, too?"

It was odd. She'd initially invited Naasir, Janvier, and Ash. The small team had become a tight unit during the fighting and she knew Naasir hadn't yet had a chance to catch up with Ash. All three had accepted the invitation, but the weird thing was, suddenly every member of the Seven who was in the vicinity had the night off to join them.

Illium's golden eyes gleamed beneath the blue-tipped black of his eyelashes. "Oh, yes, I'm definitely coming to dinner."

Elena wasn't an idiot. "What are you expecting Naasir to do?"

Illium dived toward the water at breathtaking speed, came up at a steep angle. "Word is," he said, "Naasir's bringing you a present."

That didn't sound ominous . . . until she considered who they were talking about.

Illium shot up to the sun before she could question him about Naasir's gift-giving proclivities.

Elena kept to a more lazy flight homeward. Montgomery had promised her double chocolate fudge cake, and, whatever Naasir's present, it couldn't hold a candle to the butler's double chocolate fudge cake—Montgomery made it himself from scratch, guarded the recipe like a dragon with his treasure.

When her phone rang, she answered it with a smile. "I was waiting to hear from you," she said to her younger sister Eve. "How did the exam go?"

"It wasn't as hard as my friends and I thought it would be," Eve said, voice ebullient, and the two of them fell into an easy conversation.

Landing on the snow-covered lawn of her and Raphael's Enclave home not long after she and Eve said good-bye, she watched Illium come down fast and neat. Aodhan dropped out of the sky at a slower pace, the early evening light fracturing off him in dazzling sparks.

"How's the wing feel?" she asked, having noticed the last-minute correction he'd made to keep from toppling sideways.

"Significant weakness, but I must continue to exercise it at this stage of the healing process." He stretched both wings out to their full breadth, folded them back in again.

Never, she thought, would she get used to the impossibility of Aodhan, to the feathers and hair that seemed coated with crushed diamonds that refracted light in endless shards. "Just make sure you don't push it too far." Hunters and Tower personnel, they both chafed at being grounded. Aodhan hadn't mentioned pain, but she knew it had to be bad.

The immortal ability to survive brutal wounds came at an agonizing price.

"Don't worry, Ellie." Illium bumped a fist gently off Aodhan's jaw, his skin warm gold against the sunshine-touched alabaster of Aodhan's. "I sicced Keir on him two days ago when he refused to listen to reason. You haven't seen a set-down until you've seen Keir delivering it." A wince. "Poor Sparkle."

Aodhan did something she didn't quite catch, and suddenly, Illium was on the ground, flat on his back in the snow. The shocked look on his face was almost as good as Aodhan's studiously blank one. "Shall we go inside, Elena?"

"How about helping me up first?" Illium scowled and held up a hand. "Now my back's all wet."

Aodhan hauled him up with his good arm. "Poor Bluebell."

Elena's lips twitched. It was starting to become clear why Aodhan and Illium had become friends. Aodhan might be quiet, but he could hold his own against the blue-winged angel—who remained the only person Aodhan could bear to have touch him. Elena didn't know what had traumatized Aodhan to that visceral depth, but she knew the silent battle he fought each and every day.

*"Your scars exist, but it's your courage that defines you."*

She'd said that to him a week past, received a piercing glance in return from the haunting fracture of his gaze. *"I'm afraid, every instant, that the darkness will suck me back under."*

*"But you keep going, Aodhan. Any fool can jump unawares into danger—you know exactly the risk you're taking, and yet here you are."*

In front of her, he brushed the snow off Illium's feathers and said, "Next time you call me Sparkle, I'm dumping you into the Hudson."

"I can swim."

"Come on," Elena said with a grin. "Montgomery will be waiting."

The three of them had just taken the first steps toward the house when there was a wash of wind. Jason and Mahiya landed to Illium's right a second later. The spymaster's black wings were dramatic against the white of the snow, his facial tattoo vivid even in the gray light, but it was Mahiya's spectacular wings that caught the eye. Jewel green and wild blue with strokes of black, the pattern was akin to a peacock's spray.

"Elena," Mahiya said with the gentle smile that held an inner glow. "Thank you for having us to dinner on such short notice. I'm afraid we couldn't resist the temptation."

"I'm starting to worry about Naasir's idea of a gift."

Jason stirred. "He once brought an angel a bucket of piranhas and told the angel to stick his hand inside to retrieve his gift."

"But he didn't like the angel," Illium put in, "so you should be safe. I don't know why the angel in question whined to everyone about it—he only lost a few fingers."

"At least there is nowhere for Naasir to find a live wild boar here." That came from Aodhan, Illium nodding sagely beside him. "In his defense, he had been told to bring meat to the fire."

"Gee, don't try to reassure me all at once." Leading them inside, she discovered Montgomery had set up a table in the formal dining room.

Elena and Raphael didn't normally use this room for anything but meetings with archangels or other highly ranked individuals, it was so grand. However, it took on a different air with so many of the Seven in attendance. They sprawled over the elegant furniture, dug into Montgomery's food, spoke with the ease of men who'd known one another for centuries.

That feeling only intensified when Dmitri drove his gleaming Ferrari to the front door, Honor in the passenger seat. Raphael returned home at almost the same instant, and the buzz of conversation and laughter grew to fill the house. Fifteen minutes into it and Illium had coaxed a blushing Mahiya into dancing with him in the center of the room, while Aodhan and Dmitri played a chess grudge match using a priceless hand-carved set placed on an antique parquetry table.

Honor, on the other hand, had walked over to examine the magnificent painting of the Refuge on the far wall, and Jason stood talking to Raphael as they watched Dmitri and Aodhan attempt to outthink one another.

The only ones missing were the people she'd originally invited. "Did anyone ask Naasir if he needed a ride?" Janvier and Ash she wasn't worried about, since both were locals—and they were on a case, the chilling details of which Raphael had shared with her.

Goddamn Lijuan. Elena was ready for the crazy archangel to *die* and stay dead.

"Naasir said he was coming with Janvier and his hunter." Illium twirled Mahiya back into him on those words, the gold-edged orange of the calf-length tunic she wore over black cotton leggings flaring out in a rippling circle.

The throaty purr of a powerful engine sounded just then, and Elena turned to the large windows that overlooked the drive to see a gleaming black panther of a car prowl to a stop next to Dmitri's Ferrari. "Wow."

As she watched, the driver's-side door was pushed up at the same time as the passenger door. Ash stepped out one side, Janvier the other . . . and that was when she realized Naasir was crouched on top of the car.

# 17

Ashwini got out of the incredible car Janvier had driven up in after calling to offer her a ride. Still wrestling with what she had to tell him, she should've said no, but she'd missed him. Plus, they had to talk. The fingerprints had been a bust, as had her attempt to track down witnesses and/or surveillance tapes. She'd also spoken to a professor Honor had said could be trusted, his specialty mummification.

The white-haired male had read the interim autopsy report, then stared at the attached photos for considerable time, before saying conclusively, "Not natural. Not only is the severe cell-level damage incompatible with that, *and* with the ordinary process of mummification, the appearance of the corpse is all wrong in the context of its probable age, the fragile bones and teeth even more so."

Janvier had been busy, too. He'd spent his time touching base with the "day" vampire community, and while he'd picked up a jumpy vibe, he thought that had more to do with the after-math of the battle than their victim. "Let's enjoy this dinner," he'd said after the two of them swapped information. "The clubs won't hit their stride till around eleven, and I can't think of any other way to move forward at this point."

Neither could Ashwini.

Now, she stroked her hand down the paintwork of his car, the black holding a faint shimmer that made the car appear a living shadow. "I can't believe you had this all the time."

He'd told her it had been garaged in Louisiana, that he'd hired a special truck to drop it off in New York. "Nobody," he'd said, "drives her but me."

Ashwini could understand his covetous air. This was one sexy machine. "How much did it cost?" She'd never thought of Janvier as rich, but he had to be—he was very, very smart, and the smart vamps always ended up wealthy.

"Don't worry, *cher.*" A lazy drawl that licked over her like a full-body kiss. "I can keep you in the style to which I intend you'll become accustomed."

"Such dreams you have, sugar." She patted his cheek, to his grin, before reaching inside the car and to the footwell where she'd stored the gift Naasir had bought Elena. She couldn't wait to see the look on her fellow hunter's face. "Here," she said, careful to keep her body in the way of the windows as she passed it over to the vampire.

His hands touched hers as he took the present, but her ability only reacted with a bemused shrug. It didn't know what to make of Naasir, which was fine with her. The lack permitted her to be friends with him without worry.

Looking at him, she shook her head.

Even though he'd been riding on top of the car—the maniac—the heavy silver silk of his hair had fallen back around his face in straight strands cut with a choppiness that suited him, and he looked far more civilized than she'd expected. He'd dressed in black pants and a black shirt, with an ankle-length black coat, the stark shade throwing his hair and eyes into sharp focus.

Janvier, by contrast, was in jeans and a thin, oat-colored sweater below his battered leather jacket. She could see the edge of a white T-shirt beneath the sweater. Around his neck was a burgundy scarf knit with a wool-angora blend. She'd sent it to him after the Atlanta operation, and this wasn't the first time she'd seen it around his neck—if he wore a scarf, it was this one.

As she wore the sapphire pendant he'd given her. Right against her skin.

"You better go first," Janvier said to Naasir. "Montgomery's opening the door."

Cradling his gift protectively in his arms, Naasir walked up to the door. "Hello, Montgomery."

"It is a pleasure to have you here, sir." The butler's plummy accent held real affection.

"I promise not to claw up the furniture."

"That would be most welcome," Montgomery responded, without a hitch in his butlerish tone. "Sir, Guild Hunter."

Nodding a greeting, Ashwini stepped inside to find Elena and Raphael heading toward them. She continued to have trouble comprehending how Elena could trust herself to someone that deadly and ruthless. Eyes of an excruciatingly pure blue and hair of a black darker than midnight, the Archangel of New York was in no way human, the power that pulsed off him a violent storm.

A touch on her lower back, Janvier's hand anchoring her in the present when she would've been sucked into the vortex that was Raphael's more than thousand years of life, her ability stretching out toward him like a child afraid of fire but wanting to touch it all the same. Drawing in a breath that was jagged inside her, she didn't tell Janvier to break contact, the heat of his body a talisman against her own out-of-control mind.

In front of them, Naasir bowed his head. "Sire, Consort."

Elena sighed in silent relief when she realized Naasir was holding nothing more dangerous than a potted plant, the pot wrapped in pretty foil paper. "It's nice to see you, Naasir," she said, touching Raphael's mind with her own at the same time. *The others will be disappointed. I think they were expecting something outrageous.*

"This is for you." Naasir handed her the plant. "I thank you for the gracious invitation to your home."

The hairs rose on the back of her neck at the pristine civility of the words, the tiger-on-the-hunt scent of him at odds with the sophisticated vampire who stood in front of her. "Thank you," she managed to say, wondering if she'd offended him somehow. Instinct told her Naasir was this polite only to people he didn't like.

"If Jessamy asks, tell her I followed the rules." A feral grin.

*Oh.* "I will." Glancing down, she focused on the plant in her arms. It was unusual, the red heart of the open pods lined with what appeared to be tiny barbs. Intrigued, she touched a careful finger to the red . . . and it tried to eat her.

Naasir laughed when she jumped, but it wasn't a mean laugh. Coming up beside her, he said, "It took me hours and hours to find one in your city." Pride in every word, he ran his finger over another open pod.

When the flower snapped its teeth at him, he snapped his own back. "It only eats small things."

Elena was beyond fascinated. "Like insects?"

His eyes lighting up at her obvious interest, Naasir nodded. "If you put it in your greenhouse, it'll eat any insects that bother your other plants."

Elena wasn't sure she had any insects in her greenhouse. *Raphael, where do we get food for this plant?* She'd never had a carnivorous greenhouse guest before.

*It is your gift, hunter mine.*

*Thanks a lot.* But she remained fascinated by the plant as unique as the vampire who'd given it to her. "Should we go put it in the greenhouse now, so it's warm?"

Naasir nodded. "It's like me; it doesn't enjoy the cold."

First, though, Elena took it inside to show the others. The gift was a hit.

Heading outside afterward, past an unflustered Montgomery, Elena didn't bother to put on her coat. It was freezing out, but the greenhouse wasn't far. Naasir prowled beside her, his nostrils flaring at the cold scents, the bitter night air. "Caliane is lonely," he said without warning.

Elena almost stumbled. Righting herself, she carried on along the lamplit pathway toward the greenhouse, the grow lamps within giving it a welcoming glow. "Lonely?"

The silver strands of Naasir's hair moved like liquid mercury when he nodded. "When she lived in the world before, Raphael was nearby. Now he is far from her, across an ocean, and the time she had with him at the ball did not ease her need."

If there was one thing about Caliane that Elena had never doubted, it was the Ancient's love for her son. "Can she leave her territory right now?" Amanat was a heartbeat away from Lijuan's homeland in angelic terms.

"It may be the best time. Lijuan's people are looking inward—they've put up defenses and are hunkered down behind them."

"I'll speak to Raphael." The idea of having her Ancient mother-in-law over for a visit didn't exactly make her want to jump for joy, but Caliane had appeared to be thawing toward her during their last meeting, so maybe it wouldn't be so bad. Maybe. "Thank you for telling me."

Naasir pressed his nose against the glass of the greenhouse before following her inside. She settled the carnivorous plant away from the others, not sure it wouldn't decide to change diets, and turned to find the vampire standing in the aisle with a worried frown on his face. "Are you sure you'll have enough insects?"

"Yes. I'll take care of it, I promise." A plant was a plant, even if this one had a slightly different diet. "I like plants." And plants liked her back . . . more and more these days. She'd managed to baby an incredibly delicate fern back to life after it collapsed into limp brown strands as a result of her abandonment during the battle.

Then again, the plant's recovery had probably been sheer luck.

It sat healthy and happy and green to the right, next to a cheerful pansy that had attracted Naasir. The vampire touched his fingers to the soft purple petals of the flower, stroking as if he liked the velvety texture.

"Here," she said, showing him another plant. "You can eat it." Breaking off a flower, she gave it to him.

He bit carefully, chewed. "I don't understand why people eat plants," was his succinct response, but he finished off the flower as they headed back. "We will spar?"

"I've been looking forward to it." Fast and unorthodox, he'd be an excellent opponent from whom to learn. "Though we'll have to have ground rules."

He scowled. "You said cheating was okay."

"It is—for me. Raphael's an archangel. You're a centuries-old vampire." Elena wasn't sure of Naasir's exact age, but she had the feeling it had to be around the six- or seven-hundred mark. "I'm not as strong as you." Raphael had told her she had to be blunt with Naasir.

*He is highly intelligent, but he becomes frustrated with too much subtlety. That doesn't mean he isn't capable of understanding it—but that he gets annoyed with people who force such subtleties on him.*

Tonight, Naasir looked at her with the silver eyes that held such wildness her senses kept telling her he was nothing known, nothing understood. "I could break your neck without effort," he said, as if simply stating a fact. "The sire would not like that."

"Neither would I." Her dry response made him grin, fangs flashing. "I say we do a couple of practice runs so you can gauge your strength against mine." Elena liked sparring with those stronger than her; it was the only way to get better. Their enemies sure as hell didn't go easy on her because she was significantly weaker than the average adult angel.

But, she had to be smart about it. No use being too proud and ending up dead because Naasir didn't realize he wasn't dealing with a warrior angel his own age. "How about tomorrow?"

"I will ask Janvier if he and his hunter need help with their hunt."

Elena felt her body tense again at the horror of what had been done to the Little Italy victim, at the idea that Lijuan might somehow have left a taint in their city. "I really wish the wicked witch would take a dive straight into hell."

"Did Raphael tell you I once tried to bite her?"

"No." Eyes wide, she turned to face him. "What happened?"

"I was a child. She laughed because she thought I was joking." He shrugged. "I wasn't—I wanted to kill her because she smelled like bad meat. *Wrong.*"

"In that case," Elena said, "we'll soon be best friends."

Naasir wrapped his arm around her neck, his very sharp teeth close to her ear as he said, "You smell good, Ellie." A tiny bite, playful rather than serious. "Do you think Janvier smells his hunter?"

Elena smiled at the whisper and decided to set aside thoughts of Lijuan and the death the insane archangel left in her wake. Tonight it was about loyalty, about friendship, and about the ties that bound them all to one another, angel, vampire, and mortal. "I hope so."

Janvier watched Ashwini perch on the arm of the chair where Honor had taken a seat, Ash's long, long legs clad in black jeans and her eyes bright as she listened to something Mahiya was saying to them both. His hunter appeared in good spirits despite her lack of success at unearthing a clue, but he'd felt the screaming tension in her when they'd first walked into the house. Others might've identified her response as fear at the proximity to an archangel but he knew different.

It was the history Raphael carried in his bones. At a thousand five hundred years old—give or take a decade or two—Raphael was young in relation to the other archangels. Lijuan was rumored to be ten thousand years old, while no one knew Caliane's true age; Janvier had heard guesses that went from two hundred and fifty thousand years old to double that. He couldn't imagine living that long—it made him better understand why older angels chose to Sleep for eons and why some vampires settled on a peaceful goodnight.

"You look at her as a man only looks at one woman in his lifetime, be he mortal or immortal."

Janvier met the archangel's gaze, the power in it staggering. "There has never been, nor ever will be, anyone like her."

"Such gifts don't often appear," Raphael said, his attention on Ash. "In my lifetime, I've met three others like her: mortals who needed time beyond a human life span to allow their gifts to grow to their full potential."

"Do they live?" Janvier asked, knowing the angels liked to make sure the unique and the gifted survived into eternity.

Janvier had once been sent on a mission to locate a reclusive composer who resided in a castle deep in the Caucasus Mountains. The commission had come during his years as a free agent and it had carried the seal of Astaad, Favashi, and, unexpectedly, Titus. All three archangels had loved the composer's works with such passion, they'd offered to Make him without need for a hundred-year Contract. All he'd have to do was continue to create his symphonies, fill the world with music.

A remarkable offer, yet the composer had refused it. "My music," he'd said, his eyes holding a spark Janvier had seen only in the gifted and the mad, "is precious because it is touched with my mortality. Should I become a man with eternal life, I will no longer be able to create that which brings the archangels such joy. I would become a shade, dead inside even as I lived forever."

So he wasn't surprised when Raphael said, "Two are gone, having chosen a mortal existence despite all the temptations laid at their feet. One resides in Nimra's territory, in a peaceful part of the bayou."

Janvier realized he knew exactly who Raphael meant. "Silvan." Five hundred years old, the vampire had a level of power that often eluded those twice his age. Despite that, he preferred a life of solitude over any position more lucrative and influential. "Those of my family who live in the area say he can walk in dreams."

"You'll have to ask Silvan if you wish the truth."

"Perhaps I will the next time we share chicory coffee on the dock off his home."

Raphael's lips curved. "It is true then, Cajun. You know everyone?"

"That's my job." To be the one no one feared and everyone welcomed. The task had once been Illium's, but Bluebell was now a power, a fact no amount of charm could conceal.

"You're very good at what you do." The words of an archangel to one of his men. "As to your hunter, I think you know the odds are not in your favor. Those born with deeper senses often turn down the chance at immortality for reasons we cannot understand."

Unfortunately, Janvier understood Ashwini's reasons all too well. She'd become stronger over the past twelve months, her reactions more intense. Already she lived on the edge of "normal." She feared what she'd become should she embrace immortality. Janvier knew she would be extraordinary then as she was extraordinary now, but she didn't see it that way.

"The pathologist called us earlier," he said, changing the subject to keep his mind from going around in circles. "He's completed his deep tissue analysis"—or as much as was possible given the state of the remains—"and says the victim shows conclusive signs of being a long-term donor."

If a vampire was careful, even an ongoing donor would carry no scars. Should Janvier ever taste Ash's blood, he'd lick over the wound to make sure it healed cleanly—unless he *wanted* her to bear his mark. His breath caught at the idea of it, his abdomen clenching. To have her not only offer him her vein but consent to wear the sign of his possession, it was a dream so big, he knew it might never come true.

Not every vampire, however, was careful with his donor. It led to the formation of scar tissue *beneath* the skin at the most utilized sites. Not only was that bad for the donor but, over time, it made it more difficult for the vampire to feed. The Little Italy victim's major fang sites had been so deeply scarred that the pathologist had noted it was possible she'd become useless as a donor. That could be the reason she'd been killed and thrown out with the garbage, but it still didn't explain the desiccation.

"Ash and I," he told Raphael, "are heading to the Quarter clubs after dinner to see if we can pin down the victim's identity." While there was no guarantee she'd patronized the clubs, it was a good starting point, given how many vamps first met their long-term donors in the Quarter. "It'll also give me a chance to connect with those Made who prefer the night hours."

"Stay in regular contact with Dmitri." An order. "If Lijuan did leave a taint in our city, I don't want either of you falling victim to it."

Ash looked up then, the mysterious dark of her eyes going straight to Janvier. Her laughter faded, but the connection between them . . . it continued to pulse unabated.

"No," Janvier said. "I won't take any unnecessary risks."

# 18

It took Elena a half hour into the dinner to realize that some of the wine at the table was blood red—as in *real* blood red, and that the shish kebabs Naasir was snacking on beside her were made up of cubes of seasoned but raw meat.

She could live with that. Feral as he was, there was something both innocent and wildly charming about Naasir. He truly was like a wild tiger; he might bite her hand, but only if she threatened him. At least now that he'd decided not to make a meal of her.

At that instant, he nudged his plate toward Ash, who was seated on his other side. Elena watched, wondering what the other hunter would do. Not blinking, Ash reached out and took a piece of cooked meat Naasir had ignored in favor of the raw cubes. Naasir smiled and continued to eat.

Ash clearly knew the vampire's ways better than Elena did. Unsurprising, given that the team of three "shadows" had spent days behind enemy lines with only one another for company.

"Give me a clue," she said when Naasir glanced at her.

"To what?" He bit off a chunk of meat, chewed with relish.

"To what you are," she said, her curiosity as acute now as it had been the first instant she recognized he wasn't a normal vampire in any sense. She had trouble thinking of him as a vampire at all; he might drink blood but, as his diet showed, it was hardly enough to sustain him.

Naasir grinned and took a sip of the rich red liquid in his wineglass. "You can ask me seven questions."

Catching Ash's grin on his other side, Elena considered how strongly he made her think of a big cat—an amused one right now—and decided to tie him down. "Will you answer?"

"Yes."

She wasn't about to fall for that. "Will you answer truthfully?"

Naasir flashed his fangs at her. "I'll give you at least two truthful answers."

Elena decided that was better than nothing. "Are you the only one of your kind?" she asked, conscious of not only Ash but others around them listening in.

"Yes."

She examined his extraordinary eyes, his sly half smile, his body posture—and had absolutely no idea if he was lying or not. Damn it. "Were you born or Made?"

"Both."

Angling her shoulders to face him as Illium's shook with laughter across the table, she said, "Are you part of the tiger family?" His scent, it was so wild she could almost taste the jungle, almost see the long grasses where a striped predator might hide.

Naasir leaned in so close his nose brushed hers. "No," he said with a playful snap of his teeth.

Elena wanted to strangle him. It was impossible to gauge his expression, separate truth from lie, but she wasn't about to give up. "Are you a vampire?"

He drank deeply of the blood in his glass, the dark ruby of it swirling with secrets. "No."

"I think I could be driven to bite you," she muttered. "Hard."

Naasir growled, but his eyes were laughing. "Enough?"

"No. I have three questions left." Shooting a death glare at Dmitri when he asked her if she needed assistance, all false solicitousness, she turned her attention back to Naasir. "Do you truly eat people?"

"Only if I dislike them, or if I'm very hungry." A solemn statement.

Remembering what he'd once told her about the angel who'd Made him—though she was certain he hadn't been Made in any ordinary way—as well as what he'd said about Lijuan smelling like bad meat, she figured that was a truth.

"Do you have claws?" All vampires could extend their nails, some more than others. It was part of what allowed them to climb so well. But during the battle, when she'd bandaged up Naasir's wounds, she'd thought she glimpsed a more dangerous ability out of the corner of her eye. "I don't mean normal vampire claws. *Actual* claws."

Putting down his glass, Naasir spread his hand between them. His fingers were long and strong, his skin that lush, rich brown with an undertone of gold . . . and where his nails had been, she suddenly saw wickedly curved claws as might appear on the paws of a tiger. They disappeared a heartbeat later, and she could almost imagine it had been an illusion.

"Truth," she whispered, taking his hand to examine his nail beds when he didn't seem to mind. She almost asked where his claws had gone, since there was no trace of them, but didn't want to waste a question.

"Do this, Ellie," Ash said from his other side, reaching out to playfully scratch the back of Naasir's neck, his hair brushing over her skin.

He made a rumbling sound in the back of his throat, eyes closing.

Elena copied Ash's action on his hand, got another rumble before he lifted the gorgeous, *true* silver of his lashes to say, "Last question."

"Do you change shape?" Her words made Illium erupt in gales of laughter, but Elena wasn't put off. Legends had to start somewhere. Why not with Naasir?

"Of course," he answered, then turned his body to the right and curled his arm into his chest. "See, I have just changed shape."

Making a strangling motion with her hands that had him throwing back his head and laughing in unhidden glee, Elena felt the clean kiss of the sea, of the rain in her mind. *I see you and Naasir are becoming friends.*

*What did I tell you about this new sense of humor of yours?*

She took a bite of her dinner, which she'd ignored while questioning Naasir.

*I was speaking only the truth. Naasir is currently playing with your hair.*

*He probably wants to scalp me and use my hair as a trophy.*

*True.*

Elena looked up, eyes narrowed at the far too amused archangel across the table. *I am so going to get even with you for this.* Tugs on her scalp at the same instant, as if Naasir were curling the strands around his finger, then letting go.

She turned, intending to tell him to knock it off, but then she saw his face. He looked . . . absorbed. Like a cat with a ball of yarn. She didn't care if he'd said no to the tiger question—there was something distinctly feline about him. Especially since he'd apparently talked Ash into scratching his nape again while he played his game with Elena's hair, his eyes heavy lidded in ecstasy.

She was going to unearth the truth of him, even if it took her the rest of eternity.

Janvier saw Ash run her nails affectionately over Naasir's neck and remembered the first time she'd done that. It had been about thirty minutes after meeting Naasir. Where he was standoffish and distant with most new people, Naasir had already decided he liked "Janvier's hunter," having kept track of their interactions over the years.

As a result, he'd been his normal self.

Instead of being startled by Naasir's behavior, Ash had taken to him from the start, making no effort to avoid the physical contact the other male liked to make. "He's different," she'd said with a mystified shrug when Janvier asked her about it. "It's hard to explain, but what I sense from him isn't anything that disturbs me. I'm not sure I understand most of it."

A few minutes after that, while the three of them had been crouched in a hidden access tunnel they'd been scoping out in the run-up to the battle, she'd reached out and absently scratched the back of Naasir's neck.

Janvier, having previously seen how ferociously Naasir

could react to unwanted contact, had been ready to fight for her life, but the other man had bent his head for more. Ash's startled expression as she realized what she was doing had faded into affectionate puzzlement—and Janvier realized she'd reacted to an unvoiced need in the other male.

Her friendship with Naasir was as open and free of shadows as Janvier's relationship with her was not. So much lay unsaid between them, but saying it would fix nothing. Ash knew he loved her, would always love her. Anything she wanted, he'd give her . . . except for her mortality.

He'd waited more than two hundred years for her. How could she ask him to just let her go?

# Feed

Her eyes were drenched in terror.

Raising a hand, the one-who-waited stroked her cheek as her throat worked, the scream swallowed up by the pungent miasma of her fear.

"Not tonight." A rasp, its throat a ruin. "I have fed." The hunger came often, but the one-who-waited had learned to discipline that voracious need, because without discipline it would become a slave to those urges rather than a master of them.

So it pressed its mouth to hers in a kiss that made her whimper, its lips cracked and papery against hers. Hers had been soft once, were no longer. A pity.

Releasing her jaw, the one-who-waited smiled and drew one last draft of fear-laced air before removing the temptation from view. "Soon," it promised as the wood obscured her face. "Soon."

# 19

Janvier was leaning against the wall by the window finishing off the last of the blood in his wineglass when Ash found him around ten thirty that night. Dressed in those sleek black jeans paired with red ankle boots that had a spiked heel, her long-sleeved black shirt tucked into her jeans and opened at the throat just enough to hint at skin, she looked sexy and dangerous and his.

The dangles at her ears were a cascade of hoops created with tiny beads of orange and yellow and red, the belt around her hips having a simple square buckle of gleaming silver. And her hair, that glorious hair, it was a waterfall down her back. He wanted to wrap his hand in it, arch her throat, sink his fangs into her.

Mark her.

"We should head out," she said, eating a forkful of the chocolate fudge cake on her plate.

Janvier put his possessive hunger in a stranglehold and stole a fingerlick of frosting. "Any more news from the computer teams?"

"No. They've struck out in terms of identifying her either through the tat or through missing persons reports." She stabbed her fork into the cake with unnecessary force. "Not surprising. With what we know from the signs of feeding on her body, she probably lived with her killer."

"We will find her, *cher.*"

"Yes, we will." An absolute statement as she finished off the cake.

He couldn't help it. Leaning in, he caught a crumb clinging to her lower lip and brought it to his mouth. Sucking his thumb inside, he said, "Mmm, sweet."

Her body had gone stiff at the contact, and now she moved with an unusual jerkiness to place the fork and saucer on a side table. "Let's go."

It wasn't the response he'd been hoping for, but neither was it the light, flirtatious one he'd begun to find increasingly dissatisfying. He loved playing with Ash, but not when she was using that play to keep him at a distance. This at least was a sign he'd breached the armor she used to hold him at bay.

"Any particular club you want to hit first?" he asked, after getting into the car and starting up the engine.

"I say we start at the low end and work our way up. We have no way of knowing if she was beautiful enough to be invited into the exclusive clubs." Beauty talked in the clubs, especially if sexual feeding was involved. "But if she had been a regular at one of those places, or over at Erotique"—the most elite club in the city and located outside the Quarter—"her disappearance would've created more waves."

"I haven't heard any rumors of such a disappearance," Janvier confirmed.

"Did your contact have any success in reconstructing her face?"

"Yes, I received the image during dinner. It has no life to it so we'll have to be judicious in how we utilize it." Janvier tapped a finger on the steering wheel, the streets shadowed and dark around them. "She had to be in a one-on-one relationship."

"Why?"

"You saw at Giorgio's how the cattle cling to one another. If the victim was part of a group, her housemates would have reported her missing even if her vampire didn't."

"Unless she told them she was leaving him, and he kidnapped her after allowing her—and them—to believe he'd let her go. You know how many times that happens in abusive mortal relationships. Any reason it should be different for immortals?"

Face grim, Janvier said, "No."

Blowing out a breath at the bleak ugliness of it, she ran a hand through her hair, having left it down for tonight. However, since she didn't want anyone running their fingers through it in the clubs—it was creepy how many people thought that was okay—she reached back and began to braid it tight to her skull. "The situation with Giorgio is bugging me. You don't think our victim could've been part of his harem, do you?"

Janvier shook his head. "I made it a point to check him out—all his cattle are accounted for, even the ones nudged out of the nest after becoming too old." Distaste colored his tone. "Giorgio's use of women apparently stops short of murder."

"Damn, he made such a good, smarmy suspect." She tied off her braid and considered whether to swap her heeled red boots for the hunter boots she'd left in the car. She decided to stick with the heels since this was about blending into the clubs.

"And you, *cher*—did you sense any disturbing memory echoes in his house?"

"No, but it's new. The only time I've had an overwhelming reaction to a place rather than a person was at Nazarach's home." A shiver rippled through her. "I do get a hint of it now and then with older homes, but nothing like the screams in his walls."

Janvier ran his knuckles over her cheek, the caress chasing away the shiver and wrapping another set of chains around her heart. "Even with the Tower," she said past the knot in her throat, "I don't get anything. Could be because it's continuously modernized."

"Or perhaps," Janvier said, "the reason is that it's filled with so many different souls, rather than one who dominates everyone to cowering obeisance."

Ashwini could see that; Raphael was ruthless, but he gathered strong men and women around him. Ellie, for one, had never backed down from anyone in her life, and Dmitri wasn't exactly a cream puff. Then there was Janvier. He had the ability to bend, his temperament slow to anger, but he was also very much his own man. She knew that should it ever come down to it, Janvier would walk away from the Tower rather than go against his principles.

"As for Giorgio," Janvier said, "I'm not convinced he isn't hurting his cattle." His hands tightened on the steering wheel before he seemed to consciously make himself loosen his grip. "I have people keeping an eye on the situation—there was just something too sickly sweet about it all."

"Like an abused spouse who's been charmed into forgiving and forgetting." Ashwini's stomach twisted. She knew too well what it was to want to believe in the promises of someone she loved. "The honeymoon phase, I call it. Before the next hit."

Janvier shot her a hard, dangerous glance before returning his gaze to the road. "No one hurts you."

She heard the protective rage and, below it, a kind of stunned shock. "No one has ever hit me," she clarified. "Except, of course, during my work as a hunter." Then, all was fair.

Janvier's rigid shoulders didn't relax. "You think I don't know you well enough to see through that?"

Suddenly, the space between them didn't exist, the intimacy as blinding as when he'd brushed the crumb off her lip. "I don't talk about this." Tried to not even think about it, though seeing Arvi the previous day had stirred the pain of it back up.

*No, Ashwini,* she told herself, *be brutally honest. The reason you can't find a way to tell Janvier everything is that it'll break you if he looks at you with pity in his eyes.*

The car ate up the road, a sleek piece of the night.

"When I was a boy," Janvier said into the silence that had grown too heavy, too dark, "I used to work for a man who caught crawfish and supplied them to others. It was a way to earn a little money for my family, help my mother provide for my baby sisters."

Ashwini turned in her seat, compelled by the intimate vein of memory, affection, and sadness in his tone. "How many sisters did you have?" It startled her to realize she didn't know this about him when they'd spoken so many times, trusted one another so deeply.

"Two." A smile that creased his cheeks. "Amelie arrived in time with a thunderclap one rainy day, Jöelle a year or so later in the midnight hours, both squalling and red-faced and tiny." Having reached the fringe of the Vampire Quarter, he drove around to the small lot behind a blood café, after first unlocking the gate by pressing in a code on the keypad at the entrance.

He parked, switched off the engine, then turned toward her, one arm braced on the steering wheel. "My father died in a logging accident when Amelie and Jöelle were only two and three, so it was just the four of us until my mother married again seven years later."

Meaning he'd effectively become the head of his household for those seven years. "How old were you when you began working?"

"The dates weren't so well kept then—you understand, sugar? But I was old enough. Seven or eight."

"So young?"

"It was nothing unusual, not then." A shrug. "The man I worked for, he used to hit me if I didn't move fast enough; he'd kick me at least once a day. I have never forgotten the feeling of helplessness I experienced as a small boy trapped in a position of no power against a bigger, stronger opponent."

Blood hot and hands fisted, Ashwini had to remind herself that he hadn't been that small, helpless boy for a long time.

"You'd think I learned my lesson," he continued, "but we both know I later made the decision to enter into another situation where I did not hold power, out of what I then thought was love." He smiled, as if at the foolishness of it. "I was so green, so inexperienced in the ways of the world, and Shamiya was sensual, beautiful—and she told me incredible tales of lands far beyond the bayou."

A shake of his head. "It was a deadly combination when it came to the restless young man I was then, the hunger for adventure a craving in my soul, especially when she said such sweet words to me. I did not understand that I was in the throes of infatuation, and that she was merely playing."

Ashwini could see it, see the young male he'd been, hungry to experience life and to prove himself. "Did she help you become a Candidate?" A person couldn't simply ask to be a vampire; he or she had to be chosen.

"Yes. She took me to Neha's court, where she was a favorite." He laughed. "I have never been so sick as I was on that voyage. The waters of the bayou never crashed and rolled as that ocean did, as if attempting to throw an insect off its back."

The idea of the long journey, the things he must've seen, made a thousand questions form on her tongue, but she was even more fascinated by this deeper glimpse into his path to vampirism. "Shamiya must've felt something for you to go to all that trouble," she said, unable to imagine how any woman could be so careless as to throw away the loyalty of a man like Janvier. "Even as a favorite, she still had to petition Neha." And the Queen of Poisons was an archangel, as ruthless and as deadly as Raphael.

"She felt what a child does with a new toy." He spoke the words without rancor. "I was different enough in my lack of sophistication that I was new and shiny and amusing for a period. I, on the other hand, believed myself in the grip of a grand passion"—laughing at himself, eyes dancing—"and so like a fool, I gave up gumbo for blood." There was no recrimination in his gaze, nothing but an affectionate humor directed at the young man he'd once been.

Ashwini had asked him once if he loved Shamiya still. His answer had resonated deeply with her.

*A silly question, chère. You know love cannot survive where there is no light.*

Tonight, she saw that he'd not only moved on lifetimes ago, he bore no grudge. "Have you ever seen her again?" she asked, curious. "Shamiya, I mean."

"*Oui*, many times. She is as feckless and as fickle as she always was, while I am no longer green and impressionable. I outgrew her at the infancy of my Contract." His eyes locking with hers. "But before I grew into this man I am today, I was that boy at the mercy of a brute, and that unsophisticated young man abandoned in the court of the Queen of Poisons. I am no stranger to being under the control of others."

Ashwini knew that like the small boy, that idealistic young man was long gone. Janvier had survived both his childhood and the betrayal of the woman who had lured him into vampirism, come out of it a strong, intelligent male who would never again allow himself to be powerless.

Except . . . that was *exactly* the position she'd put him in once she told him everything. And not telling him was no longer an option.

"Your sisters?" she said, choosing to focus on the good and

not the dark; there'd be plenty of time for the latter. "Did you continue to support them after you became a vampire?" The answer wasn't truly a mystery to her. She knew who he was.

"It was my task as their elder brother," he said simply, allowing Ashwini to turn the conversation back to his family. "Though Amelie and Jöelle married young to proud men who would not take my help—and that, too, is right—for my mother I was able to do a great deal."

"Her husband didn't protest?"

"*Oui*, of course." A laugh. "But there is a difference between a son who wishes to ease his mother's life and an elder brother who wishes the same for his married sisters, *non*? My stepfather knew he stood no chance, and he was a good man, understood that I had been the head of the family long before he came on the scene. We were never father and son, but we were good friends."

"I didn't realize vampires could earn income early on in their Contract." She'd always believed it was more a case of indentured servitude.

"It depends on the angel, but loyalty and a willingness to learn and work hard beyond simply fulfilling the letter of the Contract are generally rewarded." The rhythm of his voice, it held a heavier Cajun accent now, some of his words not *quite* English. "For a young man from the bayou, those rewards were staggering. I was able to get my mother anything she needed, help my nieces and nephews with their educations."

Ashwini knew they should get out, start walking to the clubs, but she wanted to know so much more, could listen to him speak forever. "Amelie and Jöelle," she said, stealing another minute, "were their marriages happy?"

That wonderful deep cheek-creasing smile again. "My sisters grew up into strong women who ran their households with iron hands—their husbands were quite henpecked and delighted about it." Unhidden love, his eyes warm with memory. "They created a legacy of children, grandchildren, and great-grandchildren.

"But even when they were '*tite* old women who'd lived such lives, *cher*"—raw pride in every word—"they would act as my baby sisters when I visited." His smile faded into poignant tenderness, the grief tempered by time. "They'd tuck themselves against my chest and complain to me of everything and nothing while I held them as I'd done since they were babies with dirty faces and a hundred kisses for their brother.

" 'Janvier,' they would say, 'dat Arnaud, he's a lazy *saleau*. He sits on his behind all day long while his *pa-pere* carries and fetches. And did you hear what Colette did? She put a *cunja* on dat *jolie jeune fille* I said you should marry.' " A thickness in his voice. "It didn't matter when I came, they always had room at their table for me, and a hundred stories to tell."

Ashwini could almost see it: him, eternally young and strong, holding his fragile mortal sisters protectively in his embrace. Until one day, there were no more complaints, no more stories. Reaching out, she comforted him the same way he'd done her so many times, her knuckles brushing his cheek in a touch that said he wasn't alone.

He took her hand, pressed his lips to her knuckles before releasing her.

"Do you stay in touch with any of their descendants?" she asked, his name written so deep in her heart, it would never be erased.

He laughed, and the sound was big and warm and gorgeous. "*Cher*, I would be hunted down and fed to a gator should I miss a single family event. Their descendants are as fierce as my sisters were, and just as glorious. I'll take you to the next *fais do-do*—or I'll say we're coming and it'll be the excuse they need for a party. Then you'll see what a wild family I call mine."

Ashwini had known some vampires kept in touch with the descendants of their original families, but she'd never met one who spoke of his family with such affection. For most, the loss of the old seemed to outweigh the delight of the new. Or they'd become too inhuman to find happiness in familial connections. "I'm up for a good *fais do-do*. As long as you haven't told them tales about me."

"Trust me, sugar, you are already a favorite. My family thinks I need someone to put me in my place."

It was so tempting to stay here, to talk and laugh and flirt, insulated from the world and from reality, but tonight their time wasn't their own. It belonged to a woman whose life had been stolen from her with heartless cruelty.

They stepped out without any need to discuss the point.

"Your fancy car will be safe here?" It was an artwork of a machine. "You don't want to put it in one of the bigger lots with security?"

"Elena owns an interest in the blood café over there," he told her, to her surprise. "She set up this lot for anyone from the Guild or the Tower who needs to use it in this part of the city—it has top-of-the-line security. Your Guild hasn't told you?"

Ashwini winced. "Memo must be in my Guild in-box. Haven't checked it for a while." Words had never been her friend. "I'm dyslexic. Got help late, and while I can read fine if I put my mind to it, it's not the relaxing thing for me that it is for others."

Janvier locked the gate behind them and they began to walk in the direction of the clubs. "I didn't learn to read until I was in Neha's court."

"It must've been hard."

"Yes, but there's a scholar in Neha's court who is very patient."

So many pieces of him she was seeing tonight, and she knew why. He was taking the first step, the first risk, being the brave one. Ashwini wasn't sure she had the courage to follow him, to take the steps that would lead to a confession that, once made, would change everything. But neither did she want to belittle his trust by withholding her own. Whether it was dangerous or not, right or wrong, they were beyond that.

"My family," she began, "is very academic."

# 20

"My father was a professor of philosophy; my mother, literature, with a particular emphasis on South Asian texts," she said, heart hurting. "You know my brother is a neurosurgeon." No matter the pain between them, Ashwini was fiercely proud of Arvi's achievements. He could've permitted the agony he'd borne to crush him—instead, he'd used it as an impetus to become the best in his field.

She just wished he'd chosen any specialty but that related to the brain. Arvi used his own skill like a razored whip with which to flagellate himself, always looking for an answer, a "fix," and coming up empty.

"One aunt is a paralegal," she continued, "the other a political strategist. My cousins run the gamut, from engineers to psychologists to biomedical researchers." Shining bright, that was the unofficial Taj family motto.

Even the rebel in the group, the laughing black sheep everyone loved and Ashwini wanted to grow up to be, had been a brilliant scholar of languages. Tanu had interceded for Ashwini more than once, but her sister had been much older, with her own life. Away at college when Ashwini's problems with the written word first became apparent, Tanu hadn't been there to mitigate the fallout at home.

"My parents were impatient with me, thought I was lazy, not trying hard enough." As a confused child who couldn't understand why she was being punished—by being banned from attending the dance lessons that healed every hurt inside her—she would stay up all night trying to teach herself to read the letters that got all confused in her head.

"They were learned people." Janvier's scowl was heavy. "Shouldn't they have known?"

"It's funny how really smart people have the most unusual holes in their worldview and perception." For Ashwini's mother, this supremely clever woman who was around words every day, reading was such a joy, such a wonderful *escape*, that she'd been unable to wrap her mind around the fact it was a struggle for her daughter.

"There was pride, too." Seeing a flashing sign that said part of the Quarter had been flooded by a burst water main, Ashwini and Janvier took a slight detour. "The idea of asking for help, of having me seen as different . . ." As an adult, she'd come to understand that the latter had been the crux of it, her entire family trying desperately to avoid looking into the blinding, eviscerating light of truth.

"Pride has often led to foolish actions."

"Yes." She had the Taj pride, too, and knew it. "Anyway, I was falling desperately behind in school before a teacher realized what was wrong and got me help." Digging up a smile, she said, "I still love books, though. Listen to a ton on audio."

"How about if I act as your personal narrator?" Janvier closed his hand around her own. "My voice is not so bad."

His voice was raw sex and molten honey. Ashwini wasn't sure she'd comprehend a word of the actual story if he read to her. "Looks like we've ended up at the exclusive end after all." Breaking the handhold out of habit, she nodded at the club coming up ahead.

The detour had funneled them to the opposite end of the Quarter from the blood café. "Might as well start here."

Club Masque was the definition of exclusive—and of dangerous. It was the center of the Flesh Market, a group of clubs that catered to the darker appetites of the sophisticated vampire upper class. Club Masque's sign for the mortal queue made the club's direction clear. It said *Fresh Meat*.

Ashwini could see at least fifty pieces of hopeful "meat" in the line.

Most would be turned away. The bouncers allowed in only the spectacularly beautiful or those handpicked by one of the VIPs inside. The hopeful were uniformly young and shiny and pretty, their flesh on display despite the cold, males included. Forget the teensy skirts and bra tops; one modelesque male with pouty lips and serious cheekbones was rocking short shorts and body glitter with biker boots.

The sight made her want to shiver. "I feel like I'm dressed for a blizzard compared to Hypothermia Central over there."

Janvier turned up his lip at the display. "Cold blood is so unappetizing." Ignoring the queue—and the eyes made in his direction by more than one clubber, he walked straight up to the bouncer.

Ashwini knew Janvier's charm could be lethal, but she didn't expect the bouncer to open the door at first sight. "Wow," she said as they walked into the black-painted hallway lit with bluish lights that created deep pools of shadow, the sound of thumping music vibrating through the floorboards. "Are you a VIV?"

"VIV?"

"Very Important Vampire."

*"Mais oui, ma belle."* Winking, he turned right and said, "Strip, sugar."

Realizing they were at the coat check, and yeah, a place this exclusive *would* have a coat check, she gave the girl behind the counter her outerwear, while Janvier took off his jacket, having left his sweater and scarf in the car. She hadn't worn any visible weapons out of politeness to being in Ellie's home, though she was certain Ellie wouldn't have cared, but that meant there were no awkward questions.

Not that the coat check girl—all breathy words and wet lips—even noticed Ashwini except as an annoyance in her attempt to seduce an amused Janvier. "So used to women throwing themselves at you that you take it in stride?" she murmured after they moved back into the corridor, using the chance to undo a couple of extra buttons on her shirt to better fit the vibe.

Janvier, somehow managing to make a simple white T-shirt look incredibly sexy, his hair just-got-out-of-bed disheveled, shrugged. "It is a burden, *cher*, but one I bear." His eyes lingered on the skin revealed at her neck, his voice rough when he next spoke. "You are dressed like an invitation."

"Janvier, I'm wearing more clothes than all the 'fresh meat' put together."

Leaning in close to her ear, his breath warm, he slipped an arm around her waist, his hand possessive on her hip. "It makes men want to unwrap you, be the only one to see what's inside." He tugged out the chain that held the pendant, knuckles rubbing across her breastbone. "It sits right between your breasts," he said on a hoarse groan before tucking it back inside the shirt. "I don't want any other male thinking about that but me."

Her nipples were suddenly painfully tight, her panties damp. Primal instinct told her to slip out of his hold if she had any hope of salvaging her shields. She didn't. It was too late for that. It was also the right decision to ensure justice for their victim. Because this was a vampire club and Janvier was a known commodity.

So was she, but not always in the best way. She'd already seen one vamp she'd hauled home to his angel. It had been three years ago, but vampires tended to have long memories about things like that.

Bracing her arm on Janvier's shoulder, elbow bent, she took in the dance floor. It was bathed in pulsing light several shades too dark to be truly comfortable for mortal eyes, but that was perfect for the older vampires. The view was otherwise relatively ordinary. Taut and toned women and pretty men danced limber and sexy in an effort to attract the attention of the bored-looking but physically stunning vampires who occasionally culled one from the herd.

She tapped her foot absently to the beat. Dancing had been in her blood as long as she could remember, but she hadn't indulged in it anywhere but inside her apartment for a long time. That wouldn't be changing in this club. Because while the dance floor was normal enough, what was above it wasn't.

The mezzanine level was basically a large wraparound balcony that looked out over the dance floor. Tables and seating arrangements were laid out in intimate groupings on that level, the stairs up to the mezzanine guarded by bouncers who, again, let up only the chosen.

In club terms, it was nothing to write home about.

However, suspended just below the mezzanine by what looked like steel cables on each of the four corners, was a sheet of transparent glass. Glass walls about two feet in height grew up from the large flat sheet on all four sides, creating a shallow box with no top. In the glass box was a live show.

Right now, from what she could tell, two male vampires dressed in full-on lace and leather, their shirts froths of white and their black leather pants so tight they appeared painted on, were feeding from a ripped mortal who was either naked or wearing a G-string. Then the two vamps threw the mortal to the glass on his front and she didn't have to guess anymore.

She could see every inch of him, including the turgid red of his erection.

One of the vampires, his hair sleek and blond, lay down on his side beside the donor, pulling up the donor's head by the hair to kiss him long and deep. When he released the breathless male from the kiss, it was to a raven-haired female vamp who'd stepped into the box. She took over the kiss, while the second male vamp watched.

Words were spoken that made the woman smile, her poison red nails on the donor's throat. Then the blond vampire stroked long white fingers down the man's back . . . and shoved him down on his distended cock right as the second male vampire sank his fangs into the donor's thigh. The woman went for his throat at the same instant.

The donor screamed, drops of blood splattering the glass, but Ashwini saw no terror on his face, only a naked sexual ecstasy.

She looked away before she ended up witnessing him spurt his semen against the glass. Not that she was sure the show would stop there. Nakedness wasn't required for feeding, so the donor had probably volunteered for public sex or pain or both. It wasn't her idea of a good time, but she wasn't about to judge as long as it was all consensual.

"Well," she murmured to Janvier, shifting her hand to play with the hair at his nape, "do you come here often?" It didn't seem his kind of thing, but maybe he had a kink she didn't know about.

He ran his hand up and down her hip. "Only so I can maintain my contacts." His lips brushed her ear as he spoke, the music too loud to permit anything else. "For me, feeding from a partner is a private thing. As is fucking." He nipped her ear with sharp teeth, the contact sending a jolt straight to the heat between her legs. "Not for public exhibition, but to be savored in hushed intimacy."

Her body was so primed, she barely resisted the urge to shove him into a dark corner and ride him to oblivion. "I'm going to the ladies'." It was the best place to find mortals in between dancing or donating, especially if she wanted to have an actual conversation.

Janvier's hand slipped low enough that he was now officially—and very possessively—cupping her ass. "I'll make sure the bouncers know to let you upstairs if we get separated. No one should bother you here, but if anyone does, feel free to fillet him or her."

"I don't need your permission for the filleting," she said, then leaned forward to bite him on the jaw.

He jerked, hand clenching convulsively.

"There"—pounding heart, shallow breath—"now no one will bother you, either, not unless they want to get filleted."

Walking away to the sight of his growing and hotly sexy smile, she felt her skin flush. What had started out as a light-hearted dig at his increasing possessiveness had instead betrayed her own. Annoyed with herself for her inability to stick to her guns until she'd told him everything, she snarled at a vamp who went to make a move on her.

His eyes gleamed, but she'd already pulled a blade and had it at his crotch. "I'm no donor."

He became erect between one heartbeat and the next. "I know. I wouldn't feed without permission, mistress. Please, hurt me. *Please*."

"Oh, for Christ's sake." She'd apparently managed to find the one vamp in this place who wanted to be prey rather than predator. "Since you asked so sweetly," she said and slashed the blade across his thigh, careful not to do anything but prick him. His eyes rolled back in his head.

Leaving him shuddering in ecstasy, she pushed open the door to the ladies' room. It was as luxurious and classy as she'd expected. In front of her was a large area with mirrors on every wall and curved seating in plush red. Several women sat on the backless red couches, touching up their makeup, talking to friends, or, in one case, snorting coke. Apparently being fresh meat wasn't enough; this one wanted to be hopped-up fresh meat.

Going through the second door, to the section with the actual stalls, she went in one, flushing it after a reasonable pause before getting out and washing her hands, all to maintain the fiction that she was just another mortal on a night out with her vampire lover. It was unlikely any of the humans would recognize her as a hunter, and even if they did, there was no law that said hunters couldn't date vamps.

"Damn," she muttered after returning to the seating area, making a show of digging into her pockets beside a gorgeous, plump brunette who was fluffing up her hair.

"You lose your ID?" the brunette asked with a sweetness that made Ashwini want to bundle her up and get her out of there ASAP.

"No, forgot my lipstick."

Her new friend opened her glittery gold clutch and took out a tube. "You can borrow mine. Just wipe it off with a tissue and use your finger." An assessing look. "I think the color would suit."

"Oh, thanks." She took a seat beside the girl . . . and noticed the bite mark on her neck. Two tiny circles, along with a nicely developing bruise. "You already donated tonight," she said with a smile, while taking a tissue from the dispenser.

"Oh, I'm with Rupert." The woman sighed, hazel eyes dreamy. "He's so nice to me. Look." She wiggled her fingers to draw attention to the large rock on her index finger.

Well, at least she had protection. "That's some ring." Ashwini took the hand, examined the jewelry. "He must really be into you."

"He is." A bright smile. "Just like that vamp you came in with is into you." The brunette waved a hand in front of her face. "God, talk about *cute*."

Ashwini didn't think Janvier was cute—he was too sexy to be cute—but she went with it. "Yeah, he's not bad," she said with a grin that implied all sorts of things.

The other woman squeaked. "Oh, that's so hot. Rupert and

I haven't, you know, because he's old-fashioned, but I'm hoping tonight . . ."

Ashwini decided she might like this vampire named Rupert. "That's nice," she said. "That he cares enough about you to wait."

"He really does."

Having stroked on the lipstick with her finger, she wiped the tube again and gave it back. "Thanks."

"You're welcome."

"Are you guys regulars here?"

"We come once or twice a week," the girl said, putting her things into her clutch. "Did you want to meet up? We can exchange numbers. I'm Lacey, by the way."

"Ash." She took Lacey's number because contacts were contacts—and because she liked the sweet brunette. "I'll call you if we come back this way, but I was wondering if you knew another donor."

"Oh, who?"

Ashwini decided against flashing the image she'd sent to her own phone from Janvier's during the drive. It was obviously not of a living person and this investigation was all about subtlety. "I'm asking for a friend who's a vamp. They had the one-night thing, you know."

Lacey's face set into lines of disapproval that would've done an eighteenth-century schoolteacher proud. "So many girls do that, but I'm a relationship girl. No spreading myself around. I even told Rupert that the first time we met, that if he was just after a quick sex feed, he could find another girl." Her cheeks dimpled. "But my Rupert's a gentleman."

Ashwini hid an inward smile. It was becoming clear Lacey and Rupert were a perfect match. "Well," she said, hoping these two would make it, "my friend never got her name, but she had a tattoo like this on her ankle."

She showed Lacey the picture of the tattoo, having had the Guild techs work with it so it now appeared to be an image she'd downloaded off the Internet. Easier than trying to explain why her "friend" would have a photo of the girl's tattoo but not her face. "Have you seen it before?"

Lacey frowned, shook her head. "But you should ask Flynn.

He knows *everyone*, I swear." Getting up, she said, "Come on, I'll introduce you."

"Thanks." She followed the brunette out the door, keeping an eye open for Janvier.

Her Cajun wasn't on the first floor. When she headed upstairs with Lacey, it was to see him sprawled in one of the groupings of sofas on the mezzanine, talking to a vampire with yards of red hair and skin like cream, her body poured into a black evening gown with plunging cleavage. Sitting in the center of her impressive breasts was a diamond that glittered even in the soft light up here.

But that wasn't what held Ashwini's attention. It was the fact that the redhead had her lips to Janvier's ear, her hand stroking his thigh, and his arm around her shoulders.

# 21

"There he is. Flynn!" Lacey called out to a square-jawed black man who immediately headed over to them. Dressed in jeans and an untucked white shirt, the sleeves rolled up to show off strong forearms, a heavy watch his only decoration, he didn't fit the hedonistic atmosphere of Masque except for the fact that he had the looks of a movie star or a model.

He and Lacey squeezed one another like best friends.

"This is my friend Ash," Lacey said when they broke apart, her face open. "She's with that *super* cute vampire who's sitting with Adele."

Neck prickling at the feel of Janvier's eyes on her though she had her back to him, Ashwini couldn't avoid Flynn's hug. The man's cheek touched hers as he held on tight and the contact made her ability come to life, as it did without warning at times even with people so young. But the resulting slap of knowledge wasn't anything she couldn't handle. Vivid and strong and with a hint of darkness, Flynn was more dangerous than Lacey, but that was a matter of degrees. A puppy would be more dangerous than Lacey.

"Ash is looking for a donor who hooked up with a friend of

hers," Lacey said with a pursing of her lips. "Do you know a girl with a tat like this? Ash, show him the photo."

Flynn looked at the picture for almost a half minute, a small frown line between his eyebrows. "I'm sure I've seen her, but not here. She's more low-key." He handed back Ashwini's phone. "I think she used to go to Hinge, but that was a while ago. I haven't been there for a year."

"Of course not." Lacey hooked her arm through his, her dimples peeking out. "As if Ko would let you go there." Her eyes grew huge the next second, her gaze focused past Ashwini's shoulder.

She didn't need to turn to know Janvier was behind her. "*Cher*"—he slid his arm around her waist—"introduce me to your beautiful friends."

Lacey giggled, blushed prettily, while Flynn's handshake was friendly.

"Ah, Rupert," Janvier said when Lacey told him the name of her vampire. "He is a good man. Try not to take advantage of him."

"Oh, I would never." Lacey dimpled again, adorably smitten. "Do you know Ko as well?"

"Benita Ko?"

Flynn nodded.

"Yes, I know Benita. Tell her Janvier said hello." He squeezed Ash's hip. "I feel restless tonight, sugar. Let us walk outside, find another bar."

Ashwini said good-bye to Lacey and Flynn, both of whom gave her a thumbs-up when Janvier momentarily glanced away. "You didn't say Ko was a good woman," she said once they were outside, winter gear back on.

"Ko is a sadist," Janvier murmured. "But as Flynn's breath caught when I applied too much pressure on his hand, enough to cause a tiny bit of pain, it appears he must be a masochist. Therefore, the two are a perfect match."

Ashwini realized he was talking about sadism in the sexual context, rather than in relation to Ko's personality. Or maybe it was both, since he clearly wasn't judgmental about the lifestyle itself. "Is she a sadist out of the bedroom, too?"

"Yes, she can be ugly." A shrug. "But she only ever has one

donor at a time and treats each well. How long did the boy say he'd been with her?"

"A year—implied."

"So, she's unlikely to be the one we search for, but I'll do a little digging, see if her tastes have altered."

"Why do immortals fixate on sex and pain? It's sad they don't seem to see everything else life has to offer."

"My darling Ashblade, your view is skewed. You see the Made who patronize such places because that is where your work takes you."

"Vamps in suburbia?"

"Complete with minivans and white picket fences."

"Flynn," she said, putting the conversation back on track, "thought our victim may have gone to Hinge at some stage in the past."

"Adele, who keeps an eye on everything in her establishment, is certain the girl wasn't a regular, so Hinge it is."

"You seem friendly with her," Ashwini said before she could stop herself. Turned out that while naïve Marie May hadn't set off her jealousy, the gorgeous, experienced Adele had turned the dial to blazing red.

"I am. She is a lush and sensual creature, Adele," Janvier said, his lips curving as if he spoke from personal, intimate experience.

"If you go for overblown and obvious." God, she needed to staple her mouth shut.

Open delight in his expression. "I've told you, I go for the unique and the dangerous."

Realizing he'd been provoking her on purpose, she elbowed him.

He touched his fingers to her nape, curled his hand gently around it when she didn't push him away. "Your body was thrumming with the music the entire time we were in the club. Shall we dance tonight?"

"Let's see what we discover first." Dancing with Janvier wouldn't be like dancing by herself or with any other man. Dancing with Janvier would be a prelude to sex. He'd touch and stroke, whisper things in her ear as he flirted with his body and his mind both. With her resolve already on increasingly shaky ground, Ashwini had no confidence in her ability to withstand him.

He linked his fingers to her own. Stubborn Cajun. This time, however, she didn't shake him off. When he shot her a smirking grin, she gave him a dark look. "Don't get too full of yourself."

Lifting her hand to his mouth, he pressed a kiss to her knuckles, the contact lips to skin since she'd forgotten her gloves tonight. "Did you dance as a child?" At her nod, he said, "What kind of a dancer were you?"

"Ballet."

He halted on the road. *"Dit mon la verite'!"*

She gave in to her laugh, he looked so comically stunned. "It *is* the truth. My mother took me to my first class when I was three. I think it was meant to give me an extracurricular activity to put on college applications later on, but I adored it."

Janvier shook his head, dislodging several errant flakes of snow that had fallen from the sky. "I cannot imagine you as a tiny sprite in a tutu, but as a long-legged ballerina, yes."

"I fully intended to become a professional dancer." Soaring through the air, free and unchained. "But . . ." She shrugged.

His eyes turned solemn. "A professional ballerina cannot always dance alone and must often be in close contact with her partner."

"Yes." She tightened her fingers on his, deciding that maybe—possibly—she could get used to holding hands. If it was Janvier. Only him. "But it didn't break my heart," she told him with utter honesty. "By the time I accepted that the constant contact would exacerbate my ability, I knew I couldn't be a professional dancer for other reasons. Do you know how much crap they take from the choreographers and the directors before they get famous enough to throw tantrums and do what they want?"

"You wouldn't throw a tantrum." Janvier's tone was dead serious, his laugh in his eyes. "You'd just shoot the person who was irritating you."

"I was tempted to do exactly that during my final years aiming for professional," she admitted. "Then I realized I didn't want fame. I only wanted to dance, and I could do that on my own."

"Where do you dance?" Janvier took her down the narrow steps to the man-made cavern that was Hinge.

"That's for me to know." She wasn't ready for him to be her audience—she had no shields when she danced, was naked in a way she wouldn't be even if she took off every stitch of clothing on her body.

"Janvier! Here to make the *misère*, my friend?"

Looking up at the statement she couldn't quite work out, she found herself facing a solid wall of a man with black hair tightly curled to his skull, his mocha skin pockmarked by acne scars and his eyes a gray-green that caught her attention and would've held it if Janvier hadn't been in her life. This was a man who'd never want for female company.

"I never make trouble, Louis." Janvier grinned and, releasing her hand, exchanged a back-slapping hug with the bouncer.

Ashwini had seen him do the same thing with another man once, back during the Atlanta operation. So she saw the difference. With Callan, it had been for show. This was genuine, affection pulsing off both men.

"This is Ash." Janvier reached back and took her hand when the two broke apart.

"*Your* Ash?" Smile huge, Louis would've hugged her if Janvier hadn't slid in between and she hadn't stepped back. Instead of being insulted, the other man laughed and said something else in the dialect he shared with Janvier.

Ashwini caught the tone, knew he was ribbing Janvier about being jealous. "I think you're getting ahead of yourself, Louis," she said. "I haven't decided whether to keep him or throw him to the gators yet."

Louis slapped a hand over his heart. "Janvier, *mon ami*, I am in love. As I see you're not carrying your blades today, I think I can take you."

"I'm not the dangerous one," Janvier drawled, his arm around her waist. "What can you tell us about Hinge?"

"It's a meat market, but safer than Masque." His expression made it clear that didn't mean much. "I can recommend a club with better music."

"We're not here to dance," Janvier told his friend. "We're looking for a girl with a tat on her ankle. *Cher?*"

Taking out her phone, she held it out to Louis. "Yeah," he

said after a couple of seconds, "I think I might've seen her here. Remember the tat because feet are the first thing I see when people come down the steps. Don't know her name or remember much else about her, but one of the regulars might."

"Can you point out the regulars?"

"Sure." Louis glanced at his watch. "I'm on break in ten minutes. I'll come join you."

There was no coat check inside Hinge, so they stripped off their outerwear and placed it on an open bar stool while ordering drinks. Ashwini had no intention of consuming hers, but with Janvier's accelerated ability to process alcohol, that'd be easy enough to cover.

Her phone vibrated in her pocket just as the bartender put the drinks in front of them with a flirtatious flash of his fangs directed at her. Sliding the phone out of her pocket, she read the message and had to bite back a cry of delight. When she looked up, it was to see Janvier looking at his own phone, a grin on his face. "Ransom?" She knew the two men were friends, often went out riding together.

"Yeah." Janvier's grin grew wider as he input a reply. "He finally did it, asked his librarian to marry him."

"And she said yes!" Ashwini sent back a congratulatory message.

Janvier's eyes lingered on her after she returned her phone to her pocket. "What about you?" he murmured, leaning in to be heard over the music, his hand on her lower back and his body heat a languorous caress over her skin. "Will you ever say yes?"

Hanging on to her control by her fingernails, she very deliberately brought her vodka mixer to her lips, forcing distance between them. "I see two women who might be donors." The glass was icy against her palm, but it did nothing to chill the heat licking over her body. "Faint bite bruise on one."

Janvier wrapped an arm around her front as she went to move past him on her way to the women. He'd pressed a kiss to her cheekbone before she could avoid it. Gritting her teeth against the craving to haul him to her, take that delicious mouth with her own, she instead moved her lips to his ear . . . and bit down hard enough on his earlobe to leave a mark.

He hissed. "You do realize many vampires consider pain

foreplay?" Hot breath against her, the muscles in his arm flexing to keep her close.

"You don't." Sliding out of his hold, she strolled over to strike up a conversation with her targets.

The conversation proved a bust, though it appeared Janvier was having some success with the bartender. Louis joined the other two males not long afterward, and she decided to head back.

A vampire shoulder-bumped her on the way, his hand sliding over hers. It should've been nothing, the contact was so fleeting . . . but it set off a deluge of nightmare that swamped her senses, threatened to take her under. Screams, he had *screams* inside him. Legs shaky and stomach threatening to revolt, she reached out to brace herself against the bar, but instead of the cold, hard edge of stone, she felt a body warm and tensile.

Sliding his arm around her with a lazy grace that belied the tension in his body, Janvier nuzzled at her. "I've got you," he murmured. "Pretend you can't get enough of me, *cher.*"

She wanted to snap off a quick retort, make light of this, but her heart was thumping too hard and her nerves trembling. Wrapping her own arm around Janvier's waist, she held on to the solid strength of him, tucking her head against his neck. Her breath came in jerky bursts, her hand clenching on his T-shirt as he murmured things she couldn't hear through the roar in her ears, but that she knew would make it seem they were indulging in a public display of affection. Sickening but normal.

Her vision eventually cleared to the point that she could see Louis watching them, a smile wreathing his face. The other man was several feet away, where Janvier must've been before he moved to intercept her. Swallowing, she took a deep breath and Janvier's scent filled her lungs: primal, earthy male.

Her chest shuddering, she rubbed her nose against his neck in a moment of weakness before raising her head. *"Merci."*

He brushed back a strand of hair that had come loose from her braid to curl against the side of her face. "No thanks between us, Ashwini. No balance sheet."

The things he said. The things he *meant.*

Releasing her grip on the cotton of his tee, she slid her hand into his hair, tugged down his head, and kissed him soft and sweet and with every ounce of the heartbreaking emotion inside her. It lasted for a fleeting fragment of time and it changed the world.

# 22

Janvier was the one who trembled this time, his arm firming to hold her tight. "Why that vampire?" he asked, voice hoarse.

"He's done horrible things." The hairs stood up on her arms at the memory. "I can't tell if it's in the present or an echo of his past, but we need to check him out."

"His name is Khalil, and I know he has darker appetites." A hard edge to his tone. "I'll put a discreet watch on him. For now, he appears occupied with a blonde barely into her womanhood, so we may go and speak to Louis."

The two of them closed the distance to the bouncer.

"Sorry for the wait." Janvier's insouciant smile invited the other man to laugh and he did.

"Some things take priority. Especially when the priority is so very beautiful."

"I like you, Louis." Ashwini tried to keep her tone playful, despite the fact that she felt scraped raw on the inside.

"If you ever decide against this no-good swamp rat, you know where you can find me." Louis slid his eyes a whisper to the right. "Brown sugar in the sequined green mini-jumpsuit thing, blonde fantasy twins, and the built guy shaved to within an inch of his life. Regular donors here. Tight foursome. High chance they would've crossed paths with your girl."

Ashwini covertly checked out the group, caught them giving Janvier a greedy appraisal. Unsurprising. He might not be dressed in leather or lace or velvet, nor have the honed beauty of the oldest vampires, but Janvier was six feet three inches of pure indulgent sex. He wasn't even trying to project that at this instant—his sexual attractiveness was innate, created by his confidence, the lithe strength of his body, the lazy smile that said he knew every sin and had invented a few new ones.

"Janvier," she said, stepping away from him, the loss of contact bruising, "we're about to have a fight. I'll be storming off with Louis."

A raised eyebrow. "Will it be a passionate fight?"

"I could slap you, but I think I'll settle for calling you a cheating bastard after Louis lets slip the news of your philandering ways."

Sighing, Janvier said, "All four?"

"They think you're delicious." She tried not to find his less than enthusiastic expression adorable and failed. "I'm the impediment."

"Rescue me in fifteen?"

"We'll see."

Louis obligingly said something right then, and she turned on Janvier. "I can't believe you did that!" She shoved at his chest, the warm muscle beneath flexing under her touch. "You cheating piece of vampire slime! I hate you!"

"Bébé." Janvier spread his arms, voice cajoling. "It was nothing, a taste onl—"

"That's it!" She inserted an infuriated high-drama scream in lieu of throwing a drink in his face. "We're done! Go taste someone else, you bastard!"

Janvier watched Ashwini stride away, her hips moving provocatively beneath the snug fit of her jeans. "Take care of her," he said quietly to his friend. "She is my eternity, Louis."

"As you pointed out, she can take care of herself," the other man replied, "but I'll keep an eye on her in case she needs backup." Grabbing Ash's jacket after Janvier slid his eyes to it, Louis went after her.

Turning to the bar, Janvier found the barkeep giving him a sympathetic look. "Women," the younger male said with a shrug. "She was seriously hot, though. The dangerous kind of hot."

Yes, his Ashblade was dangerous.

The dark-haired woman sidling over to him, her body clad in a sparkly green jumpsuit that ended barely south of her ass, was a mewling kitten in comparison.

Pretending not to see her, he nursed his drink. It was a single-malt whiskey, a good one, the flavor rich and textured.

It stood no chance against the intoxicating wildness that was the taste of his hunter.

Her kiss earlier had staggered him, enslaved him. He wasn't surprised at his body's response—he'd known for a long time that Ash owned him and always would. He just had to convince her to claim him, brand him. A public kiss? Hell, yes, he'd take that as a first step.

"Hi."

Taking his time to respond to the soft greeting, he found himself looking into a pair of uptilted brown eyes made up with glittering green and black kohl, her cheekbones sharp under glowing brown skin and her hair a sheet of ebony. "Hi." He kept his tone deliberately cool, reading her like he would an open book—the kitten, it seemed, wanted to play with a wolf.

Sinking her teeth into her plump lower lip, the gloss she wore a sheen of wet, she slid her hand down his biceps. "I saw your girlfriend leave."

When he didn't shake her off, she stepped close enough that her breasts pressed into his body, her fingers curving around his upper arm at the same time. "She didn't treat you right."

"She's passionate." A woman who loved and fought with her heart and her soul, unrestrained and furiously honest.

"I can be passionate." A husky invitation. "And I have friends."

Shifting to face the group toward which she'd nodded, the three others ensconced in an intimate seating area, he found enticing smiles pointed in his direction. "Are your friends accommodating?" He leaned back with his elbows braced on the bar.

"Oh, yes." The kitten brushed her fingers over the pulse in her neck. "Very."

Janvier found her attempts at manipulation amusing; she clearly had no idea of exactly how big a wolf she'd approached. "I don't move on the claimed."

"We aren't with anyone." A hair flip, both hands now holding on to one of his biceps. "We like our freedom."

Translated, they liked the high of fangs at the vein but didn't actually want to get into a relationship with a near-immortal. Allowing his lips to curve into a slightly predatory smile that made the woman's breath catch, her pupils dilate, he straightened and, drink in one hand, walked with her to her friends.

They'd left a spot for him in between Louis's fantasy twins. He should've taken the invitation, but he didn't. He didn't want anyone pawing him, male or female. The deception he was playing didn't alter the truth of his nature—Janvier had given himself to Ash and that was it. Playing hard to get, he sprawled in an armchair across from the twins, the male donor to his right. Green Jumpsuit perched herself on the arm of his seat, silky thighs within effortless reach.

He didn't reach, didn't stroke, but his cool attitude seemed to make the foursome even more eager to please. Before long, the entire group was clustered around him, breathless and excited and ready to go with him into one of the private booths in the back. "Unless you want to feed here," the blonde on the left said in a sultry tone. "That's okay, too."

"Only they don't allow nudity on the main floor," the other blonde added, her palm on her chest, above the low-cut neckline of a bustier of incongruously innocent white lace. "We'd like to please you in every way."

The male's pale white skin filled with a flush of color when Janvier glanced at him. "Are you as compliant and eager?"

An immediate nod. "Anything you want."

Putting down his glass, Janvier forced himself to place his hand on the thigh displayed to him, though he felt more like telling the group to get the fuck out of this life they were in. It wasn't the random fang-and-fuck lifestyle that worried him—it was the fact that a strong vampire could incapacitate all four within seconds. Janvier could do it before a scream escaped even one throat. He didn't think they understood that, believing themselves safe in a group.

It was an ignorance he'd rectify before he left, especially given how many vampires he'd noted in the room whose tendencies echoed Khalil's. Louis's meat market was becoming more deadly with each passing minute, the hum of bloodlust below the surface troubling.

"Yes." Throaty seductiveness from the girl beside him. "We're ready to be your toys. Shall I ask the bartender for a booth key?"

"I think no one has taught you the value of patience," he said in a deep purr of a tone that had the blondes squirming and the male erect beneath his tight-fitting pants. "Has no one ever spent hours with you? Taking a sip at a time, drawing out the pleasure until it is part insanity, part pain?"

"No," the blondes breathed.

"We . . . we could go to a hotel if you want." Flushing, the green-jumpsuited girl put her hand over his and rubbed her thumb gently across the back of his knuckles.

Janvier battled the violent urge to wrench it back—he didn't want to be known as available. He wasn't available, hadn't been since the day he'd met Ash, and he wanted the entire world to know that. But he was also loyal to the Tower and to Raphael, and this crime threatened the stability of the city. More, he knew his hunter would not rest easy until they gave their victim the dignity of a name.

So he played the game, eased the conversation toward the victim without alerting the four donors of his intent. He made them believe she'd fed him the last time he'd been in this club, that he couldn't quite remember her name, intimated they'd been too involved in other things to bother with exchanging such mundane information.

It was the male who said, "I think you mean Felicity." He went to his knees beside Janvier's armchair, put his hand on Janvier's own knee. "I was with her when she got her tat a couple of years ago. I got one, too. See?" He pumped up a muscle to show it off.

"It is excellent work." Janvier examined the blue-green dragon, to the boy's pleasure. The male didn't go back to his seat afterward, leaning instead against Janvier's leg like an affectionate pet.

Some old vamps treated donors as exactly that. Giorgio, Janvier thought, likely enjoyed having his women paying homage at his feet. Unfortunately for this group, Janvier had never been comfortable with such subservience, found no pleasure in the weak—though he felt nothing against them.

People were who they were, some strong, some not.

So he ran his fingers over the boy's shoulder, careful to avoid the skin displayed by his muscle shirt. He could've rejected the boy—and his friends—harshly, but Janvier didn't see the point in that; he didn't kick kittens or puppies, so why would he do the same to these harmless creatures? Though it did concern him how many of the mortals he'd seen in the clubs fell into this personality type.

That might be a fact he'd have to discuss with Dmitri—if the vampires who hooked up with such submissive men and women were caring for them, that was one thing, but if they were abusing them . . . Then again, the Tower didn't interfere in the affairs of adults unless the rules were broken. And, harmless or not, this group and others like them chose the thrill of the clubs.

As the cattle chose to give freely of their blood.

No one, however, chose to be murdered and thrown away like a piece of trash.

"Felicity?" he said as the male curled his hand around Janvier's calf, eyes closing. "A pretty name for a pretty girl."

"I guess." One of the blondes twisted her lips. "But she didn't really know how to party."

"Her last name was Johnson!" the other blonde added with a proud smile. "I just remembered."

"Felicity Johnson. *Merci.*"

"Oh, but she doesn't donate anymore," Green Jumpsuit said at once, jealousy a stabbing dagger in her eyes.

This one and the first blonde, he thought, might eventually develop claws. If they survived.

"Yeah," the male added, "ever since she hooked up with her rich boyfriend."

"We haven't seen her in months." The thigh under Janvier's hand flexed, the girl turning toward him. "I kind of didn't believe her about the rich boyfriend, but then why would she stop clubbing, if it wasn't the truth?"

"Hmm." Janvier didn't betray his reaction to what might be their first solid lead. "Who was this man?" he drawled. "I may know him."

The four looked blank. It turned out none of them had ever met the boyfriend and Felicity had been secretive about him to the point that they didn't have any details on him beyond the fact he was a rich vampire. That was disappointing, but Felicity's name was more than they'd had when he and Ash had walked into this bar.

Appearing to relax into the armchair, he let the conversation drift, wondering if Ash was planning to let him extricate himself. He could, but it'd feel exactly like abusing small, vulnerable creatures who'd handed him their trust. Deciding to take the time to give these four a lesson in safety, he said, "You're all beautiful." His words made them beam, try to get even closer. "It'd be a shame if you were damaged. Not every vampire appreciates that some treasures must be handled with care."

"We never leave with anyone without checking with each other," one of the blondes said, coming to kneel in front of him, her chin braced on his knee, her hands on his thigh.

"And," the other blonde added, "Louis gives us a signal if the vamp is one of the bad ones."

More intelligent than he'd guessed. "Good." He set aside his tumbler on a side table. "But you need to remember one other thing."

"What?" all four said at once.

He had his hands around the throats of the blondes so fast the other two froze. "That my kind," he whispered, releasing their throats with a gentle brush of his thumb over each slender column, "are not human."

Chest heaving, one of the blondes stared at him, terror in her eyes. "You moved so *fast*. I didn't even see it."

"I could paralyze you in two heartbeats, have all four of you laid out helpless before me." He was happy to see the blondes swallow and return to their sofa. "I could violate you if I wished, share you with my friends, then throw you naked and helpless into the street, at the mercy of anyone who wanted to use you. Trust me, there are a number of vampires in the room at this instant capable of doing exactly that."

Trembling, the girl wearing the jumpsuit stared at him, her pulse stuttering in her neck. "No, I don't believe you."

"Have you ever fed Khalil?" At their nods, he said, "He once tore open a woman's rib cage to feed directly from her heart." The true horror of it was that the woman had been one of his cattle who'd volunteered to pleasure her master in whatever way he pleased. "She was conscious at the time. I hear she screamed and screamed and screamed."

"Oh, God." Tears wet the eyes of the blondes, and the girl in the green jumpsuit leaned subtly away.

"So," he said, "you must be very, very careful. *Oui?*"

They nodded immediately.

"There is bloodlust in the air," he continued, able to see Khalil feeding from a willing woman ten feet away, the vampire having shoved his hand down her blouse to viciously squeeze her breast. "Warn your friends that even previously trustworthy vampires may become a risk."

Dmitri had to be briefed on this; the longer Janvier sat here, the more his instincts told him the blood was boiling beneath the surface. It wasn't yet at critical, but it would be within days if not handled with brutal decisiveness.

A rustle at his feet. "I've never met a vampire like you," the boy said, his heart in his eyes as he looked up from his position curled up against Janvier's leg. "If you're looking for a long-term donor . . ."

Janvier caught a glimpse of Ash stalking back into the bar. "You deserve a lover who will cherish you," he told the boy, being as gentle as he was capable of being. "I'm afraid I'm rather attached to the hunter about to descend on us."

The four looked like deer caught in the headlights as Ash zeroed in on them.

"You can't even last five minutes!" she yelled when she got to him. Her eyes shifted to the girl wearing the jumpsuit, her smile razor sharp. "Would you like me to separate your head from your body, sweetie?"

"N-no?"

"Then I suggest you get yourself away from my man."

Jumpsuit jumped up and so did the others, while Janvier

reveled in the claim. It was drama, but it was nice to hear the words anyway. *"Bébé,"* he said, deliberately using the term again because it totally did not fit his hunter, would amuse her. "We have just been having a drink together."

"Yeah," the male said, looking at Ash in naked awe. "You can sit with us."

Ash pointed a finger at the boy, then the blondes, then Jumpsuit. "Away. Now."

The group hauled ass.

"You're magnificent," Janvier whispered. "I think my new friends would go home as happily with you as with me."

"What now?" she murmured when he stood to place his hands on her hips, her arms still belligerently crossed.

"I seduce you into forgiving me."

# 23

Janvier was starving for the taste, the feel of Ash, but as he'd told her, for him intimacy wasn't a spectator sport. So he nuzzled at her, but didn't speak the hot, erotic words he wanted to whisper. Instead, he began to name all the liqueurs at the bar, using his sexiest voice.

"Stop that," she said, lips firmly set as she fought valiantly not to laugh.

He wanted her to laugh with him during sex, wanted her to play with him. "Do you think you've been seduced enough?"

"Did you discover her name?"

"Felicity Johnson."

"Then, I've been seduced enough."

The snow had begun to fall in earnest when they hit the street again, but there was no wind, the world a serene sheet of white. Before doing anything else, he made a call—while Ash pretended to check out the well-lit window display of the sex shop next door. His purpose was to touch base with a combat-trained Tower vampire he knew patronized a nearby dance club. Emaya didn't miss a beat when he asked her to keep an eye on Khalil.

Janvier would've preferred to do it himself, but Khalil had

already spotted him in the club, would be immediately suspicious if he glimpsed Janvier or Ash again. Khalil also knew Janvier as an individual, whereas he was unlikely to have run into Emaya—or to notice her if he did. The statuesque Emaya was more akin to Ash than she was to the prettily plump and submissive creatures Khalil preferred.

"Are you alone?" he asked her.

"No. Mateo is with me."

"Good." If Khalil was behind the murder, he'd obviously become even more sadistic as the years passed, but Emaya and Mateo had the strength to take him down should he become violent. "Stay together, keep him in your sights without alerting him, and contact me with a full report once he returns to his home."

If Khalil was the killer, he was too smart to choose a victim who could be easily linked to him, so any woman he took home tonight was safe—from death, at least. Torture remained on the cards, but Khalil had a way of finding willing victims for that, though those volunteers didn't always know the extent of what awaited. That grim truth at the forefront of his mind, Janvier said, "I want to know who he speaks to, what he does, anything that strikes you as unusual about his behavior."

"Got it."

"Even a hint of trouble, call me or the Tower."

"Will do, but my entire combat team is out blowing off steam tonight, so we have plenty of backup nearby if we need it."

Relaxing, Janvier waited until the other couple arrived in case Khalil slipped out in the interim. He covered the delay by teasing Ash about her apparent interest in the erotic toys on display. She laughed and, with her phone, snapped photos of the various items, before sending a couple of messages.

Not acknowledging Mateo or Emaya when they arrived, he sent a message through to the Tower alerting Dmitri to the ongoing situation. He also made a note that bloodlust appeared to be rising, but that it didn't appear critical at this point. *It may be a residue of the battle trauma. I think the vampire leaders should be contacted tomorrow so they can tamp things down.* The bloodlust wasn't hazardous yet, but give it a few more days and it could turn into carnage.

Janvier had once come into a town that was meant to be a

rest stop for couriers only to find every part of the small settlement sticky with rust red, and the two resident vampires feeding like gluttons on the warm, nude corpse of the woman who'd
been the lover to one. He'd executed both on the spot. It was
the only way to contain the slaughter.

Dmitri's response lit up his phone. *I've had the same report
from two other senior people in the area—we have Tower
vampires scattered through the clubs keeping an eye on the
temperature until I can talk to the leaders.*

Satisfied that the issue was being handled, Janvier said, "We
can leave now, sugar."

"Thank God." Ash slid away her phone with a groan. "There
are only so many glow-in-the-dark dildos I can look at with
wide-eyed interest."

Chuckling, he ran her braid through his fingers. "I don't
think we should go to more clubs tonight—we have Felicity's
name, and any further questions may arouse suspicion and
concern." They had to balance the needs of the investigation
with making sure it stayed under the radar.

"Agreed."

"Don't bite my head off, *cher*, but are you hurting?" He
touched his hand to his chest to indicate her scar, unable to
forget how much she'd bled in his arms, how close he'd come
to losing her. It was a nightmare that had woken him, soaked
in sweat and gasping for breath, more than once.

"I'm good. Today was all about asking questions, no real
physical strain."

Janvier had watched her carefully tonight, seen no indications of pain from her injury, so he accepted her words, and
they moved off into the delicate flakes falling from the sky.

"I love snow," Ash said with a sigh. "Bad for tracking when
it falls, but it's so forgiving on the world, so peaceful."

He watched small flecks collect on her eyelashes, knew
she'd grow ever more beautiful to him as the years passed.
Reaching for the gloves he'd slipped into his coat pockets
before leaving to pick her up for dinner, he said, "Put these on."
They were her size, ones he'd bought because she was so often
without gloves.

Tilting her head, she pinned him with the dark eyes that
saw too much. "I've realized something about you, Janvier."

He waited to hear what she'd say.

"You like to take care of people."

"Is that a bad thing?" He couldn't change his elemental nature, couldn't unmake that part of him.

"No." A spreading warmth deep within, Ashwini accepted the gloves, tugged them on over chilled fingers. It was odd to be taken care of, to be valued in such a way, but now that she'd conquered her initial confusion and fear at his tenderness, it felt like a gift. "Most hunters can take care of themselves."

"So can most vampires of my strength," he said with the confidence that made him so attractive. "That doesn't mean I would not be delighted if you showed a care for this Cajun's hide."

Ashwini thought of the way he'd looked at her after the kiss in the bar, took in the faint half smile that didn't match the shadows in his eyes, and knew it was all going wrong. In trying to protect him, she'd rejected him. "Janvier?"

"Yes?"

"I'm keeping a secret from you, a huge, terrible, bad thing." There, it was out.

He stopped in the shadow of a private club, his expression grim. "You won't tell me this secret?"

"I can't." It made her too angry, too afraid of how it would change everything between them, the cowardice closing up her throat. "But you have a right to know, and once you find out, you'll hate me for allowing this relationship to go so far."

"Ashwini, I'm yours." Utter disbelief intermingled with temper. "Hating you is an impossibility."

Her already brittle heart threatened to shatter. "You don't know what I'm keeping from you."

"I don't need to know—and neither one of us has ever been in control of the thing between us. It has its own stubborn, relentless will." He thrust one hand into his hair, began walking again, his next words so angry the heat of them seemed to melt the snow. "The only way it would die would be if you repudiated me."

Stopping again, the two of them now on the fringe of the Quarter, he faced her. "Is that what you want to do?" His tone was raw, his hands fisted. "To tell me that you don't want me?"

"You're an idiot." Hauling him to her by gripping the open

sides of his jacket, she kissed him in frustrated fury. "I'm trying to protect you." She released him, strode off ahead.

He caught up to her, his eyes bright with temper and passion both. "Well, don't. I'm a big vampire. I can handle any secret you have as long as you're mine."

"Damn you." She slipped her left hand into his right. "You'll regret this."

He wrapped his fingers around hers, the hold blatantly proprietary. "I will *never* regret you!"

Ashwini would never regret him, either.

And she knew. No more secrets, no more stealing time.

She had to tell him, show him, everything.

Forcing her mind off the heavy weight of what was to come, she said, "I shot Ransom a note with Felicity's name in case his street contacts know anything. I also fed her name to the computer tech on duty so he can troll the databases."

Vivek had been a lone ranger for a long time in the position, available twenty-four hours a day, seven days a week. He'd known everything, or so it seemed, but he was one of a kind. "How's Vivek?" she asked Janvier. "Have you seen him?" The guild hunter had chosen vampirism not for eternal life but because it would—eventually—give him back the use of his paralyzed body.

"No." Expression dark yet, Janvier said, "He asked for privacy during his transformation, and Elena has made sure of it. I don't think she's seen him, either."

She could understand why Vivek didn't want his friends to see him while he was weak and defenseless; paralyzed or not, he'd always been a force to be reckoned with. "I guess I just want to know someone has a careful eye on him. I don't know any human who's been Made after suffering such devastating long-term injuries."

"Keir himself is monitoring his progress."

Ashwini had met Keir in the aftermath of the battle. She'd been stitched up by human doctors, but the angelic healer had unexpectedly dropped by her apartment two days after she'd made Janvier leave. With uptilted eyes of warm brown set in a delicately beautiful face, his black hair sleek and his body slender as a boy's, Keir had appeared unutterably young and yet there'd been a wisdom in his gaze that told her his was a soul old and noble in its peace.

"It is past time I came to see you," he'd said with a small incline of his head.

Bemused, she'd invited him in, offered him a cup of herbal tea rather than coffee.

His response had been a smile and the words, "Yes, of course that is what I would like."

The most unfathomable thing was that she hadn't touched Keir even once, and yet she'd known he'd enjoy the tea, just as she knew he was exhausted from the work he'd been doing with the wounded at the Tower. So she'd offered him a place to rest and, to her surprise, he'd accepted, closing his eyes and dozing quietly in her favorite old armchair.

It had been strange to see angelic wings of golden brown draped over her furniture, to have someone of such age and power in her living space. "Keir," she said to Janvier, the two of them having almost reached the car, "he's so *old*." The kind of age she'd always feared. "But he doesn't make me uncomfortable. If anything, he makes everything seem peaceful, he's so gentle and centered."

She knew Keir had incredible depths to him, intricate layers of pain and living that made up any life, but there was no cruelty, none of the horror she associated with immortality.

Janvier blinked away a tiny snowflake that sought to cling stubbornly to his eyelashes. "The scholar who taught me to read," he said after they'd entered the parking lot and were inside the car, "said she'd done the same for Keir when he was a boy. She told me he was the wisest child she'd ever known, an old, old soul reborn into a new body."

"Yes. Lijuan boasted that she'd evolved to the next plane of existence, but I think Keir's the one who's done that." The healer was something better than this world, with a luminous light at his core.

Janvier's return gaze was hard. "I won't argue with you—on that point."

Gloves off and jacket unzipped in the warmth of the car, Ashwini looked out at the lightly snowy landscape as they left the Quarter. The city sparkled through the white and it felt as if they traveled inside a snow globe, like the one Arvi had given her when she was seven. She'd accidentally broken the treasured present the morning of the day he drove her to the place where they tried to "fix" her; and Arvi, he'd stared at the shards with the strangest expression on his face.

At the time, she'd thought he was angry. Now, she wondered if, just for an instant, he'd realized that what he was doing might as irretrievably shatter the sister who adored him.

"Ashwini?"

"Would you like to go for a drive?" she asked the vampire with the moss green eyes who'd branded her soul long ago and whose heart she was about to break as she'd once broken that snow globe. "I have to show you something."


Following Ash's instructions, Janvier left the city and the falling snow behind. The tires currently on his car were designed for winter conditions, so the journey was smooth despite the occasional patch of ice. He'd driven for approximately an hour on mostly empty night roads when she directed him down a side road, having not spoken much for the entirety of the drive.

The road was well maintained, though not particularly brightly lit. Janvier didn't yet have the preternatural eyesight that came with centuries-long vampirism, so he lowered their speed around the corners, in case the person on the other side was an idiot who thought he or she *could* see in the dark.

As it was, they passed only two other vehicles over the next twenty minutes.

"Turn where you can see that small signboard on the left."

The car's headlights reflecting off the discreet black-on-cream of the board, he found himself going down what appeared to be an endless private drive, winter-bare oaks lining it on either side. *"Cher,"* he said, hating the pain in her silence. "I can see large gates."

"I have the access code." She told him the code when they reached the gates, and he punched it in on the driver's side.

Lights appeared in the distance over five minutes later, a sprawling brick house that reminded him of a Georgian mansion taking shape against a backdrop of trees that were black silhouettes in the night. The drive appeared to end in a circular sweep, with what might have been a fountain in the center, though it was difficult to tell from this distance.

"Pull over here."

Not arguing with Ash's request, he brought the car to a stop some distance from the house and turned off both the headlights and the engine. "What is that place?"

Ash got out. Following, he met her at the front of the car . . . where she reached for his hand and held on tight. "It's called Banli House," she whispered. "They don't have a website or any other online presence. It's one of those places that's so exclusive, you have to know someone to get in."

Janvier's tendons went taut, jawbones grinding against one another.

"My brother was a younger doctor then," she said, "but our family was wealthy, established. One of my parents' friends must've recommended this place when . . . when things went wrong." Her breath fogged the air, her inhales shallow. "The rich usually send their drug-addicted sons and daughters here to sober them up, but Banli House is a fully accredited medical and psychiatric facility capable of handling far worse embarrassments."

Her hand was squeezing his so hard that had he been human, she would've left bruises. Janvier wanted to put a hundred bloody bruises on the man responsible for the echo of horror in her voice. "Arvi sent you to this place."

"When I was fifteen. He drove me here himself, told me the doctors would help me." A streak of wet on her cheek that broke Janvier's heart. "I wanted so much to be normal for him." Her eyes met his, huge and dark. "He was my big brother and, no matter what, he'd always looked after me." Voice cracking, she blinked rapidly. "The worst thing is, he truly believed he was doing that this time, too."

*"Cher."* He turned to wrap his other arm around her, hold her against him, his indomitable Ash who'd fought off vampires and angels hundreds of years older than her and never crumbled.

"They drugged me," she said, the words a rasp. "To make me better, that's what they said. There was more, other kinds of 'therapy.' They tied me down when I resisted, and then they pumped me full of drugs again."

Taking a deep, shaky breath, she pulled away but didn't

break the handclasp, her eyes on Banli House. Her nightmare, he thought, to be vanquished. And she'd do it with shoulders squared and head held high.

He was fucking amazed by her.

"So many people touched me and I couldn't do anything to stop it. Orderlies, doctors, nurses. Enough that I began to tune in to them." She dashed away the tears that had escaped her, stared unflinching at the facility in the distance. "Sometimes they were being nice, trying to calm me during a panic attack after I'd been strapped down, but it just made it worse—at least three of my care staff had worked with the criminally mentally ill, had horrible things inside their heads."

Her fingers flexed, squeezed his hand again.

"I was drowning in their lives and it was driving me mad, but I had to pretend the therapy was working, that I was *getting better*. Even when I slept, I couldn't let myself go too deep—I had to be awake enough to fight the nightmares. I was in there for five months."

# 24

Janvier thought of how strained she'd been in Nazarach's home, her energy contained tightly inside her skin, and couldn't imagine how she'd survived the hell of having her mind violated over and over again. "Were the walls—"

"No," she said, anticipating his question. "Banli House is too young to have become a living entity to my senses. It's safe for the time being—and if I'd been able to choose my caregivers, choose the ones who had quiet, ordinary minds, I might have been okay."

Janvier saw she didn't believe her own words; his Ash wasn't meant to be trapped and caged. Like a bird with its wings clipped, she would sicken and die. "How did you get out?" he asked through the rage that was a flood shoving against his senses.

"I convinced them I'd stabilized enough that they started to let me out on the grounds." Tiny lines flared out from the corners of her eyes, her expression wondering. "To this day, I don't know how I did it. It was as if I put on a different skin like Naasir talks about doing—beneath that skin, I was one step away from total fragmentation."

"You were tough even then."

A fast, unexpected smile. "Yes, I was." The smile faded too soon, her eyes drawn toward Banli House again. "I wanted to run the first day I glimpsed freedom, but I fought it. I knew they were watching me." Pausing, she lifted their clasped hands, rubbed her cheek against the back of his.

It was a punch right to his heart.

"So I did what they expected me to do," she said after lowering their hands again. "I sunbathed and read books like the addicts who'd gone through detox. After a while, the staff stopped paying as close attention to me. Then late one evening after final bed check, I squeezed out a window I'd wedged open, and I ran."

Janvier clenched his jaw, his entire body trembling with the storm inside him. "Where was your brother during the time you were in this place?" he asked, not sure he could ever be civil to the man again.

"Don't blame him, Janvier," she said, to his surprise. "I can't forgive him, but I know why he did it."

"No reason can excuse such abandonment." He would've died for his sisters, would've slayed dragons for them. "A brother is meant to protect."

"That's the thing." A pained whisper. "In his mind, that was exactly what he was doing." She leaned her head against his shoulder. "It wasn't until I was in here that I understood why he couldn't stand to be around me once I began to know things I shouldn't, once I ran to him as an eleven-year-old scared of the ugly things I'd glimpsed in the mind of a teacher who turned out to be a child molester."

The hurt in her voice as she spoke of her brother's rejection was old, long accepted. "In that last, Arvi didn't let me down. He had the teacher investigated, and the man ended up behind bars." A squeeze of Janvier's hand. "He's not a bad person, my brother. He's just . . . I think I'd better show you why Arvi is as he is . . . Why I am as I am." Her eyes went to the facility in the distance. "We have to go inside."

Banli House grew bigger in front of Ashwini as they approached it, a bloated beast with glowing eyes.

*No,* she thought, forcing her jaw muscles to relax, aware she was seeing the facility through the gaze of the scared, confused girl she'd once been. Banli House was no beast; rather, it was a hiding place created by the wealthy to dump their problems where the world couldn't see them.

Janvier brought the car to a smooth stop in the circular drive, near the steps that led to the entrance. There were planters on either side of it, a small manicured evergreen in each, and the fan-shaped lead glass above the door glowed from the light beyond. "It looks so warm and inviting, doesn't it?" she said through the choke hold of fear and old panic.

It was never easy, walking through those doors. But if she didn't do it every single time, the fear would win, it would own her.

Janvier braced his arm along the back of her seat. "This place wounds you. We don't need to be here."

"No. It's important."

"Then I am with you."

Ashwini skimmed her eyes over him; he wasn't wearing any visible blades or guns, but she knew he was armed. "Keep a careful eye on your weapons."

Not questioning her instruction, Janvier gave a small nod.

The front door of Banli House opened as they exited the car and she saw Carl was on duty again tonight. Neatly cut hair, straight white teeth, and creamy skin, his features symmetrical, the nurse was as attractive as every other member of staff. Ashwini had always found that strange. What did the owners think? That rich people didn't want to dump their embarrassments in a place where those embarrassments might come in contact with the less than attractive?

"Ash," the nurse said when they reached him. "It's good to see you again so soon."

"Is she awake?" Ashwini knew the answer even as she asked the question; the woman she'd come to see had always been a night owl . . . and "clock" time had little meaning to her now. She woke and slept to her own internal rhythms.

Carl nodded, his eyes skating to Janvier. "Should I place your guest on the cleared list?"

"Temporarily." There was no guarantee Janvier was "safe" in this context until Ashwini had personally cleared him.

Leading them down the hallway, Carl stopped in front of the door to the familiar corner suite. That suite was a lovely one, complete with a private sitting room and a bedroom that looked out over the grounds. It was also padded and devoid of anything that could be used as a weapon.

The antique furniture was bolted to the hardwood floor through the padding, the sheets replaced by fine blankets that couldn't be torn up and turned into a noose, the fresh flowers displayed in plastic vases that couldn't be shattered and used to slit the wrists. However, when Carl opened the door after his polite knock received a "Come in," from the other side, the modifications weren't immediately apparent.

One of the myriad reasons why Banli House was so expensive.

"Your boots," Carl reminded her.

She turned to Janvier, having forgotten the routine act in the wake of the sense of loss that so often overcame her here. "You have to take them off." A heavy tread could damage the padding.

Janvier ran his hand over her hair, in the oddly tender way that tugged at her heart, before bending to unlace his boots as she unzipped her heeled ones. They placed them to the right of the door.

Then Ashwini looked into the bayou green of his eyes one last time, drinking in the way he felt about her at this instant before everything changed . . . and led him inside.

Carl didn't come with them, but she knew he'd remain nearby in case he was needed to administer a sedative. Ashwini could tell no sedative would be needed tonight at first sight of the woman who sat by the windows, a serene smile on her face.

Seeing Ashwini, she turned and held out her hand, her features a feminine version of Arvi's, the brown-black of her hair thick and gleaming, with only a rare few strands of silver. "Ashi," she said, using the childhood nickname Ashwini heard from no one else now.

"Hello, Tanu." Ashwini settled into the chair opposite her elder sister.

Tanu's dark eyes flicked up to behind her. "Who's this?"

"Janvier." She glanced back and up at him before returning

her gaze to the sister who'd been wrenched out of her life when Ashwini was barely nine. "He's mine."

"Well," Tanu said to Janvier with the acerbic politeness that had so often put men back on their heels before they fell hard for her, "you look well nourished, so I assume you have a job?"

"It even pays in more than whiskey."

Janvier's drawling answer had Tanu's lips tugging up at the corners. "I'd watch out for this one, little sister." The last two words were in the language they'd grown up speaking with their grandparents. "He's apt to steal your virtue and slip out a window come dawn."

Ashwini found herself surprised into laughter. "Maybe I'm the one who'll steal his virtue."

"I'm not sure your Janvier has any left." Tanu's eyes danced and at that instant she was the effervescent beauty who'd once drawn three marriage proposals from total strangers during the course of a single family wedding.

Janvier tugged on Ashwini's braid. "You did not warn me I would be facing such stern scrutiny, *cher*."

Tanu didn't laugh, deep vertical lines forming between her eyebrows instead. "Where's Arvi? I tell him not to work so late, but does that dratted twin of mine ever listen?"

Ashwini sensed Janvier start behind her as he understood the true scale of the tragedy. "You know Arvi," she said. "I bet you he took 'just a glance' at a pending operation as he was about to leave, and ended up spending hours mapping it out. He's probably on his way here now." A guess that had a good chance of being true . . . because her big brother spent more time in Banli House than in his own. Arvi had lost half of himself when he'd lost Tanu, would bleed from the wound till the day he died.

"That's Arvi for you." Sighing, her sister rubbed at her temple. "God, this headache."

Ashwini didn't offer to get medication. Her sister's drug regimen was finely calibrated to make sure she didn't become an addict or end up catatonic. Ashwini hated that Tanu had to be on them, but without the drugs, her sister became manic, prone to self-harm and nightmare delusions that left her screaming.

The aim of the medication was to give her as many minutes of clarity as possible during her waking hours. Banli House was a high-class facility, after all, one that took its responsibilities seriously. If Ashwini hadn't been entombed here as a teenager, she might even have found it a soothing, caring environment.

Janvier moved from behind Ashwini's chair. "I may be able to help," he said and, hunkering down in front of Tanu, pressed his fingers to his own temples in an unusual pattern. "Try that."

Copying the motions, Tanu sighed. "Where did you learn that?"

"From my *ma-mere*—my grandmother. Sometimes what is modern is not always the best, *oui*?"

*"Oui."* Tanu laughed and patted his cheek, no indication of any tension on her face at the contact. "Yes, you're definitely trouble. Pretty trouble." Her eyes met Ashwini's. "You should chain him up."

"He probably has the key to the chains under his tongue."

Tanu's vivacious gaze dulled in front of Ashwini's eyes, her head turning toward the window that looked out into the night. "I can hear them."

"Tanu." Ashwini touched her sister on the knee.

But Tanushree Taj wasn't listening, wasn't even aware of her or Janvier any longer, lost in the cacophony of phantom voices that followed her night and day.

Rubbing her knuckles over the heavy ache in her chest, Ashwini put her hand on Janvier's shoulder, said, "We should go. She can stay like this for hours, sometimes days." Ashwini had once returned from a hunt to find her sister hooked up to a feeding tube because she'd gone into a near-catatonic state two days earlier.

Arvi had been sitting at Tanu's bedside, his voice hoarse from trying to talk her back to the world. *"Please, Tanu. I don't know how to do this without you. Please, Tanu. Please."*

Throat thick with the raw force of the memory, she wasn't ready for the intense and painful tenderness she saw in Janvier's eyes when he turned to her . . . but there was no pity. No horror. He looked at her as he'd always done when he was feeling protective, and the realization made her want to fall into his arms and ask him to never let her go.

Allowing him to tug her up once he was on his feet, she left
Tanu with a soft good-bye. "She's gone," she told Carl as she
and Janvier put their shoes back on. "Please keep an eye on
her." The voices could leave Tanu in agony, until sedation was
the only way to give her peace.

"I always do." The nurse walked with them to the front door.
"Your sister is going away more and more. You were lucky
tonight."

"Do you think you can call me when she's lucid? I'd like to
spend more time with her." Before there was no more time.
"But only if Arvi isn't here." No matter her own need to see
Tanu, Ashwini wouldn't steal Arvi's time with his twin. The
two had never made her feel anything but included as a child,
but nothing could alter the fact they'd been siblings for nineteen
years before she came on the scene.

Unlike some male/female fraternal twins, Arvi and Tanu
had never drifted apart, despite living vibrant, individual lives
of their own. Tanu had gone to a different university from
Arvi's, her social life an active whirl. Arvi, in contrast, had
buried himself in medical school, his girlfriends long-term,
where Tanu's boyfriends changed with the moon.

However, when the two came home for vacations, it was
obvious they'd kept in constant contact. They'd make com-
ments about small incidents in each other's lives, laugh over
secret jokes, tease each other mercilessly over their love lives,
give their excited little sister gifts that complemented one
another.

The only time Ashwini had seen Arvi laugh in the past
eighteen and a half years was the day five years ago when she'd
arrived for a visit to find Tanu coherent and herself. Her sister
had been doubled over in a fit of giggles, Arvi's head thrown
back in untrammeled joy as he sat on the floor with his back
to the window. When Ashwini would've backed away, Arvi
had called for her to come in, open affection in his voice.

Ashwini had walked inside, all the pain that separated them
buried beneath the wonder of that timeless instant when everything was as it should be. Her brother had held her by his side
with his arm slung around her neck, and for a single magical
hour, the three of them had been as before, Ashwini quiet and

happy just to be in the room with her older siblings while they bickered and talked and made fun of the world.

"Of course I'd be happy to call you." Carl's voice cut into the heartrending echo of memory. "I'll ask the day shift nurse to do the same." He opened the front door. "Until next time."

Leaving with a nod, she inhaled the crisp night air in deep gulps. It felt as if the stranglehold around her throat had eased at last, her lungs expanding gratefully. She hated Banli House as much as she loved Tanu. "Let's get out of here."

Janvier drove them back not directly to Manhattan but to the Enclave lookout he'd brought her to on the bike. Leaving the car, the two of them walked to the edge of the cliffs and took a seat notwithstanding the snow, their legs hanging over the side and the Hudson flowing smooth and deep below them.

The Manhattan skyline glittered in the distance, the Tower a spear of light. The brilliance of it caught on the wings of angels who flew in and out, turned the glass of nearby skyscrapers into dazzling mirrors.

"Every time I go to Banli House," Ashwini said, "I want to break her out, take her to some place better. Only the thing is, there is nothing better."

Even Arvi had accepted that.

Tanu had round-the-clock care at Banli House and friends among the other long-term residents. She was never mistreated, the staff scrupulous in following the rules about not making physical contact with her unless she initiated it or it was absolutely necessary. When it was, only a small group of people were authorized to touch her, all individuals whose minds wouldn't hurt Tanu.

If no one on the cleared list was available, Banli House called Ashwini or Arvi. And when Tanu was lucid and herself, the staff made sure she had access to whatever she wanted, be it the freedom to walk the pathways in the woods behind Banli House, eat a particular meal, or paint the hours away on a large canvas.

Once, she'd surprised Arvi by turning up to take him out to lunch. But that had been a long time ago. Tanu didn't leave the grounds now, didn't trust herself to remain coherent and rational for long enough. The voices were too loud.

Janvier held her gaze. "Your sister appears at peace."

"Sometimes I almost believe it, but—" Shaking her head, she said, "I have to start at the beginning."

Janvier turned sideways, placing one of his legs behind her, his knee bent so she could lean against him, and his hand warm on her nape. "I am here."

# 25

"Most everyone," Ashwini began, drawing strength from his unwavering support, "thinks my parents and Tanu all died in that car crash when I was nine. The truth is, only my mother and father died on impact. Tanu was badly injured but she survived."

"That is the cause of the wounds to her mind?"

"No." Terrible as that would've been, it wouldn't have torn what remained of their family to shreds. "Before I tell you about Tanu, I have to tell you about our mother."

Grief pulsed in her heart at the memory of her parents; it had dulled with time, but it would never leave her. Because while they had made mistakes, unable to understand a daughter who was so different from everything they knew, her mother and father had loved her, loved all their children. "You know my mother was a professor of literature—what I didn't tell you is that she was like me, able to see into people with a touch."

Placing one hand on Janvier's thigh, the muscle warm and taut beneath her hand, she anchored herself. "Tanu had it, too. No one in our family ever acknowledged it, ever even joked about the way they'd both occasionally know things they shouldn't. There was always a tinge of fear beneath the surface I didn't understand at the time."

"Wait." Janvier ran his thumb over her nape, a scowl on his face. "Were you and your sister both in that place at the same time?"

Ashwini shook her head. "She was moved to a satellite facility when I was moved in. Because I grew up thinking she was dead, it was decided that my coming face-to-face with her would be too big a shock." Everyone had already thought her unstable.

"But the thing was, a couple of the people who regularly interacted with me, touched me, had touched her, too. I thought I was going insane when I started getting flashes of her as if she were still alive." For a while, it had convinced her to take the medication that made her feel so fuzzy and lost.

Unlike Tanu, she hadn't needed the drugs. The medication had simply made things worse. "Then," she continued, "I realized I only got the flashes near certain people and it began to make a terrible kind of sense."

She'd confronted Arvi once she was free of Banli House, made it clear she knew the truth. "Arvi eventually told me Tanu had had a psychotic break a month before the car accident, had spent seven nights under psychiatric hold. She said the voices wouldn't leave her alone."

Ashwini couldn't imagine Arvi's pain as he watched his vivid, brilliant twin disintegrate in front of his eyes. Because the psychotic break couldn't have been the first sign—and Arvi and Tanu were too close for Arvi not to have known. Ashwini would bet her life on the fact that Arvi had tried desperately to get Tanu help, that he'd fought to save her. But Tanu was already lost.

"As soon as she was mobile after the accident, my sister apparently went into the hospital bathroom and tried to slit her wrists."

Janvier bit off a hard word. He might still never forgive Arvan Taj for what he'd done to Ash, but he could better understand the scars on the man's heart that had led to the terrible decision to institutionalize a teenage girl who'd simply been a little different. He must've believed history was about to repeat itself.

"Arvi moved Tanu temporarily to Banli after her suicide attempt." Ash looked out over the water, but he could tell she didn't see the skyline beyond. "He thought it'd be a better environment for her than a hospital ward, but the temporary stay kept being extended. Each time they thought she was better, she'd go into screaming fits for days or try to harm herself."

"I don't understand why the fact that she lived was kept from you. Your grief must've been devastating." Broken or whole, Tanu was Ash's sister, was clearly *loved* by his hunter.

"Tanu didn't want me to see her that way," Ash said, her voice rough. "Directly after her first psychotic break, she told Arvi that if she was ever institutionalized, I was to be told she was dead." Breathing in harsh gulps, she gripped his thigh more tightly. "And with the car accident . . . Arvi just said she'd died from unexpected complications."

A lie, Janvier saw, that a heartbroken child would have had no reason to disbelieve.

"Neither Tanu nor Arvi has ever said so," Ash continued in that voice shredded with pain, "but I think they wanted to give me a clean slate, no preconceptions about my future . . . because Tanu's ability was stronger than my mother's had been, and my mother had also begun to exhibit signs of mental illness in the months before the crash." Agony in her every word. "I was meant to be the one who made it . . . and I turned out to be the strongest of us all."

Staggered, Janvier saw that he'd been wrong, that until this instant, he'd had no real idea of the root of Ash's fear about immortality. "You believe the older you become, the greater your chance of becoming as she is." And a vampire's madness could last an eon.

"It's a certainty with our history. Tanu's initial psychotic break happened at twenty-eight and I'm only six months away from turning the same age." A long exhale. "It's why I've always encouraged the other hunters to see me as a little kooky, a bit crazy." Her smile was faint. "Not that I'm not, but I figured it'd make it easier to hide the first signs of degeneration."

Refusing to listen, Janvier tugged her against his chest, his jacket open. She came, swinging up her legs to lie along the cliff edge, her head on his shoulder and one arm around him as they faced the city skyline.

"Two women in a family doesn't equal an inevitable pattern," he said, his heart tearing at the idea of losing his

Ashblade to the insidious illness that had consumed her sister. "You said yourself that your ability is stronger than your sister's, and yet you're not showing any symptoms despite being so close to the age she was when she suffered her first psychotic break."

Ash pressed a kiss to his chest, searing him through the fabric of his tee. "I can feel the darkness licking at me, whispering ugly, vicious things just out of my hearing. It's coming."

"*No.* I won't accept this." More than two hundred years he'd waited for her, and now she was telling him he'd lose her in a heartbeat? No.

"I tracked down my maternal grandmother's medical records."

Janvier's blood turned to ice.

"I never knew her," Ash said. "My mother told me she died when my mother was twenty-one. What she didn't tell me is that my grandmother spent fifteen years in a psychiatric facility."

He shook his head in mute denial, but Ash wasn't finished.

"It was much harder to track my great-grandmother, but I finally found one of her girlhood friends." A ragged breath, her body rigid against him, and he knew she was fighting the same rage and pain and screaming sense of loss that had him in its grip. "She told me my great-grandmother hung herself when she was about forty, after 'the ghosts would not leave her alone'—as they hadn't *her* mother."

He knew what she was trying to tell him, didn't want to understand it.

"I'm so sorry, Janvier. I should've stopped us before—"

"Don't you say that. Don't you *ever* say that." He crushed her to him. "You were always meant to be mine." His eyes burned, his chest so painful that it felt as if his heart had burst. "Whether it's for a year or a century, it doesn't diminish who and what we are together."

Ash didn't fight his hold, the kiss she pressed to the pulse in his neck an agonizing tenderness. "I'm yours." Her fingers trembled as she curved them around the side of his neck. "Only ever yours."

He couldn't speak for a long time, and when he did, he had

to see her face. Releasing her so she could sit up, he said, "No more walls, no more distance." He wanted to shake her for keeping this from him for so long, for protecting him at the cost of the life they could've had together. "And never *any* apologies. Not between us."

His fierce, beautiful, wild storm of a lover cupped his face in her hands, her own face strong and proud and so damn vibrant it was impossible to imagine her fading into a nightmare twilight. "No walls, no distance." Raw power in every word. "You're in my soul, Janvier."

He wanted to say the same in return but his throat was too thick, too filled with the anger inside him.

Ash wouldn't let him look away, wouldn't let him hide his fury. "I want a promise, too."

"Anything." He'd split his veins for her, if that was what she wanted.

"If we're going to do this, we do it full throttle." The darkness of her eyes caught him, held him. "We live for today, not in mourning for the tomorrow that hasn't yet arrived, and we don't allow the rage to drown us."

Jawbones grinding, he defied her to look out over the water, but if the Hudson held an answer for him, it was mired in the silky dark.

"Janvier." Fingers weaving through his hair, his Ashblade's arms around his neck. "I want to play with you as we've always played. No rules, no holding back. Don't treat me as broken. Don't do that."

How could he deny her? He'd never been able to deny her anything. "Full throttle," he promised, and it was the hardest promise he'd ever had to make, the anger inside him wanting to take over his skin. "I'll show you things that'll make you laugh in delight, scream in passion, cry for the sheer joy of it."

Ash smiled in startled happiness at the words he'd first spoken to her on the train platform where they'd shared their first kiss and it was a beam of light piercing the oppressive dark. At that instant, he realized something else critical: his Ash would never permit herself to be imprisoned inside her own mind. She was a hunter, a woman who danced with danger on every job. When she felt the shadows begin to overwhelm her, she'd go out on a hunt one day and she wouldn't come home, leaving him with memories of a beautiful lover who'd died doing what she loved.

No anguish like what she and her brother suffered as they watched Tanu deteriorate.

No lingering, agonizing loss. Just a clean, sharp cut.

What she didn't realize was that he'd go with her, making a clean, sharp cut of his own. He'd lived more than two hundred years already, and the best of them, the *best* of them, had been the four since she'd entered his life.

The idea of going back to an existence where she wasn't there anymore? He couldn't do it. He'd never wanted to be a vampire to live forever. He'd done it for what he'd once believed was love, though he'd come to understand it for a false promise. *This*, this was love. The kind that forever changed a man.

If he survived Ash, he would no longer be the Janvier she knew—he'd be a man without a heart, his buried with her. In time, he'd become like the immortals he so despised, the ones for whom life held no meaning, and who'd attempt any cruelty in an effort to feel again.

No, whatever Ashwini's life span, it would be his, too.

Ashwini knew that despite the promise he'd demanded from her, Janvier didn't expect to come up to her apartment that night. He had too much honor to take advantage of her emotional state—but she needed him, wanted to greedily live every instant they had together now that she could go to him open and honest and without secrets.

"I'll walk you up," he said after parking his car in the illegal spot out in front of her building.

Taking his keys once they were through the doors, she threw them to the doorman, then dug out a generous tip. "Can you sneak the car into one of the underground parking spaces someone's not using?" Not having a car of her own, she didn't pay to keep a space.

"No problem." Nic winked. "Mrs. Beachum's in the Hamptons."

"Thanks, Nic." Not looking at Janvier, she walked to the elevators.

"Ash—"

"I don't want to waste any more time." She looked into the raw intensity of his eyes, allowed him to see her: skittering nerves, hot skin, muscles taut, she was a knot of want and need and ignorance. "I want to live, to kiss you, play with you, love you."

He closed his eyes, shuddered. "I'm too selfish when it comes to you, *cher*, to try to convince you otherwise."

Ashwini rose on tiptoe to run her lips down the stubbled edge of his jaw. "Good," she whispered, her body humming at the proximity of his.

Stepping into Ash's apartment after the too-fast elevator ride that hadn't given his spinning head and thundering pulse any time to settle, Janvier took his time in removing his jacket and dropping it on the back of one of her sofas. She did the same thing before leaning down to unzip and pull off her ankle boots. He hunkered down to take off his own boots, then watched as she walked to the glass wall that looked out at the city.

His heart felt bruised tonight, but he'd rather be nowhere else than here, with her, with his lover. Be doing nothing else than loving her, living a lifetime in a heartbeat. When his phone buzzed, he almost didn't look at the message, but Ash turned and in her face he saw the reminder that, no matter what, the victim had a prior claim on their attention.

"Khalil," he told her after scanning the details, "appears to have settled in for a night of public debauchery at Masque. Emaya and Mateo couldn't get in, but a Tower vampire named Trace was already inside when Khalil went in, and he reports that while Khalil is currently indulging his appetites on the glass platform, he's booked out a more intimate 'playroom' for the night."

"Does Masque have security protocols to protect guests in the playrooms?"

"Adele's security monitors all the rooms via a live feed." He met her gaze. "This monster appears locked up for the night, and we've heard nothing back from the computer teams tracking the victim's identity. I think, *cher*, the night is ours."

She held out a hand.

Beyond her, the falling snow blurred the hard edges of New York, made the Tower in the distance a smudged beam of light and the other buildings luminous shadows. It was the perfect background to silhouette her beauty, her resilient strength in the face of impossible odds. When he reached her, she led him into the privacy of the bedroom, the world beyond locked out the instant she closed the curtains over the balcony doors.

He'd dreamed of this moment for an eon, and now that it was here, he felt like an untried boy with his first woman. "Are you sure?" He couldn't bear for her to regret this.

Her eyes pierced him, owned him. "Oh, yes." One hand moving to caress his nape. "Touch me."

It hit him then. She was so self-assured, handling his flirtation with ease and giving back as good as she got that he'd never before thought about what her ability demanded from her sexually. *"Cher."* His fingers trembled as he cupped her face.

Lips quirking, she closed her own hands over his wrists. "Don't worry, sugar." A tease in her voice, though her pupils had expanded to turn her eyes into pools of darkness into which he could fall forever. "I might never have been able to stand to touch anyone enough to get naked with them, but that doesn't mean I'm an innocent."

"I don't know what to do," he said, lost and shaken and enslaved.

"If you try to convince me you're a virgin"—narrowed eyes—"I'm going to get out my crossbow."

# 26

Stroking his thumbs over her cheekbones, he shook his head. "It's you."

Her hands tightened on his wrists, and then she slid one hand back around to cup his nape and draw down his head. His own hands fell to her waist. She was the one who kissed him, explored him, coaxed him.

He'd been seduced many times in his long lifetime. In every instance, he'd known exactly what was happening, had allowed the seduction as part of a game in which both parties had been well satisfied. This . . . he had no control of it, was her instrument to do with as she pleased. Trembling, he sank into the kiss, into the feel of her hand stroking over his nape, her mouth playing with his.

Lips parting from his on a soft, wet sound, she met his gaze, smiled a wicked little smile, and kissed him again, his long and lean and beautiful lover. He tugged her so close there wasn't a breath between them, the feel of her body pressing against his turning the kiss molten. Ash gasped at the hard evidence of his hunger, her free hand sliding under the edge of his T-shirt to touch the skin of his waist.

He groaned, wanted to beg for more.

"I could get used to having you do exactly what I want."
Her lashes lifted, her lips moving against his, the air between
them scalding.

He found his footing in her gentle tease. "Have pity, *cher*. I
am only a man and you are . . . you." A nauseating thought hit
him out of nowhere, almost cut him off at the knees. "Am I the
only one? Is that why—"

"I've met others I can't read," she said before he could complete the question. "A small percentage of the population." Each
word punctuated by a kiss, as if she liked the taste of him.

He liked being tasted, being enjoyed, seduced in a way he
hadn't known he could be seduced.

"I even kissed some of them—out of curiosity and because
everyone needs to be touched. Even me." Another kiss, a nibble
of his lower lip. "But when you grow up conscious of every
touch, it's difficult to treat sex as a simple physical release."

The possessiveness at the heart of his nature heard the declaration hidden in her words, grabbed at it with avaricious
hands. But then she was kissing him again, and his thoughts
splintered. Shifting his hold to wrap one hand around the back
of her neck, his other hand across her lower back, he gave in
to the passion that had always been red-hot embers between
them.

Her breathing was choppy, his heartbeat ragged by the time
she kissed her way along his jaw and down his throat. He fisted
his hand in her hair as she licked out at him, made a small noise
in the back of her throat, and did it again. His body jerked, his
hips wanting to grind his rigid cock against her. Squeezing
his nape, she repeated her action, then blew on the spot. Tremors
rocked his frame. He tugged up her head, their mouths meeting
in a nakedness of need that locked its talons around his heart
and pulled.

"Let's go slow," Ash whispered when they came up for air.
"I want to do every naughty, dirty thing I've never done." The
wicked little smile was back. "Somehow, I think you know a
few sins you can teach me."

His cock felt as if it would shatter, but he was used to frustration. Being with any other woman after meeting her would've
been a betrayal, no matter that they'd been adversaries at the

time. A man knew when he'd found his woman. "I've been waiting years to play teacher with you."

Husky feminine laughter, her fingers possessive on him.

He gave her the kiss she demanded, stroking his hand down to cup her ass at the same time. Moaning into the kiss, she rubbed up against him. Not being stupid, he kept his grip where it was, squeezing and shaping the taut flesh he wanted to bite. He also wanted to bite down on the vein in her neck, in the crook of her elbow, on her wrist, on her thigh, for a far different reason: he hungered to drink from his lover as she sighed in orgasm.

Not every vampire could give pleasure with his bite, but Janvier had been able to do so since the day he first woke as a near-immortal. "I want to make you come," he said against her wet, kiss-swollen mouth. "I want to thrust my fingers inside you"—chest heaving, mouths tangling—"pump hard and deep, your musk decadent in the air and your breasts bared so I can grip and mold them like I'm doing your ass."

"God"—she bit down on his lower lip—"I love the way you talk."

Trading her kiss for kiss, he lost his words, shivered when she ran her teeth over his neck. An instant later, he took a chance and, dipping his head, scraped his own down her skin. Her hand clenched on his nape. *"Janvier."*

"Naked and sweaty, sugar. Remember?" That was when he'd told her he'd feed from her, and the reminder was as much for him as for her. His fangs ached, his cock was stone, every cell in his body starving for a taste of the woman in his arms. Feeding from a human donor had never automatically been a sexual thing for him—with her, it could be nothing else.

Eyes slumberous, Ash ran her nails over the skin of his lower back. "I give you permission."

He froze, the bloodthirsty creature inside him caught between lunging at the chance and fear it had imagined her words. "It's not nice to play with a desperate man."

A sinful, intimate laugh. "Just a taste," she whispered, lips curved and body hot against his own as she rose on her toes to fit herself against his straining erection. "Just enough to drive you crazy."

"It'll be torture," he accused, battling not to shove her to the floor or the wall and drive his cock into the tight, wet clasp of her body. "I fucking can't wait."

Dipping his head to her intoxicating smile, his pulse pounding so hard it was a roar in his ears, he licked over the point where her own pulse raced beneath her skin. He wouldn't rush this, wouldn't devour. He had to sip her like the rare vintage that she was, a vintage that was his own private reserve.

One hand splayed on her ass, the other tangled in her hair, he held her to him and sucked on the spot in her neck that made his fangs prick into his lower lip, the craving near unbearable. Ash made a very feminine sound and undulated against him. His mouth watered, his brain threatening to short-circuit.

Nipping at her, but not enough to break the skin, he asked again to make certain she was with him. "Yes?" It came out a growl, the hunger pounding in his veins.

"Yes."

He sank his fangs into her flesh, felt her jerk against him, but there was no hiss of pain, nothing but her pulse rocketing out of control. Even vampires who couldn't give pleasure with their bite had the ability to dull the pain of entry. Some, of course, liked to make it hurt, and some donors enjoyed the sharp edge of pain. Janvier wasn't about to hurt his Ashblade; he'd pumped in the pleasure-giving drug his body naturally produced before he fed.

Not much, just a touch. He wanted her addicted to *him*, not to his bite.

Then it became impossible to think. The taste of her went to his head, the feral bloodlust inside him shuddering in a pleasure so intense, it threatened to send him to his knees. He wanted to stretch out naked on top of her in a lush, comfortable bed, to sip over an hour, tasting and kissing his lover as he stroked his cock slowly in and out of her.

He wanted to drink and drink.

Breaking contact before the greed stole his mind, made him a glutton, he licked over the marks, ensuring they'd heal just slowly enough that others would know she was his. Aroused all over again by the thought, he licked once more, his veins hot and heavy, his head buzzing. "You are a drug."

Her buttocks clenched under his hold, her breath a rasp. "Jesus, you're potent."

Realizing he'd brought her to the edge of orgasm, he licked over the marks again. "I should let you suffer as I'll suffer." Despite his threat, he shifted their bodies so that his thigh was in between hers.

Urging her to ride his thigh and cursing their clothing, he sank his fangs into her one more time. He made sure it didn't hurt, but didn't pump in the pleasure-giving compound.

Her back arched at the dual wave of sensation, her cry shattered silver in the air.

Retracting his fangs before he could take more than she'd offered, he licked again and again at the wound as he rocked her against his thigh. Her nails dug into his nape, and it made the feral thing in him bare its teeth in bone-deep pleasure. The bloodthirsty beast was holding on by its claws, but that was all right. It could be patient now that she was in his arms. It could pretend to be rational for a while longer.

Going limp as the last ripples of ecstasy squeezed her dry, Ash turned her head into his neck . . . and kissed his own pulse, her arms tight around him. If he hadn't already given himself to her, he would have at that instant. Holding her close, he drowned in her scent, in her warmth, in her.

Ashwini had thought about sex before—it kind of tended to dominate the mind at times when you weren't having any, *especially* when a certain sex-on-legs Cajun kept flirting with you. But the one thing she'd never really considered was how it'd feel to be held . . . held with such fierce devotion that she could feel it in her bones.

"Don't let go," she whispered, her voice breaking. "Don't let go."

"I won't." Walking backward and taking her with him in a quiet display of strength, he tumbled them onto the bed. And then he tightened his embrace, thrust one of his thighs between her own, and locked his body around hers.

Tucking her head under his chin, she drew in the scent of him, the warmth of him, and felt things in her snap and break and knew she'd never again be the same. "I don't think I'm so tough after all, Janvier. I don't know if I can go any further." The sex she could've handled, but the way he held her, it destroyed, threatening to make her break the promise she'd asked of him.

Janvier's hand curved over her nape. "I could hold you for eternity."

Closing her eyes on that bittersweet vow, Ashwini just lay wrapped in him, and when sleep came, she went into it warmer and safer than she'd ever been. Yet the darkness lapped at the edges of her mind, showing her things she didn't want to know, didn't want to see. A vampire with skin a shade darker than her own and vivid black eyes, his razored black goatee paired with hair braided tight to his skull, used a whip on the white, white skin of a woman who screamed, welts rising over her breasts and her stomach.

Two strokes broke the skin, drew fat droplets of blood.

Yet when the vampire used the handle of the whip to violate her, the woman's scream was that of orgasm. Heavy lidded in the aftermath, she begged for him to release her from her bonds. He laughed, gave her what she wanted . . . and she crawled to abase herself at his feet, begging to pleasure him.

"Master, please."

Laughing again, he put his booted foot on her shoulder and pushed her to the floor, where he shifted his foot to her throat and held her down while he kissed a golden-skinned girl with ripe young breasts and innocence in her eyes. She couldn't have been more than sixteen and she wore only her skin and a fine gold chain around her hips. Closing his hand around her throat, the black-eyed man began to squeeze.

The girl's face went pink, then red, her eyes bloodshot. When she scrabbled at his arm in a final panic, he smiled and kissed her and continued to squeeze. Too soon, she was limp in his arms and he used his grip on her throat to throw her onto the black-sheeted bed in the center of the room. Taking his foot off the woman on the floor, he made her unzip him, then used her mouth with a vicious lack of care before kicking her in the ribs.

She curled up into a ball, her eyes wet and worshipful, but he ignored her in favor of the limp, lifeless girl on the bed. Covering her with his body, he began to feed, his throat moving in long, deep drafts . . . and his hips in a way that said he wasn't only feeding.

"No!" Coming awake on a scream, Ashwini grabbed Janvier's phone where he'd left it on the bedside table. "Call Trace," she said to Janvier, who'd woken when she did. "Find out what Khalil's done to the girl."

Janvier didn't question her, just made the call. "Adele had already entered the room after security alerted her," he said once the conversation ended, his features grim. "The girl is alive. Barely. Trace says she's twenty and a regular at Masque, extremely popular because of the illusion she gives of being even younger."

Heart thudding and skin damp, Ashwini nonetheless didn't break away from Janvier's side, his arm around her and her own around him. "Did she know she was about to be choked almost to death then sexually used when she went into that room with Khalil?"

"He has used her similarly before." Janvier put his phone back, his movements jerky, his voice rough. "I have no argument with adults who choose to play on the edges of sexuality, but in times past, when the mores were different, Khalil targeted the true innocents."

Ashwini caught a grinding anger she rarely heard in Janvier's tone. "You knew someone he hurt."

"A girl from the bayou, maybe fourteen and awestruck by the wealthy vampire who showed an interest in her. Six months after she ran away from home to be with him, the piece of shit returned her, hollow eyed, addicted to opium, and broken on the inside." His voice shook. "A year after she drowned herself, her father told me that Khalil had said she was trash, worth a little amusement but not for keeping."

"Bastard." Eyes narrowing, she focused on what Janvier had remembered. "He used the word 'trash' specifically?"

"Or something very similar." Janvier wrapped himself fully around her again. "But I wouldn't put all my faith in that, *cher*. There are too many old vampires who see humans as disposable . . . But Khalil has the cruelty to do what was done to Felicity, and the wealth and experience to hide his deadly perversions. I will make sure he is constantly under watch."

"You might not even need spies," Ashwini muttered. "I seem to have a direct surveillance feed to his life, thanks to a simple brush of skin." She banged her head against his breastbone. "I don't mind sex dreams—but why can't I have sex dreams that don't make my blood run cold and my hand itch for a gun?"

Kneading the back of her neck, Janvier shifted slightly until he was on top of her. His kiss was wet, his body weight delicious, and his skin so hot her own blood ignited. "I'm not a sex dream, but perhaps this poor Cajun will do as a substitute?"

Ashwini pretended to consider it. "It'd work even better if you took off your T-shirt."

Janvier complied. Straddling her, he said, "I'd say the same." It was a dare.

Not about to break her streak of never once turning down one of his dares, Ashwini managed to strip off her shirt. It left her dressed in a demi cup bra in polka-dotted black with pretty yellow detailing along the edges. When he scowled and gently ran his finger over her scar, she said, "It doesn't hurt and the vamp who did this is dead."

Janvier's scowl turned into a brutally satisfied smile. "Did you hear how his head bounced down the steps? Thud, splat, thud, splat."

Laughing at a conversation only the two of them would ever have in bed, she reached back and unhooked the bra.

She wasn't sure quite how it ended up off her. All she remembered was Janvier coming down over her, and then they were kissing and touching and whispering and driving each other to madness. He palmed her breasts with blunt possessiveness, bit and suckled. She ran her nails down his back and sucked a mark on his throat that made him rock his cock against the juncture of her thighs and call her a witch.

Laughter turning into a moan as he did something very naughty involving his fangs and her nipple, she bit down on his biceps. He retaliated by blowing a cool breath over her kiss-wet nipple, teasing her until she flipped their positions and did the same to him, the salt and maleness of him her new favorite dessert.

Her jeans stayed on. So did his.

But they were both sweaty and satisfied by the time they fell asleep again.

This time, she rested in peaceful warmth, the visions defeated for one night at least.

# 27

Ashwini woke to early morning birdsong tangled up in a man. She knew who he was at once—there was only one man with whom she'd ever been tangled. Easing gingerly away from his side, she looked at Janvier's face to find him watching her. "Hey," she said, the possessiveness in her veins a molten heat.

"Your phone beeped," he said, his eyes slumberous and his arm around her waist. "That's probably what woke you."

Reaching for the phone, she turned into his embrace so that he was holding her from behind, his chest pressed to her back. "It's from the Guild computer team. About Felicity Johnson."

"Mmm?"

The low, rumbling sound made her smile before she had to return to the ugliness of what had been done to their victim. "They can track her up to about twelve months ago, through a number of low-income jobs, but she falls off the grid after that. No tax return, no insurance payments, no unemployment benefits."

"Pass me my phone."

"Lazy. It's on your side of the bed."

He bit her shoulder. "Don't poke the gator."

Laughing, she twisted to get the phone . . . and he suckled the tip of her breast into his mouth. She gasped, fell back. "Tricky."

A proud smirk, his hand sliding up her rib cage. "Always." Taking the phone, he made a call.

His hair was tumbled, his eyes still a little sleepy, his voice languid. And he was hers. He knew everything and he chose to be hers. It was a gift she'd hold on to with every ounce of determination in her soul.

"Tower personnel hit the same roadblock?" she asked after he hung up.

"*Oui.*" He put his arm around her again. "It seems we must solve this the old-fashioned way."

She went to reply when his phone rang again. This time, whatever he heard made him frown, come to total wakefulness. "I have to leave to deal with a Tower matter," he said after hanging up. "I'll call you after it's done." A hard kiss, his hand stroking her body again.

It made unknown things wrench in her to watch the door close behind him a bare two minutes later. She'd never thought of herself as a woman who needed anyone, but maybe that had simply been because she'd never had someone who needed her in return. Already, she missed him.

A knock on the door as she was turning to head to the shower had her opening it without looking through the spy hole. She could feel Janvier on the other side. Not saying anything, he cupped her face and kissed the life out of her, one of his hands in her hair, the other roaming her body. She wrapped her own arms around his neck, pressed herself to the warm strength of him, the loose T-shirt she'd put on no impediment to his caresses.

"Okay," he said when they came up for air, his chest heaving, "I really have to go now, *cher.*" Janvier kissed Ash again despite his words, finding it near impossible to leave her. It felt as if he were leaving half his heart behind.

"We can do this," Ash said, her hands caressing his shoulders. "Teenagers do it all the time, right?"

"Right," he said, though he knew as well as she that what lived between them was too old, too intense to be anything as manageable as hormonal lust. Even without a time limit, they would've always been a pair once they came together, more often seen together than not. "I have to go back to Club Masque."

Ashwini's forehead furrowed. "Why?"

"I don't know. Report came in from Trace, was too garbled to make out much except the name of the club." He forced himself to release her. "Do what you can about Felicity. I'll call once I know what's up at Masque." This time, he made himself jog to the emergency exit and the stairs. Waiting for the elevator was what had gotten the better of his self-control the first time.

"Watch out for Khalil!" Ash called out after him.

"I will!" he yelled back.

However, when he reached Masque—after a hurried stop at the Tower to pick up his kukris—he discovered it wasn't Khalil who was the threat. Trace was outside the club, a blood-soaked cloth being held to his throat by Adele. Scarlet drops dotted the snow despite the club owner's efforts to stanch the flow.

"I'm fine," the slender male said when Janvier reached him, his voice still a little wet with blood. "Situation inside—vamp named Rupert's in full bloodlust and pumped up so he's stronger than he should be." Coughing up blood on the snow, Trace waved Adele and her cloth away. The claw marks on his throat said he'd come close to having his spine ripped out, but Trace was old enough that he'd survive.

"Did you call the Tower?"

Trace shook his head, dark green eyes pained but cogent. "It's only one vamp, and I knew you and Naasir could take him, since we managed to trap him inside. Naasir's on his way."

It was a good call on Trace's part, with the Tower's resources so strained. "Casualties or hostages?"

"The club was mostly empty," Adele said, taking a bottle of blood from a curvy Hispanic woman who'd run down the street with a box full of them, her indoor outfit of sleek black pants and blue velvet vest over a white lace shirt making it clear she was a local in the Quarter. "Trace, drink."

As the vampire drank in an effort to speed up his healing, Adele continued to speak, the ordinarily flawless cream of her skin splotchy. "Only people left inside were the ones in the private rooms, and they were locked automatically inside those rooms when I activated the alarm for trouble on the floor."

"That's not good." Janvier slipped out his kukris, the curved blades an extension of his body.

"No." Adele gave Trace another bottle of blood. "There are mortals trapped in those rooms, and you know how quickly bloodlust can spread. Khalil had a look in his eye I didn't like last night—that's why I was up and watching the monitors myself, with Trace for company."

*Rupert.* The name finally penetrated.

*Merde.*

"His woman," Janvier said. "A pretty, plump brunette?" He searched his memory for her name. "Lacey."

"Dead," Trace answered, wiping the back of his hand over his mouth. "He tore her apart in front of us, did it under the sheets—looked like he was going down on her. Must've put his hand over her mouth to stop her screams."

"We weren't paying attention to him." Adele's distress was open, the club owner oddly softhearted for one running such an establishment. "I mean, it was *Rupert.* Worst kink he has is staying in the Masque rooms when he knows they're monitored. A little exhibitionism, that was his thing. He never hurt his women; and this one, he *adored.* It was their first night being intimate."

Trace twisted the lid off a third bottle. "She didn't stand a chance, and he was fucking out the door before Adele could initiate the lockdown." A string of harsh words. "I thought I could handle him, but he's faster and stronger than he should be—no way Rupert should've been able to grab me, much less throw me off the mezzanine to the first floor."

Janvier had once seen a vampire in bloodlust make an impossible leap across a canyon, almost as if he were flying. A large percentage, though, went into bloodthrall after their first kill, a torporlike state caused by their gluttonous feeding that made them easy to hunt down. It didn't sound like Rupert was one of the latter. "Can I enter the club without going through the passageway?" He'd be the most vulnerable there, the narrow space negating the advantage of his blades.

Naasir jumped down from the roof at that instant, apparently having raced to the location by running along the "lower skyroad," as he called it. "There is a skylight," he told Janvier, shoving his hair out of his eyes.

Adele stirred. "It's reinforced glass. You won't be able to break it."

Sheathing his weapons of choice, Janvier met Naasir's eyes, caught his nod, and then they were climbing, the other vampire in the lead. When they reached the snow-covered skylight, Naasir raised his hands and slammed down with his claws. Cracks spread out from the point of contact. Janvier used the butt of a kukri to deepen the cracks, and then the two of them backed off . . . and ran to jump on the skylight, coming down in a hail of glass that sliced shards through both of them.

Rolling to a standing position, Janvier saw Naasir already pinned down, the once-urbane Rupert on top of him like a ravening beast, Rupert's face a mask of blood. Naasir should've been able to take him without problem—except it appeared Rupert must've hit Naasir in midfall, causing the vampire to land on a huge shard of glass that had effectively skewered him to the floor.

All that went through Janvier's mind in a split second. In position as he rose, he threw one of his blades with the flat spinning motion he'd learned during his time in Neha's court. The lethally sharp and perfectly balanced kukri spun like one of Ash's throwing stars, coming to a quivering stop in the wall behind Rupert.

Whose head toppled off his body a second later, the blade having sliced it clean through.

Growling, Naasir shoved off the body, which was spurting blood all over him. "Why did you do that?" he snarled, pulling himself off the glass shard with a look of irritation on his face. "I was about to break his neck."

"You're welcome," Janvier said, pulling his blade from the wall. He wiped it on his jeans leg, but didn't put it back in the sheath. As Adele had said, bloodlust could spread with deadly speed. "Are you badly injured?" As far as he could tell, the glass had gone straight through Naasir, but hadn't penetrated any major organs. It must've been the shock of the sudden injury that had kept him from reacting as fast as usual.

Naasir growled in reply. "My new shirt from Honor is torn and bloody."

Figuring that meant the other vampire was fine, Janvier ran to Adele's control room with Naasir at his back and scanned the feeds. Two of the vampires were pacing in an erratic pattern, but Khalil appeared in control, his women unharmed. Hitting the button that unlocked all the doors, Janvier glanced at Naasir.

"Go scare them out of incipient bloodlust. And get Trace to keep following Khalil if his wounds allow it—if not, can you do it?"

Naasir gave him a feral smile and a nod. "I wouldn't mind eating Khalil's liver. I hope he gives me an excuse."

Knowing even Khalil wouldn't mess with the silver-eyed vampire, Janvier returned to Rupert. "Damn it, what the fuck happened to you?" The cultured art collector *had* been a good man, as Janvier had said last night, but when he examined the body, he saw Rupert had been wearing a necklace of intestines, the flesh slick and bloody.

Pressing his fist to his mouth to control the gorge that rose in him, Janvier forced himself to walk to the private room with the blood-soaked sheets he'd glimpsed on the surveillance feeds. At first, he couldn't see Lacey. It was the glint of light off the ring on her finger that alerted him to the fact she was on the floor on the far side of the bed, her outflung hand the only part of her he could see.

When he came around, he wished he hadn't. The sweet, giggling woman who'd blushed at him while proudly calling herself Rupert's had been disemboweled. From the state of Rupert's face, it appeared the bloodlust-ridden vampire had torn into her stomach with his fangs, then used his hands to pull out the ropes of her intestines. Her jaw was broken, her tongue ripped out.

It made no sense. None.

Until Janvier stepped on something that felt slippery beneath his boot. Frowning, he bent down and found it to be a tiny plastic ziplock bag. There was nothing inside, but he knew what tests would reveal. "Umber."

Ashwini met up with Ransom at Guild Academy a half hour after Janvier left the apartment. Her fellow hunter had responded to her message about a meeting earlier than she'd expected, and now the two of them sat on the lowest row of the tiered seating that overlooked the outdoor training ground. Ransom's leg, his cast covered with signatures, including her own, was perched on a piece of wood she'd found to ensure the cast was protected from the snow, his crutches beside him.

The training ground in front of them was a mess of dirty snow and crushed ice from the early morning session that had already occurred. The Guild never cleaned up this yard, never put up shields against the wind or the rain. Sessions occurred no matter what the weather. "I remember getting my ass kicked by Bracken one winter while hail pelted down on my head and face." She winced at the memory. "Damn, but that hurt."

"That's nothing," Ransom said. "One year, we had a category three storm hit—full-on rain, gale-force winds, flying debris—and he made my group come out here and complete our session."

"Please. I once had to fight Bracken in a flood. The water was up to my thighs."

Ransom snorted. "Dude, there was that time cats fell from the sky, claws out."

They looked at each other and began to laugh. It was a ritual among all hunters who'd graduated from the Academy in the past twenty years, the attempt to one-up each other with Bracken training stories. The outdoor sessions were mandatory for every trainee, but the all-weather stuff was reserved for the final year—because vampires were tougher, more resistant to the weather.

"A hunter who melts at the sight of a little snow—" Ashwini began.

"—is a hunter who'll soon be lying in a nice, quiet grave," Ransom finished, and then, in a hysterical imitation of the weathered Academy trainer, added, "Is that what you want, princess? Is it? I didn't think so. Now, *move!*"

They laughed again.

"If he came out here now," Ransom said, "and told me I had detention and had to do a hundred rounds of the yard on my crutches, I'd say 'yes, sir' and start moving."

"Me, too," Ashwini admitted. "I think he's one of the few people on the planet I'm actually scared of."

"Only idiots aren't scared of Bracken."

"Saki seems to handle him fine."

"They're having sex on a regular basis. An option unavailable to us." Ransom drank some of the coffee he'd brought out in a carry cup. "So, Felicity Johnson."

"Were you able to find out anything about her? We know she was a club girl who disappeared after hooking up with a rich sugar daddy."

Ransom took a doughnut from the box of four she'd managed to sneak past the other hunters who were here early—to prep for sessions they were teaching. Biting into it, he chewed and swallowed before answering. "That part is right," he said. "A few of the working girls I know said Felicity used to be one of them for a couple of months, starting about a year back."

That fit with when she'd dropped off the grid in terms of more vanilla jobs. "Pimp?"

"No, but the girls said she was vulnerable to male attention, that something in her made her crave their approval." Taking another sip of his coffee, he continued. "She avoided the pimps because she wasn't going into the life long-term—she got out fast once she realized the johns might permanently hurt her if she wasn't careful. Word is she worked under the table cleaning, and was down to her final cents at times, but she didn't come back to the streets."

"She knew if she got into it too deep," Ashwini said, starting to see more of their victim, "she'd be stuck at the low end forever."

A nod from Ransom. "Working girls have a hard life and it shows. No way to glide into a new, better life if the old one is stamped onto your face and body. The thing is, none of the women I talked to had anything bad to say about Felicity—she got out, but she never forgot her friends.

"She helped out with free babysitting for one of the women two or three times, and when she hooked up with her rich lover, she lent another woman a little money so she could pay for a plane ticket out of town for a family emergency."

A good person, a loyal one, too. "When's the last time any of them had contact with her?"

# 28

"Seven months ago. Visit before that, she'd told them she was going to go with her lover to Europe, so they didn't worry about it. The other women were happy for her, thought she'd made it, had the life she'd always wanted." He finished off the doughnut and his coffee at the same time. "They were surprised she dropped them cold, but knowing her as they did, they figured maybe her rich guy had her on a short leash and she'd get back in touch once things had eased."

But Felicity, Ashwini thought, was likely already in a desperate situation by that time. "Will the women talk to me?" she asked Ransom, conscious how protective he was of his friends on the street.

"Yeah. They want to find out who hurt her—I hope you nail the fucker." Pulling out his phone, he sent her names and contact numbers, told her the women were waiting for her call. "I know I don't have to ask, but be careful of them."

"I will." She stared out at the training ground, the rucked-up snow glittering under the sun. "Janvier's working this with me. Can I take him along?"

"No problem. I cleared it with the women—Tower's not

going to have any interest in them aside from this case and, like I said, they really liked Felicity."

Enough, Ashwini thought, to stick their necks out. That told her a lot about her victim. "So," she said after a couple of minutes of comfortable silence, "how come you're in so early? I thought you and Nyree would be celebrating. Hope my request didn't mess anything up."

"Nah, I saw your message after our celebration. Easy enough to make the calls while Nyree was catching her breath." A glow in the green of his eyes, his handsome face happily smug. "Two of the librarians at her work came down with a bad case of the flu, so she went in to cover. I was meant to teach a class this afternoon, but I swapped with Demarco for a morning session so I can take off when Nyree's shift is over."

"You better invite me to your wedding."

"Are you kidding?" Ransom grinned. "I plan to have one hell of a party. Shit, I'm getting married." He shook his head, like a dog shaking off wet. "And I *want* to do it."

Well aware of his dating history, Ashwini squeezed his shoulder. "I'm happy for you, Ransom."

She met Janvier an hour later, at the little warehouse that housed the blood café in which Ellie had an interest. Blood-for-Less was closed for the day, but there was an employee out back handling donors coming in to sell blood. The stocky male vampire—who looked more like a schoolteacher than someone who should be in the Quarter—let them into the main sitting area and promised to send in the three women when they arrived.

Ashwini had picked the location because it wouldn't put the women in an awkward position if they were seen. There was nothing strange about a working girl getting a bit of extra cash by selling blood. Right now, however, Ashwini's attention was on Janvier. Deep grooves marked the sides of his mouth, his eyes dull.

Touching her fingers to his jaw in the muted light inside the blood café, she said, "What is it? What's wrong?" That was when she noticed he'd showered, changed. His blades sat openly on his back, over a plain black T-shirt, his jacket and scarf discarded on the back of a wine red sofa.

"Sit with me."

Once they were down, he took one of her hands in his and told her of the horror that had occurred in Masque that morning. "Lacey?" Shock held her frozen; she couldn't believe that the sweet, friendly woman who'd been so adorably besotted with her lover was gone, murdered at the hands of that lover. "You're sure?"

"I'm sorry, *cher.* I wish I could tell you she felt no pain, but it would be a lie."

Still having trouble processing the horror of it, she focused on him, pressing a kiss to his temple and running her hand down his back. "I'm sorry you had to see that."

Leaning forward, his shoulders taut, he blew out a breath. "This drug is appearing more and more like a poison intended to cause this effect."

Ashwini heard more than Janvier said. She knew how protective he was of women, knew part of him would be going over and over every interaction from the previous night, trying to figure out if he could've prevented this. "Rupert was a good person until he took the drug," she reminded him, thinking of how she'd found herself liking the vampire from Lacey's description of their relationship. "He made the choice to use the drug, no one else. Not even Raphael could've stopped him unless he was in the room at the instant Rupert decided to eat Umber."

Janvier put his hand on her thigh. "Thank you," he said after over a minute. "I needed to hear that—you expect the ones who go to vampires like Khalil to die, but this . . ."

She curled her hand around his arm, her head against his shoulder. Lacey had died in horrible agony, but as a woman who loved, Ashwini knew the worst pain would've been of Rupert's betrayal. Lacey's heart would've broken long before her body. "She was so harmless, Janvier."

He shifted to wrap an arm around her, pressing his lips to her hair. "At times, I forget I'm not human. Not today."

Ashwini wasn't about to let that go. Lifting her head to pin him with her gaze, she held the raw honesty of the eye contact. "Humanity is what we make it." She'd seen too much horror done by mortals to believe them free of the taint of evil. "You're sad about Lacey. You're sad about Rupert, too. And you're angry at the loss of life that didn't have to happen." Two happy flames snuffed out because someone had decided to create a seductive poison. "That's humanity and it lives in you."

His throat worked, his eyes red rimmed. "Be in my arms," he said at last. "I need to hold you."

She slipped into his embrace in silence and that was how they sat until they heard voices from the back of the café. Breaking reluctantly apart, the two of them were on their feet by the time Aaliyah, Carys, and Sina came in as a group.

It was obvious that Carys, a brassy blonde with cool blue eyes and a sprinkling of freckles across the bridge of her nose, was the leader. Aaliyah, dark skinned and model tall with delicate bones, spoke in a soft tone heavy with grief. Sina, in contrast, her emerald green hair cut in a blunt fringe above slanted eyes set in a broad, pale-skinned face, smiled easily but it didn't reach her eyes.

"Please," Janvier said after the café employee showed them in, "take a seat."

The women hesitated, but then sat side by side on the sofa that faced the one Ashwini and Janvier sat back down on. When the café employee came in with a tray of orange juice and cookies, the three women exchanged raised eyebrows. Ashwini rose and thanked the young vampire, made a quiet request in his ear. The small bottle of blood appeared moments later.

This time, Sina's smile was assessing. "Most people don't realize I'm a vampire."

"I'm a hunter." Even then, it had taken her a minute—Sina's fangs were the smallest she'd ever seen, small enough to be mistaken for human canines.

"Fangs work fine, in case you were wondering," the lushly curved vampire said, opening the bottle to take a sip while the others picked up the unopened bottles of juice and twisted off the lids. "Just a weird genetic thing."

Ashwini didn't ask the other question she wanted to know the answer to, but she caught the understanding of it in Janvier's eyes, knew they'd discuss it later. For now, she showed the women the facial image created by Janvier's contact. "Is this your friend?"

"She never looked that flat, was always moving her hands when she talked. Used to drive me nuts." Her voice hard in an effort to hide the tremor beneath, Carys pushed away the photo. "Her hair was dark gold, not white-blonde, but yeah, that's Felicity. Big bluey-green eyes and all."

Identity confirmed as far as possible, Ashwini asked the women to go over the details the three had shared with Ransom. Afterward, she said, "Do you remember exactly *when* she began talking about her new boyfriend?"

Sina frowned. "Eight months ago."

"You sound very sure," Ashwini said.

"She told me on my birthday, that's why. We'd gone out for a drink, the four of us, and she was bursting with news. Do you guys remember?"

The other two women backed up her recollection.

It was Aaliyah who spoke next. "Few weeks after that, Felicity was so happy because her guy had said he'd take her to Europe, buy her things in Paris, Milan, Rome. She was always into the fashion magazines."

Carys rubbed at the faux-fur collar of her thigh-length coat like it was a worry stone. "Girl used to blow too much money on the rags, but she said it made her happy to look at that stuff."

"Any idea when she was meant to go to Europe?" Ashwini leaned forward, forearms braced on her thighs.

All three women shook their heads. "She just said it'd be soon." Sina rolled her lips inside, bit down with her teeth. "That was the last time I saw her—about seven months ago. Does that help?"

"We'll check airline records." Ashwini would bet her entire year's income that Felicity had never left the country, the promise of Europe a lure designed to lay a false trail.

"Do you know where your friend lived before she found her lover?" Janvier nudged the cookies toward Aaliyah, received a small smile in return.

"Yeah." Carys told them an address in a not particularly nice part of Queens.

"And Felicity never mentioned her lover's name, where he lived, anything?" Ashwini asked, wanting to be certain. "Even the color of his hair."

Carys and Sina shook their heads, but Aaliyah suddenly sat

up straight. "One time she said she'd be moving into a nice Quarter house like the rich bitches, and that she was going to invite us for coffee and cakes, and we'd have to wear fancy hats and say 'oh, yes, my dear' and 'toodles.'" Blinking rapidly, Aaliyah whispered, "We laughed so hard."

It was a tenuous link, but it *was* a link directly to the Quarter. "Do you remember anything else?"

"No . . . but I did ask her why she didn't point out her rich john to us, you know, on the sly."

"Aaliyah!" Sina's mouth fell open. "You never told us that."

"I didn't want to make Felicity look bad, 'cause her man sounded like a first-class dickhead." Rubbing off her tears using the sleeve of her black coat, she said, "Jerkoff told her that if she even hinted they were involved before he took her to Europe for a makeover so she'd 'fit his lifestyle,' the whole deal was off. Felicity wanted it *so* much, she didn't want to jinx it by telling even us."

A pause before Aaliyah added, "It was weird . . . Felicity never had a pimp, but, looking back, this guy, he got into her head like a pimp does, made her believe the whole 'daddy' shtick."

That he was omnipotent, Ashwini thought, gut boiling, that if he had to be cruel, it was because Felicity had let him down. *Bastard.*

"We didn't give you enough, did we?" Carys asked, blunt and up-front.

"You gave us another point on the timeline." Ashwini didn't disrespect the women by sugarcoating reality. "Each step gets us closer to finding out what happened to her."

"Will you . . ." Sina took a deep breath, her breasts threatening to overflow the low-cut top she wore beneath her deep pink puffer jacket. "Will you tell us what you discover?"

"I promise."

"We don't have a lot"—Carys stuck her jaw out, shoulders held tight—"but we want to make sure she has a gravestone, a proper burial. Girl ain't got no family, grew up in foster care after her grandparents got swept away in a flood when she was a kid."

Ashwini felt no surprise that Felicity's murderer had zeroed in on wounded prey, on a woman so hungry for love and a stable life that she'd been willing to erase herself to achieve it. "The man whose son discovered the body also wants to help," she told the women as she took out her phone. "He's a good guy. Maybe you can work with him to organize Felicity's funeral once her ashes are released."

Five minutes later, the women left with Tony Rocco's contact number, and Ashwini was back in Janvier's car, having caught the subway to meet him at Blood-for-Less. As they pulled out, she asked what she hadn't inside. "How can a vampire be forced to work the streets? Is it part of her Contract?" Never before had she realized that might be a possibility.

"No," Janvier said. "Certain things are expressly prohibited under the Contract, by order of Cadres ongoing, including the selling of the body for profit. The punishment isn't worth the risk. Of course, that doesn't mean there aren't myriad other ways the Contracted can be used and abused."

Ashwini thought of what she'd seen in Nazarach's court, of the two women on their knees, one on either side of the angel, their faces white and muscles quivering beneath couture evening gowns. "Do you wonder sometimes, about Simone and Monique?"

"*Non*. They both made their beds—as Sina may have." He stopped behind a gleaming black town car that was attempting to parallel park in a minuscule space. "She's around a hundred and fifty."

"That means she would've received a payment when she completed her Contract." Word was, even if a vamp were given only the minimum mandated amount, it was enough to support a person for a year.

Slipping around the town car, Janvier said, "Vampires aren't immune from bad decisions, or bad luck." His voice held dark memories of the carnage he'd witnessed that morning, of the bad decision that had ended two lives. "There's also the possibility that she chooses this existence—for some, even a hundred years is too much life and they become bored. It may be a rush for her to get into cars with strange men, to use the body to take control."

Every time Ashwini thought she understood people, she learned something that told her even her abilities couldn't predict everything. "The calculating bastard set Felicity up with the Europe trip."

"That's my take. He had to know she'd tell her friends, brag about it a little."

"She was excited to be so close to touching her dreams." In her mind's eye, Felicity was becoming fully formed, a vulnerable woman who was loyal to her friends, and who was driven by hope for a better future. "Then he took her and he hurt her."

"But she didn't die until recently." Janvier's words were ground out. "He kept her for months."

"When we find this son of a bitch, I will personally nail his nuts to the floor before slicing him to ribbons."

"I think you will have to get in line, *cher*." A grim smile. "But perhaps I will share."

Dmitri stood in the center of Masque and considered Janvier's earlier report. The Cajun had been in the Tower for a scarce fifteen minutes to shower and change before he'd left to meet his hunter, but it had been long enough.

"The bloodlust situation wasn't at urgency last night," he'd said, his voice harder than Dmitri had ever heard it, "but this morning changes everything."

Dmitri agreed with the other male's assessment. He'd watched a recording of Adele's surveillance footage, seen crimson tinge the irises of two vampires trapped in the private rooms. He'd also sensed the ugly energy in the air when he'd deliberately walked along the block to reach the club: a vicious mix of scrabbling fear and stimulated excitement.

The swift actions Trace, Janvier, and Naasir had taken in dealing with Rupert that morning had added depth to that fear, but the violent thrill of bloodlust was thick in the air and becoming thicker by the second. The fight against Lijuan had unleashed aggression in a large number of the Made, and now they wanted to surrender to those urges rather than deal with the aftermath of war.

"Dmitri." Adele's long red hair brushed her butt as she walked toward him, her sophisticated features and dress not reflecting the pragmatic earthiness at the heart of her nature. "What do you plan to do about this?"

He half smiled; he'd always liked Adele, even more so now that she'd fought with grim fury to defeat Lijuan's vermin. "I saw you move like a warrior, Adele." Hair braided around her skull, her weapon of choice a war hammer, she'd annihilated the reborn in her sector. "Why do you run this den of iniquity rather than becoming part of the Tower?"

Adele snorted. "You forget, Dmitri. I've known you for five hundred years—sin and sex and pain, you've enjoyed them all."

Enjoyed, Dmitri thought, wasn't the right word. He'd drowned himself in sensation in a futile effort to forget a loss that had beaten his heart to a pulp and left him dead on the inside. But Adele didn't know his past, had no right to it.

"I want you to contact every vampire leader in the Quarter." The ones outside it had been doing their jobs, the vampires who looked up to them in no danger of slipping the leash into carnage. "Tell them they are to be at the Tower on the stroke of six." It was a risk to push the meet to later in the day, but he was making a judgment call that news of the summons would have an immediate and permanent chilling effect on the rising bloodlust. "Lateness is strongly discouraged."

Adele raised an eyebrow. "You plan to put the fear of Dmitri in them?"

Dmitri knew he could be ruthless; it was an asset. The current situation, however, required stronger firepower. "The audience isn't with me, Adele. Raphael has requested their presence." He'd spoken to Raphael the previous night, when the reports first came in, received the go-ahead to take this action if he deemed it necessary—because the archangel who was his friend caused bone-deep fear in mortals and immortals both.

"It appears," Dmitri purred to a rapidly paling Adele, "that the Made need to be reminded that the Tower never stops watching."

Adele's swallow was audible. "Who will die tonight?" she asked on a whisper of sound.

"All those who have forgotten that they are not the apex predators in this city."

# 29

Felicity's apartment building, blackened with the grit and smog of the city, had the downtrodden look of a woman who'd once been beautiful but had long since surrendered to the march of time. She didn't even bother with makeup: window coverings were absent or hanging in a lopsided way, and at least a third of the dirty panes of glass had cracks running through them. Two had given in to the pull of gravity and were totally missing, the holes covered up with black plastic.

A tenant on the third floor had made an effort—Ashwini could see greenery against the window, what looked like the curling tendrils of a luxuriant fern. The attempt at beauty only threw the decrepitude of the rest of the building into sharp focus. That lack of care was visible inside as well. Graffiti crawled across the walls just inside the entranceway, and the scuff marks on the linoleum floor had worn through to the concrete.

"I understand why she wanted out." The leaden despair soaked into the concrete and glass and wood of the building was powerful enough to brush against her senses, but far, *far* beneath, she could almost glimpse tiny, struggling seeds of hope.

Felicity had planted one of those seeds, would've given hope to her neighbors when she made it out. Seeing this, feeling the fragility that lay underneath the hardened surface, it made the cruelty of what had been done to the young woman even worse. Not only had the monster who'd killed her stolen her life, he'd made a mockery of her spirit. "The person responsible for Felicity's torture and death deserves every circle of hell."

"We will ensure he—or she—ends up roasting for a long, long time." Janvier nodded to the left, to a sign that, judging from the richness of the ink, had been recently defaced by a blue marker that told the reader to "Fock of!" It'd be funny if it wasn't so sad. Below the misspelled profanity was the word *Office* and an arrow pointing down the corridor.

"I do not have high hopes of anyone actually being in the office," Janvier said, "but the world is full of surprises."

"Most of them bloody and nasty and deadly." Walking with him down the narrow corridor, Ashwini took the dimly lit stairs down to a basement level. In front of her was a closed door plastered with advertising flyers, neighborhood promos by people struggling to create a sense of community in this hopeless place, and small posters asking for help in finding lost pets. Raising her hand, she rapped on the door with her knuckles.

To her astonishment, it opened almost immediately to reveal a big, bearded guy with skin so sallow it was clear soaking up the sun wasn't his favorite pastime.

"Yeah?" He scowled before Ashwini could identify herself and spoke again. "You're a hunter. Which schmuck vamp is hiding out here?"

Perceptive, she thought. He might actually be of some help. "No vamp," she said, "but we have questions about a former tenant."

The man, who appeared to be in his early thirties, scratched his belly, the size of it hinting at a love of beer and fast food. "Right. Come in." Backing away from the door, he waved them into an office that held a television set currently showing a rerun of a crime show, a sagging sofa with denim upholstery, a desk buried under paper, and several rickety chairs.

He switched off the TV and said, "You want to sit?"

Not sure the chairs would hold, Ashwini shook her head.

"You're the super?" she asked to make certain—for all she knew, he could be the owner.

Reaching up, he scratched his jaw this time, the frizzy black curls of his beard rasping against his skin. "Ah, yep, had the gig going on ten years now," he said. "Name's Seth. I'm a student—on my second doctorate, so this job's great, especially since it comes with a room out back." He made a face. "I do what I can, fix what I can, but the owners don't give me much money, so I have to let the inessential stuff—like the endless fucking graffiti—go." Rubbing his hands over his face, he blew out a breath. "But you didn't come here to listen to me moan. Who's the tenant?"

"Felicity Johnson."

His animated face froze, then crumpled noticeably. "Aw, damn, something happened to her, didn't it? I knew she'd never leave Taffy like that."

"I'm afraid she was murdered." Ashwini watched him for any signs of possible guilt as she delivered the news, saw only pain.

"Who'd do that?" A bewildered question. "She was no threat to anyone."

"You remember her," Janvier said, leaning against the door he'd closed.

"Yeah, she was sweet. Real nice." His sallow face even more pale and his previously steady body swaying a fraction, he took a seat behind his desk. "You sure it's her?"

"We haven't yet been able to run DNA or find a fingerprint match," Ashwini said more gently than she might have before witnessing his reaction, "but yes, we believe it's her." It was too much to hope that Felicity's room remained untenanted, but if Seth had kept her tenancy application, then fingerprints might be a possibility.

"Most tenants in a place like this," the super said, staring at his overflowing desk, "they get so hard, so angry with life that they just want someone to blame—I'm an easy target. But Felicity isn't . . . wasn't like that." A shaky smile. "When I fixed her door after it threatened to fall off its hinges, she baked me muffins. I never had fresh-baked muffins before."

Another glimpse of who Felicity had been, another stab of

fury at the person who'd ended the life of a woman with stars in her eyes. "Who's Taffy?"

"Oh, Taffy . . . was her cat."

Deciding to risk it, Ashwini flipped around one of the chairs and sat with her arms along the back. "How long ago did Felicity leave?"

"Well, 'bout eight months ago she started going away for a day or two. She asked me to check in on Taffy, that's how come I know."

That fit with Sina's account of when Felicity had met her mysterious rich boyfriend. "Go on."

"Then she started staying away for longer and longer." He swallowed, his voice hoarse. "I figured she'd give up her lease, but she didn't, popped in and out until about six months ago."

*One more month, we're closer by one more month,* Ashwini thought on a fierce wave of exultation, but didn't interrupt the desolate man.

"The last couple of times I saw her, maybe two weeks apart," Seth said, his eyes bleak, "she didn't look so good. See, the thing with Felicity was, no matter how bad it got, no matter how low she was on funds—" He broke off, started again. "I cut her a bit of slack now and then. Gave her a little extra time to get the rent to me; I knew she'd be good for it."

He shook his head. "Anyway, the thing was, she was always happy, you know? Like a bunny or something. All peppy and shit." His shoulders began to shake, sudden tears rolling down his face. His sobs were loud, harsh, and real, a dam that had burst without warning.

Janvier ran his hand over her hair before she could reach out to the distraught man, then moved past her to squeeze Seth's shoulder. He returned to his previous position only when the other man began to calm.

"Sorry," the super gasped out, lifting the bottom of his T-shirt to wipe his face. "I kept hoping that she was living the high life on a yacht in the Mediterranean or something, but I knew, I *knew* she wouldn't leave Taffy."

A meow sounded right then. A small gray cat slid through the gap in the door behind the desk on its heels. Seth's face crumpled again at the sight of the cat, but he pulled himself together on a shuddering breath. "Come 'ere, Taffy," he said, and the cat jumped up into his lap. "She's as sweet as Felicity. I never was a cat guy, but then Felicity didn't come back . . ." Shoulders slumped, he petted the purring animal.

"I'm sorry." The words were inadequate, but they were all she had until they tracked down the person who'd hurt Felicity.

"I want to help," Seth said, wiping the back of his hand over his eyes and lifting his head. "Felicity, I never saw her down, you know? But those last two times, it was like she was . . . fading. As if someone was stealing her spirit." A vein pulsed along his temple. "I asked her if her boyfriend was hitting her, but she said she'd just given too much blood."

"So," Ashwini said, thinking through what he'd shared, "she wasn't really living here those last months but she never took Taffy?"

"No, said her guy didn't like cats. I told her no man was worth giving up Taffy, but she just laughed." He petted the cat again, the repetitive action easing the tension in his body. "I couldn't figure out why she kept the apartment, wasted her money. She knew I'd take care of Taffy if she really needed it . . . I hope she knew."

"I think she did." To Ashwini, Felicity's actions said the other woman had felt safe here, and that she'd had enough misgivings about her new life to cling to that safety as long as she could. "Can you remember the exact date of the last time you saw her?"

"No, but I can find it." Opening a big black diary scrawled with so many notations, Ashwini didn't know how he made sense of it, he backtracked until he found the note of her visit. "No, it was shredded," he said when Ashwini asked about the tenancy agreement. "Did you want to look at her things instead?"

Ashwini's heart kicked. "You kept them?" Felicity's belongings could provide a near-foolproof source of DNA and/or fingerprints.

"The landlord sold off most of it to pay the back rent after she didn't come back," Seth said, "but I went in beforehand and gathered up the stuff I knew meant something to her. Rest of it was furniture she got from Goodwill, few clothes and books."

"It'd be helpful if we could take Felicity's things with us."

Getting up at Ashwini's reply, Seth retrieved the slain woman's belongings from the back room. "I hid it there in case the landlord figured out I saved stuff for her." His face crumpled again. "I kept hoping she'd come back."

He placed the pitifully small box on the table in front of Ashwini, then sat down and rubbed Taffy's head with his fingers when the cat returned to her perch on his lap. "After you're done . . . could I maybe have the picture in the red frame? It's of us after we went out to a ball game one time with some other friends."

That was when she understood the keening note of anguish beneath his sadness. It was love. Felicity had been deeply loved and had never known it . . . or perhaps she had, but was unable to reciprocate it for reasons of her own. People didn't always love who they should, or the ones who were good for them. "I'll make sure you get it back," she said.

"Her funeral . . ."

"Do you know Sina, Carys, and Aaliyah?"

A jerky nod. "I'll talk to them, take care of Felicity."

So many lives, Ashwini thought, Felicity had touched so many lives.

Not able to leave Seth sitting there alone with the cat in his arms and tears in his eyes, she said, "Do you have family in the city? Friends?"

"Yeah." A rough answer. "But I need to be alone right now. I need to try to understand it."

Ashwini didn't have the heart to tell him there could be no understanding this. Leaving him to his grief, she didn't say anything until they'd stowed the box of Felicity's belongings in the car. Their first stop afterward was the Guild forensics lab, where a senior technician looked in the box and commandeered a black picture frame he said had a good surface for prints.

It held an image of Felicity standing on a rooftop, her arms raised and feet spread as she looked toward the Tower. A classic tourist shot—and Felicity, she looked so young and brimming with hope.

The forensic tech also took a small hairbrush with a carved

wooden handle. "I can see several hairs we might be able to use for DNA . . . yes, the follicle is attached," the bespectacled man said as he meticulously picked the strands out.

Meanwhile, the no-nonsense woman who took care of fingerprints lifted several from the picture frame. A number were too big to be Felicity's, likely Seth's. But the smaller ones matched the body they'd found. To confirm, the tech also printed an ID card from a fast-food chain that had Felicity's name and face on it.

"No doubt, it's a match," she said.

The DNA would put the final stamp on the identification, but there was no longer any question in Ashwini's mind that Felicity Johnson was their victim.

Taking the rest of Felicity's belongings, she turned to Janvier. "Let's go to a pretty place to look at this." It seemed an insult to Felicity's hopes to do it in such hard, clinical surroundings.

"I know a spot," Janvier said, and they headed back to his car.

Watching the city pass by, the snow ground into ice and dirt in places, pristine in others, she kept her silence. There was no need to speak. She'd seen the same grim sorrow that lived in her heart on Janvier's face. When he pulled into a parking garage near Chelsea Market, she thought he meant for them to go into a tea shop inside, but he led her through to the High Line.

Originally elevated railway tracks used by freight trains, the area had been converted into a living green space. Summer days and nights saw it filled with New Yorkers out to grab a little sun, take a stroll, or just hang out. And it wasn't popular only with mortals and vampires. Angels liked to drop by, often sitting on the specially reinforced railings, their wings hanging over the sides. Ashwini had once seen two of them eating ice cream and watching the stream of yellow taxis below while a curious boy of about seven leaned on the railing beside them and asked a million questions.

Long grasses and wildflowers, trailing vines set up on trellises, innovative pieces of sculpture in among the greenery, the mood of the High Line changed at the whim of the gardeners and curators, making it a place that was new again and again and again. Then there were the birds and the butterflies, their song and color filling the air on sunlit summer days.

The sunshine today couldn't banish the cold snow on the deep wooden seats where people liked to lounge in warmer weather, but it remained a pretty place surrounded by the pulsing heart of the city. The gardeners allowed the plants and trees to grow freely in winter, so that instead of the barren lines of a manicured park, here there were waving grasses that had beaten the snow with grit and resilience, bare tree limbs stark against the sky.

Janvier placed the box of Felicity's belongings on a small wooden block that he brushed free of snow, then walked toward a winter-barren tree in the center of the garden. "Come here, *cher*. Look at this."

Joining Janvier under it, she sucked in a gasped breath. A delicate and secretive new sculpture had been added to the tree. Tiny bronze fairies sat on the branches, peeked out of a small hole in the trunk, tiptoed along in readiness to pounce on friends who sat gossiping. Each was exquisite in its detail, its features unique.

"Did you know it was here?" she asked, heart aching at the ephemeral beauty of the piece—because visitors who glimpsed the secret wouldn't be able to resist; they'd take a fairy or two home as a treasure.

"It's one of Aodhan's," Janvier told her. "He put it here three nights past with Illium's help. He says they are for taking—tiny sparks of laughter caught in bronze, meant to travel where wonder will bear them." Picking up a fairy who sat with her chin in her hands, her face expressive with delight at the world before her, he gave it to Ashwini. "For when Felicity is put to rest. I think it suits a woman who was never sad."

Ashwini pressed a kiss to his cheek on a wave of raw emotion and tucked the tiny creature carefully into her pocket, making sure the fairy's face popped out so she could continue to drink in the world. Then, brushing aside the snow from a couple of the seats, they sat opposite one another, the wooden block between them.

Though tall buildings looked down on them, Ashwini didn't feel enclosed. The rush of traffic, the car horns, and the fragmented conversations that drifted up from the street, added to the bite in the air, the shadow of angel wings on the snow as a squadron passed overhead, it all spoke of freedom. This was a good place to step into Felicity's past, to see who she'd been before a monster decided to treat her as disposable.

Ashwini lifted the lid off the box.

# 30

Felicity's box held an impossibly small amount for an entire life.

A pretty gold chain with a heart-shaped locket sat inside a decorative wooden box with a blue velvet lining. Opening the locket, Ashwini saw pictures of a man and woman who looked to be in their fifties or early sixties. "Probably her grandparents."

There were three more photos. The one of Seth with Felicity, both of them laughing and waving foam fingers in the air with one hand, the other closed around hot dogs bursting with all the fixings. Felicity was beaming at the camera, Seth at her. "She knew," Ashwini said, running a thumb over the red of the frame to brush away a fleck of dust. "She couldn't look at this photograph and not know how he felt about her."

Janvier picked up the second-to-last photograph, its frame sparkly pink. "This one, too, holds those who loved her." He turned it to show her an image of Felicity with Carys, Sina, and Aaliyah, the four women laughingly holding up pretty-colored drinks at a bar. Felicity was wearing a body-hugging white dress and had a silky-looking scarf of sunny yellow around her neck, purple butterflies on the fabric. She looked young and pretty and happy.

The last photograph was of the older couple in the locket again. Ashwini traced the tractor in the background, took in the endless turned earth, caught the glint of a shovel in the corner of the frame, the sun lines that marked the faces of the two smiling people who looked out of the image. "She was a country girl."

Janvier's eyes became chips of malachite, hard and icy. "One who came to the city to make a better life for herself, find a man who'd offer her the security she craved."

"Except she found a predator instead." It was too common a story, the predators as often human as immortal, but that didn't mean each and every victim didn't deserve justice.

Her resolve firm, Ashwini returned to the contents of the box. A small figurine of a cat chasing a ball, chipped in one corner, a white teapot with pretty blue flowers, and a pen from a chain hotel sat on top of a shoe box filled with stubs and papers. Setting the shoe box aside for the moment, Ashwini and Janvier went through the rest.

It wasn't much. More inexpensive ornaments that had meant something to Felicity, but that she'd been too embarrassed to bring into her new "home." Given what Ashwini knew of Felicity's nature by now, she was certain the shame and embarrassment had been fostered in her by another.

The woman who'd been cheerful and hopeful and bouncy as a bunny, the woman who'd had every intention of inviting her working-girl friends to tea in her Vampire Quarter house, wouldn't have felt it herself without outside pressure.

"That's it," Janvier said after removing two books from the box.

There were no notations on the dog-eared pages, no scraps of paper hidden within.

"Shoe box," she said, hoping against hope that Felicity had left them a thread to tug, a trail to follow.

"She didn't keep a proper grocery list." Ashwini showed Janvier how Felicity had scribbled herself a reminder to buy milk around a recipe she'd ripped out of a magazine. "But she was compulsive about her finances." Those documents were neatly bound by a rubber band.

"When you are poor," Janvier said, "you never forget the value of money, *non*?"

Ashwini ran her finger under the rubber band. "I was never poor, except for the time I was on my own." She'd always remember the day she ran from Banli House, racing from the terror of it in flimsy slippers not meant for gravel and tarmac. The soles of her feet had been bloodied lumps of meat afterward, tiny stones embedded into her flesh.

The pain hadn't mattered. She'd found the lonely dark of the road, waved a truck to a stop, and taken her life in her hands when she'd jumped into the cab. Better, she'd thought in her panicked and angry state, to die in freedom at the hands of a maniac truck driver than end up insane in the prison of Banli.

As it was, the driver hadn't been a maniac. He'd just been a lonely man who wanted some conversation on the road and who hadn't seen any reason not to give her a ride to her grandma's home out of state. Of course, Ashwini didn't have a grandparent out of state, but it had been as good a story as any.

"On your own at fifteen, *cher*," Janvier said gently. "I think you understand the meaning of poor."

Ashwini thought of how she'd begged her way into a dishwashing job at the diner where the trucker had dropped her off, her wages paid in meals. She'd slept rough in the woods nearby, moved on after a bare three days, afraid she hadn't run far enough. By then, she'd scoped out the drivers who patronized the diner, deliberately using her ability for the first time in her life to separate the good from the bad. And the good ones took her far enough away that she'd finally felt safe.

"The funny thing is," she said, her eyes on the shoe box, "I ran in the opposite direction to Felicity."

"A rural area?"

Ashwini nodded. "I'd seen a documentary, knew the big fruit orchards always needed fruit pickers." She'd timed her escape for summer, conscious she'd never make it in winter without the right gear. "I turned up and worked hard and lived in a barn or two to save money for winter. I snuck in after everyone else went home, snuck out before the farmers woke up."

"Will you tell me how you came to the Guild?" Janvier asked, his voice dark music that seduced and coaxed and made her feel alive.

Ashwini let the music sink into her bones as she opened the door into the past. "I was three months into my new life and out of work when Saki found me asleep in her parents' barn. She was the toughest woman I'd ever met"—all honed strength and patience—"but instead of kicking me out, she sat down on a hay bale and asked me why I thought this existence was better than home."

Janvier watched her with a quiet intensity. "You told her the truth."

"Yes." To this day she didn't know why, but that conversation had changed the course of her life. "She told me about the Guild, said my independence and resilience would stand me in good stead."

The choice had been easy; it was the first time in her life anyone had said she might succeed at something without having to alter her very nature. "It sounded too good to be true, and I was sure they'd reject me, but they didn't." Her defiant facade had cracked at the acceptance, left her exposed to Saki's keen eyes. That was when the other woman had taught her the first rule of the Guild: *Your fellow hunters will always have your back. We will never use what we know about you against you.*

"I was scared to return to New York to attend the Academy, afraid Arvi would put me back in Banli House. But . . . I missed my brother, too." Love was never uncomplicated; she could hate Arvi and love him at the same time. Once, she'd tried to tell herself that she felt nothing, but the lie had been too big to carry. "The Guild psychologist was the one who made sure I wouldn't be committed again. So I came home, did everything in my power to be a normal teenager."

"And your brother?" Janvier asked softly. "Did you see him on your return?"

Ashwini's mind flashed back to that instant so many years ago when Arvi slammed into the conference room at Guild HQ. She'd never forget the wild look in his eyes, his hair a tumble and his jaw shadowed with a coarse beard.

He'd stopped halfway to her, his chest heaving. "You're safe. Alive."

The agonizing relief in those words would live with Ashwini forever. "Yes," she'd whispered, her hand clenching on the back of a chair as she stared across the gulf between them. She'd wanted to run into his arms and she'd wanted to punch and scream at him, the equally powerful urges crashing up against each other to lock her feet to the floor. "I would've died in that place."

Arvi had flinched. "I was trying to save you."

"I know." Thanks to Saki, she also knew he'd filed a missing persons report on her, had hired countless private investigators in an effort to find her. Not only that, but he'd been personally talking to every bus driver and train conductor he could find, in the hope that someone might remember her. "Thank you for searching for me." It had been her fear, and yet to know that he had, that he hadn't simply written her off . . . it made her want to cry despite the confusion and anger inside her.

Arvi's expression had been stark. "There was never any question."

That was the only time the two of them had ever spoken of what he'd done by putting her in Banli House. "Yes," she told Janvier now. "I saw Arvi." Throat thick, she swallowed. "He'd looked for me," she said simply, unable to face the tangled knot of emotions incited by the memory. "But he didn't stand in my way when it came to the Guild, didn't try to reassert guardianship."

Safe from the threat of committal, Ashwini had narrowed her focus to her Guild studies, determined to forget the other part of her existed. Having learned the truth about Tanu and her mother by then—after confronting Arvi a month after her return—she'd seen her "gift" as a curse that had destroyed her family and she'd wanted no part of it. "I was nineteen before I accepted who I was, what I had inside me." It was seeing Tanu behind a locked door one day that had done it; she'd vowed she'd never be so trapped . . . and realized she'd imprisoned herself.

Janvier's smile was faint, his eyes dark. "So many years in so short a story. One day, you will tell me the rest of it."

Ashwini shrugged. "I was luckier than a million others."

"And the predators?" Janvier asked, tone quiet but shoulders tense. "You must've been a beautiful girl, tall and long limbed."

"More like skinny and dirty." Not that such things stopped the monsters. "I had a couple of close calls—ironically not from the strangers I was so vigilant about, but from two of the farm laborers I'd gotten to know over the summer."

One man had cornered her in a disused drying shed she'd

thought to use for sleep, while another had grabbed her in the
fields when she'd made a mistake and been the last one to leave.
"But I'd been a cornered animal once before," she said to the
vampire who had death in his eyes right now. "I still had that
feral strength in me, along with the knives I'd bought with my
first bits of money."

Janvier's expression didn't soften. "These men didn't wish
to make trouble for you after you hurt them?"

"They may have, but I hopped a freight train to another farm
state the same night in both cases. I knew I couldn't win against
them." The helplessness had grated at her, but her survival
instincts had won out over pride.

"I feel a compulsion to visit these areas."

"No need. I went back when I was a fully trained hunter.
Neither will bother another girl ever again." At Janvier's raised
eyebrow, she said, "They're not dead, just . . . out of commission in certain bodily functions."

"Good." A slow, dangerous smile, before Janvier bent his
head to the papers again. "The spreadsheets stop seven months
ago, so she didn't do one for the last month Seth saw her alive."

"She may finally have become totally dependent on the
bastard who killed her."

Eyes narrowing, Janvier passed her a ticket stub that had
become stuck inside the financial documents. "Opera. Nothing
Felicity could afford and the performance was in that final
month."

Ashwini took it, eyes on the bar code. "Good chance we
can track this."

Nodding, Janvier went back to the financial documents
while she combed through the other pieces of paper.

"Her income goes down over the last five weeks of record
keeping," he said a few minutes later. "Far as I can see, that's
when she stopped doing her cleaning jobs."

Ashwini turned over the stub for an art house movie. No
bar code. No way to chase down a single patron from six and
a half months ago. Setting it aside, she said, "The sugar daddy
convinced her to quit, but was generous on his terms." Paying
for things but giving her no financial independence. "Seems
like something an abuser would do."

"Controlling her under a veneer of devotion." Janvier's jaw

muscles moved. "He has done this before. It was too smooth an operation."

"Yes." The realization that Felicity hadn't been the first, the other victims lost and forgotten, infuriated her. "Opera, art house flick, receipt for a designer dress—" She frowned, looked at the total. "Five grand, paid in cash." It must've been a prop, meant to draw Felicity deeper into the spider's web. Five thousand was loose change for an old, rich vampire.

"Either an old vampire uneasy with other methods of payment," Janvier said, "or a young one showing off."

"I'd go for old with how well orchestrated this was, how *patient*, but why limit it to vampires?" She raised an eyebrow. "Angels can be even more twisted." Nazarach had taught her that. "Could be an angel is behind this and the vampire who bit her is simply the one who did the dirty work."

"I'll do some discreet digging, see if any angel is known for tastes that might have morphed into this kind of ugliness." Opening a bank statement still in its envelope, as if it had come after Felicity last visited her apartment, he stopped. "She bought something at a store that's unusually high end for a woman with as little income as Felicity. Maxed out her credit card . . . and that card was paid off in full a few weeks later."

Ashwini glanced at the charge, saw the reference, and looked up at the billboard plastered on the wall of a building a block down. "A man's watch," she said, blood a roar in her ears. "She bought the bastard a gift."

Janvier followed her gaze. "He's cold, calculated. Banks can be worse than cops, so he made sure they wouldn't come looking."

"But a store like that," she said on the wave of her rage, "will have surveillance." Maybe, just maybe, the monster had been with Felicity when she bought the gift.

# 31

Four hours after his visit to the Quarter, Dmitri finished his call with Astaad's second—who had the bad taste to be sleeping with Michaela, but was otherwise sane—and walked up to the roof. He and Raphael needed to discuss the upcoming meeting with the vampire leaders.

As he'd predicted, the bloodlust had begun to cool the instant the order rippled through the vampire community. Seven of the leaders had contacted him already, the tremor in their voices barely hidden. "Please tell the sire I have taken care of the problem," had been the message of each, though the exact words may have differed.

It was too little too late. What Raphael needed from Dmitri was to know the names of the worst offenders, the ones who had encouraged the lack of discipline through their own actions or inaction. It hadn't taken Dmitri long to gather that information, not with the reports recently filed by Trace and Janvier, as well as input from Illium about the Made who wielded the most authority over others.

Dmitri had also had a long and interesting conversation with Adele that had clarified certain matters. She might refuse to join the Tower officially, but Adele's loyalties were unquestionable—and she knew as well as he did that punishment could not be avoided once the crime had been committed. While Raphael wasn't capricious or brutal without cause, he was also ruthless when it came to maintaining order in his territory.

Bloodlust equaled carnage. It would never be acceptable.

However, when Dmitri exited out into the glassed-in enclosure that housed the elevator, he was surprised to find Naasir and Elena on the other side. They were using the flat surface of the roof as a training ground and going at each other no holds barred. No, he thought after a second glance, that wasn't true. Naasir wasn't moving with anywhere near his ordinary speed.

It wasn't because he'd been injured that morning—the wound had looked bad, but was comparatively minor relative to Naasir's age and strength. No, it was because the two of them were still gauging each other's strength.

"She calls him a tiger creature."

Dmitri turned to the archangel who'd come up behind him. Raphael didn't use the elevators, so he had to have used the stairs. That, too, was highly unusual. Dmitri guessed he hadn't wanted to fly up, disrupting the practice session outside. "Well, she's heading in the right direction." Naasir's Making was a unique and terrible thing. "He did actually tell her several truths at dinner."

Lips curving, Raphael kept his eyes on Elena and Naasir. They were stepping it up now, Elena's knives slicing faster as Naasir moved with a swift grace that was fascinating to watch. Venom was as fast, but more sinuous, with the startling and jagged speed of a viper. Naasir's strikes were fluid, feline, and oddly stealthy for being so feral.

"She's holding her own—that's something." Elena had once slit Dmitri's throat on a busy Manhattan street, so the hunter had considerable skill, but she was up against a very dangerous vampire of over six hundred with nowhere to run; she couldn't even take off fast enough to avoid Naasir. "You have warned Naasir that she's not yet fully immortal?" The other male wouldn't fatally hurt her on purpose, but he might not realize he was doing so without an advance caution.

"Yes." Raphael's smile deepened. "Even with having to restrain himself, he's laughing. You know what that means."

"He's enjoying himself." There were an extremely limited number of people who could put that look on Naasir's face, especially in a sparring session. "It's because she's as unpredictable as he is. No rules, just do what's needed." That balanced out the fact that Elena wasn't strong enough to take his blows at full strength.

"Her sessions with Janvier have honed that aspect of her hand-to-hand combat skills."

"Good." Dmitri was the one who'd recommended Elena train with Janvier. The Cajun was one hell of a street fighter and Elena needed every skill she could learn; a considerable number of people would like to see her dead. She was, after all, a living, breathing manifestation of Raphael's heart.

Continuing to watch the session outside, he slipped his hands into the pockets of his black pants. "Trace got in touch earlier." The elegant vampire with his taste for poetry and art had healed enough to take over the watch on Khalil a couple of hours back, only to have to hand it off to Emaya and Mateo forty-five minutes ago. "He found the Umber dealer—unfortunately, it appears the man's head was separated from his body late last night.

"Trace believes his supplier didn't like the fact that he couldn't keep his mouth shut, and I agree with him." Whoever was behind this did not want to be famous or to have his name known to the Tower. "The dealer himself was low-level scum who was in all probability chosen for his contacts among the bored and the rich. I don't expect Trace to find anything to connect the dealer with his supplier."

Raphael's expression changed to the merciless focus that made him a member of the Cadre. "It's no coincidence this drug has made its appearance now."

"Yes. The weak fear what may yet come." The clash in the skies above New York had only been the first battle. "But the malaise is generally restricted to the cowardly pleasure seekers who scuttled into hiding rather than fight." Dmitri had been happy not to have to deal with their pathetic uselessness during the hostilities. "I am sorry about Rupert. He fought with courage. He must've taken the Umber in a moment of foolishness."

"Is his death and devolution chilling the ardor for the drug?"

"On the surface, but to some, the incident has lent it a deadly glamour." Russian roulette played with a crystalline substance, murderous bloodlust only a taste away. "If we don't shut off the pipeline, we'll have more incidents."

Raphael's eyes tracked Elena as she managed to swipe Naasir on the thigh, but got her wing twisted in the process. "A mistake," he murmured. "She won't do that again."

They watched the two outside for another minute before returning to their conversation.

"There's a chance this drug is another move by Charisemnon or a different member of the Cadre who seeks to weaken the city." The intense black of Raphael's hair gleamed blue-black in the light pouring through the glass. "I've spoken to Keir and he tells me a drug of such virulent effect on the Made would be near impossible to manufacture using known chemicals."

Dmitri agreed, especially since their own labs were having difficulty analyzing the compound. "The latest tests say it has an organic rather than manufactured base, but that doesn't get us much closer to breaking it down."

"Jason?"

"He's spread the word among his operatives—he'll have a report for us tonight from the other courts. So far, Umber appears to be a localized problem." Folding his arms, Dmitri met the violent blue of Raphael's eyes. "Of the vampire leaders, Severin and Anais are the worst offenders. Both have fed violently in public in the past two weeks." Not disallowed in and of itself, but a stupid choice at the present time.

The two had to have known their actions would embolden and incite others.

"It appears Anais and Severin wish to be my guests. Let's accommodate them after the meeting," Raphael said, his tone ice-cold. "The three of us will have a private discussion after I clear this Cadre matter."

"Michaela is truly continuing to insist that Lijuan's territory be taken and split up?"

"Yes, and now Charisemnon is threatening to declare war on her. No one is taking either one of them seriously, but it's a nuisance that needs to be handled."

"The Refuge?" Meant to be neutral ground, the home of

angelkind and the sanctuary of their young had suffered sporadic fighting during Lijuan's offensive. Galen and Venom had been forced to stay in the Refuge to defend Raphael's stronghold there against attack.

"It is safe," Raphael answered. "Michaela won't make the same mistake as Lijuan. She's far too smart and cunning, where Lijuan was arrogant."

Dmitri understood the difference. One relied on power, the other on manipulation and playing the tides right. "In many ways, Michaela is the perfect political animal. The vicious, manipulative kind who'd sell out her own mother to gain points."

"There is a reason you're my second, Dmitri."

"I was speaking to Dahariel earlier—I can't imagine why a man as intelligent as he is slides into bed with her."

"Have you told him that, like the spider that eats its mate, she has a habit of being the final woman her men ever touch?"

Dmitri felt his lips tug up at the corners. "I may have reminded him of the long-dead Archangel of Byzantium, and of the more recently departed Uram." He pointed beyond the window, where Naasir had Elena backed up to the very edge of the roof. "Perhaps you should intervene." An uncontrolled fall could smash her into the Tower.

"No, I think not."

Elena swiped Naasir's legs out from under him the next second and got herself back onto the main part of the roof. She was breathing hard, Naasir growling. Flipping over and to his feet, he clawed at her in seemingly undisciplined anger. Elena fell for it and was on the ground with Naasir's hand at her throat a heartbeat later.

She slapped the cold, hard surface and Naasir released her, reaching down to help her up. From Naasir, that was a compliment—it meant he'd found his opponent worthy enough that he was sticking around. Otherwise, he'd just walk away.

"Naasir won't want to leave." The other man could work apart from the others of the Seven, but his nature rebelled against long-term isolation from his family. "Venom isn't strong enough to permanently take his place in Amanat and we need the others here." It meant that of all the Seven, Naasir was the only one who'd be on his own—and he'd already been that way for ten months.

"Naasir may not wish to go," Raphael said, "but he will." An archangel's absolute confidence in one of his men. "He understands the need."

"Does he have a lover at least?" Naasir didn't do well without physical contact, especially when separated from Raphael and the others of the Seven, and his partner in Amanat, while lethal, was an ascetic who did not indulge in pleasures of the flesh.

Quiet amusement turned the Archangel of New York back into the man who had been Dmitri's friend for a thousand years. "He is a wild creature in an elegant, civilized city. What do you think his chances are?"

"He's drowning in women who're fascinated with him." No wonder Caliane was attempting to civilize him. "Your mother must fear he'll tempt one of her maidens away into danger."

"I've eased her mind on that point. Naasir may snack on the sweet and lovely, but when he chooses a mate, she will be a fierce creature with claws that bloody him and a heart as wild as his own."

Laughing because Raphael was right, Dmitri watched as, outside, Naasir took two of Elena's knives and pretended he didn't know what to do with them so Elena would show him how. "Be careful, Raphael," he said, well aware Naasir's loyalty was as unflinching as his own. "The tiger creature is flirting with your consort."

"Of course he is. She, too, is a fierce creature with a wild heart." Raphael pushed through the door, his hand snapping up to catch the knife Elena threw in his direction.

# 32

Janvier could tell Ashwini wanted to kick a hole in the wall when the officious man at the opera box office told them the tickets had been bought at the door, paid for in cash.

After having discovered that the jewelry store where the watch had been bought had wiped its surveillance footage, and the designer shop that had sold the five-thousand-dollar dress had no record of who'd bought it, it was the last straw.

"Damn it, it can't end like this," she said, every muscle in her body taut enough to snap. "This evil monster isn't going to get away with it!"

Cupping her face, he just held her, touched her.

At first, she almost vibrated against him, ready to tear away . . . but she didn't. Sliding his hands down to wrap his arms around her when she leaned into him, he held her close, her own arms wrapping around him in turn. They stood in silence, uncaring of the people who streamed past them on the sidewalk.

His heart hurt.

The things she'd told him, the future she'd predicted, it threatened to crush him.

*Full throttle,* he reminded himself. It was how they'd always lived, would live, to the last flicker of the flame that was his Ashblade's clever, vivid mind.

"Let's go for a walk," she said when she drew back after an unexpected kiss to his throat. "Clear our heads, try to think of other avenues to explore." Then, to his delight, she reached up and fixed the scarf that was about to slide off one side of his neck.

She scowled at the smile that creased his cheeks. "Don't try to hold hands."

So, of course he did. Not to tease her, but because it felt good to have her palm sliding against his . . . especially when she curled her fingers around his with a tug of her lips. It felt like coming home.

They walked through the businesspeople and the tourists, the occasional mother with a pram, the restaurant hawkers trying to talk them inside for a meal, the roadside stall owners calling out to them about "genuine imitation" gold watches and "faux designer" handbags. It was loud and chaotic and it was New York.

"I wasn't sure I would like this city," he said to her. "Yet the mad spirit of it has a way of getting under a man's skin."

"You miss the bayou, though, don't you?" Rich and dark, her eyes saw to the heart of him, and that was her right. "That old hut I tracked you to once—"

"You mean the place where you threatened to bury me in a swamp hole then douse me in fire ants?"

Ashwini bared her teeth at the taunting vampire who was the only person who'd ever totally "got" her. That time in the bayou, he'd answered the door barefoot and wearing jeans only partially buttoned, his body lazily relaxed as he leaned up against the doorjamb of the house surrounded by water on almost every side. The half-submerged cypress trees in that water had been lush with foliage and heavy with Spanish moss in the thick humidity, the landscape unearthly in its beauty.

A different, bright green moss had grown up the sides of the hut, turning it into a part of the bayou, and to the right she could see a hammock slung between two submerged trees with enough height to make it worthwhile. At any other time, she'd have climbed into that hammock and let out a sigh, happy to spend the afternoon watching the bayou water move slow and sinuous as a woman intent on seduction.

Right then, however, she'd been sorely tempted to shoot Janvier in the gut. "You made me traipse through the bayou for weeks," she muttered now. "Then, right when I had you, you made nice with the angel you'd pissed off." It wasn't the first time he'd done that, either. "You knew how mad that made me—why did you keep doing it?"

Lifting their clasped hands, he pressed a kiss to her knuckles. "I was courting you."

"Only someone with a twisted sense of humor would consider that a courtship." Turned out she was one of those people, but damn if she hadn't had fun when she didn't want to kill him. "I was going to ask if that place is yours."

"Yes. It is close to where I grew up." She saw him train a single look at a street thief who'd been eyeing them, and suddenly, the curly-haired teen with spotty skin decided he had to be across the road. "It is a simple, quiet place. There is no rush there, *non*?"

"Yes." She could imagine relaxing into the hammock with him, feeling all the cares of the world slide away. "Let's go there . . . after this is over. After Felicity can rest."

Eyes the shade of his homeland held hers, his accent evoking the lush, humid, haunting welcome of it as he said, "After Felicity can rest."

They kept walking, going nowhere in particular, the air cold in their lungs and the sunshine bright from a winter blue sky. When Ashwini's phone buzzed, she took it out with her free hand. "Guild confirmed her accounts have all been closed, and our contacts in banking say it appears she did it herself."

"Her killer talked her into it," Janvier said with absolute confidence. "Told her he'd take care of her, that if she loved him, she'd do as he asked."

Ashwini could almost hear the bastard convincing Felicity to do just that. Except . . . "She kept her apartment as long as she could, didn't give up her cat," she said slowly. "I bet you she set up an account somewhere else."

"Or," Janvier said, "left money with someone she trusted."

"No." Ashwini shook her head. "He'd cut her off from her

friends by that time. I'll get the Guild cyber-geniuses to search across all possible banking institutions."

She sent the message, but wasn't hopeful they'd find anything that'd lead them to Felicity's murderer—regardless of her attempts at maintaining her independence, it was clear the young woman had been almost totally dependent on her "lover" by the end. In all probability, she'd been imprisoned soon after she was last seen, giving her no chance to access any money she *had* managed to hide away.

"I'm going to quietly track down and talk to the servants who work in the houses of the angels and vampires who may be capable of such cruelty," Janvier said, the strokable mahogany of his hair lifting in the breeze. "Often, they are aware of more than their masters know."

It was a good idea. "I might be able to help with that. I generally come into contact with the younger vamps, and a lot of them are at the servant level."

"We'll make a list, start circulating." He was quiet for a minute. "*Cher*, something Aaliyah said is gnawing at me."

"About how the vamp ordered Felicity not to say anything about their being a couple until she had her 'makeover'?" That had been niggling at her, a sharp barb in her gut.

"Yes, exactly. I don't believe she was ever part of his official cattle, that he held that out as a lure—if she was good enough, pleased him enough, she'd become one of the chosen." A punishing edge in every word. "In the interim, he must've arranged to meet her outside his usual haunts, where there would be little chance he'd be seen with her."

The more Ashwini learned about the man who'd tortured and killed Felicity after suffocating her spirit, the more she hated him. "It puts all our suspects back in the pool." And still there remained the question of *how* he was causing fatal injuries so eerily similar to the results of Lijuan's feeding. "But the servant angle is still worth following—one may have noticed signs of a woman he or she never saw."

Janvier shoved a hand through his hair. "I wish we didn't have to tiptoe through this investigation. *Someone* had to have seen her with the bastard, if we could only ask!"

Even as he bit out the words, his eyes lingered on a giggling child who'd just tugged his mother to a window display, then took in a group of women clustered around a nearby café table, heads bent in laughing secrecy. "But to give Felicity justice, we would have to rip open the wounds of a city that has barely stopped bleeding."

Ashwini had no answers, torn between the same competing forces.

Eight hours later, keeping the details of Felicity's death under wraps was no longer an issue.

Having split from Janvier earlier to follow through with their plan of speaking to those who staffed the homes of the powerful and wealthy and cruel, Ashwini ran into the intensive care section of the hospital to find he'd beaten her there.

"Where is she?" It came out a gasp, her heart pumping; she'd received the call while at Guild HQ, giving Sara a progress report, had decided to leg it rather than try to negotiate the heavy traffic in a cab.

"In a room down the hall." Janvier's jacket was open over his black T-shirt, his scarf missing. "This way."

She fell into step with him. "Have you spoken to her?"

A shake of his head. "The physicians are with her. I think she'll react better to a woman, in any case."

Painfully conscious of what Janvier didn't say—the torture the woman may have suffered at male hands—Ashwini met the gaze of the angel who stood guard beside the closed door at the end of the hall, wings of silver-blue pressed against the wall. "You brought her here?"

"Yes," Illium said, his golden eyes colder than she'd ever seen them. "She ran out of Central Park, naked and screaming, collapsed on the street."

"Jesus." Ashwini thought of the bitter cold, the ice. "Hypothermia?"

"A hint of frostbite—I picked her up almost as soon as she was spotted."

Which meant she'd been dropped off somewhere nearby, abandoned close enough to traffic to get herself help and attention. Not, Ashwini thought, for her good, but because the sadistic monster behind this wanted it to be front-page news. It was eight now, so the victim had run out during the busy time when people were leaving work or heading out to dinner.

"The tracks circled back to another street entrance," Janvier said, answering the question she'd been about to ask.

"Of course they did," she muttered. "Security cameras?"

"I alerted the Tower and Guild teams to go through any feeds they could find," Janvier said. "So far, nothing."

Ashwini girded her stomach. "How bad?"

Illium had parted his lips to answer when the door was pulled open from the inside and a tall, thin vampire with sandy brown hair, and aristocratic features in a pale-skinned face stepped out. He was wearing green scrubs, held a chart in one hand. "She's lost over half the blood in her body," he said, shoving a hand through his hair, leaving it standing on its ends. "However, that doesn't explain her appearance. I've never seen its like and I've been a physician for lifetimes."

Ashwini could feel the vampire's age pressing against her skin, knew he had to be at least seven hundred years old. "Is there anything you can tell us?"

"Nothing useful."

Another doctor stepped out then, a mortal woman, her hair a silver cap vivid against the deep brown of her skin. "The poor girl." Pressing the bridge of her nose between thumb and forefinger, she met each of their intent looks in turn. "One of you can go in, but we had to sedate her to get her to stop screaming, so I'm not sure how much sense you'll get out of her."

Janvier and Illium stayed outside while Ashwini went in. Closing the door behind her with a quiet snick and steeling herself for what she might see, she faced the bed. They'd put the victim in a private room with a sprawling view of the field of fallen stars that was the night-draped city. The woman on the bed, however, wasn't concerned with the scenery.

She lay flat on her back, staring up at the ceiling with dull brown eyes that were sharply slanted. Paired with the knife-edge cheekbones that now pushed painfully against her skin, those eyes would've given her a feline kind of beauty once, stunning and sensual. Her only flaw, for those who would see it that way, was the birthmark that covered the left side of her face and part of her neck, the color dark as port wine.

Once again, the killer had chosen a woman who may well have been vulnerable, a target wounded by the world until she'd been willing to overlook the danger signs in hope of love and safety.

Her face had shrunken in on itself, the majority of her skin a papery white that appeared leathery from a distance; Ashwini was certain that was an illusion, that it would prove as thin and brittle as Felicity's. The woman's fingernails were cracked and broken, her frame emaciated, and her black hair so thin, it felt as if a touch would turn it to dust.

A bandage covered her throat, the flesh below no doubt torn and ripped.

When Ashwini gently lifted the sheet, she saw bruises and bite marks on every inch of skin exposed by the thin hospital gown. That, however, was where the resemblance to Felicity ended. Where Felicity had been a mummified husk, this woman still had some blood in her body, some flesh on her bones. As if she'd escaped before the process was complete.

Ashwini was certain she'd been released on purpose.

Replacing the sheet, careful not to nudge the IV lines that dripped into the woman, she said, "I'm Ash. My job is to find out who did this to you. Help me."

No response.

Not about to give up, she grabbed a chair from the corner and took a seat beside the bed. Then she started talking about Felicity, about what they'd found so far. "This," she said at the end, "what the bastard's done to you, what he did to Felicity, it isn't right and it needs to be stopped."

Nothing.

Ashwini wasn't even sure the victim had blinked the entire time she'd been talking. Accepting that perhaps the woman simply couldn't reply, that she'd been broken on too deep a level, Ashwini rose to her feet and put the chair back where it had been. However, when she would've left the room, something made her turn back.

No change, not even a whisper, and yet . . .

She returned to the bed, stared at the hand that lay so fragile and emaciated inches from her. It hadn't been visible when she'd replaced the sheet. "Speak to me," Ashwini whispered, but the woman continued to stare up at the ceiling.

Yet her hand, it lay in front of Ashwini like an invitation.

Throat working and skin hot, she flexed and unflexed her own hand. Her instincts screamed that she had permission, that the woman trapped in that shell of a body was crying out to her on a frequency no one else could hear. Still, she hesitated. This wouldn't be like with old and wise Keir, or with the young and teary-eyed teenager who'd discovered Felicity's body.

Whoever this woman had once been, she'd carry horror in her veins now.

Ashwini had never told Honor, never would, but after Honor's abduction, there'd been so many screams in her body that the noise had been deafening, a howling terror that swamped Ashwini. She'd thrown up from the pummeling force of it more than once, but she'd sat with Honor at the hospital night after night regardless, her hand locked tight with her best friend's.

Honor had *survived* that vile darkness, had needed Ashwini to be strong enough to fight its echoes, be at her side.

As this woman did now.

"I'm here," Ashwini said . . . and touched her fingertips to the back of the victim's hand.

# 33

The contact was a bruising punch to the stomach delivered by a fist of cold iron, one that knocked the breath right out of her. Then came the nausea, tied to an overwhelming and dread-laced panic that made her want to curl up into a ball in the corner and rock herself to oblivion. Breaking the contact, she braced her hands on the bed and sucked in desperate gulps of air.

"*Cher.*"

She'd sensed Janvier walk inside, didn't startle at his worried tone. "I don't know how to do this." It came out like broken glass, rough and jagged. "I don't know how to get past her terror."

Moving in so close that his body heat licked over her skin, Janvier picked up one of her hands and lifted it to his mouth in the way that had so quickly become familiar. The kiss was soft, a lazy seduction, and it had nothing to do with the ugliness that had consumed their victim. The gentle pleasure of it made the nausea retreat, her heart rate calm.

Lifting their clasped hands, she rubbed her cheek against the back of his hand.

"What if I stay?" he asked. "Will the touch anchor you?"

"I don't know." This was uncharted territory. "All my life, I've tried to minimize this, what I can do. Very rarely, I sense good things, but too many times, it's cruelty and evil. So I don't look, don't want to look."

"It is nothing to be ashamed of. No one can live life mired in horror."

How did he do that? See her so easily? "Sometimes I think I became a hunter so that I could ease my shame," she whispered. "That I choose to face physical danger because I can't face this."

"Yet," Janvier said, "I've heard other hunters say you saved their lives by warning them to take extra weapons or backup when the intel suggested no need for either."

"That's different. I know things now and then."

"And there are no nightmares? You pay no price for this knowledge?"

Ashwini couldn't hold his gaze. Because there had been dreams before each of her warnings to fellow hunters, dreams that had left her soaked in sweat, her heart racing so hard and fast that it had caused physical pain. "Stay," she said, her trust in him so deep, it was a part of her soul. "If . . . if it looks like I might start screaming, haul me away." It was her secret horror, that the madness might suck her under before she even knew it was there.

"Have I ever left? Hmm?" A slow smile that made her heart ache. "Even when you wished me to perdition. Or was it to a bog infested with leeches?"

"No, I'm pretty sure it was a pit filled with fresh elephant dung."

"Ah, we must be clear." Another kiss to her knuckles.

Centered by the playful interaction, she clenched her fingers on his and then she reached out with her other hand and closed it with infinite care over the exposed part of the victim's arm.

Again, the impact shoved into her like an ice pick to the brain. Every second of the terror and the pain the victim had endured, all of it concentrated into this agonizing and brutalizing force. Feeling her hand clamp down on Janvier's while remaining gentle on the victim's arm, Ashwini tried to see through the shriek of it but it was too viscous, too loud.

A bead of sweat formed on her temple, started to roll down.

Her stomach threatened to revolt. Stifling the urge with sheer effort of will, she shuddered and thought of Janvier, of the hunt through the bayou that had left her sticky and bad tempered and bitten by what felt like a thousand mosquitoes, forget about the other bugs.

The visceral memory cleared a pathway through the rage of screaming emotion, a thin ribbon of a road that was a verdant moss green. It didn't stop the panic, the horror, but the emotions formed a curving wall of terrible ugliness on either side of the road now, ready to smother her again should she falter in her will. Sucking in shallow breaths of air, Ashwini stepped on the road, followed it down . . . and then she was falling in a gut-churning spiral, the evil baying at her, mocking her.

Ashwini slid out one of her knives. *No one* was ever again going to imprison her. Slicing the howling darkness to shreds, she stepped out and . . . "Oh."

The woman who lay so motionless on the hospital bed was not as she was now, but as she must've been: that stunning face with its unique beauty, of medium height and curvy, with silky black hair down to her waist.

"Hello," Ashwini said. "I've been looking for you."

"We don't have much time. I'm going."

"No." Ashwini reached out, took her hand. "You'll make it."

The woman's smile was sad and resolute both, her shoulders firm. "No, I don't want to stay, don't want that life. I'm not what he made me."

Thinking of the shell on the bed, her bones as fragile as a bird's, her heart a flutter beneath Ashwini's touch, and her eyes hollow, Ashwini understood that this woman would never again live, even should her body survive. "Are you sure?"

"Yes." The victim's fingers grew thinner . . . No, they were fading. "Not enough time."

"Tell me his name." Ashwini fought to hold on to her for another heartbeat. "The one who hurt you."

"I don't remember." No distress, as if she'd traveled beyond that. "It's already gone. I know my name. Lilli Ying. I have a mother, a father. Please tell them I didn't suffer."

It was a lie, but a lie Ashwini would speak as if it were the truth. "I promise. Can you tell me anything about the person who hurt you?"

"The first monster wanted to cause us pain. It gave him sexual pleasure." A flicker of fear pierced the peace, was quickly erased. "But then . . . then the other one came, and it was worse." Her features faded, her voice a faraway whisper. "The other one had wings. And he drank my life from me."

"Wait, don't go!" Ashwini felt as if she were attempting to hold on to a wisp of air, a streamer of mist. "I need a trail to follow to find the monsters. Something. Anything!"

The echo of the victim tilted her head, looked at her a little blankly. But then she said, "It smelled like peanuts, where they kept me. Strange. Made me want peanut butter muffins. Peanuts. Such a big place that smelled of peanuts." The air dissipated, the words less than a memory of thought. "I have to go."

"Where?" Ashwini asked, the question one that haunted her after all the screams she'd touched in the world, all the pain she'd witnessed. "Is it a good place?"

Her only answer was a piercing beep that shattered the world into a million sharp, glittering shards.

Janvier easily took Ashwini's weight when she staggered back from the bed. Alarms sounded from all around them, the heart monitor showing a flat line. But the woman on the bed . . . she had a smile on her face, a final muscle movement made the instant before the alarms shrilled into high-pitched panic.

Holding Ash as the doctors rushed back in, he heard her whisper, "No, let her go," in a voice so hoarse, he only heard it because her breath kissed his jaw on the words. "She wants to go."

Janvier gave the order in a louder voice and, when the doctors hesitated, said, "I'll take full responsibility. Give her the peace she wants."

It was the mortal doctor who put her hand on the vampire physician. "He's right. She suffered too much trauma. We'd only prolong her pain if we managed to resuscitate her."

Shoulders falling, the vampire physician reached out and pressed several buttons.

The alarms went silent, the only sound Janvier could hear that of Ash's shallow breathing. Struggling to lift her lashes and failing, his Ashblade parted her lips, spoke again. "She said it smelled of p—" Her body became dead weight, her bruised mind losing the battle with consciousness.

Wrapping one arm around her waist, he held her upright so no one else would realize her condition. In the corridor, he didn't request that Illium fly her out. The blue-winged angel was a man Janvier would trust at his back anytime, but he was also an angel hundreds of years old, with memories Janvier couldn't hope to know and that might cause Ash further pain even in her unconscious state.

"Can you make sure the victim's body undergoes a thorough examination and autopsy?" he asked the other man instead. "Take her to the Guild morgue and to the pathologist who examined Felicity."

"I'll make sure it's done." Golden eyes took in Ash's lax body, the shimmer of perspiration on her skin. "Do you need a ride?"

Shaking his head, Janvier said, "Tell Dmitri I'm off the grid until I get back in touch."

A curt nod.

Thirty seconds later, Janvier had Ash in the elevator. Stabbing the button for the underground garage, he said, "Almost there, *cher*." For some unknown reason, he'd taken the car to his interviews when the bike would've been easier, the decision one he'd consider later. "Not that I'm complaining about having you pasted to me."

"Ha-ha." Her voice sounded weak and drugged, the words slurred. "Your hand . . ."

"You crushed it to pieces," he said against her temple, maintaining a rigid hold on his emotions. "Now you will have to kiss it better, inch by inch."

No sound, her body losing all tension again. Swinging her up into his arms, he stepped out of the elevator and strode straight to his car.

He'd never seen her like this, and he hated it. She wasn't meant to be so still, so lifeless. Ash was life and wickedness and wildness. Starting the engine after clipping in her seat belt, he drove not to his spacious Tower apartment but to her home. She'd be more comfortable in her nest, and, truth be told, he liked it, too. The Tower didn't have the scent of home for him.

It didn't have the scent of her.

At her building, he parked in the same space her doorman had used the previous night. It took him a bare two minutes to carry her to the elevator and get into her apartment after he dug out the key he knew she carried in her left jeans pocket. Placing her on the bed, he tugged off her boots and jacket, removed her weapons. "Not the way I want to undress you," he said to fill the silence that was vicious metal claws around his heart.

No, he'd never survive her loss.

Her skin was a little hot when he checked, but her breathing was steady.

Janvier wasn't about to risk anything; he called the Guild and a medic was at the door within seven minutes. Ripping off his motorcycle jacket and dropping his helmet on the carpet, the heavyset male checked her over. "Her vitals are within safe levels." A piercing look at Janvier after he made that pronouncement. "Sara sent me because I've stitched Ash up before. I know what she can do. If that's what's caused this, we'll have to monitor her and see what happens."

"I'll do it."

The medic didn't argue with Janvier, simply showed him what to do to check her vitals, then said, "I'm not far." He gave Janvier his direct line. "Call me the instant you think she's in distress."

Kicking off his boots after the other man left, Janvier stripped off his jacket and blade holster, as well as his belt to ensure the buckle wouldn't dig into her. An instant later, he was curled around her. Ashwini was so vivid in life that he forgot how fragile she was as a mortal—today, he couldn't help but notice that despite the toned muscle that made her so beautiful and dangerous in motion, her limbs were slender, her bones all too breakable under his vampiric strength.

And her mind . . .

Sliding one arm under her head and refusing point-blank to go into a future that wasn't yet written in stone, he undid her braid with his other to make her more comfortable, murmuring to her in the language he'd spoken as a boy, skinny and wild and often hungry. "The first time I saw you, you had a crossbow pointed at me and a seriously pissed-off look on your face."

The memory was one of his favorites: she'd had a streak of

oil on her cheek, her olive green tank top smudged with dirt, and her combat boots planted a foot apart, black cargo pants hiding her long, long legs. He'd wanted to wrap his hand around her ponytail and pull back her head to arch her throat for a blood kiss that would ram erotic pleasure through both their bodies.

"Never had I felt such lust," he said, stroking his hand down her arm to lace his fingers with her own. "I could've devoured you, even had I to pay for it in crossbow wounds." He chuckled. "Imagine if you'd permitted me to seduce you then, *cher*."

No movement, her skin temperature clammy enough to make a ball of fear lodge in his gut. "Don't go." It was a harsh plea, his heart and soul laid at her feet. "Please don't go. It's not our time. Not yet. Not so soon."

# 34

Dmitri was briefing Raphael about the second victim when Elena appeared in the doorway to Raphael's Tower office.

*Hello,* hbeebti.

*Hello, Archangel.*

She leaned against the doorjamb and he watched as she and his second acknowledged each other with a glance. The two had come to an understanding that they both had the best interests of the city—and its archangel—at heart. Not that it stopped either one from sharpening their knives on each other.

Today, however, Dmitri had more critical matters on his plate. "A distraction won't work this time," the vampire said. "Too many people saw the victim, even with how quickly Illium picked her up, and while the media knows not to push the Tower, the talking heads are speculating on every channel."

"Shut it down." Raphael would permit no one to seed fear in his city. Not the enemy and not its own citizens.

"It won't cure the problem," Dmitri responded, proving why he was Raphael's second. Where many would've snapped to his command, Dmitri had the confidence and the intelligence to dispute Raphael's decisions when necessary. "The rumors will continue to circulate beneath the surface, doing worse damage."

"Suggestions?"

"Ahem."

"You have an idea, Consort?" Raphael asked the hunter who stood with her arms crossed and her wings held off the floor as per Galen's training—of course, Elena would say his weapons-master had beaten the habit into her, but the end result was that she had the posture of a warrior.

Her lips twitched at his formal address. "I was about to suggest we tell the truth."

Dmitri's expression was distinctly sardonic. "The Tower does not share its concerns."

Rolling her eyes, Elena sauntered into the room to stand with her hands on her hips at Raphael's side. "I wasn't suggesting we start doing a daily Tower broadcast. But what's the harm in pointing out that our enemies are attempting to use underhanded techniques to disrupt the city?"

Raphael had changed with the times. Unlike many of the older angels, he didn't look down his nose at the modern world, believing the old to be better. His Tower was fully integrated with current technology, with Illium in charge of ensuring that continued uninterrupted. The blue-winged angel was fascinated with both mortal and immortal ingenuity and had the kind of agile mind that could quickly process new concepts.

So Raphael wasn't stuck in the "stone age," as Illium had been heard to mutter about certain other vampires and angels. He had, however, long believed that mortals were safer in their ignorance of the bloody details of the immortal world. The irony of the fact that he was standing in the same room as two former mortals, one his heart, the other his closest friend, wasn't lost on him.

Neither was the cold truth that mortals could not play in their world.

Dmitri's friendship with Raphael had cost him his cherished family, the vampire spending a thousand years in purgatory. Elena had broken her back when Raphael had hauled her into an immortal problem, her body a bleeding, shattered doll in his arms. Without the kiss of immortality, his hunter's light would've been extinguished that violent day above Manhattan when he fought Uram. "Humans," he said, "cannot become used to demanding an answer from the Tower and getting it."

Elena's eyes, the gray ringed by a luminous rim of silver that whispered of her growing immortality, were open, without shadows, when they met his. "I know."

The two of them had been negotiating their viewpoints—her mortal heart against his immortal mind—since the day they met, but it was no longer a pitched battle. "Then why suggest a response?" he asked, conscious his consort's ability to understand the people of this city was oftentimes better than his own.

"Because it can work if we do it right." She tapped her foot, her forehead creased in a frown. "I say Dmitri calls a couple of the reporters who stuck around during the battle, the ones who risked their lives to cover it—and who, incidentally, made the Tower look damn good."

Dmitri nodded slowly. "I'll have a quiet conversation with them, bring them into the inner circle, shape the story as we wish."

"I don't know that manipulation is necessary," Elena countered. "The city is on our side. Give them a sign that the Tower knows that, that's all—people just want to feel included, to feel as if they have a part to play."

"Try it," Raphael said to Dmitri. "The Cascade will bring many more such decisions our way, so we must begin to establish what works."

An hour later, news hit the networks that the tortured woman reported to have run out of Central Park had been the victim of a cowardly attempt by their enemies to disrupt the city's recovery. While no one from the Tower appeared to confirm the reports, the Legion made an impressive flyover across the city that night, accompanied by two full squadrons led by Illium.

A half hour after that, Raphael's second told him the mood in the media had altered from fear to proud outrage. " 'No one has the guts to hit us head-on,' " Dmitri said, reading out a comment on an article. "That encapsulates the direction of the conversation." Sliding away his phone, he came to stand beside Raphael on the edge of a high Tower balcony. "Elena was right."

"There, Dmitri, you did not melt at admitting that."

His second laughed and the sound was one that was becoming familiar again after a thousand years of silence. It wasn't only his city that was healing, Raphael thought, his eyes catching the refracted light that betrayed Aodhan's presence in the sky; his people were, too. And it had all begun with a single, vulnerable mortal who did not accept that to be an archangel was to be always right.

# 35

Janvier didn't sleep for the ten hours that Ash was out, motionless and so deep in her mind that the life of her was a muted shadow. She finally stirred as the city was awakening, the high-rises wreathed in mist and coated with a light layer of snow he'd watched fall an hour before through the sliding doors off her bedroom.

Stretching against him, she made a sound in the back of her throat. He imagined it was his name, knew he was fooling himself. But then she turned to nuzzle his throat. "I knew it was you, *cher*." A sleepy, drowsy statement.

Janvier wanted to smile, to tease her in delight about his name being the first word on her lips, but he couldn't stop the convulsive shudder that shook his body, his arms locking around her.

"Shh." Wiggling until she could get both arms around his neck, Ash held him to her in a bruising grip that still wasn't tight enough for him. "I'm sorry," she said, rubbing her cheek against the roughness of his. "I didn't know that was going to happen."

He couldn't speak, the hand that had been choking him for

the past ten excruciating hours slow to release its punishing grasp.

Ash continued to murmur apologies, pressing soft, unexpected kisses along his temple and jaw. *"Mujhe maaf kardo na, cher."*

The private, intimate intermixing of language, it broke through the icy fear, made the choke hold ease, his breath no longer jagged rocks in his lungs. Shifting to brace himself on one forearm, he thrust a hand into her hair. "What did I tell you about apologies?"

He'd never forget those ten endless hours, but neither would he forget her dazzling, sinful smile as she said, "I'm not sleepy anymore."

Naked joy in his blood, he hauled her up over him, her unbound hair creating a curtain of black silk around their faces as they drank one another in. "Where did you come from?" Ash whispered in the hushed space. "I wasn't looking for you."

"Are you planning to throw me back?"

"Never."

The single empathetic word was better than any flowery declaration of love.

Coming down, she rested her head on his heart, not disputing his right to run his fingers through her hair. "I can't remember what I said in the hospital. Did I tell you about the peanuts?"

"You tried to say something, but you didn't complete your sentence."

"Damn." She jerked up into a sitting position. "Lilli told m—" A pause, her voice ragged and her hands fisted to bloodless tightness as she said, "That was her name. Lilli Ying."

"I won't forget." He couldn't take the agony of her gift from her, but he could help her carry the names of the lost. "What did Lilli say?"

"That she could smell peanuts during her captivity and that the space where she was held was a large one."

Squelching his need to continue to hold her, Janvier grabbed his phone. "I'll get the computer teams on to creating a list of possible locations."

"Good." She thrust her fingers through her hair, pushing it back from her face. "I'll update Sara, then I'm going to shower."

He watched her swing out of bed, sway on her feet. He was beside her with vampiric speed, but she held out a hand. "Give me a sec."

Stretching carefully, she said, "I'm a little light-headed, but I've felt like this before. Lots of liquids, a bit of protein, and I'll be fine." Clouds darkened her expression. "It's Felicity who needs our help. Lilli's gone, but I don't think Felicity is." She rubbed a fist over her heart, her eyes pools of shadow that saw into another realm. "We need to give her justice, give her peace."

It took Janvier a few short minutes to shower and change into fresh clothes after they arrived at his Tower apartment. Deciding to wait for him since there'd been no word from the computer teams yet, Ashwini took in the breathtaking view of the city through the floor-to-ceiling span of his living room windows.

Wonder unfurled in her when she caught sight of an angel gliding down inches from the windows, his wings spread to their full breadth. Those wings were so bright as to hurt the eye, diamond dust sprinkled on every filament.

*Aodhan.*

No matter how much darkness she saw in the immortal world, there was no doubting the splendor of angelic flight—the angels' physical beauty was less intriguing to her than their skill and grace in the air. Aodhan angled out of sight the same instant Janvier stepped out of his bedroom, hair damp and jaw shaved. Both their phones vibrated right then, the computer teams having compiled a preliminary list.

Taking a bottle of blood from his fridge, Janvier led her down to the Tower's dedicated tech floor.

"Why are you drinking budget blood?" she asked with a laugh after seeing the label: *Blood-for-Less.*

He shot her a minatory look. "You know why."

"Sucking up to the boss's consort?" Ashwini set her face into lines of mock disappointment. "I thought better of you."

"Very funny. I'm being supportive." Scowling, he drank half the bottle. "None of us want Elena's first business venture to go down in flames. And anyway," he said a little defensively, "this is a bottle of their premium line."

"Right." Delighted at the idea of all these tough Tower vamps throwing their weight behind a fledgling blood café, she rose up on her toes and pressed her lips to his jaw. His devastating smile was her reward . . . and if it lit the candle of guilt inside her, she snuffed it out just as quickly.

*Full throttle.* That was the promise they'd made to each other, and it was a promise she would keep. To live for today, for him, and not always in anticipation of the awful mental degeneration that awaited in her future.

They walked into tech central seconds later. The Guild techs were already patched in, the two teams having been working together to create the list of locations. Illium and Dmitri were both at a big glass table in the center and waved them over. "I've spoken to the Guild Director," Dmitri said when they reached the table. "She's putting together teams that will assist ours in clearing the possible locations."

"We have ten so far." Illium pointed out the *X*s on the map on the table. "Six of them are peripheral—either because the scent would've faded long ago or because of their distance from the city. Places like boarded up movie theaters and old factories."

"If you're right about the perpetrator being arrogant and smug," Janvier said to Ashwini, "and I think you are, then he would want a place he could control. His castle."

"Something appropriate to his wealth and image of himself." Ashwini couldn't see him being satisfied with a musty old theater or a factory unless he'd upgraded it inside. "Any sign the six were renovated anytime in the past five years?" she asked, knowing they had to cast a wide net—there was no knowing how long the bastard had been doing this. Even five years could be too small a window, but they had to start somewhere.

Illium told the computer experts to see what they could dig up on that point, then moved on to the four remaining properties.

"This one here," he said, pointing to an *X* in Harlem, his wings held tightly to his back in an astonishing fall of color, "was a restaurant that shut up shop three months ago."

"Their gimmick," Dmitri continued, "was to give all the patrons a free miniature jar of handmade peanut butter."

Ashwini remembered the place—she'd gone once with Demarco. The food had been terrible. Even peanut butter couldn't save it. "Three months is too short a window unless the abuse began elsewhere."

"What about these two?" Janvier pressed his fingers to twin Xs not far from the port where Raphael had blasted and sunk a ship full of Lijuan's infectious reborn.

"Warehouses with the same owner." Illium's golden eyes gleamed. "Giorgio."

Ashwini's skin prickled, but she knew they couldn't rush to judgment. Too many of the older immortals enjoyed pleasure that was perverse to anyone who possessed an ounce of humanity. But the hairs were rising on the back of her neck, the image of Giorgio's "perfect" brainwashed harem front and center. The man was a master manipulator.

Good enough to string along vulnerable women who wanted to believe in hope.

"The warehouses are in active use," Dmitri added, "but the computer searches picked up an interesting fact—they're consistently only being used to half their capacity."

Ashwini folded her arms. "So one could be empty?"

"Or one is in full use, the second only utilized enough to provide cover for other movements in and out," Janvier pointed out. "The extra space could've been made into a grotesque 'playroom.'"

It made an ugly kind of sense. Why risk hiding the women in a residential area when the warehouse and port district had enough ongoing noise to provide cover for any screams in the daytime? As for the night—aside from the odd security guard, the area would be deserted. Giorgio could have redone the interior or a part of it to his standards before moving his captives in.

A perfect prison within relatively short reach of his Vampire Quarter residence.

"Does he import nuts or items that would have the scent?" Janvier asked, the tension across his shoulders telling her his instincts were shouting exactly the same things as her own.

"Yes." Dmitri brought up a manifest on a tablet, handed it over. "He's not the only one who imports such goods, but the other shipments are all stored in warehouses shared between multiple companies."

"And this last?" Putting the manifest down on the table, Janvier tapped the final *X*.

"A midsized factory that packaged peanuts. Shut down a year ago and left boarded up by the owners." He brought up images of the four properties on a part of the glass table that Ashwini belatedly realized wasn't a simple table at all. "The factory also has enough space that your killer could've set up a private room inside—and Khalil was one of the financiers behind the venture."

Janvier hissed at the sadistic vampire's name, but shook his head. "We check the factory out, but I say it's Giorgio. Khalil is vicious, evil at times, but he's never been this *sly*."

Yes, she thought, that was the right word. There was a cruel slyness about it all, a sense that the monster had been laughing at his victims; such meanness fit Giorgio with his shiny new house, false bonhomie, and herd of devoted cattle. And there was something else, something she'd seen and forgotten, something *important*.

She heard Dmitri speak again, mention that Trace had found a dead drug dealer in the same general area, a man who'd been dealing Umber. It was a coincidence too good to be true. But that wasn't what held her attention, what occupied her mind.

Felicity was whispering to her.

What she had to say changed everything.

*"The watch!"* Violent anger tore through her, made her voice shake. "Janvier, when we interviewed Giorgio, the bastard was wearing the watch Felicity bought him!" It hadn't registered at the time except as part of his entire getup. "He was taunting us even then."

Janvier's response was a stream of Cajun-flavored cursing that turned the air blue.

Things moved at rapid-fire speed after that. Dmitri authorized them to use whatever force was necessary to bring Giorgio in and rescue any other hostages. Illium and a mixed angelic/ Legion squadron would provide aerial backup. Meanwhile,

Dmitri would coordinate with Sara to clear the other possible properties, on the slim chance that Giorgio wasn't the killer.

Ashwini was used to working alone for the most part, but she had no problem being on a team. Especially when the core of that team was made up of her, Janvier, and Naasir. They knew one another's rhythms, could predict split-second decisions with near-total accuracy and make the necessary course corrections.

Now, the three of them made their way to the suspicious warehouses while another unit cleared Giorgio's house. If he was there, they'd take him into custody. Ashwini didn't care about that at this instant—she wanted the bastard to pay, but her first priority was to rescue any other women he'd caged.

Leaving the car some distance away in order to maintain stealth—the one thing they did not want was for Giorgio to murder his victims in a fit of rage—the three of them went onward on foot. "Up," she said to the two men.

Grinning, Naasir jumped onto a rooftop with a feral grace that was magnetic. But not as compelling to her eyes as Janvier's fluid leap up. She made the motion for "Go" and they headed onward. The two would take Naasir's lower skyroad, while she'd go in on the ground, and their aerial backup would drop down from above the cloud layer on their signal.

She tugged down the ball cap under which she'd hidden her hair after dirtying up her face, made sure her battered and patched sunglasses were on her nose, and slouched forward with her hands in the pockets of her raggedy black coat. A young vampire at the Tower had dug up the ankle-length piece out of God knew where.

On her feet were sneakers as ragged. She hated being without her boots, but they were the thing that most often gave people's true motives away, especially hunters and military types. It was something Saki had taught her soon after her admittance into the Guild.

*Shoes and wristwatches, that's where folks slip up.*

So she slouched along, just another street person looking for a place to get out of the cold, pitiful and not the least bit intimidating. When she reached the first warehouse, she made as if to see if she could get around the back and, when that proved impossible, tried the door, muttering nonsense under her breath for effect.

The door was wrenched open from within, the muscle-bound vampire on the other side dressed in a navy suit sans tie, his complexion so white it was eerie. "Git!" He shoved at her shoulder with bruising force, while another body moved in the shadows behind him. "Out! Pestilent vermin."

Allowing herself to stumble and fall to the concrete frontage swept clean of snow, she held out hands clad in holey gloves. "S-sorry. Sorry. Didn't know it was occupied."

The door slammed shut.

Pushing up to her feet, hands over her ears as she rocked, she tried the same thing at the next warehouse, this time more furtively, giving the appearance that she was afraid of being caught again. No response this time, and she picked up not even a hint of sound.

Going with her gut, she said, "First warehouse," into the tiny microphone attached to the collar of her coat. "Two vampire guards that I saw, armed with guns and possibly knives." Retrieving her gun from a coat pocket, the silencer already on, she held it in one hand; the coat's sleeves were long enough to conceal the weapon. "I didn't hear or see anything to suggest a bigger contingent, but there could be more toward the back."

Naasir's voice came through the receiver in her ear. "I will listen." A minute later. "I hear male laughter, movement, but it is small. No more than two or three."

Another voice followed Naasir's. "Giorgio," Dmitri said, "is not at his home or at any of his known haunts. His cattle are accounted for except for the one named Brooke. She left with him around three a.m."

Ashwini's blood ran hot. There was a good chance the bastard was inside the warehouse and he probably had Brooke with him. Not only had she tarnished his name, but her actions had drawn Tower attention; it may have been enough to make Giorgio break pattern and attack a woman who could be linked back to him.

"Give us a minute," she said to Dmitri and Illium both, then she signaled to Janvier and Naasir.

Quiet as ghosts, the two men whispered across the roof to

jump down behind the target warehouse, while she shuffled her way back to the front. Hesitating and mumbling to give them enough time to get in position, she surreptitiously undid her coat to expose the thin T-shirt she wore underneath before knocking on the door.

# 36

It was pulled open by the same vampire who'd shoved her to the ground.

"You still here?" he snarled. "I told you to git!" Fangs glinted in the sunlight. "Or do you want me to get nasty?"

A vicious guard dog, she decided, one who'd do anything for money. "I was just wondering," she said, imitating the jerky, scratchy movements of a junkie. No one to worry about. No one important. No one who'd be missed. "Do you have, like, a dollar?" A jerk that made her coat half fall off her shoulder, drawing his attention to her body. "For coffee?"

His eyes gleamed red, dropping to her breasts. "I think we can work out a deal."

He was reaching to maul her breasts when there was a shout from inside the warehouse. As he turned, Ashwini shot him straight through the temple. He dropped to the floor with a bone-cracking slam, but didn't die, his shoulders and legs twitching and bloody froth gathering at the corners of his mouth.

Before she put in another bullet at the precise point in his spine that would paralyze him long enough to get this done, she looked inside to find Naasir and Janvier only a few feet away. It appeared the guards had been playing poker around a table close to the entrance. Naasir had ripped out the throat of a second guard with unusual care. The male was seriously damaged, but would survive to face Tower justice. Janvier, on the other hand, had a sweating vampire on his knees, one of his kukris held to the dark-skinned male's throat.

Since they needed only one conscious and able to talk, she put the bullet in the first vampire's spine, then contacted Illium. "We have this under control," she said, stepping over the guard's body to head to Janvier. "I think your squadron should clear the second warehouse before joining us."

"Consider it done."

In front of her, Janvier hauled his captive to his feet and slid away his blade. "See Naasir over there? He's hungry. Don't run unless you want him to chase you."

Naasir obligingly smiled his most feral smile.

The whites of his eyes showing, the guard nodded.

Together, the three of them and their captive moved deeper into the warehouse via the clear aisle in the center, shelving and boxes on either side. Normal enough. Until they reached the center.

On the left were more goods, including several large crates situated a short distance from where the shelving ended. On the right, however, the shelving continued uninterrupted, but the goods went in only a few feet deep. Beyond floated gauzy hangings Naasir tore down to reveal a plush black carpet.

On the carpet sat a four-poster bed with rumpled satin sheets. It was fitted with leather restraints as well as heavy black-on-black damask curtains that had been tied to the sides with glossy gold ropes that ended in tassels. Two large arm-chairs upholstered in a deep red fabric sat nearby, at an angle that would provide the occupants with an uninterrupted view of the bed.

One of those armchairs had a back meant to accommodate wings.

Beside each was a beautifully crafted round wooden table etched with designs in gold, its feet curved.

Fury a burn in her blood, Ashwini strode to the bed, touched the sheets. Cold. But though she couldn't see it against the black satin, she could smell the blood, feel the slight stickiness of it against her fingertips. Spinning to face the guard, she said, "Where are the women?"

When the man refused to speak, Janvier shoved him back to his knees and had the kukri at his throat before the guard had time to even draw breath.

"Oops," Janvier said, beads of dark red beginning to form on the sweating vampire's neck. "I'm a little shaky today." His smile was so chilly, she would've been surprised it came from him if she hadn't known how much he hated men who hurt women.

Ashwini knew the victims had to be here, but the warehouse was massive. Thick with shadows, it had shelving large enough to hold human-sized cages and could take considerable time to search. To judge from the bloodstained sheets on the bed, a woman could die in the interim.

"Where are they, you piece of shit?" She strode over to slam the muzzle of her gun to the guard's temple as wings of silver-blue appeared in her peripheral vision. *"Talk."*

"I would do as she says," Janvier drawled without removing the blade from the man's throat. "She can be trigger-happy."

"I'm more scared of him than of you," the guard said through his cowardly quivering.

Ashwini thought they could change that, her current mood without mercy, but Naasir suddenly froze, his nostrils flaring. "I have them." He took off in the direction where she'd noted the large wooden crates.

*No,* she thought and ran.

Janvier ran right beside her, leaving the gibbering guard to Illium. "Ash!"

Half turning without lessening her speed, she caught the crowbar Janvier looked to have picked up from the final—and mostly empty—shelves on the left. He grabbed a hammer that was lying there after throwing her the crowbar.

Naasir was already using his claws to wrench the slats off one box, his strength ferocious. She went to a second, while Janvier took a third. Three of the Legion arrived two seconds later and joined in.

Ashwini hoped with her every breath that Naasir was wrong, that they'd find nothing more interesting than schmaltzy souvenirs, but she could smell what Lilli had, understood now why the scent had made such a strong impression on the tortured woman. "These crates used to hold peanuts," she said, using the crowbar to wrench up a slat.

Naasir growled loud enough to raise every tiny hair on her body and, throwing aside a slat, picked up an emaciated woman from the crate he'd demolished. Thrusting her into the arms of one of the Legion, he said, "Fly!" Every member of the team had been briefed as to where to take any injured they might find.

Ashwini could see that her crate wasn't empty now and she renewed her efforts, Naasir coming over to help. It took another excruciating half second to get the slats off enough that she could see the woman. Pressing her fingers against the victim's throat, Ashwini prayed for a beat. Nothing. No, wait. There it was. A faint flutter. "She's alive!" she yelled at the same time that Janvier yelled the same.

Naasir lifted out the woman just as the victim Janvier had discovered began to scream, high-pitched and piercing. Ashwini ran over, guessing it was seeing a male that had set her off. Janvier backed out of view at the same time.

The shock of recognition was instant. "It's all right," she said to Brooke. "You're safe." Nude body bruised and bloodied, one of her eyes swollen half-shut and her lip split open, the auburn-haired woman was nonetheless still whole. "We're taking you to a hospital."

Brooke was already fading, eyes glazed by shock and face pale, but she struggled to speak. "Giorgio . . . hurt . . ."

"We'll get him," Ashwini promised. "Conserve your strength."

Ignoring the words, Brooke forced out, "M-monster w-watched . . ."

Lights, sirens on the doorstep.

"Janvier!" Ashwini called out. "Help me carry her to the ambulance." She could've done it in a fireman's carry but that might aggravate any internal injuries Brooke had sustained, and with the wounded woman having lost her battle with unconsciousness, she wouldn't be traumatized by the contact with a male.

Janvier lifted Brooke into his arms with utmost gentleness. "I have her, *cher.*"

Knowing he'd be careful with her, Ashwini turned to make

sure all the crates had been opened and there were no more victims.

When Janvier returned, he, Ashwini, Naasir, and Illium compared notes. Brooke wasn't the only one who'd been conscious. The girl Naasir had rescued first had also managed to speak.

"'Monster,'" Naasir repeated, his eyes gleaming so violently in the semidark of the warehouse that Ashwini realized they were actually reflective . . . like a tiger's. "She kept saying 'monster.' I thought she was confused, talking about me."

"The second armchair," Ashwini pointed out, "it had a back modified for wings."

"An angelic partner may explain the desiccation," Illium said, features grim. "The emergence of new abilities among our kind isn't always telegraphed ahead of time."

"We go over this warehouse inch by inch." Janvier's voice had lost its languid rhythm, become hard, ruthless. "Feathers at Giorgio's home could belong to innocent angelic guests, but anything here is near certain to belong to his partner."

Not wasting time, they walked to one end of the warehouse to form a horizontal line across the huge space with others of the squadron. Not the Legion fighters, however—according to what Ashwini had picked up from talking to Tower personnel, while the Legion were skilled in the air, they weren't very good at delicate tasks. Not yet.

Using high-powered torches flown in by the Legion to light shadowy areas and illuminate aisles between the shelving, the line was almost to the other end of the warehouse when Janvier called for them to stop.

Positioned only a couple of feet to his left, Ashwini watched him crouch down and pick up something from the ground. "Feather," he said, fierce exultation in his tone. "Red."

*Red?*

As far as she knew, there were no red-winged angels in the city, but she was no expert. Many angels also had delicate markings—one could have tiny red feathers on the inner curve of a wing, for example. "Do you recognize it?" Angelic colors tended to be highly distinctive. No one in New York would ever mistake one of Illium's for one of Raphael's, or one of Jason's for one of Aodhan's.

"No." Janvier rose to his feet, handed the feather to Illium. "You know who this is?"

A chill iced Illium's expression. "There are two options that make sense."

"Red," Naasir said, a growl in his voice, "is unusual among angels." His eyes met Illium's. "Xi and Cornelius."

Ashwini's mind filled with an image of wings of gray streaked by vivid red, her skin pebbling. "Wasn't Xi—"

"—one of Lijuan's generals?" Illium completed. "Yes."

Naasir spoke again. "Not the oldest or the most powerful, but favored because of his intelligence."

"Cornelius," Illium added, "is a lower-ranked general. His wings are a heavy cream for the most part except for a scattering of red across the top arches."

"Illium!"

Turning toward the doorway, Ashwini saw a slender black-haired vampire with a scarf around his neck walking toward them. He must've arrived in the area after them, she realized when Janvier introduced him as Trace.

His voice was hoarse as he said, "I had a hunch, with Giorgio being scientifically trained. Dug around in the other warehouse." Trace opened his palm. On it sat a tiny ziplock bag with a few crystalline granules colored a reddish brown.

Ashwini recognized it from Janvier's description of the new designer vampire drug that was the reason for Lacey's horrific murder.

"Supply or creation?" Illium asked after taking the bag.

"Creation. There are tools. Nothing elaborate, but enough." Trace glanced around. "Giorgio must've separated out his drug operation from his sadistic games"—utter distaste in his voice—"because the other warehouse already had the right setup for it."

"See if you can discover anything else about the origins of the drug," Illium said, his glance taking in all four of them. "I'll alert Raphael that it appears either Cornelius or Xi somehow managed to remain behind in the city, or return to it after the rest of Lijuan's forces retreated."

The angel couldn't technically give Ashwini an order, but this was one order with which she had no argument. First, however, they finished going over the warehouse. Ashwini found another tiny red feather, this one with a tip of rich cream. Xi, she remembered, had no cream in his wings. Still, she double-checked with Naasir and Janvier, received the same answer.

That narrowed their target down to a single angel: *Cornelius.*

"They were careful," Janvier said, his hand touching her lower back. "Must've picked up any larger feathers."

"No." She stared at the tiny feather as Naasir contacted Illium with the updated information. "They had no reason to be careful—Giorgio was so sure he couldn't be tracked that he used a warehouse held under his own name. There's something *wrong* with this feather." Holding it cupped carefully in the palm of her hand, she walked outside into the light. "Do you see it?"

First Janvier, then Naasir examined the feather. Even Trace. None could see anything wrong, and when she looked at it in their hands, she couldn't, either. But as soon as she took it, she felt it again, the wrongness. "There's something wrong with Cornelius, then," she said, skin crawling. "Very, very wrong."

Sliding the disturbing thing into her pocket, after rooting around in there for something to act as a bag and finding a crushed plastic sleeve that had once held tissues, she walked with the men across to the other warehouse.

It was identical to the first one in size and shape, but the lighting was much better, most of the space filled with what appeared to be normal goods. They opened a few boxes to be sure, found the kinds of things a man who served the luxury market might acquire—exotic spices, antiques, rich bolts of silk.

The back right of the warehouse, however, was sectioned off into its own room with a single small window. It said *Office* on the door, and at first glance that was what it appeared to be. Tall filing cabinets, a desk, invoices, a phone. There was even a tiny sink behind the filing cabinets, as well as a camp stove.

It was under that sink that Trace had found a clear plastic box that held a steel bowl, a dirty syringe, a tiny spoon, and what looked like a bunch of ordinary sugar crystals alongside more ziplock bags. Putting everything on the sink, Trace said, "Either the foreman who ran this warehouse was oblivious to his master's activities or he was the cook.

"The bag I found was crushed under the bowl, must've been missed when they made the last batch." He held the syringe up to show them the brownish residue inside before putting it back down. "In all honesty I'm not sure how or what they were doing, but I believe they must've needed water and the stove. The actual raw materials are nowhere in evidence."

Naasir sniffed the air. "I smell blood."

Frowning, Ashwini, Janvier, and Trace spread out, looking for any evidence someone had been held or hurt in here. "I don't see any blood," she said. "Janvier?"

"Nothing."

Trace's response was the same.

Naasir sniffed the air again, walking closer and closer to the sink until he had his nose in the bowl. "Blood," he said definitively. "Strong blood. Angel blood."

"They made a drug out of the *blood* of an angel?" Ashwini just stared at the wild silver of Naasir's gaze.

# 37

"Yes." Naasir sniffed again, his eyes going flat. "This blood is *wrong*." He hissed, drawing away from the bowl. "Bad to drink." He came to Ashwini. "Show me the feather again."

Taking it out of her pocket, she removed it from the plastic sleeve. Naasir didn't take it, just put his hand under hers and lowered his nose to the feather. The silver liquid of his hair slid forward to kiss her skin. "Yes," he said, rising to his full height. "You were right—the feather smells wrong, too, but it's much more subtle."

Ashwini put it away in her pocket. "No question it's the same angel?"

"None."

The deep, deep green of Trace's eyes glinted. "That explains why Umber is so exclusive—even an angel can't donate blood every day without consequences."

"It also," Janvier said, "confirms the *why* of the drug."

"A poison." Naasir's features set into piercingly intelligent lines, his feral nature taking a backseat. "The aim was always to kill or cause bloodlust."

"Yes." Trace stared at the wall, his mind clearly working. "Either they're adding something to the blood or the angel's blood is poison. Given what you said about the feather, my bet is the latter."

That left the question of how the blood had been poisoned in the first place—but if their man *was* Cornelius, well, he was Lijuan's protégé, and the Archangel of China had created infectious reborn. Not a stretch to say that one of her minions hadn't been "blessed" with poisonous blood courtesy of his goddess.

"Can you track the scent?" she asked Naasir.

"Yes," Naasir said. "But there is no fresh trail outside—the snow has buried what was there. We'll need to narrow down the location."

"We may as well start at Giorgio's house," Janvier said. "Ash and Naasir and I can do that. Trace, can you get this to the Tower"— his nod took in the drug paraphernalia—"and have it tested?"

"I'll have it fast-tracked."

Leaving the vampire in the warehouse, a number of the Legion on guard over both properties, the three of them went directly to Giorgio's tony Vampire Quarter town house. Allowed in by the guards Dmitri had left at the door, they decided to start at the top and work their way down. The town house's décor was, as she'd noticed on her first visit, far more modern than the velvet and lace Giorgio favored on himself and his cattle.

It was also sumptuous. Three-hundred-count Egyptian cotton sheets, designer curtains, granite counters in the bathroom, and fixtures polished to perfection. Ashwini found plenty of evidence that the women were welcome in the master bedroom—not the least of which was a crumpled pair of lace panties.

Not touching the panties and the discarded seamed stockings hung over the back of a chair, Ashwini tapped the walls to check for hidden compartments. She didn't find anything, and neither did either of the two men. Naasir shook his head when they met again in the downstairs hallway, having split up during the search of the lower half of the house. "No scent."

"Giorgio has other properties." She scanned the information that had come through on her phone from the combined Guild/ Tower team. "Small rental homes, shares in a hotel . . ."

"The desiccated dog," Janvier reminded her, "was found in

the Quarter, so our angel may be comfortable in this area. Even if he isn't, the Quarter is Giorgio's milieu. I can't see him putting up his guest anywhere that would take him too far out of his way."

Ashwini frowned. "None of the places on this list are anywhere near the Quarter."

The three of them headed to the closest property regardless, with Dmitri and Sara having already dispatched teams to clear the others.

Eight hours of fruitless searching later, Ashwini kicked the punching bag in the Guild Academy gym. She'd been working out her frustration on the bag since the final possible location was cleared forty-five minutes past, but wasn't having much success in calming herself down.

Not only had an angel with freaking *red* in his wings disappeared into thin air, to the point that no one they'd questioned in the Quarter recalled ever seeing him, but so had Giorgio, leaving behind only his bewildered and distraught showpiece cattle. All had seemed genuinely upset when Ashwini interviewed them.

Apparently, even psychopathic bastards had their fans.

As for the vampire guards from the warehouse, they were the vicious brutes Ashwini had tagged them; Giorgio had trusted none of the three with details of his plans. Their only task was to guard that sickening torture chamber while it wasn't in use. When it was, they played guard dogs outside the warehouse.

None had ever seen the angel's face—at least according to the one who could speak, Giorgio's partner had always arrived covered in a black cloak, the hood shadowing his features. The guard said they'd all assumed it was another vampire, because there was no indication of wings beneath the cloak. That, of course, should've been impossible. The guard had also admitted to taking advantage of a captive and said his partners had, too.

Punching the bag in renewed fury, her hands protected by boxing gloves, she swung out with a hard kick. The bag swung, exposing the lean form of the man who stood against the wall on the other side. Stilling the bag using her hands, her chest heaving, she said, "How did you get in here?" He was neither student nor instructor nor hunter. Right now, it was only the latter two in here, the students being at dinner.

"I am a teacher, *cher*," he said, strolling closer.

She raised an eyebrow.

"Truth." He held up his hands before taking hold of the bag and keeping it steady while she threw a few more punches. "I volunteered my services for your final-year students."

"You're playing prey?" Every student had to successfully complete a "hunt" before graduating. "Usually one of us does that."

"Not that you are not brilliant, my darling, devious Ash, but you aren't a vampire. We do have certain tricks."

"You have more than most." No vamp but Janvier had ever come close to outwitting her on a hunt. "How many have caught you so far?"

"All," he said. "I am not here to destroy their confidence, only to make them work hard and earn the collar, and each has done that."

At that instant, he could've been any hunter in the room, at once proud of the students and concerned with making sure they went out into the world with the right tools to survive. Tools Giorgio's victims had never had. "We've hit a dead end, haven't we?" She went through a rapid series of punches and kicks.

Moss green eyes shadowed, Janvier stopped the bag from spinning. "Yes, but every vampire and angel in the city has been alerted to be on the lookout. Neither Giorgio nor Cornelius will be able to show his face without being picked up. Need will draw them out."

She knew he was right. Even if Giorgio had a store of blood, it wouldn't last forever. And if they found Giorgio, they'd find the angel. "I hate waiting," she said, though at this point, there was no other option. The Guild's financial whiz was running through Giorgio's finances with her counterpart at the Tower; if the vampire had hidden any properties under shell corporations, the two would find it. All his accounts had also been flagged to send up an alert should he attempt to access them.

Ashwini knew she wouldn't be any good to Felicity, Lilli,

and the other victims if she didn't have her head in the right
space when the information came through. Modulating her
breathing with conscious effort of will, she tugged off her
gloves. "I have to shower," she said. "You're taking me to dinner after we drop my gear off at home."

"Then will you *be* my dinner?"

Skin shimmering at the reminder of how potent he was, she
said, "Play your cards right and I just might."

His wicked smile followed her into the shower, scoured
some of the frustration off. Not all of it. Nothing could do that
until they'd hunted down the evil behind the torture and deaths
of so many hopeful young lives, but she could breathe, could
think . . . could remember that she, too, had a life.

*Full throttle.*

Exiting the locker room after her shower, her duffel over
her shoulder, she found Janvier chatting to Ransom. The other
hunter was on his crutches but dressed in workout clothes that
likely meant he'd come to lift weights, his hair pulled back in
a tight twisting braid. Flicking it, she said, "Pretty."

"Nyree did it." A smug smile.

Never had she thought she'd see Ransom gaga over a
woman. It was cute. "So, when's the wedding?"

"We haven't decided, but it won't be long. I figure if I'm
going to do this, I'm going to do it." A glance from her to
Janvier. "So . . ."

Her scowl made his grin widen. "Have a nice dinner!" he
called out as they left, loud enough to alert the others in the
gym. "Call me if you want any tips about doing dirty, dirty
things on the back of a motorcycle!"

Their fellow hunters hooted and whistled.

Instead of snapping a quick comeback as she would've done
before, Ashwini swiveled to haul Janvier down to her with a
grip on his leather jacket and claimed his mouth in a deep, wet,
possessive kiss that set the entire gym hollering. When she
released him, he looked like he'd been hit over the head with
a baseball bat. She took his hand, ignored the ruckus, and
headed outside.

He didn't speak until they were at his bike and she'd swung
up behind him, the duffel slung across her back. Then he leaned
backward into her, his hand on her thigh. *"Merci, cher."*

She wrapped her arms around his neck, her position on the bike giving her the extra height. "I should've done it a long time ago." Publicly claimed him for her own.

"You weren't ready—and this is a moment I will never forget." Sitting up, he passed over her helmet and put on his own.

The traffic was heavy but they made good time despite that, thanks to Janvier's driving. It would've been reckless in another, less capable man. With him, it was simply exhilarating and they were back in her apartment not long afterward, both of them pumped and laughing.

When Janvier pushed her up against the wall after they entered and kissed her, his hand curving around her neck, she wrapped one leg around his and thrust her hands into his hair, sank into the heat and the strength of him. It felt so good to touch and be touched, but it wasn't simply that. It was because this was him.

Her man.

He'd kissed her with a half smile, half laugh on his face and it felt like sunshine in her blood. Licking and tasting him, as he did her in turn, she bit down on his lower lip. "How am I doing?"

"You need lots of practice." A glint in his eye. "On me. I insist."

She bit him again for that, before sucking his lip and flicking her tongue over the sensual punishment. "Don't complain if I wear you out, then." Returning to the kiss with a smile that echoed his, she drank in the taste of him. "I like kissing you, cuddlebunny."

His shoulders shook. Scraping his fangs lightly over her lips, he slid his hands down to cup her ass. "I acquiesce to being your cuddlebunny, if you'll meet my terms. They involve naked cuddling and blood."

"Done." Laughing, she just drank in his smile, and then they were kissing again. Their breaths grew shorter, his body harder, hotter. Skin burning under her touch, he shrugged off his jacket to drop it to the floor. Ashwini ran her hands up his back, over the leather of the holster. "Knives," she murmured, kissing his jaw, his throat.

Janvier's muscles shifted, his arms crossing over his back. The slide of blade against scabbard and then the thump of two blades being embedded into the walls on either side of her head. She laughed softly. "You're fixing the holes."

"It will be my pleasure." He busied himself kissing her neck as she undid the strap across his chest and pushed the holster off his muscular shoulders. Sometimes, she forgot how strong he was, but it was impossible to do that with him so close, his muscles fluid beneath his skin.

The holster and scabbards hit the carpet with a dull thud.

Sucking on her neck, Janvier pushed off and reached for the gun she wore in the thigh holster. "Will you shoot me if I touch your gun?"

"Not today."

Deep male laughter, his cheeks creasing beautifully. Unable to resist, she pulled him back to her mouth and demanded another kiss. He gave it to her, but then broke off. "I do not intend to get accidentally shot in the family jewels, *cher*."

"No, that would be a shame." She tugged up his T-shirt and slid her hands over the hard ridges of his abdomen.

"That is not helping." He groaned but managed to get the gun out of the holster. Making sure the safety was on, he put it on the entranceway table.

"Nuh-uh." She pushed at him. "Not here."

Instead of complaining, he let her go and used the chance to rip off his T-shirt. By the time she made it to the bedroom and put the gun on the bedside table, he'd shucked his boots and socks and was working on undoing his belt, having left a trail of discarded items behind him as he followed her. Her mouth watered. God, he was sexy with his hair all mussed up and his lips wet from her kisses, his body bared for her eyes only.

Pulling the belt out of its loops, he dropped it to the floor.

She walked over, put her hands on his hips, then slid down to press her lips to his navel, just above the button he'd flicked open on his jeans.

He said words she didn't know in his native tongue, thrust his hand into her hair, and shuddered. "You cannot do that, sugar. Or I will embarrass myself."

Rising slowly, kiss by kiss, she met his mouth with her own. He hauled her close, his erection pushing demandingly against her abdomen and his body heat a pulse. She ran her hands over him, loving the feel of him, the scent of him. He smelled . . . of Janvier. Masculine and hot and just Janvier.

When she reached down and stroked him through his jeans, he broke the kiss to press his forehead to hers, his breathing strained. "Ashwini." A hoarse whisper. "I have no defenses against you."

Seduced, intoxicated, she tugged down the zipper, wanting to feel him in her hand, to pleasure him as he did her with his every touch. "You're not wearing underwear." She used her teeth to tug on the lobe of his ear. "I should've known."

Gripping the back of her neck, he kissed her again as she closed her fingers around the thick heat of his erection. His cock felt like iron, but his skin there, it was so delicate, so fine. Fascinated, her own pulse a hammer and her blood so scalding it was near ignition, she stroked gently to the tip, felt the wetness there. Her next stroke slicked that bead of wetness over him, turned his body even more rigid.

"Harder." It was a harsh murmur against her ear.

"I don't want to hurt you."

He chuckled. "There is a reason orgasm is called *la petite mort*." Closing his hand over hers, he showed her a rhythm so rough she would've never done it on her own. But since he'd asked . . .

Releasing her on a groan when she proved an apt pupil, he locked his hand in her hair, kissed her, deep and voracious and raw. It was mouth sex and it scrambled her neurons. Her hand, though, it knew what to do, did it fast and hard until he broke off the kiss to throw back his head, muscle and tendon standing out in stark relief as his hips pumped into the fist of her fingers.

# 38

Ashwini looked down, watched him come for her, and it was the most erotic sight she'd seen in her life. When his muscles relaxed, she released him to bite at his throat, over his pulse. He shivered, then nuzzled at her, one hand cupping the side of her face. His eyes were lazy, his body languid as he walked her backward.

When the bed hit the backs of her knees, she fell onto it with a gasp. "My hand," she murmured to the delicious man above her, one who looked as if he'd just rolled out of bed and was ready to crawl back in—with her.

A smile that was pure male. "I'll take care of it." Zipping up just enough to keep his jeans on, he moved with vampiric speed, was back from the bathroom in the time it took for her to inhale, the stickiness on her hand an erotic reminder of their intimacy.

Using a wet facecloth to wipe it off, he dropped the cloth over the side of the bed. "I'm not always so . . . civilized," he said afterward, lifting one of her legs and pulling off her boot and sock. "Would you wear me on your skin?" Kissing her ankle, he put down that leg and picked up her other one.

Ashwini, her breathing less than even, found herself

watching the way the muscles of his abdomen flexed and eased
as he took off her other boot and sock. He looked up and, smiling, stepped between her thighs and braced himself with his
palms on either side of her. Coming down in an effortless move,
biceps taut, he flicked his tongue over her lips in a wet tease.

"You're hot, sugar."

"Yes."

"You should take off your jacket."

"That's not the kind of heat I'm talking about." Her body
felt as if it were melting from the inside out, her bones honey.
However, when he pushed back into a standing position again,
she sat up and shrugged off her jacket, as well as the thin
sweater she'd pulled on directly over her bra.

Janvier moved with that dangerous, beautiful speed again,
his hands on her waist before she'd pushed the strands of hair
off her face. Picking her up, he dropped her higher on the bed,
so that her legs were no longer half hanging off the side.

It should've scared her, the evidence of his strength. Without
her weapons, she'd never take him. But she wasn't scared, not of
Janvier, never of him. She welcomed him as he joined her
on the bed, his shoulders blocking out the light. With his jeans
barely hanging on to his hips, she had plenty of gorgeous male
flesh to explore with her hands while he tasted and licked her
throat.

Bracing himself on one forearm, he tugged down the cup
of her bra. Her breasts were ordinary size; she'd never win a
wet T-shirt contest. But Janvier groaned and dipped his head
to suck not just her nipple but part of her breast into his mouth.

Spine arching, she thrust the back of her hand against her
mouth to stifle her scream as he sucked. Each hot, wet pull
went straight to her core. Her panties were so wet she could
feel her arousal threatening to soak through her jeans. She
didn't care. Holding him to her, she undulated her body toward
his in an attempt to rub up against the delicious friction of his
cock.

When he lifted his head, she said, "No."

Dropping a kiss to her nipple, he shifted his attention to her
other breast and it was just as good. It tightened her stomach
muscles, made her thighs clench around him. *"Janvier."*

"Let me, *ma belle sorcière*."

She gave in, allowed him to do what he would, and was panting so hard by the time he lifted his head again that she had no breath to form words. Janvier stroked his hand down her ribs, then reached underneath and up to undo her bra clasp. When that proved difficult with her on her back, he grinned at her. "I'll replace it." Lace and cotton tore and her top half was nude to him.

Stroking her, shoulder to thigh, he kissed her mouth, her jaw, whispering sweet, dirty things in her ear that had her hips rising toward him even before he undid her jeans and slid his hand inside her panties. The shock of contact would've lifted her off the bed if he hadn't been pinning her down with his body.

"So wet for me, *cher*." His breathing as harsh as her own, he accompanied each word with a kiss. "You make me lose my mind."

Her own mind a chaos of sensation, she clutched at his shoulders and, unable to resist the temptation, looked down. The sight of his hand between her thighs, his muscular forearm lightly dusted with hair, made her moan. She needed his kiss, needed to find an anchor again. He bent his head, gave her what she wanted without a word passing between them.

When he withdrew his hand ten seconds later, she dug her nails into his shoulders.

"I would see you." Going down off the bed with those words—with a pause for a kiss or three along her body—he hooked his fingers at the sides and pulled off her jeans and panties in one strong tug. Dropping them onto the floor, he came to kneel between her thighs, taking hold of her knees to spread her wide.

Fingers closing on the sheets, she watched him watch her. His eyes were heavy lidded, his cheeks flushed at the arch of his cheekbones, his breathing ragged. And when she ran her eyes down his body, it was to see that he was thickly aroused, the zipper of his jeans doing a very bad job of containing his length.

"Take off your jeans." She wanted to see him, too, wanted to have every inch of him touch every inch of her.

"In a minute." Inserting his hand back between her thighs, he began to stroke her lightly, so lightly. Again and again and again until her skin shimmered and she was rising up against him, caught on the edge of a pleasure so intense, she could feel it building under her skin like an electrical storm surge.

He withdrew his hand.

She threatened to murder him in creative ways.

Janvier's responding smile imprisoned her, seduced her. When he kissed her, she bit him. It only made his smile deepen. Wrapping her legs around his hips had no effect. He made his way down her body, and then . . .

The scream that came out her mouth as his own closed over her clit was a thin echo, her lungs devoid of air. He sucked hard, eating her up like she was candy, and the storm surge crested, collided. Her mind splintered, rode the crest . . . and he kept on kissing her, long slow licks, small sucks, and quick flicks that had her riding the wave for so long that she was boneless when it passed, her muscles quivering.

Pressing a kiss to her inner thigh, Janvier rose and got rid of his jeans at last.

*Beautiful,* she thought but couldn't say, her mind too fuzzy from the exquisite, erotic thing he'd done to her.

"You are the beautiful one, sugar."

She frowned, but then he was coming over and she had other things to think about. His naked body on hers, it felt even better than she'd imagined, all heat and strength and a wholly masculine weight, his skin silk under her possessive hands.

Rubbing against her, Janvier reached down to stroke her again. She shivered, sensitive but not in a bad way. "Yes," she murmured, before he could ask the question.

He kissed her again, and this time she kept her eyes open. So did he. The intimacy was blinding. When he slid his finger inside her, she shuddered but didn't break the eye contact. Neither did he . . . and nudged in another finger. Spreading his fingers slightly inside her, he curved them to stroke her deep and slow.

Feeling the storm surge begin to build again, she stroked his cheek. "Together this time."

Turning his head, he kissed her palm.

Her heart squeezed.

She ran her fingers through his hair and down over his nape as he removed his hand from between her legs and shifted position. When he slid his palm down her inner left thigh, she let him push her thigh out wider, and then he was nudging at her with his cock. She moaned at the feel of him pushing into her, the blunt head of his cock wide enough that she definitely felt it, her muscles stretching in an effort to accommodate him.

A small sound escaped her throat. He went motionless.

Tightening her legs around his hips, she rocked up. "I want you inside me." Kisses on his lips, his cheeks, his throat, her hands cupping his face. "I need you."

"*Ashwini.*" The fingers of one hand digging into her hip, he took a shaky breath and pushed.

It burned but the hurt was a good one.

He slid in another inch, both of them sucked in a breath . . . and he began to retreat. But he pushed back before she could complain, going in an inch deeper. Again, and again. By the time he got to the fifth stroke, she'd forgotten the edge of discomfort and was thinking only of the pleasure. Muscles clenching around him, she heard him swear and then there was no more thinking.

Just heat and sex and Janvier's body stroking in and out of her, their mouths ravenous on one another and their eyes open. She gave him her soul, took his, and it was as it had always been meant to be.

Elena landed on the Tower roof late that night, after assisting a fellow hunter with a vamp who'd turned into a squirrelly runner. The small, slippery woman had been fast, weaving in and out through the city with the agility of the acrobat she'd apparently once been. Elena had found herself admiring her—even more so after her response to being caught. "I should've never listened to Bill," the petite runner had muttered in disgust. "Loophole, my ass! And now that very nice ass is toast!"

Wondering how many others Demarco's accountant target

had infected with his "loophole" lunacy, Elena reached out to Raphael. *Archangel?*

No response.

Frowning because she'd assumed he was at the Tower, she walked inside and to his office to find it empty. Her next stop was Dmitri's office. The vampire was dressed in black jeans and a black T-shirt today, his hair messy, as if he'd been running his hand through it. There was no doubt that Dmitri was a gorgeous, sexy man. There was also no doubt that he liked blood and pain a little too much.

His relationship with Honor was nothing Elena would've ever predicted—because the fact that Dmitri loved his wife was never in question. He saw no one else when Honor was in the room, his dark eyes only for her. Anyone who dared hurt the other hunter would soon find themselves very dead, likely after significant torture.

"Ellie," he said, curling a tendril of scent around her senses. *Fur and champagne and the promise of agonizing sin.*

Tensing her muscles against the impact because she knew damn well he did it only to test her, she gritted her teeth until the first wave passed. "Is that a report on the victims Ashwini's team found?"

A nod, features grim. "The one named Brooke has the most broken bones and internal injuries, but her chances of survival are nonetheless better than the ones Cornelius fed on."

"It's certain, then, that it's Cornelius?" Elena had kept up with the ongoing situation despite her other duties. The request for assistance from her hunter pal had come in only forty-five minutes before; she'd spent the rest of the day flying across wider New York. Raphael had asked her to take a Legion squadron and visit the well-behaving vampire leaders.

*An indication that their control of their people has been noticed, and a reminder that the Tower never stops watching.*

Having seen bloodlust in action a number of times as a hunter, the carnage sickening, Elena had no problem with doing what she could to ensure their city didn't descend into a bloodbath. As it was, the men and women she'd met today had all been on edge. News of Anais's and Severin's detainment at the Tower, entwined with the blood-chilling fear of the others who'd come face-to-face with a coldly furious Raphael the previous day, had spread through the community like wildfire.

Elena had reassured the vampire leaders that Raphael had noticed their attention to their duties and that they were in no danger of being called to a meeting with a pissed-off archangel. Her simple presence, the fact that she knew their names, had been enough to drive home Raphael's second point while simultaneously making the leaders feel appreciated.

Her wing muscles ached from the hours of flight, her body exhausted, but it had been worth it to reinforce the calm of the city. Even the Quarter had been free of any hint of bloodlust when she'd dropped by prior to answering Hilda's call for an angelic assist. Her Guild colleagues had begun to utilize her in specific incidents where an aerial view would be helpful and it gave Elena a way to keep her hand in, even as she spent more time on Tower business.

Her hunter soul, however, wished she'd been able to help Ash and Janvier also, the ugliness of what they'd discovered enraging her. *No one* had the right to do that to another living being, to take sick pleasure in the terror of another.

"My gut says it's Cornelius," Dmitri answered now, dropping the report on his desk. "It all lines up too well—the way the victims are emaciated, the red and cream feathers, and the fact that Giorgio spent half a century in Lijuan's court at the beginning of his Contract. That last's something I've just learned." He put his hands on his hips, raised an eyebrow. "But Janvier and the hunter are chasing this trail. What can I do for you, esteemed consort?"

Her fingers itched for a blade. "Have you seen Raphael?"

"Ah." He walked closer. "I'm afraid one of your favorite people has come to visit."

"If you tell me Michaela is here, I'll have to stab you for being the messenger." Raphael had personally escorted the other archangel out of his territory prior to the battle, after Michaela pretended to be pregnant to gain their sympathy—or for some other Machiavellian purpose they hadn't yet worked out.

"Such kinky things you say, Ellie." A purr of sound, before the scents around her became intoxicating enough to strangle her breath.

"Dmitri, stop baiting Ellie." Having entered behind Elena, Honor went to poke her husband in the side, a scowl on her face. "What are you doing to her?"

Wrapping an arm around Honor's shoulders, Dmitri held her close. "Keeping her strong." His eyes watched Elena, unblinking as a predator's. "Her scent susceptibility is a weakness others haven't yet learned to exploit, but they will."

Elena wished she could disagree, but, bastard though he was, Dmitri was right. Forcing air into her lungs, she said, "Spit it out. Who's here?"

"Caliane."

Her mind simply refused to compute that. So did Honor's, judging from the way her jaw fell.

*"Caliane?"* they both said in unison.

"Yes."

"But she's an ocean away!" Elena pointed out in desperation. "She can't just leave her city and fly over." Elena had spoken to Raphael about Naasir's report of Caliane's loneliness, but he'd said nothing about his mother visiting so soon. "What about the shield that protects her people? Lijuan's generals are just a short flight away."

"It appears Raphael's mother has secrets like any Ancient," Dmitri said, a faint curve to his mouth. "I've been in touch with Venom—the shield is active, and Venom didn't even know she was gone until I called him. Caliane told her people she would be sequestered with her maidens for some days."

Elena rubbed her face. "Oh, *God*," she moaned. "My mother-in-law has arrived for a visit and the house isn't even ready! Is she there?"

Amusement open, Dmitri said, "She was spotted by a far-advance scout—Raphael has flown out over the water to escort her the rest of the way home. You have at least an hour and I've alerted Montgomery that a suite needs to be made up." The drugging tendrils of scent retracted, the vampire taking pity on her. "Trust your butler."

Excellent advice, even considering the source. "I need to get home, change." She had grease and blood on her from the capture, the acrobat having led her and Hilda into a junkyard. "Why didn't you give me a call earlier?"

"The sire stated an hour's warning would be enough. It's all the time you need."

*According to whom?* Elena wanted to yell. "Damn it, Honor, what do I do with an Ancient mother-in-law who thinks I'm a bug?" One that had infested the life of Caliane's beloved son.

# 39

The other hunter winced, lifted her shoulders. "Sorry, Ellie. I don't have any experience in that field." Biting down on her lower lip, she snapped her fingers. "Wait, didn't Keir come in last night? I bet Caliane likes Keir."

"You're a genius!" Kissing the other woman on the cheek, Elena ran out the balcony door and swept down to the infirmary floor. Keir was amused at her panic but promised to join them for a late supper if Caliane was not exhausted and wanted company.

"She has come to see her son, Elena," the healer said, his hand gentle on her cheek and his eyes warm. "I think she will require little entertaining."

Hoping that was true, and that Caliane would decide to ignore her for the most part, Elena flew homeward, the Legion fighters who fell in with her silent shadows. The Enclave house was lit up like a glowing beacon, and Montgomery—damn, but the man deserved a raise—had set up hundreds of tiny candles in the snowy yard, each protected from the elements and the wind generated by angelic landings by a glass cage.

It was astonishingly beautiful from the air.

Landing in the circular area that had been left clear for that purpose, Elena walked inside to find the house in a bother. It was highly efficient, but everyone had somewhere to be, and no time to waste. Montgomery actually had a hair out of place. "Guild Hunter," he said, his relief obvious. "I took the liberty of putting out one of your gowns in readiness."

"Great, thanks." Elena took the stairs two at a time, while Montgomery kept pace with her. "Is there anything else I need to handle?"

"I've prepared the blue suite for Lady Caliane, and Sivya is ensuring we'll have plenty of dishes for her to choose from," he said as she walked into her and Raphael's rooms and began to unstrap her weapons.

Crossbow, knives, the throwing stars Ash had given her, the blade sticks that had been a gift from Mahiya. Leaving it all in a pile on a table, although she usually made sure to clean and neatly store her tools, she began to unlace and pull off her boots. "It sounds like you're on top of things." She frowned, tried to think like a consort. "Run her a bath so it's ready and at the right temperature when she arrives. She's had a long journey."

"Of course."

"And get a few flowering potted plants from the greenhouse," she said, remembering the lush gardens of Amanat. "Put them in her suite and her bathing chamber."

"I'll do it now."

"What about clothes?" Elena's head jerked up. "If she came alone, she might not have brought anything." Nothing of Elena's would fit her, Caliane being smaller and with more curves.

Montgomery looked momentarily green, but pulled himself together with commendable speed. "I'll contact the tailor. He must have a suitable piece he can alter quickly, and I'll have him work through the night to produce others." The butler pulled the door shut behind himself.

Tearing off her clothes, Elena showered at the speed of light, then slipped into the dress Montgomery had chosen. It was wildfire white with a haunting shimmer and, as far as gowns went, it was comfortable, being a column that began at her neck and skimmed down her body, but split into four overlapping panels at the hips.

The overlap meant her modesty was preserved, while she

had the ability to stride about—and to fight. The back was open
to accommodate her wings; she normally didn't like showing
that much skin, but it worked with the severe front, and honestly, she was happy not to have to figure out any straps or
wing-slit buttons at the moment. Button the collar at the side
of her neck, the closure discreet, and the dress was done.

Montgomery *really* deserved a raise.

Brushing out her hair, she pulled it into the twist Sara had
taught her, then anchored it using Mahiya's blade sticks.

Still feeling naked and weaponless, but knowing she
couldn't plaster herself with knives, had to find more baubles
instead, she opened the wooden jewelry box that sat on the
vanity. Her eye fell on the sweet, sweet blade that Raphael had
given her. The sheath and handle embedded with gemstones,
it appeared decorative—and could slice through bone if used
correctly.

Yes, her lover knew her.

"I love you, Archangel," she said with a smile as she fixed
the soft black sheath around her upper arm, the blade sparkling
shiny and fancy in contrast to the white of the dress.

She poked small diamond earrings into her pierced earlobes,
dusted on makeup, and, deciding that would have to do, raced
on to the next critical thing on her list—a face-to-face call with
Jessamy. The slender angel's eyes, a rich burnt sienna, went
huge when Elena told her what was about to happen. "This is
a highly unusual situation, Ellie," the other woman said, flipping rapidly through her books. "You are greeting an Ancient
who is the mother of your consort, but he is also an archangel."
Lines marred her smooth forehead. "It all complicates the usual
order of things."

"Give me something, Jess," Elena pleaded. "It's her first
visit to our home." Caliane had Slept for over a thousand years,
rising to consciousness less than a year past, during Lijuan's
first overt attack on Raphael. Since then, Raphael's mother had
remained in the lost city that had arisen with her, focusing on
the well-being of her people.

Elena ran a hand over her face. "It's critical I make a good
impression." Not because she cared for Caliane's approval, but
because Caliane was Raphael's mother.

If her own mother could come back, could pierce the veil

of death, she thought on a wave of grief that had never ceased to hurt, Elena would want her and Raphael to be friends, to like one another. The latter was improbable with Caliane, but at least the two of them could have a cordial relationship that might, in, oh, ten thousand years or so, thaw into mild liking.

"This will have to do," Jessamy muttered. "It's an account of a younger archangel greeting an Ancient. You're not an archangel, but as Raphael's consort, you carry his status by association in this situation."

Five minutes of swift instruction later, Elena headed downstairs, the slippers that matched her dress in one hand. Leaving them by the door, she went into the kitchens to discover controlled chaos. Waiting for a pause in the movement, she said, "Thank you. I know it'll mean a lot to Raphael that you're giving his mother such a welcome."

Smiles on each and every face, the stress draining away.

She made sure to personally thank Montgomery as well. Maybe she didn't know exactly how to be a consort, but she knew the members of a team functioned better with acknowledgment. And these people were all part of her team now—part of her family.

Then the rain, the crashing sea, was in her mind. *Guild Hunter, I give you a five-minute warning.*

*A five-hour warning would've been better.* She slipped her feet into the flat evening slippers and headed out into the snow to find that Montgomery had arranged for a pristine black carpet to be rolled to the landing area. *We're going to have a discussion when you get home about your idea of appropriate prep time.* Though she had to admit he'd been right to cut it so fine—the rush had given her no real time to stress.

A kiss against her mind. *I did not wish to steal your enjoyment in chasing your vampire rat.*

*What did I tell you about your new sense of humor?* Conscious of Montgomery walking briskly outside, to stop several feet behind and to the left of her, she looked toward Manhattan.

Raphael's wings were as distinctive to her in silhouette as they were in color, his wingspan extraordinary against the night sky, the white fire of them dazzling. That had to be Caliane by his side, smaller but with the same exquisite flight control.

A full squadron flew at their back.

Dmitri must've organized a welcome escort, but the escort fell back halfway across the Hudson, and it was Raphael and Caliane alone who landed in front of her. Eyes of excruciating blue and hair of midnight, there was no doubting they were mother and son.

"Lady Caliane," Elena said, stepping forward with both hands extended as Jessamy had decided would be acceptable. "You are welcome in our home."

Part of her was expecting the Ancient, dressed in weathered red-brown traveling leathers but with a bearing as regal as always, to reject the overture. She was ready to pretend it didn't matter, for the sake of keeping the peace, but Caliane's fingers closed over her own, the power in her bones a hum against Elena's skin.

"I thank you for your generosity," Caliane responded before breaking the handclasp. "I should've sent word of my journey."

"This is your son's home," Elena said, going with her gut. "You are always welcome."

Raphael's eyes met hers. *You are kind to my mother, hbeebti. I think she is embarrassed at her impetuous behavior now that she is here.*

*Thanks for the heads-up.* Smiling at Caliane, Elena waved toward the house. "Everyone is excited to meet you."

Caliane hesitated for a second, then fell in step with her. When Elena introduced Montgomery, Raphael's mother was pure grace, as she was with the other staff members who'd lined up to meet her, every single one spic and span.

Showing Caliane to her rooms afterward—her fingers discreetly crossed that Montgomery had managed to arrange a gown—Elena said, "Please take your time. We'll wait for you in the library. The dining room is a little too grand for family."

"Consort." Caliane's eyes were intense, her expression unreadable.

Elena's hand tightened on the doorknob, the hairs rising on the back of her neck. Her primal hindbrain recognized Caliane as a threat, screamed at her to run, but of course that wasn't an option. "Lady?"

"This house . . . it has a heart. I am glad my son lives in a house with a heart."

Unsure whether that was a compliment or a simple statement, Elena inclined her head and left Caliane when the
Ancient made to walk to the bath. She didn't blow out a relieved
breath until she was in the master bedroom. Walking straight
into Raphael's arms, she let him wrap his wings around her
and the two of them stood there, ready to face this extraordinary visit as they'd faced everything else: together.

Ashwini dreamed of Felicity, woke with the young woman's
face at the forefront of her mind. It frustrated her beyond bearing to know that Giorgio and Cornelius remained free to exercise their perversions. Leaving the bed to find Janvier on the
balcony on his phone, she put on a large T-shirt, stuffed her
feet into thick socks, then went out to hug him from the back.

He was wearing just his jeans, his body warm against her
in spite of the cold. Turning, he held her close with one arm
around her shoulders as he spoke to Dmitri. "Giorgio has been
connected to Lijuan," he told her before returning to his
conversation.

She could see from the lack of a smile in his eyes that there'd
been no further breakthroughs. Stifling the urge to scream at
the sky, she pressed a kiss to his chest, then ducked inside to
shower and dress. She was putting her hair in a ponytail when
she heard the sound of angelic wings nearby. Glancing out the
balcony doors, she was just in time to catch the heartbreaking
light of Aodhan's wings sweeping back up.

Janvier walked in with a duffel the next instant. "Fresh
clothes."

"What exactly do you have on him that he'll play courier
for you?" she asked, bemused at the idea of being with a man
who could call in angelic help like she could a ride from a fellow hunter.

Walking backward into the bathroom, he winked. "That is
between me and Sparkle, my *khoobsurat* and gorgeously dangerous Ashblade."

Happy despite her raw emotions at the sense that Felicity
remained lost, unable to move on, she left him to his shower
and walked into the kitchen to make coffee. "I'm not giving

up," she said to the ghost of the woman who'd been punished for wanting only to believe in hope, in a future where she was cherished. "The evil pieces of shit *will* go down. I promise you that."

A wintry sigh across her skin that made it pebble, her breath suddenly frosting the air as her lungs fought to deal with the sudden, excruciating cold . . . then warmth rushing back into her, and she knew that for the moment, Felicity was gone.

The kiss on the back of her neck ten minutes later was accompanied by the fresh, clean scent of soap and man. Facing him, she held up her coffee, having already eaten a couple of pieces of toast. "Sip?"

He nodded and took a drink, absorbing the pleasure of the taste with a sensuality that made her lower body clench. The chemistry between them was impossibly more powerful this morning, their bodies having learned exactly what they could do to one another.

Indulging herself by caressing him with her gaze, she caught the fine edge of tension in the line of his jaw. "When did you last feed?" She put aside her coffee.

"I'm not about to keel over, *cher*." A slow smile. "I can pick up a bottle from the Tower."

She tugged up the cuff of her black V-necked sweater to bare her wrist and raised it to brush his lips. His eyes went heavy lidded, his chest expanding on a deep inhale. "There is no obligation."

"I know." Stroking her fingers down his neck, she leaned in even closer, the side of her body aligned to his.

He shuddered, cupped the other side of her wrist, and pressed a kiss to her rapidly beating pulse. Then he licked out, drew in another long breath. Her blood seemed to rush to that one tiny point. Nipples rubbing against her bra and skin tight, she waited. When his fangs scraped over her skin, she bit back a moan.

His eyes flicked up. In them was pure sex and the lazy, possessive affection that had tied her up in knots long before she'd admitted he was far more than just a job to her. "Now," she said, tone husky.

A sinful smile before his fangs pierced her flesh.

His lashes came down, his throat moving as he fed . . . and her blood, it turned to honey. Legs trembling, she shifted to lean against the counter. He followed, one hand going to her lower back to caress her lightly as he continued to feed.

He wasn't drawing much blood, she realized with the part of her mind that wasn't dazed. He'd taken most of what he needed in the first two pulls, was now sipping . . . enjoying. She was enjoying it, too. The arousal kept building and building, a fist low in her belly. It was different from sex, not as intimate . . . except this was Janvier. Slipping his fingers under her top to caress her skin, he lifted his lashes again, their eyes connected, and the fist exploded outward.

Shivering through the ripples, she opened eyes she didn't remember closing to see him licking the wound closed. He did it several times, until she couldn't see anything but tiny pinpricks that would fade in a day. Satisfied, he slid a hand around her nape and jaw, running the thumb of his other hand over her lower lip. "I could become used to this breakfast."

She nipped at his thumb. "Gotta say, it's not a bad morning wake-up." Yeah, he'd turned her inside out, but he wasn't exactly in control, either, his erection aggressive against the zipper of his jeans. "Maybe next time we should do it before we get out of bed."

"I vote yes." Rubbing up against her, he groaned. "We have—"

Both their phones beeped at once. The message was identical. *One victim awake. Wishes to talk.*

Arousal doused, they headed out and to the hospital without further conversation. It was Brooke who was awake and stable enough to talk. Fear was a metallic taste in the air around the brutalized woman, but when she grabbed for Ashwini's hand, Ashwini didn't protest.

Stomach muscles clenched against the barrage of pain and panic that made nausea shove at her throat, she met Brooke's bruised brown eyes. "You're tough," she said. "Good. The bastards wouldn't have expected that."

Brooke's smile turned into a grimace as her abused facial muscles attempted to stretch. "You haven't found—" She coughed, but waved off the chips of ice Ashwini offered from the cup on the bedside table.

"No," Ashwini answered, putting the ice back. "We haven't tracked them down yet, but we will. Do you know any place Giorgio might hide?" Pulling out her phone, she went through each of the properties they'd already cleared.

"You got them all." Rasping, barely audible words. "Only . . ."

# 40

"Only?" Ashwini could tell Brooke was in severe pain, but the woman had nixed pain medication prior to this meeting because she wanted to talk, wanted to help. Ashwini wasn't about to second-guess her courage.

"Cattle." Brooke whispered, her hand tightening on Ashwini's. "Cattle give him things."

Ashwini frowned, focusing ruthlessly on the facts rather than the silent scream of terror that continued to slap at her, making her skull throb. "How?" she asked. "His pattern seems to be going after women who have little." Even the showpiece cattle had all proven to be from modest or deprived backgrounds. Brooke herself had been an exotic dancer in a low-rent part of town before Giorgio plucked her for his adoring harem.

Despite that, the financial wizards had checked them out, found no properties.

"Pattern right." Brooke coughed again, accepted the ice chips this time, her breathing a serrated scrape. "Make us grateful."

"He's a predator." Ashwini squeezed the other woman's hand. "One who's had hundreds of years to hone his skills. Don't you *ever* blame yourself for what he is."

A shaky nod. "Th-thanks. Needed to hear." The other woman seemed to be about to lose consciousness, but blinked rapidly, managed to stay awake. "Cattle poor . . . but Penelope got in-in-inh . . ."

"Inheritance?"

Another faint nod. "T-turned out her McScrooge aunt was rich. L-left it all to her five y-y-years ago." Air noisy in her lungs, her hand spasmed on Ashwini's. "It's in sp—" Throat dry, she couldn't speak until Ashwini had eased more ice into her mouth. "Aunt didn't like Giorgio," the hurt woman said clearly, eyes so bright it was clear she was fighting desperately to communicate all she knew. "House is in special legal trust where Pen can use it till death, but she has no . . ." A wracking cough.

Mind racing, Ashwini said, "She has no control over it— can't sell it or sign it across to Giorgio?" That had to be the reason why it hadn't shown up in the searches. Penelope's name wasn't on the deed.

Brooke nodded. "The women d-don't know 'bout him." A pained inhale. "Don't hurt them."

"Don't worry. They won't be punished for his crimes. And Brooke—thank you. What you've just told me changes every-thing."

Brooke's smile was a shadow, her eyes closing.

Leaving the sleeping woman after freeing her hand, Ash-wini walked out to where Janvier stood waiting in the hospital hallway . . . and staggered, would've gone to her knees if Jan-vier hadn't caught her.

"A minute," she said, holding on to him, letting his heat warm up the ice in her veins.

"As long as you need." Arms steel and voice rough, he pressed his lips to her temple.

She wished she could stay in his embrace forever, but she'd made a promise to Felicity, to Brooke, to all of the victims.

Pulling away after that single precious minute, her nausea and pounding head at a more manageable level, she kissed him once before returning to the horror. "Penelope," she said, already dialing the data team. "She has access to a property." Rattling off everything she knew to the tech who answered, she put a rush on the information. "Find the aunt and you'll find the house."

She'd barely hung up when Carys's name appeared on her phone. "Two girls are missing," the woman told Ashwini. "They had a call-out last night, told another girl they were going to be rich, maybe even bag a sugar daddy who'd get them into a Quarter house."

A knot formed in Ashwini's gut at the eerie similarity to the line Felicity had been fed. "It's only overnight," she said, trying not to leap to a deadly conclusion. "That unusual?"

"Yeah, if Bridget and Marta were overnighting, they would've told us. It's how we look out for one another."

"Send me their photos. Is there anything else you can think of that might help us find them?"

A pause. "You actually going to help? You're taking me seriously?"

Nonplussed, Ashwini said, "Why wouldn't I? You don't seem like the kind of woman who'd lie."

"I'm not, but cops don't take hookers missing overnight seriously."

"I'm not a cop."

"Yeah, you're a hunter." It sounded like a compliment. "Ransom said you were solid." A crackling rustle in the background. "Okay, I talked to the girls, as well as a few of the guys who work that area, and the girls were picked up in a black SUV, tinted windows. But it wasn't a guy inside. It was a woman. I wrote down the description—brunette in her late twenties, good condition. One of the girls noticed she had a nice mani—"

"Gold with diamantés?"

"Yeah, you know the bitch?"

"Yes, I know the bitch." Hanging up after making sure Carys didn't have any other useful information, she turned to Janvier and told him Carys's news. "Penelope knew what Giorgio was the entire time. I fell for her sweet 'we're all loyal to one another' act." So, she thought, had the brave woman in the hospital bed; Brooke's only crime was that she'd loved a monster.

Even Dmitri had put only a light watch on the cattle, more

to make them feel safe in the hotel where they were currently staying than to lock them in. It would've been simple for Penelope to slip out. "I bet you she's been luring women for him, playing chauffeur. That's why no one ever saw Giorgio with Felicity."

Janvier's eyes blazed.

Not needing him to speak to understand the cold rage in his bones, Ashwini added the information about the black SUV to what she'd already given the data team. It wasn't much, but if Giorgio or one of the women had a black SUV registered in his or her name, it might give them another way to track the bastard.

The property information came through three minutes later. Turned out the aunt had *two* properties, both tied up in a complicated legal framework that made actual beneficial ownership unclear. "We'll take the one on the Lower East Side," she told the tech, she and Janvier having reached his bike. "It's closer to the hospital."

"Naasir says he can handle the one on the Upper West Side," came the response. "Illium's going with him."

"Tell them to call if they find anything." Hanging up, she shared the address with Janvier, and the two of them roared out.

Her phone had another message on it when she checked it after they parked a block down from the three-level freestanding house that had belonged to Penelope's aunt. "The vehicle's registered to Marie May," she told Janvier as they got off the bike. "Guild's put out an alert." It would go out to cops, Tower personnel, any hunters in the vicinity.

Janvier, having hung their helmets on either side of the handlebars, stared down the street. "I don't think that'll be necessary."

Following his gaze, Ashwini saw it. "Son of a bitch." A black SUV with tinted windows was parked directly across from the house.

No way in hell was that a coincidence.

"We can't wait," she said. "He's already had those two women for hours."

"Front or back?" Janvier asked, sending in a request for urgent backup.

She looked at the building. "You know that climbing thing

you do? Can you get up to that third-floor window, figure out a way to get inside?"

Janvier followed her gaze to the closed but not particularly secure-looking window. "Child's play."

"You go in, work your way down. I'll enter through the front." She caught his scowl, shook her head. "I'll go in like I'm following up on Penelope, making sure she's all right after the trauma of discovering Giorgio's crimes."

"It's still a risk."

Ashwini smiled. So did Janvier. Then they split.

She walked down the sidewalk and up the steps to the front door of the house, while Janvier went left and over the fence of the house on the corner. By the time she rang the front doorbell, she figured he had to be climbing the side of the house.

When no one answered on the first ring, she leaned on it, acting irritated for the benefit of the surveillance camera trained on the doorstep. Meanwhile her stomach churned, her ability picking up something so horrible that she had to shove it aside or she wouldn't be able to function. Glancing at her watch at the continued lack of an answer from within, she took out her cell phone and rang Penelope. She heard it ring inside the house before it was silenced. The door swung open five seconds later.

No gold choker or silk top this time, but the thigh length robe of deep blue was richly embroidered.

"Oh, hi!" said the brunette, her eyes glittering and her cheeks flushed. "Sorry about the wait." A small laugh. "I was shaving my legs."

Ashwini didn't glance down, simply smiled as if she'd swallowed the excuse. "I wanted to check up on you," she said, wondering what lay in the darkness of the hallway behind the woman who played aide to a sadistic psychopath. "Brooke told us you might be here when we couldn't find you at the hotel with the others."

Penelope's mouth thinned at the sound of Brooke's name, but she recovered quickly. "Oh, I hope I'm not in trouble—I wanted to be in my own home." She opened the door a little wider. "You can tell everyone I'm fine. And Brooke?" Bright, hard eyes. "She'll be okay?"

"Yes, the doctors say she'll make a full recovery." Ashwini patted the brick cladding. "This is a great place."

"Isn't it? My aunt left it to me." Lower lip quivering, Penelope hugged herself, her distinctive gold and diamanté nails vivid against the dark blue of the robe. "I can't believe Giorgio did those things, hurt Brooke. I loved him."

She was, Ashwini thought, a pathologically good liar. She was also now a step outside the doorway, having instinctively followed Ashwini when she shifted back. Continuing to smile, Ashwini leaned in toward her and said, "I can blow a hole through your gut in the time it takes for you to scream, so don't."

Penelope froze midbreath, her mouth open like that of a blowfish.

Remaining close to block the expression on Penelope's face from the camera, she said, "Is Giorgio inside that house?" She dug the gun into Penelope's side when the other woman didn't answer quickly enough, no mercy in her with the memory of Brooke's battered face at the forefront of her mind.

"Y-yes."

"Who else?"

A twist of her lips. "Nothing but two whores I picked up off the street."

Ashwini flicked off the safety. "Don't lie to me. I don't like you and I'll have no hesitation in putting a bullet through your pretty face to mess it up."

Smugness wiped away, Penelope whimpered. "You can't do that."

"Self-defense. Who do you think the Guild is going to believe? Me or a dead blood junkie who sold out her sister?"

"Brooke isn't my sister! She's a piece of trash who shamed our master."

"One last chance." Ashwini shoved in the gun hard enough that it would bruise, her voice ice-cold. "Who else is inside the house?"

Goose bumps on her skin, Penelope crumbled. "The other master," she whispered. "The old one."

"Who watches the surveillance feed?"

"The master," she said. "He'll see you." She began to smirk.

Ashwini reached out as if to hug Penelope and stabbed two fingers into a particular part of her throat. It made the brunette's eyes go wide, a retching sound escaping her before she slumped. Slinging an arm around the dazed woman, she gave up any attempt at stealth and shoved the door fully open to see no one lying in wait.

She dumped a moaning Penelope in the hallway and, pulling out the belt of the woman's elaborate robe, used it to hog-tie her, hands behind her back and ankles lashed to her wrists. A slash with one of her blades and she had another piece of the robe to use as a gag. "Wouldn't want you calling out to your precious Giorgio at the wrong time," she muttered. Finished, she set Penelope on her side to make sure she could breathe.

The entire operation took her under a minute and her skin crawled the whole time, but she figured Giorgio was too much of a coward to come at her straight-on. No, the pencil-dicked bastard would be hiding somewhere, ready to ambush her like he'd ambushed the women who had trusted him.

Ignoring the daggers Penelope was throwing at her with her eyes, she slid away the knife she'd used to cut up the robe and pulled out her secondary gun from an ankle sheath. Both guns held out, she took a step toward the first closed door on this floor.

Having scrambled up the side of the building, Janvier got to the old-fashioned bay window and looking through the parted curtains, confirmed the room beyond was empty. He could've broken a pane to get in, but the noise might alert anyone up here—so he used a trick he'd learned from a jewel thief, and broke the hinges instead, using a sharp blade and vampiric strength.

Grabbing the falling half of the window, he lowered it quietly to the floor, then slid in, his kukris in hand the instant his feet touched the carpet. One ear open for Ash, he scanned the room to find it comparatively bare, though there were a few feminine accoutrements lying about.

Including a pretty yellow scarf with purple butterflies half hanging out of a drawer.

His mind flashed to the photo of Felicity with her friends, all with cocktails in hand . . . and Felicity with that scarf around her neck.

This had to be where she, Lilli, and the other victims had lived before Giorgio put them in the crates. The place where they'd tried to become "good enough" to move into Giorgio's Vampire Quarter house. Clamping down his rage, and taking a quick look around to make sure he wasn't missing anything, he stepped out into the corridor.

To the left was what proved to be a bathroom when he pushed the door open. It, too, was empty. As was the room next to it. That room had a tiny decorative balcony on the side not visible from the street, but it was so small he could see no one was on it from a glance through the sliding doors. That left the right-hand side of the floor.

It had two doors, and the first one was locked. Sliding away one of his blades, he took a small metal wire from his pocket, another little trick he'd learned from his larcenous friend. Ten seconds later, there was a small click that said he was in. The sound was tiny, but Janvier knew some older vamps had hearing that was preternaturally acute. Putting away the wire, he waited, listening at the door.

Sounds from within, but they were odd, muffled.

He very carefully nudged the door open while keeping his body out of the way. When there was no other sound, he pushed it fully open and slammed his back against the corridor wall again.

More muffled sounds, louder now.

He glanced in, saw a woman bound hand and foot, something stuffed in her mouth and her curly black hair a tangle against the thick gray carpet. Mascara ran down the clammy white skin of her face, terror in her eyes. Lifting a finger to his lips, he checked the rest of the room and found no evidence of another individual. He looked out into the corridor to ensure it remained clear, then went down beside her.

"I'm going to untie you," he said quietly. "But if you start crying or making any other kind of noise, I might not be able to get you out." There was no knowing if Giorgio had guards in this place and Cornelius was a powerful angel, even without Lijuan feeding him energy. "Nod if you understand."

A frantic nod.

Janvier took out the gag first. It turned out to be a balled-up sock.

"My friend, Marta," she whispered through her dry mouth and cracked lips. "The brunette who brought us here took her."

"We'll find her." Cutting the ropes, he led her to the room with the sliding doors. They proved to be locked by a keyed dead bolt. It took him precious seconds to pick the lock, but when he slid the doors open, he saw his hunch had been right: rusted but with no indications of dangerous wear, there was a large pipe on the outer wall that went all the way to the ground.

It had enough joins to provide a grip.

Shrugging off his leather jacket, he gave it to the woman who'd confirmed her name was Bridget. Her skintight jeans and little boots would protect her legs from the cold, but she wore only a bustier on her top half. "I'm going to help you over the railing to that pipe." Thinking of her hands on the icy metal, he remembered he had Ash's gloves in his jacket pockets, told her to slip them on. "Climb down as silently as you can."

"What about Marta?" she asked, having wiped the backs of her hands across her face. It had further smeared her makeup, but her eyes held more anger than fear.

"I'll get her. It'll go better if I don't have to worry about you as well."

Giving a jerky nod, she pulled on the gloves. "Should I call the cops after I get down?"

"They're already on their way. Can you operate a motorcycle?" At the negative shake of her head, he said, "Go down the street and hide behind the house on the corner." He'd noticed it was empty when he came through. "Our backup should arrive within minutes."

She didn't speak again until he'd helped her out. "Please help my friend."

"I will." Waiting just long enough to see that she was steady on the pipe, he went back out to the corridor and quickly looked in on the rooms he'd already cleared. The final door on the right was a master bedroom, opulently male in design. Janvier smelled the same cologne he'd smelled in Giorgio's home, saw a cravat on the bed, a shirt with a fall of lace at the cuffs on a chair.

Of Giorgio himself, however, there was no sign.

He started down the stairs to the second level.

# 41

Looking right as she moved down the hallway, Ashwini found a spacious living area. Her eye went immediately to the tumbler of red liquid on the antique sideboard, beside a crystal decanter of the same.

*Blood.*

Nothing else had that same consistency, a consistency that was obvious to her even from her current position. Stepping inside with care, she scanned the large room. There really was only one place anyone could hide and that was behind the sofa by the windows. Instead of walking over, she dropped to the floor and looked beneath the cream-colored sofa with curved wooden legs. Nothing.

She confirmed that by crossing the room and taking a second look.

Now she had a choice to make. Go through the door from the living room to the room on the other side, or enter the other room from the corridor. Eyes narrowed, she looked around and found an ornate chair that was heavy but that she could carry without dragging it on the floor. She moved it to under the knob of the internal access door, blocking it as an exit route, then returned to the corridor.

Back near the entrance, Penelope was flopping around, hair all over her face as she attempted to move, one bare breast and thigh exposed. Confirming with a glance that the other woman wouldn't be going anywhere, Ashwini opened a door on the left. It proved to be a closet filled with velvet and lace coats, along with what appeared to be a hooded black cape. Closing it, she cleared the two other rooms on the left while keeping an eye on the open doorway that led into the room off the living area.

The first room on the left was some kind of rumpus room with a television and surprisingly laid-back furniture. Either Giorgio hadn't gotten around to updating it or it was for the women. The other room was a toilet covered in fancy tile. So, likely, the remaining room hadn't yet been updated. Dead certain someone was in the room she'd left for last, she made her way to the door.

At the same time, she swapped out her guns for knives. They'd make far less noise and not alert anyone else in the house. Then she drop-rolled into the room—to a rushing attack from a supernaturally pretty vampire with waves of golden hair. But Giorgio wasn't used to fighting for his life. He went for where her body should've been, rather than where she actually was.

She'd come up into a crouch and thrust a knife into his gut before he could stop his headlong rush. His blood stained his white shirt scarlet. Well aware how quickly vamps his age could shrug off a gut wound, she thrust a second knife directly into his heart seconds after the first, then rose to stab a third into his neck from the side.

It severed his jugular, blood pumping out in hot spurts to splatter the warm yellow walls of what turned out to be the kitchen, but he still kept coming, trying to gurgle something that sounded like "whore."

"Better a whore than a sadistic piece of shit like you," she said and, grabbing the hunting knife from her belt, slammed it into his brain through his left ear, then twisted.

A shocked look on his face, Giorgio collapsed at last.

Ashwini knew he wasn't dead—she'd made certain of it. She wanted Giorgio to suffer immortal justice. It could last years. The blade in his brain should keep him down for a day at least, but she wasn't going to risk it, with all the weirdness in this case. For all she fucking knew, Giorgio was part reborn and would shamble back to life as soon as she turned her back.

Raiding the kitchen in lieu of using up her own knives, she methodically put carbon-steel steak knives through his palms, forearms, and shoulders, careful not to make skin-to-skin contact. After which she brought a meat cleaver down on his thigh, snapping the bone. She did the same to his other femur.

Unlike Giorgio, she took no pleasure in causing the injuries. Her only motive was to keep him in place. Except for the last two knives she'd found—narrow and sharp filleting blades.

"This is for every woman you've ever hurt," she said and pinned the bastard's testicles to the floor, the knives slicing easily through his pants. "I hope that fucking hurts when you wake up."

Judging him contained, she got up and headed out into the hallway again.

The sirens she could already hear told her backup would arrive long before Giorgio had any chance of rising. Taking the stairs to the second floor, she went up on silent feet . . . to see Janvier coming down from the third floor. She jerked up her head. He said, "One girl safe," in a low tone, then zeroed in on the blood on her jacket.

"Giorgio's."

Touching his fingers to her jaw, he looked down the corridor. "Cornelius must be on this floor if he's here."

"He is." The nauseating ugliness she'd sensed even from the outside dominated the air here, acrid and *old*. Fighting the sick feeling in her gut, she slipped her guns back out. Knives wouldn't do much good against an angel, but a brain full of lead might slow him down enough for Janvier to behead him.

They went down the corridor side by side, clearing two rooms before Ashwini's churning stomach told her they were at the right one. Communicating that to Janvier with a single glance, she didn't argue when he nodded at her to open the door so he could go in first. As a vampire, he had more chance of surviving a pissed-off angel than she did. And she had a better chance of keeping him safe if she went in with guns blazing behind him.

Turning the knob, she shoved it open before swinging around to go in behind Janvier. He went in as low and as quiet as she had in the kitchen and came up ready to defend against an attack . . . except there was no attack.

There was, however, an angel in the room.

Ashwini kept her guns up, her eyes refusing to believe what they saw in front of them. When she chanced a quick look at Janvier, it was to see the same disbelief in his eyes.

Janvier had shown her a photo of Cornelius soon after they'd first found his feathers. The male in the image had had a heavy build, his hair a glossy chestnut so dark it was near black, his eyes a deep greenish hazel, and his skin a sun-stroked brown that—when paired with his sculptured features—spoke of the Mediterranean or northern Africa. His wings had been spread in the image, warrior strong and ready for flight.

In front of the windows stood . . . she didn't know what to call him. He might've once been an angel but his wings were now two lumps of petrified cartilage and bone, the cream of his feathers visible only in sporadic patches, the red all but gone. When he turned to face them, she saw his cheeks were sunken in, his skin stark white, and that his dusty-brown hair evidenced the same molting as his wings, the skin on the exposed parts of his skull reminiscent of tanned hide.

Ashwini could've circled his upper arm with her forefinger and thumb. It was as if he'd lost all body fat and muscle mass. But even his bones weren't quite right, his jaw sticking out in an odd way and his right leg appearing to have a second knee that pushed at the thin red silk pants that hung over his emaciated form, his upper half bare to reveal a rib cage that was crushed on one side.

His eyes were a filmy blue, his teeth jagged . . . and covered with blood, the same blood that ringed his mouth and dripped down his chest.

Smiling grotesquely at them, he slid to his knees and went as if to feed again from the woman on the floor, her hair a pool of magenta and her skin a pale brown. Ashwini shot him through the head, hoping it wouldn't blow his skull to smithereens. With a normal angel, that wouldn't be a risk, but with this one . . .

Cornelius fell forward but his head was whole. Good. He, too, needed to face immortal justice.

Janvier pulled the enemy angel's body off the woman, while

Ashwini checked her for a pulse. She had to use the wrist—the woman's throat was too bloody a mess.

"Come on," she whispered, seeing only the most minor signs of long-term damage on the victim—her skin was a touch drier than it should be, the sheen of her dyed hair dulled but not absent. It gave Ashwini hope that they weren't too late. "Come on."

Then there it was: a pulse, thready but present.

Hearing boots slamming up the stairs, she ran to the door, saw Trace. "Get the paramedics!"

He nodded and disappeared back down the way he'd come.

The paramedics were in the room a half minute later.

Fourteen hours after that, the city dark, Ashwini leaned against the wall of a large windowless room in the center of the Tower. Janvier stood beside her, one booted foot up against the wall, his arms folded. Elena was next to Ashwini, while Dmitri flanked Janvier. Naasir had growled when told of the capture and said he'd get the report from them. The idea of being closed up with "walking rancid meat" hadn't appealed to the vampire.

Ashwini wasn't exactly happy about it, either, but she had to see this through no matter what. Staying strong against the vortex of Raphael's power was actually giving her a counterbalance to the bile-inducing horror of Cornelius's evil . . . and Janvier's shoulder touching her own was a physical anchor.

Raphael stood in the center facing Cornelius—who'd finally healed enough to speak, but not to stand for an extended period. It shouldn't have taken an angel of his age anywhere near that long to shake off a bullet wound, but Cornelius wasn't exactly a normal angel anymore. He sat in a chair that was the only piece of furniture in the room, his face wreathed in a grimace of a smile.

Ashwini ground her teeth against the urge to go for a gun again. Marta, the woman they'd rescued, was alive, but the damage done to her was more than skin-deep. Her bones had aged ten years, with her internal organs showing signs of the same. According to the doctors, she'd be fine with supplements, but her life span had been permanently shortened.

All so a monster could live another day.

"Cornelius," Raphael said, his wings glowing in a way that no one ever wanted to see, because when an archangel glowed, people died. "You are not as you were."

"My goddess gave me a gift."

"She fed from you because you were disposable and strong." A pitiless rejoinder. "My spymaster has confirmed that Xi retreated with the troops, as did Alastair and Philomena. Their injuries and the deaths of Lijuan's other generals came at the hands of my people, not from Lijuan."

Cornelius's smile didn't slip. "I offered myself to enhance her greatness, to become part of her." He broke off into a rattling cough. "Alas, she could not complete the feeding in the midst of the final strike, could not take the fullness of my soul into herself."

That explained Cornelius's half-desiccated state.

"And the women?" Raphael asked in an ice-cold tone that had Ashwini's heart freezing. As long as she lived, she would *never* understand how Ellie got into bed with him. Even more so now that Ashwini had personally experienced the shattering vulnerability that came with sex.

Janvier shot her a look at that instant, his eyes glittering, and it was as if he'd read her mind. She scowled. He grinned and closed his hand over her own. "I could tear off your head with a single wrench," he said in a low tone that reached only her.

"Stop reading my thoughts." She wasn't worried in the least about his strength. If he'd wanted to hurt her, he'd have done it long ago. Instead, he'd put himself in the path of danger for her more than once.

Frowning, Janvier said, "But you spoke aloud."

She blinked, leaned in to speak against his ear. "No, I didn't."

They stared at each other.

"We'll talk about it later," she finally whispered and they returned their attention to the interrogation.

Cornelius admitted to using the women to maintain his strength as he awaited his "goddess's return," but refused to admit he'd fed on animals before he tracked down Giorgio.

"Saving face," Dmitri murmured. "To feed on animals makes him an animal himself."

"What did animals ever do to you that you'd insult them like that?"

Ashwini's muttered rejoinder made Dmitri's lips curve. "My apologies. You are, of course, correct. He is an unnatural abomination."

"What will Raphael do to him?" she asked.

"He'll ask the surviving victims their will and then he'll make sure it's carried out, on both Cornelius and Giorgio."

"Good." Had it been up to her, Ashwini would've told Raphael to shut the bastards up in a room together, where Cornelius could feed on Giorgio until the vampire died, then starve to death himself. It'd take a long, long time, even given his current state.

Maybe she'd mention the idea to the living victims.

"You are bloodthirsty, my Ashblade."

When she glared at him, Janvier scowled. "You didn't say that aloud, either?"

"No." She pushed off the wall when Raphael turned to leave, indicating the questioning was over.

He left Cornelius in the room and Dmitri locked the door behind them.

"I have spoken to Giorgio," Raphael said, his wing brushing over Elena's.

"Already?" Ashwini said before she realized she was interrupting an archangel. "I didn't think he was powerful enough to heal so fast."

Raphael held her gaze, the blue of his eyes violent. "He isn't."

But Raphael, she understood, keeping a white-knuckled grip on her ability so she wouldn't be sucked into the force of him, was an archangel. No way of knowing how he'd made Giorgio talk, and it was probably better if she didn't; she had enough nightmares inside her skull.

Raphael's eyes didn't move off her, the power in them chilling. "You did an extraordinary job of containing him without causing a deadly injury."

Ashwini decided she wasn't delirious. Raphael definitely sounded amused. "I might have gone a bit overboard," she admitted with a wince. "I just didn't want to risk that he'd crawl away, escape justice to carry on his reign of torture and death."

"A worthy motive," Raphael said, his expression growing chilly again as he added, "He deserves the pain."

"You have to teach me the knife-through-the-brain trick," Elena said, giving Ashwini an excuse to look away from the archangel who had noticed her. No sane person wanted an archangel's notice. *Ever.*

"There's a twist at the end," she said, curling her fingers surreptitiously around Janvier's. He curled back in turn, warm and strong.

And it became easier to breathe. "That's what you have to be careful about," she told Ellie. "Otherwise, you scramble the brains too badly for the vamp to recover."

The other hunter's eyes gleamed. "We'll talk." She looked up at her consort. "So, what did that slimy coward have to say for himself?"

"That he was no traitor." Cold disgust in Raphael's words. "In truth, he had no true loyalties, did only what was good for Giorgio. Cornelius had known him in the past, and when he saw Giorgio in the Quarter, he tracked him to his home and asked for sanctuary, convincing Giorgio that he'd be rewarded when Lijuan arose anew."

"Sire," Janvier said, "Giorgio wasn't always thus. He was a great physician. Is it the madness of age?"

Raphael's answer was absolute. "No. He simply became bored with eternity and this was his entertainment." The pure male beauty of the archangel's features did nothing to hide the ruthlessness that made him one of the Cadre. "I believe he accepted Cornelius not because of any belief in Lijuan's resurrection, but because he wished for a partner in his perversions."

"Giorgio shouldn't have been able to get away with his misuse of women for as long as he did," Dmitri said, his voice stripped of all traces of civility.

Thinking of Carys's surprise at Ashwini's response to the report of the two missing pros, she said, "You need a better way to stay in touch with the vulnerable."

"Ash is right," Janvier said. "There's a gray world beneath the surface of the city, and it's from this pool that predators like Giorgio pick their prey. I'm also concerned about how many submissive mortals I saw in the Quarter clubs."

Dmitri frowned. "We have a network in place, but its focus is on keeping an eye on the immortals, rather than on mortals who might become prey. It's a gap we need to work out a way to plug."

What the Tower needed, Ashwini thought, was someone like Ransom, someone trusted on the streets and protective of its denizens, *but* who wasn't mortal. It had to be a vampire, a man or woman who'd already made the choice to live in the immortal world.

"We can discuss this further tomorrow," Raphael said. "For now, the predators are locked up, and you both"—those eyes full of *power* noticing Ashwini and Janvier again—"have earned the night off. Enjoy the peace while it lasts."

There was no doubting it was an order.

"Sire," Janvier said, and the two of them left to head out. He'd already grabbed a black and red motorcycle jacket to replace the jacket he'd given to the woman he'd rescued, so there was only one other thing to remember.

"Grab a few bottles of blood," she said to him once they were in the main corridor. "You need more than I can give you."

His smile was wicked. "You give me plenty, sugar. And it's all good."

Rolling her eyes, she leaned in and kissed him on that pretty mouth. "Thank you." For figuring out she'd needed a smile and giving it to her.

"No thanks necessary," he said and took her hand again. "Just always be mine."

*I want to grow old with you,* she thought on a heartbreaking surge of love, *to see the world with you, to fight with you, to kiss your sinful, laughing mouth a million times.*

Giorgio had become bored with eternity, when Ashwini would give her soul to experience a single mortal lifetime with the vampire by her side without the specter of a psychological breakdown that would eventually fragment her into myriad tiny pieces.

Bitterness threatened, but she'd made her decision a long time ago, and she wasn't about to permit a monster to shake the foundations of her world. No, she'd think of her sister, of Felicity, of Lilli. None had had a chance to experience love in this way, to walk hand in hand with a man who would lay down his life for her. A day, a week, a month, a year—no matter how long she lived as a whole person, she would do it with an open heart and an unfettered spirit.

"I love you," she said as they walked to his Tower apartment, pressing her lips to his jaw.

*"Cher."* He turned to cup her cheek, his eyes startlingly vulnerable.

Heart raw, she stroked her fingers through his hair. "You know I do. You have to."

"Yes." A gorgeous, wild smile. "But it is nice to hear you admit it."

Kissing her laughing mouth, he murmured his own words of love, told her she owned his heart and always would. "Let's stay here," he said, sliding his hand under her jacket and sweater. "We can go to your place in the morning."

"Deal," she said just as her phone buzzed.

Holding the moss and sunlight of his gaze, one hand on his nape, she reached into her pocket with the other. "I have to check the caller ID." It could be Banli House.

"I know," said the man who understood her, accepted her.

Eyes burning, she leaned into him as she looked at the name on the screen. It wasn't Banli House, but it was a call she had to answer.

"Tanu is Tanu tonight," Arvi said, his voice holding a smile. "She'd like to see you."

# 42

Elena walked out to a Tower balcony with Raphael. Dmitri had just left to handle an emergency situation with Sorrow, the young woman who'd been taken by a mad archangel and changed in inexplicable ways. Honor had been training Sorrow in how to handle herself in the dark, Naasir hanging out with them, when Sorrow had had one of her unpredictable violent episodes.

Everyone was physically fine, but Sorrow was near a mental breakdown. Since Dmitri seemed to be the one person who could get through to her, Honor had called him in. Elena would never forget finding Sorrow, covered in blood and naked, in the old shed meters from the chamber of horrors that had held the remains of her friends. It infuriated her that the young woman continued to pay the price for another's evil; she hoped Sorrow would find a way to fight the poison inside her, to make it.

The survivors of Giorgio's and Cornelius's crimes would have a road as difficult to travel. Of those found in the crates, it appeared Brooke alone might be able to live a normal life and she was badly traumatized. The others had the bodies of infirm elderly people, their minds nearly broken. "Will you really let the victims choose the punishment?" she asked her archangel.

"It's the only satisfaction I can give them."

"What if they choose mercy?" Elena wouldn't, but then, she liked her justice bloody.

Raphael faced the night winds. "I would honor their wish— and I would also lock both Giorgio and Cornelius in barren cells underground, so that they can live in mercy till their deaths."

"That's why I love you, Archangel." She spread her wings, folded them back in. "Your mother seems happy." Caliane had remained at the Enclave property since her arrival, content to spend time with Raphael and to speak to Keir, though she'd also taken a liking to Montgomery.

"Yes." Turning to face Elena, Raphael held her close, their eyes locked together. "You make me proud to be yours, *hbeebti*." Power in every word, his emotions a fury. "I know she is difficult, but you are treating her with grace and compassion."

"She's your mom, Raphael, and she loves you." It was as simple as that. "Speaking of Caliane, we should fly back. She said she can only stay another day without putting Amanat at risk and you've already had to be at the Tower for hours to deal with Cornelius and Giorgio."

His kiss was a storm inside her, making her body ignite. "We will continue this when we are alone." With that, he fell backward off the balcony before twisting in midair and rising.

*Show-off.* Taking flight herself, she waved to her Legion escort, recognizing him now. The Legion were like identical twins, times seven hundred and seventy-seven. Each was the same, and yet once you got to know them, each was unique.

This one was a sweetheart and not the least bit creepy on his own.

He waved back, and when she went to her greenhouse after landing, he came with her. *Go spend time with your mother, Raphael,* she said when her archangel frowned at her. *Caliane and I, we've made our peace.* Or at least begun the process. *That doesn't mean we want to see each other any more than necessary.*

His lips curved, the sea a crashing wildness in her mind. *I will see you in our bed, Guild Hunter.*

*Count on it, Archangel.*

Ashwini walked into Banli House to be told that Tanu and Arvi were in the winter-and-night-cloaked gardens. Stepping outside, Janvier by her side, she followed the sound of animated voices to find her sister sitting on a wrought-iron garden seat under the moonlight, Arvi by her side. Tanu had a thick blanket wrapped around her, while Arvi was wearing his coat.

They were both smiling, their conversation fluid.

"Ashi!" Tanu's face lit up. "Come, sit." She held her blanket open.

Heart breaking into a thousand shards of pain and hope, Ashwini accepted the welcome and leaned into her sister's side. Arvi rose at the same instant, held out his hand. "We never met properly. I'm Arvan, Ashwini's older brother."

"Janvier."

The men shook hands, then Arvi retook his seat beside Tanu, while Janvier located a metal outdoor chair, brushed off the snow, and set it up to Ashwini's left in front of the seat. Then the four of them sat talking under the moonlight. Carl brought out coffee at some stage, and, warmed by the liquid, they remained outside for hours more.

Tanu was vivacious and intelligent and occasionally sharply sarcastic in her replies as she'd been before the degeneration. And Arvi, he laughed helplessly at several of Tanu's retorts. But for that single incident five years past, Ashwini hadn't seen him that way since she was a young girl. It made her realize just how much of her brother had broken when Tanu fragmented.

Throat tight, she looked helplessly toward Janvier. He reached quietly under the blanket to take her hand. The two of them were silent for the most part, Ashwini content to sit with her sister's arm around her while Tanu and Arvi spoke, two pieces of a whole that had been torn apart and who'd found one another again for this single magical night.

"It's time," Tanu said with a smile as fire kissed the sky on the horizon, dawn whispering its arrival. "I'm so happy to have spent this time with you and your Janvier, Ashi." Her sister hugged her tight before releasing her from the blanket. "You grew up as smart and as wild and as beautiful as I always knew you would."

Reluctant to go, but knowing she had to, Ashwini rose to her feet to find herself pulled into her brother's warm, strong arms. "I'm sorry for not being the big brother you needed," Arvi said against her ear. "But I have always, *always* loved you. I am so proud of you for what you've become."

Tears choking her throat, she hugged him with all her might. "It's okay, Arvi. I understand."

She hugged Tanu again as well, her arms wanting to hold on forever. "I love you, Tanu. You and Arvi both."

Face devoid of darkness, Tanu kissed her on both cheeks. "Live an extraordinary life, won't you, Ashi? Fate has promised me you'll make it."

Ashwini couldn't speak. Nodding jerkily, she grabbed Janvier's hand and left the garden. It wasn't until they were in the car halfway down the long drive that she let the sobs come.

*"Cher."* Janvier pulled over to the side, beside a winter-barren oak and hauled her across the stick shift into his lap. "Ashwini, what's wrong?" One hand on her hair, he held her against him, his other arm locked around her waist. "Please talk to me."

She couldn't, not for a long time. The first wave of the sun's rays had warmed up the sky when she whispered, "They're gone."

Janvier grew motionless around her. When he moved, it was to press a kiss to her hair. Voice thick, he said, "You knew they were saying good-bye."

"Arvi started dying the day Tanu began to disappear." Her brother had done what was necessary to bring Ashwini up, had even become a celebrated surgeon, but he'd been a ghost of the Arvi she'd once known. "Tonight . . . today, Tanu was herself, *truly* herself, for the first time in years, and I saw Arvi again."

"They made the decision together."

"Yes. Everyone used to say Arvi was the alpha of the twins, but they were always equal." And so, after years of saving Tanu from herself, Arvi had waited for her to come back long enough to make certain of her wishes, waited for a decision uncontaminated by the mysterious disease that haunted the women of their family.

Swallowing past the lump of grief inside her, she reached into her jacket pocket. "Arvi gave me this." He'd slid it in during the final hug she would ever receive from her big brother.

Janvier took the small envelope, shook it open in the passenger seat. A golden key fell out, along with a folded piece of paper. "I think it's to a safe-deposit box."

She smiled through the sadness. "That's Arvi, organized to the end."

When Janvier passed her the notepaper, she unfolded it to find instructions on how to access the box. Arvi had written in his strong, sloping hand:

> *Everything you need to settle our estates is in there. I know we're leaving you alone, but I've made sure you'll be able to afford every resource you could ever need.*
>
> *Tanu says she's dreamed a dazzling future for you, and I want to believe her, but if fate isn't so kind, then you'll have the money to fight it. I couldn't find the answer, but another surgeon might.*
>
> *Make sure Tanu's brain is autopsied; compare it to the results of Mom's autopsy—I had it done privately after the accident. The report is in the safe-deposit box, along with full scans of her brain. The associated slides are in a special medical storage facility you'll find the details of in the box. Make sure the pathologist follows the format exactly so you get all the required information. If he balks once he has cause of death, hire a private pathologist to redo that part.*
>
> *You've lived without fear for so long. Keep on doing it, keep on being the strongest of us all.*
>
> *With all my love—Arvi*

The grief slammed into her anew and with it a beam of blinding knowledge. "Don't go with me, Janvier." She sat up, held the beautiful moss green eyes that had laughed with her across the world. "Don't make that choice when it happens for me."

Arms locked around her, Janvier shook his head, his jaw set in a way she'd seen only rarely. She'd lost the argument every single time. "No," he said, "that you cannot ask of me."

"Yes, I can." She gripped his jacket on either side, tried to shake him. "Think of Arvi—he saved so *many* lives." Angry tears formed. Blinking them away, she said, "Those gifted hands will never again pick up a scalpel, never again give someone hope."

"He lived a shadow life," Janvier growled. "You said it your-self. It was his choice to go today, when he was happier than he'd been for decades!"

"Arvi has been heading toward this since the day Tanu was first diagnosed! You're whole, healthy."

"I won't be after you!" His fury filled the car, his voice raw. "I won't be me after you."

"Honor came back for Dmitri," Ashwini whispered, sharing a secret she'd spoken to no other. "I promise you I'll come back for you." She might not wear the same face, the same name, but she'd know him. Always, she'd know him. "No matter what it takes. I'll come back."

His eyes glittering wet, Janvier's fingers dug into her hips. "You're sentencing me to an eon alone. How can you ask that?"

"Because you're strong enough to bear the pain."

"No, I'm not."

She kissed him, her hand curved around his neck. "You need to be. I need to know you'll be here when I return."

He wouldn't look at her, his muscles rigid, and she knew she'd lost the battle today. But it wasn't over. The disease inside her might snuff out her light, but she would not let it snuff out Janvier's.

Fourteen days later and a week after Felicity and Lilli were laid to rest, Janvier drove his Ashblade high into the mountains, where she scattered the ashes of her sister and her brother on the wind. According to the autopsies, Tanushree and Arvan Taj had died of heart failure. Inexplicable, said the pathologist, but not unheard-of in twins. Whatever it was that connected them, it sometimes snipped both lives short when only one was wounded.

Two syringes had been found in Arvan Taj's pocket, filled with a drug that would've stopped their hearts if the needle was stabbed into the organ, the plunger pushed down. Neither syringe had been uncapped, much less used. The siblings bore no marks on their bodies.

It was as if once they'd made the decision to go, their hearts had simply stopped beating. They'd been found at peace on the wrought-iron seat where Ashwini and Janvier had last seen them, Arvan's arm around Tanu's shoulders and her head against his chest, their eyes closed and the sunrise warm on their faces.

The pathologist had done the specialist autopsy requested on Tanu's brain, but the results had appeared ordinary at first glance. However, when Ash took that report and its associated findings, as well as her mother's, to a neurosurgeon who had been a friend of Arvan's, the doctor had discovered an abnormality deep in the temporal lobe. A tiny, *tiny* malformation that was identical in mother and daughter, except that Tanu's was slightly larger.

"It's like nothing I've ever seen," the doctor had said. "*No one* could've ever picked it up without having the two slides side by side." His brow had furrowed. "I don't think it had anything to do with her death," he'd told Ash, unaware of the Taj history on the female side. "But even if it was malignant, there would've been nothing we could do. It's in an inoperable location and I don't know of any drug created to deal with something like this."

Ash had taken the news better than Janvier. It was Ash who'd held him, who had comforted him. His strong, beautiful lover.

"There," she whispered now, putting down the second urn. "I felt them go. I think they were waiting to make sure I was all right." The long white cotton scarf she wore around her neck, the same color as her tunic and leggings, threw the sorrow on her face into sharp relief, the wind blowing back the rich silk of her hair.

Sliding his arm around her, he stood with her on the mountaintop and he thought of the promise she'd asked him to make.

"If you're right and people sometimes come back, then I'll come back with you." He couldn't imagine it any other way. His soul would find hers, no matter the unknown beyond death.

"You are an awful, mule-stubborn man."

"I love you, too."

A quiet, husky laugh as she tilted up her head. "I made a promise to myself that I wouldn't let this thing in my head take you, too."

"I'm over two hundred years old," he reminded her. "By rights, I should already be dust in the earth. Eternal life for its own sake has no meaning for me—I'm angry only because I won't get to live it with you."

Reaching up to stroke her fingers through his hair, she sighed. "Let's have hope in Tanu's dream and discuss your stubbornness another time." A hard pull of his hair that made him wince. "When I have a kukri at your throat."

He nipped her lower lip, smiled. "Full throttle all the way, *cher.*"

Her eyes warmed. "All the way, cuddlebunny."

# 43

Titus arrived with only three warriors the night before the block party was scheduled to begin. Elena didn't have to be told that the small unit was both a gesture of trust and a display of his confidence in his own strength. Folding in his wings as he landed on the Tower roof, his warriors coming down behind him—two males and one female—Titus headed toward Elena and Raphael.

"Titus." Raphael walked forward to meet the other man halfway and held out his arm. "You are welcome."

Titus grabbed Raphael's forearm, Raphael's own hand closing over his in the clasp of warriors. "I am glad you are here to welcome me, Raphael," he said, his words a boom that made Elena realize the archangel usually modulated his voice so as not to drown out everyone else in his vicinity. "You are a pup, but a strong one I'd have at my back in any battle."

"And I would have you, though you are heading toward frail old age."

Titus's laugh at Raphael's riposte was huge. "Well met, young pup. Well met."

Breaking the handclasp with a deep smile, Raphael turned to Elena. "My consort."

She stepped forward. "Archangel Titus," she said, keeping it formal until he gave an indication that informality was welcome.

Her restraint was thanks to Jessamy. Elena had been in Remedial Protocol School that afternoon, since this was the first time she was welcoming an archangel to her city who had no consort and who was unrelated to Raphael, *but* who'd known Raphael as a boy and had, in fact, helped train him.

All of which, apparently, changed everything.

At this rate, she thought with an inward snort, she'd have the protocol thing sorted in, oh, another nine hundred years, give or take. "You made good time."

Titus made his reply in the softer tone she was used to hearing from him. "A good wind."

"If you and your people would follow us," she said, hoping Raphael was right and Titus was laid-back enough that she could soon drop the protocol crap. It was making her head ache. At least she hadn't had to put on a gown for this. "We have prepared suites for you."

"A short moment to wash, nothing more," Titus said. "I would explore your city. It has been an age since I have visited these lands."

Elena led the group over the side of the roof and down to a guest balcony where Dmitri was waiting. He greeted Titus with the familiarity of old acquaintance and mutual respect, then led the escort through to their rooms, while Elena showed Titus to his. Turned out that since Raphael had a consort, he couldn't do certain tasks himself if she was able, without it being taken as an insult.

"I hope everything is to your liking," she said to Titus.

He surprised her by throwing back his head and laughing with the smile-inducing lack of inhibition she'd already come to expect from him. "Ah, you must forgive me," he said when he caught his breath. "I see this role sits ill on you—you are meant for battle, not for such niceties."

Elena grinned. "I can rock a dress when I put my mind to it."

"Perhaps I will see this at the celebration you have planned."

"You never know." Walking forward, she held out her arm as Raphael had done, saying, "I'm not yet as immortal as you," at the last minute as she remembered Raphael's warning about Titus treating her as a blooded angelic warrior.

Titus clasped her forearm. It was hard enough to jar her teeth, but not hard enough to break anything. "You will be," he said. "Then I will say I knew you when you were a fledgling." Another huge laugh. "As I knew your consort when he was a pup."

Leaving him to freshen up, she stepped out to join Raphael on the balcony. "You were right," she said. "I like him. He's like a hunter—only much more powerful."

"You should trust your consort."

Sliding her wing over his, she leaned her shoulder against his. "I wish the thing with Cornelius and Giorgio hadn't happened, that we could go into this celebration without that ugliness." Her heart hurt for Ash, too, though the other hunter seemed to have a serene peace inside her when it came to the loss of her brother and sister.

She'd returned Elena's fierce hug after the funerals, murmuring, "Don't be so sad, Ellie. Your sisters aren't trapped in that house; they're flying on their own wings."

Elena couldn't explain how Ash knew that the funerals had brought back visceral memories of the deaths of her own sisters, or how she knew about the horror that had taken them, but Elena held the other woman's words close to her heart. Ash had always glimpsed more than anyone should, seen beyond this world. If she said Ariel and Mirabelle were no longer imprisoned in the blood-soaked house that had once been their childhood home, then Elena could do nothing but believe it.

Raphael slid his arm around her waist. "I feel your sorrow."

"Just working through stuff," she said, her emotions heavy but not agonizing. "Thinking about how some people are so kind and generous, others the opposite." Not many would've reached out across their own grief to ease that of another, as Ash had done for her, and it was a kindness Elena would never forget. "The world would be a better place if we could erase all the Corneliuses and Giorgios from it."

"I've lived long enough to understand that there will always be some ugliness in the world." Raphael stroked a tendril of hair that had escaped her braid back behind her ear. "We cannot erase it, for it acts as the foil for joy, for goodness."

"I guess I'm not old enough to accept that yet." It didn't matter that Cornelius and Giorgio were currently serving out their brutal and ongoing punishments in distant underground bunkers. "I feel so much fury for the pain caused, the scars left on the hearts of good people."

"Never lose that part of yourself, Elena." Raphael's eyes held a lick of wildfire in their depths that spoke of the changes going on inside him. "Before you, I had become jaded, unable to see the light or the dark. It is not an existence to which anyone should aspire."

Rubbing her cheek against his hand, she said to hell with shocking their guest should he step outside and drew her archangel down for a kiss. "To life."

"To life, *hbeebti*."

Ashwini sat with her legs hanging off the edge of the Tower roof, watching the revelers on the rooftops around them and in the streets far below. Music came from every side, merging and mixing and becoming a wild, vibrant melody. Wings passed overhead, the area a sea of angels landing on roofs and on the tarmac as they joined in the celebration in different areas.

Illium flew down to the under-renovation Legion building right then, the silver in his wings shimmering in the lights beaming out of the Tower. The Legion fighters were, for the most part, sitting in crouched positions on different parts of the Tower. Ashwini hadn't yet figured out if they were bemused by the entire thing or fascinated.

A male head was suddenly in her lap, hair of liquid silver on the black of her jeans.

"You'll fall," she said to Naasir, petting his hair as she knew he wanted.

"No, I won't," he said easily, staying stretched out on the edge. "I came to see you. I never had any brothers or sisters, but I would be angry and sad if something happened to my people . . . like it did to Aodhan once." Silver eyes held her own. "I'll fight with you if you want."

The offer, she knew, was genuine. He'd allow her to cut him up if it would make her feel better. Because she was one of Naasir's people now. As he was part of her family. Affection had her pressing a kiss to his forehead. "Thank you, but I think

I'm okay," she said through her lingering sorrow at Tanu and Arvi's loss.

Knowing that they had wanted to go didn't change the hole in her heart, didn't make it any less painful to accept the fact that she'd never again witness Tanu's acerbic wit or hear Arvi's voice. What did help were the people around her. Like the wild creature in her lap and the hunters who were the family she'd created. They'd stood shoulder to shoulder with her as she laid her siblings to rest, done a thousand small things to make it more bearable.

And Janvier . . . he'd been her rock throughout, solid, protective, and unwavering. She didn't know how she would continue to function, to exist, if anything ever happened to him, and in that agony of thought, she'd finally understood his own stubborn refusal to stay after she was gone. That didn't mean she planned to accept it. He had a wild, beautiful, adventurous eternity ahead of him and she'd fight to make sure he claimed it.

"This is a fun party," Naasir said into the lazy quiet between them, the repetitive motion of stroking the cool silver of his hair having relaxed her as much as it had him. "I think Ellie should be in charge of all immortal parties."

Ashwini laughed at the idea of Ellie let loose on stuffy angelic balls. "Go have some of that fun," she urged him, conscious he was returning to Amanat in twenty-four hours. She'd miss him, might have to bag herself a hunt in Japan so she could swing by for a visit. "I saw the pretty little angel with the auburn hair giving you the eye earlier. She's over there trying to scorch me to a crisp with her mind, if you want to go soothe her feelings."

"No," Naasir said definitively. "I want a mate and I've decided to go hunting for her. The little angel didn't smell like her."

Ashwini felt a twinge of sympathy for all the smitten women he'd be smelling and rejecting until he found his mate. "You realize it can take time? You can't force it."

Eyes closing under her continued petting, he made a rumbling sound in his chest. "A mate would do this for me."

Her lips quirked. "Yes. Or you might do it for her."

Eyes flicking up, Naasir grinned, his fangs flashing in the light. "Does Janvier pet you?"

She pulled at his nose.

He laughed and, bending one leg at the knee, closed his eyes again, the silver fan of his lashes vivid against the rich brown of his skin, the undertone a gorgeous, warm gold. At that instant, she almost imagined she saw faint stripes underneath. Startled, she stared . . . to see his usual skin. Strokable enough to have women begging to touch him, but otherwise normal for Naasir.

Clearly, Ellie's "tiger creature" theory was starting to affect her subconscious.

"Where's Janvier?"

"Catching up with friends." Those bonds were important to them both. "Why have you suddenly decided you want a mate?"

Naasir stretched lazily before settling back into his previous position. "I'm old enough now, and I want someone to play with like you play with Janvier and Raphael does with Elena. Even Dmitri plays with Honor." This seemed to fascinate him. "The rules are secret in each game. I want to have secret rules with a woman who . . ." A long pause. "A woman who knows me, understands what I am, and who wants to have secret rules with me."

It was a very Naasir definition of love and it was wonderful. "I think your mate will be a lucky woman."

Naasir's gaze was oddly solemn when he lifted his lashes. "I'm different, Ash. Deep inside. I'll never be like other men."

"I'm different, too," she whispered. "Janvier loves me exactly as I am." As she did him, stubborn Cajun will or not.

Elena took a seat beside Izak where the injured angel lay propped up in a bed next to a large window that gave him a great view of the partiers on the roof to the left, as well as of the angels flying back and forth. "I brought you something." She lifted the saucer holding a piece of cake. "Red velvet with cream cheese icing."

Izak's smile was shy. "My arms . . ."

"You have me." She scooped up a bite of cake, using the fork she'd brought with her, and fed it to him, aware of the fact his body had prioritized the healing of his skull and his spinal cord over broken bones. "So?"

Swallowing, he said, "How did you know it was my favorite?"

"I know everything. I also know Montgomery."

He laughed, and it was a brilliant sound, the light back in his eyes. "You shouldn't be taking care of me. I'm going to be in your Guard."

"Who made that rule?" Feeding him another small bite, she said, "Way I hear it from Hannah—who, as *you* pointed out in your pitch, already has a Guard and is thus an expert—while my Guard is meant to be my shield if necessary, I'm also meant to ensure they have what they need. Right now, you need cake."

The young angel grinned this time. He truly was adorable. It was going to be difficult for her to treat him as a warrior, but she figured she'd just handle him as a hunter in training until he grew up a little more. "I smuggled in something else for you." Glancing around to make sure the healers weren't paying any attention to them, she took out a small bottle from the ankle sheath that usually held a gun.

Opening it, she slid in a straw she'd concealed down the side of a knife sheath and held the drink to his lips. "Sip," she ordered before he could take a long draw. "It's Illium's secret recipe and it's lethal."

Eyes brightening, he took a drink and went, "Whoa."

"Yeah, that's what I said. Lots of angels drinking and flying today—I hope none of them fall into the Hudson."

Izak laughed. "Alcohol wears off very fast in angelic bodies. I don't think it has any effect on angels as old as Aodhan and Illium."

"No wonder he makes it so strong." She cut Izak off when he became a touch too smiley. "Let's wait for it to wear off on you before you have the rest." Baby that he was, half a bottle was clearly plenty for Izzy.

"Janvier told me Titus is here."

Elena leaned in close. "You didn't hear it from me," she whispered, "but last I saw, Titus was carousing in the street, kissing a different willing woman every five minutes." More than one human was going to wake up the next day with a surreal memory she'd probably put down to too many shots. "And—Hmm, I'm not sure I should be saying this to such tender ears . . ."

"What?" His eyes went huge. "I want to know."

Far too adorable. It was ridiculous. "Well," she said in a conspiratorial tone, "I'm pretty sure there are shenanigans going on high in the sky tonight." Anyone who had a telescope pointed up toward the stars might just get an eyeful.

"People are *dancing*?" A small pout. "I want to be outside."

Shoulders shaking, because he was clearly still feeling the effects of Illium's concoction, she patted his face. "You'll have plenty of opportunities to seduce and be seduced, Izzy."

"Can I have more cake?"

She fed the remaining half to him. His eyes were starting to flutter shut by the end, and when she rose to her feet, he was in a peaceful sleep. Pressing a kiss to his cheek, she glanced at the doorway to see Keir exchanging an intimate look with a heavily muscled male warrior. The warrior angel's hand was curved around the side of Keir's neck, his head bent toward Keir's shorter and more slender form. Whatever he said made the healer laugh before he slipped out of the warrior's hold and into the infirmary.

Seeing Elena, he came over. "You look puzzled, Ellie."

"I am. Last time I saw you with anyone"—back in the Refuge—"it was a woman." And he, without a doubt, had stubble burn on the dusky skin of his throat right now. Which meant he'd been getting frisky only seconds before she saw him; Keir was too old for the mark not to have faded otherwise.

Smile gentle, he said, "I have been alive thousands of years, have learned that love does not always wear a single face." A warmth in his eyes. "Ah, but it will for you, will it not?"

"Yes." Raphael was her heart, would always be her heart. "So, you're a player?" She sighed. "All this time, I thought you were a nice guy. I introduced you to my single friends, like that sweet squadron leader."

His laugh soft, he allowed his wing to brush hers. "If I could find what you have with Raphael, I would stop playing. Until then, I will share pleasure with smaller loves—perhaps even your rather lovely squadron leader." Reaching down to tug a blanket over Izzy, he said, "The boy is doing well. I think he is even more in love with you, however."

"A little cake and punch and everybody loves me." Leaving him with a kiss on his cheek, she went to talk to an angel who was down with severed legs, but was able to sit up on her own.

She had a drink in her hand and a plate of goodies on the table next to her. "This celebration was a wonderful idea, Ellie."

Before the battle, none of the squadron but Izak had called her Ellie. It was a welcome change. "How are the legs?" she said, able to ask as she could a fellow hunter.

"It hurts, but the injuries are healing faster than anticipated." The woman's dark eyes went to where Raphael was speaking with two other wounded fighters, one an angel, the other a vampire. "The sire is responsible for that."

Elena didn't nod, didn't need to. Raphael's ability to heal remained nascent, but it was shaving days, sometimes weeks off the recovery time of the injured. According to Keir, what Raphael was doing wasn't healing as he knew it. Keir's current theory was that Raphael was sharing power.

Lijuan, Elena thought, shared death. Raphael shared life.

His eyes met hers across the width of the room at that instant, and she saw pride burning in his gaze, the same pride that filled her veins. For their people, who had survived the unimaginable with their spirits intact; for their city, that had stood strong against an unprovoked attack. There was no need for either of them to articulate that. They saw and understood each other in a way few people ever did, mortal or immortal.

For her, love would only ever have a single face, and it was his.

# 44

Janvier tracked Keir down three hours into the party. Catching the healer's eye, he ducked out into a small room off the corridor.

This, what he had to ask, it was a private thing, an important thing.

"Janvier," Keir's wings made a whisper of sound in the doorway. "I am glad to see you are not dead yet."

Janvier tried to smile at the old joke, but the urgency of what he had to ask tore at him too desperately to allow for levity.

Keir's expression altered, wise eyes in an ageless face turning solemn. "What is it?"

"You can't speak about it to anyone else."

"I will not." It was the oath of a healer. "Not even should the Cadre ask."

Hope a white-hot flame inside him, he said, "It's about Ash."

Ashwini felt a prickle on the back of her neck that told her Janvier was near, even before Honor said, "Here comes your Cajun." A shoulder nudge from her best friend, the two of them having spent the past half hour talking. "I'm off to debauch my deliciously sexy husband—you should do the same with Janvier."

Janvier slid down beside her as Honor left; his thigh pressed against hers, strong and warm, the city spread out below them.

"I thought you went to catch up with your friends from out of town." He'd brought her a cocktail earlier, danced with her on the roof, then slipped away while she chatted with Honor. Naasir had prowled off before that, in full mate-hunting mode.

"I was speaking to Keir."

"I didn't realize you two were friends."

Janvier took her hand, his expression unexpectedly serious. "I'm going to tell you something, *cher*, and I want you to listen. Don't dismiss it out of hand. Promise me."

A tremor shook her on the inside, incited by the fear that he'd ask her to embrace vampirism after all, but her trust in him was stronger than her dread of endless madness. "I promise."

Leaning forward with his forearms braced on his thighs and his eyes on the angels flying over the city, he said, "I know why you don't want to become a vampire. An illness of the mind can last centuries for those of my kind."

Relief rained over her senses. "I could live millennia as a broken shadow." It was her worst nightmare.

"There's Dmitri," he said in an apparent non sequitur. "Do you see him?"

Glancing over her shoulder, she smiled. "Yes, he's dancing with Honor." The dark, dangerous vampire was whispering things in Honor's ear as the two of them swayed to a slow and sensual ballad.

"Keir knew him when he first became a vampire," Janvier said, "and now a thousand years later, he says that while Dmitri has changed physically, it is in strength and a refining of his features. He hasn't truly aged."

Ashwini frowned. "Vampirism doesn't stop time."

"No, but it slows it down to an insect's crawl. Every aspect of aging slows down—including changes in the brain." His hand squeezed hers. "Keir has seen this in the brains of vampires who have died in accidents or battles. Tumors and fragile blood vessels, among other things, both of which are mortal ailments the centuries-old fallen must've had *before* embracing near-immortality—because in the normal course of things, with no strange archangelic powers in the mix, *vampires don't get sick*."

Ashwini wanted to grab on to hope, desperate for a lifetime with him, but there was one problem. "Vampires go insane just like mortals."

"Yes," Janvier agreed, his voice fierce, "but not from an organic cause. The degeneration is psychological, as with Giorgio. He isn't insane, but he would've been, given enough time, and it had *nothing* to do with his brain."

No, Ashwini thought, it had to do with a breakdown in his conscience. She had no fear of that happening to her—not with Janvier acting as her balance, and her acting as his. "Could Keir give us any kind of a timeline?"

Bayou green eyes slammed into her own. "A single human year could equal a thousand years as a vampire. A month could mean a hundred years or more."

All the air rushed out of her lungs. "And then?" she whispered. "When the time comes? Whether after a hundred years or a thousand?"

"Then we go together." A quiet promise. "When you're ready, I'll ask Raphael to erase us with angelfire. You won't be trapped in an existence you do not wish."

Ashwini's heart was in her mouth, her pulse a roar. "Tanu and Arvi gave me this chance." Without her sister's death and her brother's instructions on the autopsy, she'd never have known the apparent insanity had a physical cause.

"There's no guarantee, *cher*." Janvier lifted their clasped hands to his mouth, pressed his lips over her knuckles. "You are unique. The change to vampirism could have an adverse reaction, as it does with a small number, and consume you in madness." His hand trembled. "I could lose you in a heartbeat." Voice breaking, he took long seconds to continue. "I almost didn't tell you of the option when Keir spelled out the risk. I would rather have you for a single fleeting day than take the risk. I would be that selfish."

It was her choice, Ashwini thought, and no matter what she decided, he would fight to come with her, ending his near-immortal existence.

"No," he said, the word harsh. "Don't you make this

decision for me. The decision must be yours or I will never forgive you."

"Stop reading my mind." She glared at him.

"You're the one with the power." He glared back. "Stop thinking at me."

"I don't know how to stop." Frowning, she thought of how sexy she found his butt, then stared at him.

He threw up his hands. "I have nothing."

"Good." She'd have to figure out how to make the block subconscious. "I was imagining sinking my teeth into your butt. You know it's been on my to-do list for a while."

His cheeks creased. "I'm available anytime."

Resting her head on his shoulder, she kicked out her legs like a child. "If we do this, we could get everything or we could get nothing."

"I already have everything." He kissed her knuckles again. "If you agree, you would have to sign on to serve Raphael for a hundred years. I have no fears the sire will do anything but treat you as the gift you are—he does not waste his assets." Absolute certainty in his tone. "There's also the risk the transition will either erase your ability or make it painfully more vivid."

Ashwini ran her free hand up his arm, the earthy, masculine scent of him in her every breath. "Nothing's guaranteed. I have an impressive scar across my chest to prove it." The world was in a state of flux as the most powerful beings on the planet jostled for power, war a promise rather than a probability. "We're both fighters, hunters." Lifting her head, she kissed his jaw, her eyes holding his. "Our life is never going to be rainbows and puppies."

"I don't know." Smiling, he kissed her fully on the mouth. "I had a pup when I was a boy. I miss his slobbery face."

She touched noses with him. "You want a dog?"

"Yes."

"Where are we going to keep a dog in our apartment?"

"I have a house in the Enclave."

Her mouth fell open. "You have a house in the *Enclave*?" That was the most exclusive piece of real estate in the country. "Vampires your age aren't that rich." She poked him in the side. "Did you forget to tell me you were in the vamp mafia?"

"I'm the don." A solemn face belied by laughing eyes. "I have the house because it was a gift a hundred years ago from an old angel for whom I retrieved a precious object. It's not grand, but it has a yard and a view over the cliffs."

Still astonished at the idea that he owned an Enclave house—and not simply a house, but one with a cliff view, she said, "Why don't you live there?"

He gave her a *look*.

"Right." An Enclave home was not the kind of place you lived in alone. "Is it vacant?"

"No, but the angel who leases it from me is leaving for another territory in a month. Will you choose the new paint and furniture with me?"

"Are you sure you trust my judgment? You've seen my idea of interior design."

"Your apartment is my favorite place in the city."

"Sweet talker." Realizing she was being soppy and silly, she nonetheless kissed him, one of his arms wrapped right around her waist, her hands on his face, and a smile on both their mouths.

"A*hem*." The interruption was courtesy of Illium. The blue-winged angel hovered in front of them, his hair disheveled and a red lipstick mark on his cheek. "Do you not have a room?"

"Do you?" Janvier responded with a raised eyebrow.

"Many, many rooms." Flipping backward, the angelic male dropped down like a bullet.

"I think he's been drinking his own brew." Ashwini pointed out Illium's acrobatics below them just as the sky exploded in color, fireworks painting the velvet black.

Janvier's laugh was deep, delighted. "Sugar, remember—"

"One of your best ideas, *cher*."

*Secret rules,* she thought, her eyes on his profile as he watched the sky rain color, *secret play*. When he met her eyes, his own reflecting the sky, she said, "Full throttle."

The smile faded from his lips, raw emotion in his voice as he repeated the vow. "Full throttle."

# Epilogue

Ash spun out with a kick. Stopping it with one hand, Janvier pushed at her foot in a way intended to make her lose her balance. Wise to him, she shifted her weight and, grabbing his other forearm, twisted under and back—or would have if he hadn't broken the hold to spin around to face her . . . and they were back to where they'd been before she'd chanced the kick.

Facing one another, legs spread and forearms up, grins on their faces.

"Truce?" Janvier asked, blood pumping. "I'm getting kind of hungry." He also knew that her body had to ache by now.

His Ashblade had rebuilt her strength with teeth-gritted focus after waking from the transformation to vampirism with, as she'd put it, "muscles like noodles." It was, however, taking time for her to regain her endurance. Not everyone had this severe a physical reaction to the process, but neither one of them was complaining about the side effect. Because she'd also woken with her mind alert and active, her personality unaltered.

"Truce," she said, lowering her arms to stretch up on her toes before coming down flat on her feet and reaching up to rub the back of her neck.

He just watched her, drank her in. The time she'd spent unconscious during the transition had been the loneliest of his life, the breath-stealing pain of it not yet faded. But it wasn't the most powerful emotion that held him prisoner. That was naked joy.

"Hey." Dark eyes on him, his lover drew him into a slow, hot kiss that was a stamp of possession. "I love the way you look at me."

"Good. I intend to do it for eternity." Clasping her hand in his, he drew her to their home. As he'd told her, it wasn't grand, but it was perfect for them. With four bedrooms, there was plenty of space for friends and his family to drop by—which the entire clan would be doing en masse in a month's time—and the polished wood floor of the sprawling living area gave Ash a built-in dance studio.

The first time she'd danced for him, he'd felt as if she'd gifted him with her soul. It was a gift he treasured with ferocious protectiveness.

"Look," she whispered, pointing to the happily exhausted form of their new chocolate-colored mutt of a puppy. "He's adorable, but what's even more adorable is when you try to teach him to do tricks and he just wants to lick and love you to death."

"I am not giving up," Janvier vowed. "He will fetch something for me eventually." They'd adopted the scraggly furball after someone abandoned him as a newborn at Dr. Shamar's veterinary clinic, and right now, he was dreaming doggy dreams on the verandah, dark against the white of the walls.

Ash and Janvier—with help from Guild and Tower friends— had stripped the old paint a month earlier and put on a fresh coat of creamy white. It suited the house with its delicate cornices and wraparound verandah. Inside, his Ash indulged her liking for color, turning each room into a warm, welcoming haven.

It was the pieces she'd restored and saved that he most loved.

She was the one who'd figured out how to polish up the double swing with an iron frame that he'd found in a junk shop, the two of them working together to create the large flat cushions for the seat and the back. The rejuvenated swing sat on the back part of the verandah, facing their small but breathtaking view of Manhattan.

Taking a seat on the swing, the puppy curled up underneath in his favorite spot, the two of them unlaced and took off their boots and socks. "Yesterday," Ash said, eyes sparkling, "when Bluebell dropped by, I asked him to take off his boots before he came inside and he accused me of having an unnatural relationship with our wooden floor."

"Does he not know it is a most decadent ménage à trois?" Janvier slapped a hand over his heart. "My dear, honeyed floor, let me count the ways I love thee."

Ashwini laughed at the languid seduction of his voice. "She is a divine other woman." It was in the two months directly after she woke as a near-immortal that she and Janvier had worked on the floor. She'd been painfully weak then and the repetitive motions needed to strip and polish the wood had acted as low-impact physical therapy.

Four months on, every time she looked at that floor, she remembered lying in the then-empty room with Janvier, the sun's kiss on their bodies and their hands linked as they discussed their plans for the house . . . and for the future. There was, of course, no way to see the malformation in her brain, but six months on and she felt no different from prior to her Making.

"The countdown is now frozen in amber," Keir had told her, his hands gentle on her face, "or as close to it as matters not. Live without fear."

The echo of Arvi's words had made her eyes burn, her breath stuck in her chest. The hole in her heart that was the space where Arvi and Tanu had lived would always hurt, but she would honor the gift they had given her. For the first time in her life, she no longer knew when she would cease to exist, and that was a wonderful gift.

"How was your meeting with Dmitri?" Janvier asked as they walked inside.

"Good." Hitching herself onto the counter, she said, "I was able to give him a heads-up on that creepazoid vamp Carys mentioned." Ashwini was currently working for the Tower in the role of liaison with the people who lived in the gray that had been Giorgio's hunting ground, though she'd also received dispensation to work for the Guild in her off time.

"It would be idiotic of us to deprive the Guild of one of its best hunters when the hunters do a task that makes our job easier," Dmitri had said point-blank. "You and Janvier, however, will also work as a team directly under my authority to hunt down older vampires wanted for crimes beyond the purview of the Guild."

That was a job she could sink her teeth into, with the *best* partner she could imagine. That partner's eyes widened slightly when she added, "Ellie grabbed me as I was leaving and made us an offer. Turns out she needs a Guard. Founding member is Izzy, with Vivek having just come onboard."

Janvier handed her a bottle of blood from the fridge. "Both of us?"

"We're a pair." It was an irrefutable truth. "She told Raphael she was planning to steal you and he said she'd made an excellent choice."

Janvier's smile was slow. "I see no downside, *cher*. We will be expected to undergo intensive training over time, and to come in if Elena needs us—"

"We'd do that anyway." Ellie was family.

"Exactly. Otherwise, we'll be kept busy with any number of tasks, much like the Seven." He came to stand between her knees. "I say yes."

"Me, too." Ashwini had the feeling Ellie had no idea what to actually *do* with a Guard—it'd be fun to figure it out with her, hold on tight to that friendship into eternity.

"Speaking of Vivek," Janvier said, "did you hear he regained the use of his right hand last night?"

Having put the bottle on the counter, Ash pumped her fists in the air . . . then frowned. "*Wait* a minute. Everyone said it might take over a year for him to regain any voluntary movement below the neck and he has an entire hand already?"

Janvier's eyes glinted. "Something is afoot, but I do not know what." Palms braced on the counter on either side of her after he put his bottle down, too, he said, "Aodhan was responsible for Vivek's Making, but there are rumors Keir was in the room at the time. He must've done something."

"I suppose it doesn't matter if we ever figure out what," Ashwini said, though her curiosity was a sharp, nibbling creature inside her. "I'm happy for V."

"Yes." He picked up her bottle of blood. "You have to drink, sugar."

Running her fingernails over his scalp, to his shiver, she leaned in to nuzzle at his throat. "I don't like cold blood."

Janvier wove his hand into her hair, unraveling her braid and holding her to his neck. "Then it is a good thing I am addicted to your bite." He jerked slightly when she sank her fangs into him, his pulse thudding as the taste of him—hot, dark, sinful—filled her mouth.

Unlike Janvier, she couldn't give pleasure with her bite, but that wasn't a problem. Not when the two of them always ended up naked after she fed from him, the erotic connection so powerful that they were helpless to fight it. It was why she could *never*, *ever* feed from him in public. Her own pulse a racing train, she fumbled with his pants as he tore down the sweats she'd worn for their session, taking her panties with it.

He thrust his hand between her thighs, drove two fingers into her before she could push his own pants down. Crying out, she clung to his shoulders. Her brain was hazy, her balance off. They went to the floor in a tangle of limbs the next second, Janvier twisting to take the brunt of the impact—without ever stopping in his caresses.

Tugging desperately at his workout pants and underwear, she managed to free his cock and realized to her frustration that her sweats were caught at her knees, leaving her unable to straddle him. Janvier gave her no time to sit up to finish the task; he flipped them . . . and then he flipped her. Tugging her up onto her knees, he thrust into her from behind, his entry shockingly, searingly tight because of the way her legs were held together.

Sweat, heat . . . his fangs sinking into her shoulder . . . and boom.

"We really need to get a handle on that," she said some time later, her legs finally free of clothing.

She was on top of Janvier, licking up the two thin trails of blood that had escaped her bite because she hadn't had the presence of mind to seal the wound before he blew her brains out. That wound was now healing, but he'd carry the bruise for a few days. She kinda liked that, which was why she kept biting him on the neck.

"Why?" He ran his hand down her back and over her butt, luxuriating in her body with an earthy sensuality that made her boneless. "I'm not complaining about quickies straight out of a porn movie."

She snorted with laughter. "Porn? Seriously?"

His slow, wicked smile caught her heart, made her glad all over again that she'd taken the jump into the unknown. "Didn't we do it on the bathroom floor last night?" he said. "Today, I have you sans pants in the kitchen. Seems pornish to me."

Bursting out laughing again, she kissed his gorgeous, playful mouth. "Is this normal? The insane sexual connection?"

"Not that I've heard. It is our little gift." He squeezed her butt. "One that I hope will continue for a long, long, *long* time."

Sitting up on him, the T-shirt she'd worn to work out in doing its best to preserve her modesty—and failing spectacularly, if the glint in his eye was any indication—she pushed back her hair and spread her hands over his chest. "I'm happy, Janvier." A whispered confession. "I'm so happy to be here, to be with you. It hurts my heart, the happiness."

His amusement faded, his expression naked with emotion. "Your heart bruise is a perfect match to mine." Tugging her down, he cupped the sides of her face, spoke words low and rough that made her feel whole in parts she hadn't even known were broken.

"Marry me," she whispered. "I'll show you things that'll make you laugh in delight, scream in passion, cry for the sheer joy of it."

The light in his eyes, it was her whole world. "Done."

# Author's Note

I hope you enjoyed Ashwini and Janvier's story! As mentioned in the book, the first time these two worked together, going from adversaries to allies, was during their visit to Atlanta—when they came face-to-face with the cruel and deadly angel Nazarach as well as the Beaumont vampire family.

If you haven't yet read the story of that mission, you can find it in *Angels' Pawn*. This short is available on its own as an ebook, or you can read it as part of the Guild Hunter anthology *Angels' Flight* (available in ebook, puperback, and audio). You can find excerpts for *Angels' Pawn* and the other *Angels' Flight* novellas on my website. nalinislngh.com/flight.php.

Happy reading!

# Acknowledgments

As Janvier was born over two hundred years ago in Louisiana, he speaks Cajun French perfectly. He also speaks French as it is spoken in France, thanks to his years spent acting as a courier, but Cajun French is his mother tongue and a language I wanted to incorporate into the book because it's an integral part of him.

I would like to thank Lori and Michael Leger for translating a number of words and terms into Cajun French for me. I'd also like to thank the many people who maintain online websites dedicated to the Cajun French language.

Of particular help were Louisiana State University's Cajun French–English glossary, Learn Louisiana French's list of proverbs and sayings, LouisianaCajunSlang .com's list of expressions, and Clarence's list of Cajun Cuss Words on CajunRadio.org. (Be careful when speaking French in Louisiana! Some words that wouldn't be considered rude in France will be in Louisiana, and vice versa.)

My thanks also to Laura Florand for help with standard French terms.

Last but never least, I'd like to thank my readers, many of whom pointed me in the direction of various resources when I posted the research request online. You are awesome covered in awesome-sauce.

Any errors in the language or its usage are, of course, mine. I also admit to a bit of artistic license in using terms and phrases originating from a number of different regions within Louisiana. I figure a vampire who has lived over two centuries would have traveled and picked up bits and pieces here and there (maybe from other immortals and near-immortals!).

Before I go, I'd like to make a note about the use of the word *cher*. It is sometimes believed that this is an incorrect usage of the word *chère*. However, *cher* (pronounced *sha*) is part of the Cajun French language. It is a fluid word whose meaning can change in context or with the tone of the speaker. When it comes to Janvier, he only ever uses it with Ashwini, no one else. It is very much a term of affection, of love for his one and only Ashblade.

Turn the page to read an excerpt
from Nalini's novella

# Secrets at Midnight

Available November 25, 2014,
in the anthology *Night Shift*.
And in summer 2015, look out for the next book
in Nalini's extraordinary Psy-Changeling series,
followed by the next Guild Hunter
adventure later in the year.
In the meantime, Nalini invites you to
visit her website and join her newsletter for free
short stories as well as exclusive sneak peeks.

Vivid green eyes watched her with an unwavering focus that raised the tiny hairs on Kirby's arms, made her stomach go tight, a strange breathlessness in her chest. She didn't recognize the tall, muscled male with skin tanned a beautiful gold, but he had to be part of the DarkRiver leopard pack—there was something feline about the way he stood, a stealthy predator at rest. She had the insane urge to go up to him, touch him, *curl up naked against him, skin to skin*.

The wild, uncharacteristic thought snapped Kirby back to her senses, and all at once, she was aware of Vera looking at her quizzically. Not sure how long she'd been staring at the stranger, she held up the small white box in her arms and said, "I baked yesterday," even as her pulse thudded hard and rapid against her skin. "I thought I'd drop off half the cake for you, since I know you like black forest."

"I like black forest, too." A deep male voice that brushed over her senses like fur, the lips that shaped the words curved in a teasing smile, until she could almost believe she'd imagined the feral intensity of him when he'd first looked at her.

Tapping her cane on the ground, Vera looked up into that

green-eyed face that had twisted Kirby's insides into a tangled snarl. "I suppose you want some?"

"Yes, please." Hands behind his back, expression as innocent as a five-year-old's.

Snorting, Vera jerked her head toward Kirby. "This is Bastien. Don't let him charm you—next thing you know, you'll be naked."

Kirby's face filled with heat, burning her skin, the rush of blood so loud in her ears that she almost missed Bastien's protests. Ignoring them both, Vera walked toward her door at a spry pace, a grace to her movements even at this age that made it clear she was changeling. Not able to look Bastien in the face when her own was no doubt the color of an overripe tomato, Kirby began to follow . . . and realized she'd acquired a six-foot-plus shadow.

"I feel I have to defend myself," he murmured, the words a purr of sound against her ears.

"Really?" she managed to say, the scent of clean, fresh soap and warm-blooded male in her every breath. "You don't like making women naked?" It was a response driven by some hereto hidden part of her that told her to show him her claws . . . despite the fact she was human, didn't *have* claws. No matter if it felt as if the tips were shoving against her skin.

A pause.

Kirby had the feeling she'd surprised him, but he recovered quickly. "Oh, I do." His voice had dropped, acquired a rougher edge. "However, and despite Vera's refusal to believe me, I'm very particular about who I make naked now that I'm no longer a hormone-driven teenager. Of course, when I was a teenager, a naked woman would've ended things rather abruptly, biologically speaking."

Skin burning again when it had just settled, Kirby nonetheless refused to back down. "I hope your ability to stand . . . firm"—*Was she really saying this?*—"against temptation has improved with time?" She'd never flirted this way, hadn't known she could.

A hand on her lower back, his breath warm against her earlobe as he bent close to say, "You have no idea, little cat."

Fighting the shiver that threatened, she walked into Vera's

house and to the kitchen, where she placed the cake on the counter, and said, "I'll make the coffee."

It gave her something to do, though if she'd thought it'd help her ignore Bastien, that proved a futile effort. Sprawled in a chair at the kitchen table opposite Vera, he was saying something that had the older woman laughing.

"Why are you dressed up so spiffy?" Vera asked once her laughter had faded, lifting her fashionable but unnecessary cane to tap Bastien's forearm. "Was it for the girl selection?"

Bastien dropped his head in his hands, the stunning dark red of his hair catching the sunlight pouring through the kitchen windows, all of which overlooked woods filled with tall green firs. His white shirt was pulled taut over his shoulders in this position, his strength apparent. "I thought Mom needed my help with the furniture," he growled when he raised his head. "If I'd known it was about matchmaking, I'd have worn my rattiest jeans and a stained T-shirt."

Ears straining to hear every word, Kirby found the cups as the coffee began to percolate.

"Your mother loves you." Vera glared at Bastien. "You're in fine form, prime of your life, should find a girl before you get old and crinkly."

"Gee, thanks, Vera." A masculine mutter as he leaned back again, one arm braced lazily against the back of his chair, his big body loose limbed, very much a cat at rest. "I was hoping I had a few more years yet."

Vera's response was a grin bright and full of anticipation. "I'll enjoy watching you fall, Bastien Smith. I bet she wraps you around her finger."

A shrug, those broad shoulders catching Kirby's attention again. "Of course she will." Impossible as it was, it felt as if his voice was pitched to stroke over Kirby's senses. "What would be the point otherwise?"

Vera's smile turned affectionate. "I'm glad to see you understand that." Glancing up as Kirby brought across the tray holding the coffee, Vera's expression softened. "And you, Kirby?" She tugged Kirby into a seat. "Have you found someone yet?"

"I've only been in the city two weeks," she said, conscious of Bastien going preternaturally still for a single, taut moment, the green of his eyes no longer human, before he rose to get the cake.

"From the accent," he said, "I'm guessing . . . Georgia?"

Kirby nodded, happy he'd changed the subject, but Vera wasn't done.

"Two weeks, schmoo weeks. It's never too early to start looking." The older woman's eyes glinted, flicking from Kirby to Bastien. "You two would make pretty cubs together."

Kirby wanted to die. Dig a hole, jump inside, bury herself for good measure.

Bastien, on the other hand, served up the cake without missing a beat, his body heat lapping against her like a tactile caress where he stood between her and Vera. "Undoubtedly," he said, "but not if you terrify Kirby away with warnings about the likelihood of ending up naked while with me."

Kirby responded in pure self-defense, driven by that strangeness in her that said she couldn't permit him to overwhelm her. Not now, not ever. She might not be a dominant, but it was critical he didn't see her as weak. "That likelihood is getting less and less with every word you speak," she said, ignoring the strange thoughts in her head, the continuing stinging in her fingertips.

Laughing, Vera slapped her hand against the table as Bastien took his seat with a meek expression belied by the fact he'd shifted his chair so his thigh pressed against Kirby's. It incited an escalation in her clawing awareness of him, her skin prickling in a way that felt as if it came from inside and out both. Almost as if she had a leopard under her skin, too, one that was rubbing up against it in an effort to get closer to this gorgeous cat who made her nerve endings go haywire.

Shaking off the odd sensation, she focused on his conversation with Vera. Intelligent, witty, a little bit wicked, Bastien was definitely the kind of man who'd never have trouble attracting a woman. Kirby was far from immune. If she was brutally honest, she'd never reacted to anyone as she'd done to Bastien.

That raw wave of need, of *want*, at the start, followed by an increasing desire to know more about him, know everything . . . It was unsettling. As was the tearing disappointment that had her nails digging into her palms when he glanced at his watch and said, "I'd better get into the office. With the instability caused by the Psy political situation, I have to keep an extra-sharp eye on things."

"All work and no play." Vera shook her head as Kirby stared deliberately into her half-empty coffee cup in an effort to hide her disturbing reaction, her skin flushing alternately hot then cold. "Be careful you don't become a dull boy."

"I thought I was making women naked on a regular basis?" Rising with that quip, Bastien went around to kiss Vera on the cheek. "Can I give you a ride anywhere, Kirby?" he asked, his hand on the back of her chair.

Scared by how much she wanted to lean back, rub her cheek against his arm, tug him down to her mouth, she shook her head.

"Don't be silly," Vera said. "You haven't got a car."

Her fingers flexed, the tingling in her fingertips increasing in strength. "It's no trouble to catch the—"

Bastien's breath whispered hot and silken over her ear, his face a caress away from her own. "I promise I don't bite." It was a dare.

# NEW IN THE PSY/CHANGELING SERIES FROM THE *NEW YORK TIMES* BESTSELLING AUTHOR

Praise for the novels of Nalini Singh:

"Nalini is brilliant." —*USA Today*

"Paranormal romance at its best." —*Publishers Weekly*

nalinisingh.com
facebook.com/AuthorNaliniSingh
facebook.com/ProjectParanormalBooks
penguin.com

FROM *NEW YORK TIMES* BESTSELLING AUTHOR
# NALINI SINGH

# Heart of Obsidian

## A PSY-CHANGELING NOVEL

A dangerous, volatile rebel, hands stained bloodred.
A woman whose very existence has been erased.
A love story so dark, it may shatter the world itself.
A deadly price that must be paid.

The day of reckoning is here.

### PRAISE FOR THE PSY-CHANGELING SERIES:

"A phenomenal series."
—*Joyfully Reviewed*

'I don't think there is a single paranormal series as well
planned, well written, and downright fantabulous
as Ms. Singh's Psy-Changeling series."
—*All About Romance*

nalinisingh.com
facebook.com/AuthorNaliniSingh
facebook.com/ProjectParanormalBooks
penguin.com